Peter May was born and raised in Scotland. He was an award-winning journalist at the age of twenty-one and a published novelist at twenty-six. When his first book was adapted as a major drama series for the BBC, he quit journalism and during the high-octane fifteen years that followed, became one of Scotland's most successful television dramatists. He created three prime-time drama series, presided over two of the highest-rated serials in his homeland as script editor and producer, and worked on more than 1,000 episodes of ratings-topping drama before deciding to leave television to return to his first love, writing novels.

His passion for detailed research for his books has taken him behind the closed doors of the Chinese Police force, to the kitchen of a three-star Michelin chef, and down the Paris catacombs; he has worked as an online private detective, was inducted as a Chevalier of the Grand Order of Gaillac wines and earned honorary membership of the Chinese Crime Writers' Association.

He has won several literature awards in France and received the USA's Barry Award for *The Blackhouse*, the first in his internationally bestselling Lewis Trilogy, and the ITV Crime Thriller Awards Book Club Best Read for *Entry Island*.

He now lives in south-west France with his wife, writer Janice Hally.

PETER MAY

THE
FIRE
MAKER

Quercus

First published in Great Britain in 1999 by Coronet Books
This paperback edition published in 2016 by

Quercus Publishing Ltd
Carmelite House
50 Victoria Embankment
London EC4Y 0DZ

An Hachette UK company

A CIP catalogue record for this book is available
from the British Library

ISBN 978 0 85705 396 1
EBOOK ISBN 978 1 78087 956 7

10 9 8 7 6 5 4 3 2 1

Typeset by CC Book Production

Printed and bound in Great Britain by Clays Ltd, St Ives plc

For my parents

'Be not deceived; God is not mocked: for whatsoever a man soweth, that shall he also reap.'

Galations 6:7

INTRODUCTION

My first visit to the People's Republic was pure chance. I was in Hong Kong researching another book which was going to be set in South-East Asia, and my hotel was advertising a one-day trip to Shenzhen in southern China. I jumped at the chance.

We went by train and by coach, and when we stepped off the bus in Shenzhen itself it was as if we had arrived on another planet. It was 1983, just a handful of years after the end of the Cultural Revolution, and very little had changed since the Communists took power in 1949. The streets were jammed with bicycles, and everyone still wore their blue Mao suits. Little old ladies hobbled around on bound feet – a horrible hangover from the days of Imperial China.

The open air markets were like medieval street scenes: animals being hacked up on long wooden tables with huge bloodied choppers, bone and fur and flesh everywhere. Westerners were an irresistible curiosity. Almost nobody had a television set, and the country had been closed to the outside world for decades. And if I thought the Chinese were strange, they thought I was even stranger. There I was, six foot-two, blond hair, ginger beard, a completely alien sight on the streets of China. And huge crowds of people simply followed me around, staring open-mouthed.

I had an extraordinary sense of having arrived somewhere special, a society preserved as in aspic, and I knew immediately that I wanted to write about it.

I went away and spent the next eight years reading everything I could about the country – its history, its politics, its culture, its cuisine – and watched with the rest of the world as the horrors of Tiananmen Square unravelled before me on my television screen in 1989.

In 1991 I returned, this time in search of a story. I went to Beijing on a tourist visa, but spent my days and nights exploring the city, talking to people, getting a sense of the place. Although the new, modern Beijing, under Deng Xiaoping, was already springing up around me, it still felt hugely alien. No one spoke English. Street signs, menus, shop names, maps, everything was written in Chinese characters. Even the Pinyin romanisation of Chinese was rare.

At that time they had built six ring roads around the city, all of which were eerily empty. Vast bike lanes flowed with a stream of blue-suited, black-haired humanity, and people still gawped at us everywhere we went.

I befriended a tour guide who was eager to talk to me about the events in Tiananmen Square two years before. One night he took us to his home at the end of a line of squat, concrete pillboxes in a dark, unlit alley. He, his wife, their baby, and their babysitter (a peasant girl from the country) lived in one tiny room that contained two beds, a table, a couple of armchairs and a huge television set. The kitchen was a concrete cubicle barely big enough to turn around in. An outside toilet was shared with the other residents of the block.

He showed us illicit video taken during the Tiananmen Square protests, and warned us to be careful when we left, because the Street Committee would be watching us. We rode back through the city well after midnight in an almost empty bus, the only other passengers on it with their eyes fixed on us.

I had thought that my story might revolve around events before, after or during the events of June 1989, and arranged by telephone to visit the offices of CNN in Wangfujing Street to see their archive of unbroadcast footage taken in and around the square. As it happened, there was a power cut (there were many in Beijing in those days), and when I reached the block where CNN had their offices on the fourth floor, the elevator was not available and I had to walk up.

When I got there the office was empty, except for bureau chief Mike Chinoy and an assistant provided by the Chinese government. But, of course, without power it was impossible to view the footage, and although I was able to sit and chat to Mike about the events of two years before, I always wondered if it was more than coincidence that prevented me from seeing that video.

I left Beijing empty-handed on that trip, but had learned a great deal, and was even more determined to use China as a setting for my next book. No one had set a crime thriller in Beijing at that point, just as no one had used Moscow as a setting before *Gorky Park*. I was absolutely intent on being the first to do it in China.

In the end, it was another six years before I returned. But this time I had a story, and a precious introduction to the Chinese police from a man revered by the country's top cops.

The late Dr. Richard Ward was an American criminologist who started life as a detective in the New York City police department. Sickened by the corruption he encountered on a daily basis, he quit to enrol at university and take a degree in criminology. His rise to acclaim by the international justice community followed quickly. He became the vice-chancellor of the University of Illinois in Chicago, where he set up an organisation called the Office of International Criminal Justice (OICJ), which brought police departments around the world together in an exchange of methods and information.

Then during the 1990s he spent several years in Shanghai training the top five hundred Chinese police officers in the latest Western policing techniques, and became a legend in the Chinese police.

Dick was my starting point when I began research on what was to become *The Firemaker*. I knew what my story would be, and that my two central characters would be a Beijing cop and an American female pathologist. I had already found technical advisors on pathology, and genetics (the subject of my story). But getting even a foothold on the steep learning curve that would be required to write authoritatively about the Chinese police was proving next to impossible. There was simply no information about their structure or methods anywhere, not in libraries or bookstores, nor on an internet then still in its infancy.

A contact put me in touch with Dr. Ward, and I wrote and asked if he would help me. He suggested we meet. He was giving a speech in Paris at a conference on international terrorism, and I was in France at the time. So we met for dinner in the French capital. I think, during that meal, I must have passed some kind of invisible litmus test, because texts, phone calls and emails then began flooding out of Dick's office in Chicago to the Chinese capital. And when I arrived on that first research trip in June 1997, the doors to the Chinese police – normally firmly closed to foreigners – were thrown wide open for me.

I was the first Western writer to get this kind of access, taken under the wing of the Beijing police and admitted into an arcane world of oriental policing, unusual in its embrace of both ancient and traditional Chinese methods, and the very latest international forensic and computing techniques. Over the next seven years, during frequent trips back and forth to China, I was given privileged insights into the workings of police departments in Beijing and Shanghai, allowed access to forensics and pathology facilities in both cities, visited police stations and holding cells, detectives' offices and interrogation rooms. I rode in squad cars and ate in police canteens. And such was the influence of the Chinese police, that if I wanted access to anything not normally available to foreigners, they arranged it.

Interestingly, the branch of the Beijing Ministry of Public

Security which hosted me, was the propaganda department. I quickly discovered that the Chinese interpretation of 'propaganda' was a little different from ours in the West. This department of the Ministry was headed up by a top cop, Wu He Peng, and his job was to make movies and TV cop shows and publish crime fiction. He would, for example, have made the Chinese equivalent of *Taggart*, and the Chinese had been publishing the Sherlock Holmes stories and Agatha Christie, among others, all through the twentieth century.

Their philosophy was to show police and their investigations in a good light. Cops were always the good guys, and the baddies always got caught. That was the propaganda element of the job.

Wu He Peng had been appointed to this job as reward for catching four notorious criminals who had been robbing museums of priceless artefacts and smuggling them out of the country. One of the first things he did in his new job was make an eight-hour drama based on that investigation. He wrote it, produced it, and starred in it as himself, bringing him instant fame throughout China, where the average nightly television audience is 500 million.

I also discovered that not only were the Chinese police avid consumers of crime fiction, they also loved to write stories. So much so that there is a course at the Beijing University of Public Security (the police university) entirely devoted to the history of Western crime fiction, and the propaganda department publishes several monthly magazines featuring short crime stories written by serving police officers.

The very first day of my first research trip I was taken to the University of Public Security. There I was introduced to the dean of the facility, and to a young serving police officer who had graduated some years before but returned from time to time to lecture to students. He was unusually tall and his nickname was 'Clinton' (Bill was still then US President) because it rhymed with his name, Lin Tong. I spent some time chatting to 'Clinton' after our initial meeting, and was hugely impressed by his quiet presence and thoughtful modesty. He immediately became the model for my Chinese cop, Li Yan.

That first research trip for *The Firemaker* was also my introduction to the man who would become my great friend and mentor, Dai Yisheng. He had been a firm friend of Dick Ward, and now became my *sherpa* during that and all subsequent visits to China. Mr Dai was a retired policeman, and one of the most educated and well-read people I have ever met. A graduate of the American University in Beijing in the late nineteen-forties, he won a post-grad place at Cambridge University in England. For better or worse, this coincided with the Communist Party's creation of the People's Republic in 1949. He was torn. Should he stay to help build the new China, or take up his place at Cambridge? He decided to stay. But as an intellectual, perhaps considered dangerous to the new regime, he was ordered to become a policeman – in Tibet.

He and his wife were dispatched from their home in Sichuan Province, and told they would have to walk to his new job in Tibet. It took them three perilous months, traversing rivers in flood, trekking through forests, climbing mountains, before they finally reached his posting.

His life was a turbulent one: thrown in jail during the Cultural Revolution before finally being brought back to Beijing and receiving a high-ranking post in an influential police department. Now retired, however, he had all the time in the world to devote to me and my researches. He took me places in Beijing that no foreigner had ever been. From him I gained invaluable insights into Chinese history and culture, the Chinese mentality in both everyday life and police investigations. I met the most extraordinary array of people inside and outside the justice system, and remember one night being smuggled by taxi from a backstreet restaurant, where I had been questioned by the local police, to the top secret HQ of the Beijing serious crime squad off a dark alleyway buried in the depths of the city.

Usually I met Mr Dai in the lobby of my hotel, and we would head off for our destination together on bicycles. But once I visited his home in a seedy, 1950s soviet-style apartment block, where old men played chess in the basement. And it seemed like an ignominious end to the career and life of such a noble and intelligent man.

Mr Dai became the inspiration for Li's Uncle Yifu.

By the time I had returned in '97 on that first research trip, English had become more widespread. Many restaurants were now featuring menus in English or Pinyin. And those ring roads were beginning to start filling up with more than taxis and buses and official vehicles. The great move away from the bicycle towards private cars was already underway.

And during all my subsequent visits, right up until 2004, I bore witness to the transformation of a country, from the closed, almost medieval world of Mao Zedong, to the vision of modern China set in train by Deng Xioaping. Those changes are reflected in the six books of *The China Thrillers*, which span probably the greatest and fastest period of change in Chinese history.

As I look back now, I can see the books as bearing witness to that change. From six empty ring roads to nine ring roads jammed end to end with private and commercial vehicles. From rivers of bicycles to the merest trickle of cyclists. From the Mongolian *siheyuan* courtyards which had been the traditional home of Beijingers for centuries, to high-rise modern apartment blocks.

It was a breathtaking transformation, reflected in each of the books.

The 'bread cars' – the ubiquitous yellow vans used as taxis, and referred to frequently in *The Firemaker* – had been banned by the time I returned in 1999 in an attempt to reduce pollution.

The 50th anniversary of the People's Republic that year saw the abolition of the old green military-style police uniform, to a new smart black uniform similar to those found in police forces elsewhere around the world.

In the run-up to the 2008 Beijing Olympics, great swathes of the city were demolished by armies of hammer-wielding workmen, transforming the capital in the space of little more than twelve months into a bustling modern metropolis, with little sign of the history and *hutongs* that had been so apparent when I first arrived.

Mao suits disappeared, to be replaced by the latest Western fashions. Everyone got mobile phones. Showrooms sprang up everywhere selling Mercedes and BMW. The insidious invasion of foreign culture brought McDonald's to Beijing street corners and, God forbid, even a Starbucks in the Forbidden City. English was becoming the common currency.

I feel privileged to have experienced Beijing and China as it had once been, and to have borne witness to its metamorphosis. *The China Thrillers* could hardly have been set at a time of greater change. And so I view the books now almost as modern historical documents. They tell us not only about the evolution in the relationship between Deputy Section Chief Li Yan and American pathologist Margaret Campbell, but bear testament to one of the most astonishing cultural transformations in recent history.

An approximate time scale of the series is as follows:

The Firemaker – Summer of 1999
The Fourth Sacrifice – Summer into autumn of 1999
The Killing Room – Winter of 2000
Snakehead – Summer of 2001
The Runner – Winter of 2003
Chinese Whispers – Autumn into winter of 2004

Peter May
Spring 2016

PROLOGUE

The laughter of the children peals through the early morning quiet like bells ringing for the dead. Hair straight, dark and club-cut, bobs above the frilled white and pink of the girls' blouses as they run along Ritan Park's dusty paths in the gloomy green Beijing dawn. Their dark oriental eyes burn with the fire of youth. So much life and innocence a breath away from that first encounter with death, and the taint of mortality that will stain their lives for ever.

Their mother had asked the baby-sitter, a dull country girl, to take the twins to the park early, before kindergarten. A treat in the cool of the morning, before the sun would rise and bleach all colour and substance from the day.

An old man in Mao pyjamas and white gloves practises t'ai chi among the trees, slow-motion graceful, arms outstretched, one leg so slowly lifting, exerting a control of his body that he has never had of his life. The girls barely see him, drawn by the strange sounds coming from around the next corner. They run ahead in breathless anticipation, ignoring the calls of the baby-sitter asking them to wait. Past a group of people who stand reading sheets of poetry strung between the trees; past a bench with two grey-haired old ladies in carpet slippers and grey cardigans who shake their heads at such a wanton display of free spirits. Even had they been allowed, in their day bound and bleeding feet would have put a stop to it.

The sounds that draw them, like strange music, grow louder as the children turn into a large paved circle bound by a high wall. They stop and stare in open-mouthed amazement. Dozens of couples – young, middle-aged, elderly; civil servants, office workers, army officers – shuffle in bizarre embrace. All heads are turned for guidance to the steps of an ancient sacrificial altar in the centre of the circle. At the top of the steps, where once blood was spilled as an offering to the sun, a young couple all in black confidently demonstrate the steps of the cha-cha in time to music scratching out from an old gramophone.

There is such joy in all their expressions that the children stand for a moment entranced, listening to the alien melody and rhythms of the music. Their baby-sitter catches them up at last, flushed and breathless. She stops, too, and gawps bewildered at the dancers. The city is such a strange, unfathomable place. She knows she could never settle here. From the far side of the circle she sees men wielding long, silver-bladed swords in slow, deliberate acts of contained aggression, slicing the air in grotesque parody of some medieval battle. The dancers ignore them, but the baby-sitter is afraid, and she shoos the reluctant children down a path, away from the people and the noise.

But now another distraction. Smoke filtering through the leaves, descending like a mist, thick and blue. A strange smell, the baby-sitter thinks, like meat on an open fire. And then she sees the flicker of flames through the green gloom and is gripped by a sudden desperate fore-boding. The children have run ahead again, scrambling up a dusty path among the trees, and ignore her calls to wait. She runs after them, a shady pavilion that overhangs the lake dropping away to her left.

The wailing call of a single-stringed violin reaches her as she crests the rise through the trees and follows the children into a clearing where the flames lick upwards from a huddled central mass. The girls stand staring curiously. The baby-sitter stops. She feels the heat on her face and shades her eyes from the glare, trying to see what it is that burns so fiercely. At its heart something moves. Something strangely human. The scream that comes from the nearest girl somehow sharpens the baby-sitter's focus, and she realises that what moved was a charred black hand reaching out towards her.

CHAPTER ONE

I

Monday Afternoon

The world tilted and the sun flashed back at her, reflected in a fractured mosaic like the pieces of a shattered mirror. Her body was telling her it was two in the morning and that she should be asleep. Her brain was informing her that it was mid-afternoon and that sleep was likely to be a distant prospect. Sleep. In twenty-one hours of travelling, it had successfully eluded her every attempt to embrace it. Although in these past weeks even sleep had provided no escape. She was not sure which was worse – the waking regrets and recriminations, or the restless nightmares. The gentle oblivion induced by the vodka tonics she had swallowed gratefully during the early hours of the flight had long since passed, leaving her with a dry mouth and a headache that swam somewhere just beyond consciousness. She glanced at the health declaration she had filled in earlier, still clutched in her hand . . .

WELCOME TO CHINA
FOR A BETTER & HEALTHIER TOMORROW

She had drawn a line through the space left for 'Content of Declaration'. She had nothing to declare, except for a broken heart and a wasted life – and neither of these, as far as she was aware, was infectious, contagious, or carried in the blood.

The world tilted again, and now she saw that the dazzling mosaic of light was in fact a pattern of water divided and subdivided into misshapen squares and oblongs. The reflection of a culture five thousand years old. Green shoots of rice pushing up through the paddies to feed a billion hungry mouths. Beyond the haze, to the north, lay the dusty plains of the Gobi desert.

An air hostess walked through the cabin spraying disinfectant into the atmosphere from an aerosol. Chinese regulations, she told them. And the captain announced that they would be landing at Beijing Capital Airport in just under fifteen minutes. Ground temperature was a sticky 35 degrees. Centigrade. That was 96 degrees Fahrenheit for the uninitiated. One of countless differences she supposed she would have to get used to in the next six weeks. She closed her eyes and braced herself for the landing. Of all the means of escape she might have picked, why had she chosen to fly? She hated airplanes.

The overcrowded shuttle bus, filled with the odour of bodies that had not washed for more than twenty hours, lurched to a halt outside the terminal building and spilled its passengers into the simmering afternoon. She headed quickly indoors in search of air-conditioning. There was none. If anything, it was hotter inside, the air thick and unbreathable. She was assailed by the sights and sounds and smells of China. People everywhere, as if every flight of the day had arrived at once, passengers fighting for places in the long queues forming at lines of immigration desks. Even in this international transit hall, Margaret drew odd looks from strange oriental faces who regarded her as the strange face in their midst. And, indeed, she was. Curling fair hair held back from her face in clasps, and tumbling over her shoulders. Ivory pale skin and clear blue eyes. The contrast with the black-haired, dark-eyed uniformity of the Han Chinese could not have been starker. She felt her stress level rising and took a deep breath.

'Maggot Cambo! Maggot Cambo!' A shrill voice pierced the hubbub. She looked to see a square, uniformed woman of indeterminate middle age pushing brusquely through the advancing passengers holding aloft a piece of card with the name MAGRET CAMPELL scrawled upon it in clumsy capital letters. It took Margaret a moment to connect the name she saw, and the one being called out, with herself.

'Uh . . . I think you might be looking for me,' she shouted above the noise, and thought how foolish that sounded. Of course they were looking for her. The square woman swivelled and glared at her through thick, horn-rimmed glasses.

'Doctah Maggot Cambo?'

'Margaret,' Margaret said. 'Campbell.'

'Okay, you gimme your passport.'

Margaret fumbled for the blue, eagle-crested passport in her bag, but hesitated in handing it over. 'And you are . . . ?'

'Constable Li Li Peng.' She pronounced it *Lily Ping*. And she straightened her back, the better to display the senior constable's three stars on the epaulets of her khaki-green short-sleeve shirt. Her skipped green hat with its yellow braid and its gold, red and blue crest of the Ministry of Public Security was slightly too large and pushed the square cut of her fringe down over the tops of her glasses. '*Waiban* has appointed me to look after you.'

'*Waiban*?'

'Foreign affairs office of your *danwei*.'

Margaret felt sure she should know these things. No doubt it would be there, somewhere, in all the briefing material they had given her. '*Danwei*?'

Lily's irritation was ill concealed. 'Your work unit – at the university.'

'Oh. Right.' Margaret felt she had revealed too much ignorance already and handed over her passport.

Lily glanced at it briefly. 'Okay. I take care of immigration and we get your bags.'

A dark grey BMW stood idling just outside the door of the terminal building. The trunk lid swung up and a waif-like girl in uniform leapt out of the car to load Margaret's luggage. The two large cases were almost as big as she was, and she struggled to heave them off the trolley. Margaret moved to help her, but was quickly steered into the back seat by Lily. 'Driver get bags. You keep door shut for air-conditioning.' And to reinforce the point, she slammed the door firmly closed. Margaret breathed in the almost-chill air and sank back into the seat. Waves of fatigue washed over her. All she wanted now was her bed.

Lily slid into the front passenger seat. 'Okay, so now we go to headquarters Beijing Municipal Police to pick up Mistah Wade. He send apology for not being here to meet you, but he have business there. Then we go straight to People's University of Public Security and you meet Professah Jiang. Okay? And tonight we have banquet.' Margaret almost groaned. The prospect of bed receded into some distant, misty future. That much-quoted line from Frost's poem came back to her . . . 'and miles to go before I sleep'. Then she frowned, replaying Lily's words. Did she say *banquet*?

The BMW sped along the airport expressway, bypassing the toll gates and quickly reaching the outskirts of the city. Margaret watched with amazement through the darkened side windows as the city rose up around her. Towering office blocks, new hotels, trade centres, upscale apartments. Everywhere the traditional single-storey tile-roofed *siheyuan* courtyards in the narrow *hutongs* were being demolished to make way for the transition from 'developing' country to 'first world' status. Whatever Margaret had expected – and she was not certain what her expectations had been – it had not been this. The only thing 'Chinese' that she could see in any of it were the ornamental curled eaves grafted on to the tops of skyscrapers. Long gone the huge character posters urging comrades to greater effort on behalf of the motherland. In their place gigantic adverts for Sharp, Fuji, Volvo. Capitalism was the spur now. They passed a McDonald's burger joint, a blur of red and yellow. Her preconceptions of streets thick with cyclists all uniformly dressed in Mao pyjamas were blown away in the clouds of carbon monoxide issuing from the buses, trucks, taxis and private cars that choked the six lanes of the Third Ring Road as it swept round the eastern fringes of the city. Just like Chicago, she thought. Very 'first world'. Except for the bicycle lanes.

The driver hugged the outside lane as they approached the city centre past the Beijing Hotel and Wangfujing Street. In the distance Margaret could see the ornate towering gate of the Forbidden City, with its huge portrait of Mao gazing down on Tiananmen Square. Heaven's Gate. It was the backdrop, it seemed, to every CNN report from Beijing. A giant cliché of China. Margaret recalled seeing the pictures on TV of Mao's portrait defaced with red paint by the democracy demonstrators in the square in '89. A student herself then, still at medical school, she had been shocked and outraged by the bloody events of that spring. And now here she was, a decade on. She wondered how much things had changed. Or even if they had.

Their car took a sudden left, to the accompaniment of a chorus of horns, and they slipped unexpectedly into a leafy side street with gardens down its centre and locust trees on either side forming a shady canopy. Here they might have been in the old quarter of any European city, elegant Victorian and colonial buildings on either side. Lily half turned, pointing to a high wall on their right.

'Ministry of Public Security in there. Used to be British embassy compound before Chinese government threw them out. This old legation area.'

Further down, past some older apartment blocks that didn't look remotely European, they took another left into Dong Jiaominxiang Lane, a narrower street where the light was almost completely obscured by overhanging trees. A couple of bicycle repairmen had set up shop on the sidewalk, making the most of the shade. Cars and bicycles crowded the road. On their right, a gateway opened on to a vast modern white building at the top of a sweep of steps guarded by two lions. High above the entrance hung a huge red-and-gold crest. 'China Supreme Court,' Lily said, and Margaret barely had time to look before the car swung left and squealed to a sudden halt. There was a bump and a clatter. Their driver threw her hands in the air with a gasp of incredulity and jumped out of the car.

Margaret craned forward to see what was happening. They had been in the act of turning through an arched gateway into a sprawling compound and had collided with a cyclist. Margaret heard the shrill voice of their driver berating the cyclist, who was getting back to his feet, apparently unhurt. As he stood, she saw that he was a police officer, in his early thirties, his neatly pressed uniform crumpled and dusty. A trickle of blood ran down his forearm from a nasty graze on his elbow. He pulled himself up to his full height and glared down at the little driver, who suddenly stopped shrieking and wilted under his gaze. She bent down timidly to retrieve his cap and held it out like a peace offering. He snatched it from her, but peace was the last thing on his mind. He unleashed, it appeared to Margaret, a mouthful of abusive language at the shrinking waif. Lily, in the front seat, emitted a strange grunting noise and hurriedly climbed out of the car. Margaret, too, thought it was time to interface, and opened the back door.

As she got out, Lily was picking up the bicycle and making apologetic noises. The policeman appeared to turn his wrath on her. More venom issued forth. Margaret approached. 'What's the problem here, Lily? This guy got something against women drivers?' All three stopped and looked at her in amazement.

The young policeman regarded her coldly. 'American?'

'Sure.'

And in perfect English, 'Then why don't you mind your own business?' He was almost shaking with anger. 'You were in the back seat and couldn't possibly have seen what happened.'

From somewhere deep inside, Margaret felt the first stirrings of her fiery Celtic temper. 'Oh yeah? Well, maybe if you hadn't been so busy looking at me in the back seat, you would have been watching where you were going.'

Lily was horrified. 'Doctah Cambo!'

The young policeman stood for a moment glaring at Margaret. Then he snatched his bicycle from Lily, dusted down his cap and replaced it firmly on his close-cropped head before turning and wheeling his bike away in the direction of a European-style redbrick building just inside the compound.

Lily shook her head, clearly distraught. 'That's terrible thing to say, Doctah Cambo.'

'What?' Margaret was at a loss.

'You make him lose *mianzi*.'

'Lose what?'

'Face. You make him lose face.'

Margaret was incredulous. 'Face?'

'Chinese have problem with face.'

'With a face like his, I'm not surprised! And what about you? Your . . . *mianzi*? You didn't have to stand there and take all that. I mean, you outrank him, for heaven's sake!'

'Outrank him?' Lily looked astonished. 'No.'

'Well, he only had two stars . . .' She patted her shoulder. '. . . and you've got three.'

Lily shook her head. 'Three star, *one* stripe. He got *three* stripe. He is Supervisor Li, senior detective Section One, Beijing Municipal Police.'

Margaret was taken aback. 'A detective? In uniform?'

'Uniform not normal.' Lily looked very grave. 'He must be go some ve-ery important meeting.'

II

Li stormed through the front door of the redbrick building that still housed the headquarters of the Criminal Investigation Department and made his way quickly to the toilet. The blood on his forearm was congealing with the dirt from the side-walk. He ran it under the tap and jumped back cursing as water splashed darkly all over the pale green of his shirt. He looked at himself in the mirror above the washbasin. He was dusty and dishevelled, splashed with water, bleeding from the elbow, and had a dirty smudge on his forehead. In addition to which his dignity was severely dented – and in front of two Chinese women of inferior rank he had just lost face to a foreigner. '*Yangguizi!*' He almost spat the word back at himself in the mirror. *Foreign devil!* After two hours of sweating over his uncle's ironing board, neatly pressing every crease and flap of his shirt and trousers; after an uncomfortable hour in the barber's chair that morning having his hair shorn to a bristling quarter-inch all over; after fifteen minutes in a cool shower to wash away the sweat and dust of the day; he should have looked and felt his best going into the most important interview of his career. Instead, he looked – and felt – awful.

He sluiced his face with water and dabbed away the blood on his arm with paper towels. His anger at the incident at the gate was giving way again to the butterflies that had been fluttering inside his ribcage all morning.

When the position of Deputy Section Chief had become vacant there was an automatic assumption among his peers that Li would get the job. Still only thirty-three, he was one of the most experienced detectives in Section One. He had broken a record number of homicides and armed robberies since his graduation to the section from the University of Public Security, where he had been the top student of his year.

Li himself had felt that he was ready for the job, but he was not in a position to apply for it. The decision on his eligibility or otherwise would be made in the Promotions Department, with a final decision being taken by the Chief of Police. Cosy assumptions of promotion from within had, however, been thrown into disarray by rumours that a senior detective of the Shanghai CID was being recommended for the post. It had been impossible to ascertain the veracity of the rumour and, through the long bureaucratic process, Li did not know if he was even being considered. Until his summons to attend an interview with the divisional head of the CID, Commissioner Hu Yisheng. And even now he had no idea what to expect. His immediate boss at Section One, Chen Anming, had been tight-lipped and grim-faced. Li feared the worst. He took a deep breath, straightened his cap, tugged at his shirt, and stepped out of the toilet.

Commissioner Hu Yisheng sat in shirtsleeves behind his desk in a high-backed leather chair, his jacket carefully draped over the back of it. Behind him, rows of hardback books in a glass-fronted bookcase, a red Chinese flag hanging limp in the heat, various photographs and certificates framed on the wall. He leaned over his desk, writing slowly, tight, careful characters in a large open notebook. His mirror image gazed back at him from the highly polished surface. He waved Li to a seat without looking up. Li slowly lowered his hand from an unseen salute and perched uncomfortably on the edge of a seat opposite the Commissioner. The silence was broken only by the gentle whirring of a fan lifting the edges of papers at one side of the desk – and by the heavy scratching of the Commissioner's fountain pen. Li cleared his throat nervously and the Commissioner glanced up at him for a moment, perhaps suspecting impatience. Then he returned to his writing. It was important, Li decided, that he didn't clear his throat again. And almost as the thought formed, so the phlegm seemed to gather in his throat, tempting him to clear it. Like an itch you can't scratch. He swallowed.

After what seemed an eternity, the Commissioner finally placed the top back on his pen and closed the book. He folded his hands in front of him and regarded Li almost speculatively.

'So,' he said. 'How is your uncle?'

'He is very well, Commissioner. He sends his regards.'

The Commissioner smiled, and there was genuine affection in it. 'A very great man,' he said. 'He suffered more than most, you know, during the Smashing of the Four Olds.'

'I know.' Li nodded. He had heard it all before.

'He was my inspiration when the Cultural Revolution ended. There was no bitterness in him, you see. After everything that happened, Old Yifu would only look forward. "No use worrying over the might-have-beens," he used to say to me. "It is a happy thing to have a broken mirror reshaped." It was the spirit of men like your uncle that put this country back on the rails.'

Li smiled his dutiful agreement and felt a sudden foreboding creep over him.

'Unfortunately, it makes it very difficult,' said the

Commissioner. 'For you – and us. You understand, of course, it is the policy of the Party to discourage nepotism in all its insidious forms.'

And Li knew then that he hadn't got the job. He loved his Uncle Yifu dearly. He was the kindest, fairest, wisest man he knew. But he was also a legend in the Beijing police. Even five years after his retirement. And legends cast long shadows.

'It is incumbent upon you to be better than the rest, and for us to examine your record more critically.' The Commissioner sat back and took in a long, slow breath through his nose. 'Just as well we are both good at our jobs, eh?' A twinkle in his eye. 'As of 8 a.m. tomorrow you are promoted to the rank of Senior Supervisor, Class Three, and to the position of Deputy Section Chief, Section One.' A broad smile split his face suddenly and he rose to his feet, extending an arm towards the bewildered Li. 'Congratulations.'

III

The car sat idling in the somnolent shade of a tree just inside the rear entrance to police headquarters, across the compound from the door of the redbrick building that Supervisor Li had passed through more than fifteen minutes earlier.

'That Mistah Wade now.'

If Margaret had lapsed into gentle snoring in the back seat Lily gave no sign of having heard it. She leaned across and unlocked the door. Bob Wade slipped in beside Margaret. He was incredibly tall and skinny and seemed to have to fold himself up to fit in the car.

'Hey, you guys, I'm really sorry to keep you waiting.' He pumped Margaret's hand enthusiastically. 'Hi. You must be Dr Campbell.'

'Margaret,' she said.

'Okay, Margaret. Bob Wade. Jeez, it's hot out there.' He took a grubby-looking handkerchief and wiped away the beads of sweat forming across a high, receding forehead. 'Lily looking after you okay?'

'Sure.' Margaret nodded slowly. 'Lily's a real gem.'

Lily flicked her a look, and Bob was not slow to detect Margaret's tone. He leaned forward to the driver. 'How about we hot-tail it to the university, Shimei? We're running a bit behind schedule.'

Shimei gunned the engine and backed out into the compound before swinging round towards the gate. As they passed under the arch, Margaret noticed Supervisor Li emerging from the redbrick building. His whole demeanour had changed – a spring in his step, a smile on his face. He didn't even see their car. His shoulders were pushed back and Margaret realised that he was very tall for a Chinese, maybe six feet. He pulled his cap down over his flat-top crew cut. Its peak cast a shadow over his square-jawed high-cheekboned face and, as he disappeared from view, she thought how unattractive he was.

'You must be pretty tired.' She turned to find Bob examining her closely. He would be around fifty-five – the age she felt right now.

She nodded. 'I've been on the go something like twenty-two hours. It seems like one hell of a long day. Only it's tomorrow already and I've still got nearly half of it to go.'

He grinned. 'Yeah, I know. You're chasing the day until about halfway across the Pacific and suddenly you jump a day ahead.' He leaned towards her, lowering his voice. 'What happened with Lily?'

'Oh . . .' Margaret didn't want to go through it all again. 'Just a little misunderstanding.'

'You mustn't mind her really. She's not *all* bad. Bark's worse than her bite. You know, she was a Red Guard during the Cultural Revolution. A real old-fashioned comrade. Only her kind of communism's not really in vogue any more, so she'll stay at the bottom of the pile. Never be anything more than a three-star constable.'

The Cultural Revolution was something Margaret had always meant to read up on. She'd heard of it often enough without ever really knowing what it was – except that it had been a bad time in China. She decided, however, not to display her ignorance to Bob.

'So what made you decide to come to China?' he asked.

The truth wasn't an option for Margaret. She shrugged vaguely. 'Oh, you know . . . I was always kind of interested in the place. The Mysterious East and all that. I was doing some lecturing, part-time, at the University of Illinois in Chicago, and this guy from the Office of International Criminal Justice . . .'

'Dick Goldman.'

'Yeah, that's him. He said the OICJ were looking for

someone to do a six-week stint at the People's University of Public Security in Beijing, lecturing on forensic pathology, and was I interested. I thought, hell, it beats chasing fire engines for the Cook County Medical Examiner's office. Lot of fires in Chicago in June.'

Bob smiled. 'You'll find they do things a lot differently here than Chicago. I've been out here nearly two years and I'm still trying to get my lecture notes photocopied.'

'You're kidding.'

'You ever heard of the Three Ps?' She shook her head. 'Well, they represent the three things you must have to survive in this country. That's Patience, Patience and Patience. The Chinese have their own way of doing things. I'm not saying they do them any worse or any better than we do. Just different. And they've got a totally different perspective on the world.'

'In what way?'

'Well, for example, you come here thinking: I'm an American citizen. I live in the richest and most powerful country in the world. And you think that makes you pretty damned superior. But the humblest peasant working fifteen hours a day in the paddy fields will look down his nose at you. Why? Because you're not Chinese and he is. Because he is a citizen of the Middle Kingdom. That's their name for China. So called because it is, of course, the centre of the world, and everything beyond its borders is peripheral and inferior, populated by *yangguizi* – foreign devils like you and me.'

She snorted. 'That's just empty arrogance.'

Bob raised an eyebrow. 'Is it? The Chinese were weaving silk three thousand years ago. They were casting iron eighteen hundred years before the Europeans figured out how to do it. They invented paper, and were printing books hundreds of years before Gutenberg built his first printing press. By comparison, we Americans are just a pimple on the face of history.'

Margaret wondered how often he'd delivered this little homily to visiting American lecturers. He probably thought it made him seem more knowledgeable, and China more daunting. And he was right.

'Biggest single difference – culturally?'

She shrugged her complete ignorance.

'The Chinese focus on and reward group efforts, rather than individual ones. They're team players. And the individual is expected to put the team's interests way ahead of his own. And that's a pretty big deal in a country of 1.2 billion people. Guess that's why they've been around for five thousand years.'

Margaret was getting tired of her cultural studies lesson. 'So what happens now?'

Bob became brisk and businesslike. 'Okay. We'll get you settled in at the university, meet the people you've got to meet, then you can go and get changed and freshened up for the banquet.'

Lily's words came back from earlier. 'Banquet?'

'Yeah, at the famous Quanjude Beijing Duck restaurant. It's a traditional welcome. Didn't you get an OICJ briefing document?'

'Yes, of course.' Margaret didn't like to confess that she

hadn't read it. She had *meant* to. If she could stay awake long enough she would do it tonight.

'There's a lot of etiquette associated with these things. Do's and don'ts. Chinese can be a bit touchy, you know what I mean? But don't worry, I'll be around to keep you right.'

Margaret didn't know whether to be pleased or pissed. Bob, she thought, could become pretty tiresome.

They were heading due west now along another six-lane highway running through a canyon of modern tower blocks. The sun was dipping lower in the late afternoon, dazzling through the dust and insects that caked the windscreen. Out of the haze, a sweeping flyover rose up from the road ahead. But at the last moment they bore right on to a smaller road thick with cyclists, and then right again into what looked like a building site.

'Here we are,' Bob said.

'We are?' Margaret looked with some horror.

They bumped across a pot-holed yard, raising a cloud of dust in their wake, and turned through a gate where a policeman stood endlessly to attention in the searing heat. He saluted as they passed. No one bothered to acknowledge him. Then suddenly they were on a private tree-lined road, a large all-weather games pitch behind a high fence on their left. They pulled up outside a tall white building with curled eaves and ornamental brown pillars.

Margaret got stiffly out of the car and was nearly knocked over by the heat. In the cool, cloistered air-conditioning of the BMW, she had forgotten how hot it was out there.

Bob pointed to a twenty-storey building beyond the administration block. 'Staff live in there.'

'What?' Margaret was incredulous. 'How many staff are there?'

'Oh, about a thousand.' He steered her through double doors and up dark marble steps in the cool interior.

'And how many students?'

'Around three thousand.'

Margaret gasped. A three-to-one student-teacher ratio was unheard of in the States.

'It's kind of like the West Point for police in China. Down here.' And they set off down a long featureless corridor.

Margaret had had no idea the university was on such a small scale. She was seriously regretting now not having read her briefing material.

'Of course,' Bob went on, enjoying his possession of superior knowledge, 'you'll be interested in the pathology department and the forensics. That's all down the far end of the playing fields. The Centre of Material Evidence Determination. They got some pretty sophisticated stuff down there, including a brand-new block with all the latest laboratory testing facilities – DNA, you name it. Stuff from all over China gets sent there. Christ, they even take ear-prints – you know, like fingerprints, only ears. But I got to admit, I can't see many perps leaving their ear-prints at the scene of a crime, unless they've beaten somebody to death with their hearing aid.' He laughed at his own joke. But Margaret was distracted. His smile faded. 'Not my field, of course.'

'What *is* your field?'

'Computer profiling. I've been helping them set up a system here that's going to be as good as anything the FBI've got back home. In here.' He opened the door into a tiny office, no bigger than eight feet square, with one small window at ceiling height. There were two desks pushed together, three small plastic chairs of the stacking variety, and a single filing cabinet. Three cardboard boxes stood side by side on one of the desks. 'This is you.'

Margaret looked at him in consternation. 'This is me what?'

'Your office. And think yourself lucky. Space is at a premium.'

She was about to voice an opinion on Bob's definition of the word 'lucky', but was prevented from doing so by the arrival of two middle-aged men and a woman all wearing the uniform of senior police officers. They smiled and bowed and Margaret smiled and bowed back, and then glanced anxiously at Bob for help.

'These are your colleagues in the Criminal Investigation Department here at the university.' He rattled off something in Chinese and they all bowed and smiled again. Margaret bowed and smiled back. 'Professors Tian and Bai, and the delightful Dr Mu,' Bob introduced them. They all shook hands, and then one by one solemnly produced their business cards and presented them to Margaret, the corners held between thumb and forefinger, the English translations of their names facing towards her. She took them each in turn and fumbled in her bag for her own cards and handed one back to each.

'*Ni hau*,' she said, exercising the only Chinese she knew.

'You're supposed to present your cards to them the way they did to you,' Bob said.

'Am I?' She was flustered by this, but it was too late to do anything about it now.

'Didn't you read your briefing material?'

'Sorry, I forgot.'

She smiled at them again and they all smiled back, then one by one lifted a cardboard box from the desk and left.

Margaret looked around in despair. 'This is hopeless, Bob. I can't work in this space for six weeks.'

'What's wrong with it?'

'Wrong with it? It's like a cell. I'll be banging my head off the walls after a week in here.'

'Well, I wouldn't mention it to Professors Tian, Bai and Dr Mu.'

'Why?'

'Because I don't think you'd find them very sympathetic. They probably don't like you very much already.'

Margaret couldn't believe she was hearing this. 'Why wouldn't they like me? They've only just met me.'

'Well, for one thing . . .' Bob sat on the edge of one of the desks, '. . . you probably make more in a week than they earn in a year. And for another . . . they've just been moved out of their office to make way for you.'

Margaret's jaw slackened.

'Anyway . . .' Bob stood up. '. . . time you met Professor Jiang. He'll be waiting for you.'

*

Professor Jiang was a thickset man in his late fifties, who looked like he'd been scrubbed and freshly pressed for the meeting. He had a head of beautifully cut thick hair, greying in attractive streaks, and wore the rank-equivalent uniform of a Senior Commissioner. His dark-rimmed glasses seemed a little too large for his face. He rose expectantly as Bob ushered Margaret into the reception room. It was cool in here, blinds drawn to keep the sun at bay, two rows of soft low chairs facing each other across the room, even lower tables in front of each, bottles of chilled water placed before every chair. Also rising to greet them were a younger man in uniform, and a pretty girl in her early twenties wearing a plain cream dress. Bob made the introductions. First in Chinese, then in English.

'Margaret, this is Professor Jiang, Director of the Criminal Investigation Department – your department head.' They shook hands and exchanged formal smiles. 'And his assistant, Mr Cao Min. He's a graduate of the university who's been out there doing it in the real world for a while. A real-life detective.' Mr Cao shook her hand solemnly. 'And, uh, this is Veronica.' Bob chuckled. 'Lots of Chinese girls like to give themselves English names. Come to think of it, I don't believe I know what your real name is, Veronica.'

'Veronica do fine,' Veronica said, shaking Margaret's hand and smiling sweetly. She was extraordinarily tiny, her child-like hand almost disappearing inside Margaret's. 'I translate for you.'

They all took their seats, Professor Jiang, Mr Cao and Bob on one side of the room, Margaret facing them on the other.

Veronica sat in neutral territory on a chair by the window. Margaret felt as if she were attending an interview, and sat with a strained smile on her face, waiting for whatever would happen next. After a moment, Professor Jiang composed himself, sat forward and began addressing Margaret directly in Chinese. She found it strangely disconcerting not being able to understand a word he said but being obliged, somehow, to maintain eye contact and listen with interest. Professor Jiang's voice was very soft, its cadences almost hypnotic, and Margaret caught herself beginning to sway back and forth. She had a sudden, overpowering desire to sleep. She blinked hard. The professor spoke for what seemed like an eternity before finishing with a tiny smile and sitting back in anticipation of her response.

Margaret looked to Veronica for enlightenment. Veronica thought for a long time. Then she said, 'Ah . . . Professor Jiang say he welcome you to the Chinese People's University of Public Security. Very pleased to have you here.' Margaret waited for more, but Veronica had clearly finished, and all eyes were on Margaret for her reply. She smiled and locked eyes once more with the professor.

'Uh . . . It's a very great honour, Professor, to be invited to lecture at the People's University of Public Security. I only hope that I can live up to your expectations of me, and that I can bring some enlightenment to your students.' She caught Bob winking encouragingly at her from across the room, and not for the first time that day felt an urge to punch his smug face.

Professor Jiang leaned forward again and breathed Mandarin across the room for another eternity.

'Professor Jiang say he sure you bring much light to students.'

The professor watched eagerly for Margaret's response. She was at a loss, so just smiled and nodded. Which seemed to go down well, for the professor grinned broadly and nodded back. They smiled and nodded back and forth for the next quarter of a minute before Mr Cao suddenly sat forward and said, in a West Coast American accent, 'You and I will meet tomorrow morning and go over your schedule of lectures. If you require any audiovisual facilities, or access to the pathology labs, then I can arrange this.'

Margaret was almost overwhelmed by relief at the ability to be able to communicate again in plain English. 'That's great,' she said. 'I brought quite a lot of slides, and if it's possible to arrange it, you know, I think it would be great if we could take the students through a real autopsy.'

'We can discuss this tomorrow,' Mr Cao said, his rise to his feet apparently a cue for everyone else to stand. As Margaret shook hands with them all yet again, there was a knock at the door and Lily entered, nodding her acknowledgement to Professor Jiang.

'Ready to take you to apartment, Doctah Cambo.'

'Hotel,' Margaret corrected her.

'Apartment,' Lily insisted. 'Just down street here. We have apartment for unmarried lecturer.'

'No, no. I'm staying at the Friendship Hotel. I didn't want an apartment. I made that clear in Chicago. It's all booked.'

The colour rose high on Lily's face. 'People's University of Public Security cannot afford hotel. We provide apartment for lecturer.'

Almost twenty-four hours without sleep was taking its toll on Margaret's patience. 'Look, the hotel is booked, I'm paying for it myself. It was all part of the deal. Okay?'

There was consternation on Professor's Jiang's face as he struggled to make sense of this friction between the two women. Bob stepped in quickly, smiling and speaking rapidly in Chinese in an attempt to smooth Lily's ruffled feathers. Then he turned to Margaret, still smiling. 'Just a little misunderstanding. We'll sort it all out.'

Lily looked far from mollified. She glared at Margaret, turned abruptly and marched out of the room. Bob smiled and nodded some more, uttering further soothing words in Chinese to Professor Jiang, and steering Margaret hastily out into the corridor.

'Jesus, Margaret, what the hell do you think you're playing at?'

Margaret was beside herself with indignation. 'What have I done now? The hotel is booked. It was all agreed. I didn't want to go home at night and have to start making my own bed and cooking my own meals.'

He drew her away from the reception room. 'Yeah, but Lily didn't know that. You don't just go contradicting people here, Margaret.'

'Don't tell me. I made her lose "*mianzi*".'

'Oh, so you have read your briefing notes.' Margaret resisted the temptation to put him straight. 'The thing is, Margaret, the Chinese have got a thousand ways of saying "no" without ever saying "no". And you're going to have to start learning some of them, or your six weeks here are going to seem like six years.'

Margaret sighed theatrically. 'So what *should* I have said?'

'You should have said how grateful you were for the university's offer of accommodation, but that unfortunately you had already booked a room at the Friendship Hotel.' Bob stopped her at the top of the stairs. 'I told you, they do things differently here. And if you want to get anything done, you're going to have to start getting yourself a little *guanxi* in the bank.'

'What the hell's "gwanshee"?'

'It's what makes this whole society work. A kind of old boys' network – you scratch my back, I'll scratch yours. I do you a favour, you do me one in return. And you're not doing anyone any favours by making them lose face.'

Margaret's head dropped, and to Bob she suddenly looked very small and very frail. He immediately regretted his impatience with her.

'Hey, listen . . . I'm sorry. You've had a long day . . .'

'*Two* days,' she corrected him, a hint of petulance in her tone.

'And I guess this is all pretty bizarre stuff.'

'Yeah.' Now she was fighting an unaccountable urge to burst into tears, and became aware of her foot tapping manically on the top step. Bob was aware of it, too. His voice became soothing.

'Look, Lily'll take you to the Friendship. Have a shower, get changed, maybe even grab an hour's shut-eye, and just let the banquet tonight wash over you. Enjoy it. The food's great. And as for the other stuff . . . I'll keep you right, okay?'

She flicked him a look that verged on the grateful, and a wry smile turned up the corners of her mouth. 'Sure. Thanks.'

But her reassurance lasted only as long as it took to reach the car and the scowling face of Lily Ping, and Margaret's heart sank again.

IV

The young security guard nodded to Li as he passed through the staff gate at the rear of the Jingtan joint venture hotel on Jianguomennei Avenue. Li slipped in the back door to the ground-floor kitchen and looked around for Yongli. But there was no sign of him. Sous-chefs were chopping vegetables and preparing marinades, jointing chickens and basting duck for roasting.

Li stopped one of the waitresses. 'Where's Ma Yongli?'

She nodded towards the door. 'Out front.'

Li crossed to the door, opening it a crack, and peeked out. Yongli stood by a hot plate and gas ring behind an ornate counter with a Chinese canopy. His white smock seemed to emphasise his height and his bulk, his round face solemn below his tall white chef's hat. He gazed out at the early eaters in the twenty-four-hour Café China, his mind somewhere else altogether. He was on front-of-house duty tonight, cooking dishes from the day's Special Menu in view of the customers who ordered them. But the serious diners were not yet in and, for the moment at least, he was idle, his mind free to wander. Li watched him affectionately for a moment, then issued a short, sharp whistle from between his front teeth. Yongli's head snapped round and his face lit up when he saw Li. He glanced about quickly to see if any of the managers were watching, then hurried over to the door, pushing Li back into the kitchen with an irresistible force. 'Well? Well? Come on, tell me. What happened?'

The smiled drained from Li's face and he lowered his head and shrugged. 'The Commissioner said it was Party policy to "discourage nepotism in all its insidious forms".'

All the animation left Yongli's expression. 'Aw, come on, you're shitting me, right?'

Li retained his grave demeanour. 'It's what he said.' He paused, and then a big grin split his face. 'But it didn't stop me getting the job.'

'You bastard!' Yongli grabbed at him, but Li backed off, grinning stupidly.

'Hey!' Yongli shouted out to the kitchen. And heads lifted. 'Big Li got his promotion!' And he grabbed a couple of stainless-steel ladles and started working his way up a line of hanging pots and pans, beating out a tattoo on them as he went. A cheer went up from the staff, and there was a spontaneous round of applause. Li flushed and shook his head with embarrassment, still grinning like an idiot. Yongli reached the end of the row. 'So the next time you get lifted by the cops,' he shouted, 'you can just say, hey, don't you know who I am? I'm a pal of Big Li Yan. And they'll let you go faster than hot coals.' He turned a huge, sparkling-eyed, maniacal grin on his friend and stalked down the aisle towards him, taking Li's face in two giant hands and planting a big wet kiss on his forehead. 'Congratulations, pal.' And the two embraced, to further applause from the kitchen staff.

They had been best friends since meeting on their first day at the University of Public Security nearly fifteen years before. Two kindred spirits, each instantly recognising the other. Big daft boys, then and now. It had broken Li's heart when Yongli had dropped out in their final year. His results had been deteriorating in almost precise correlation to his pursuit of women and karaoke bars and a lifestyle he could not afford. It was the essential difference between them. Li took his career more seriously than his pleasures. But to Yongli the pursuit of pleasure was all. And he had jumped at the chance to train as a chef with a Sino-American joint venture.

'The money's fantastic,' he had told Li. And, compared to the subsistence existence of a Chinese student, it was. Even after his promotion, Li would earn substantially less than his friend. Yongli's training had also included lessons in English, six months at a hotel in Switzerland learning how to cook and present European food, and three months in the States finding out how Americans liked to eat their steaks. There he had learned how to fully indulge his hedonistic inclinations, returning with a great appetite for all things American and a three-inch addition to his waistline. In many ways Li and

Yongli had grown apart, their paths in life taking very different courses, and their friendship now was sustained more by its history than by its present. But the warmth between them was still strong.

'So.' Yongli pulled off his hat and threw it to one of the other chefs, who caught it deftly. 'Tonight you and I are going to celebrate.'

'But you're working.'

Yongli twinkled. 'I made contingency arrangements – just in case the news was good. The boys await my call, and a table is booked at the Quanjude.'

'The boys?'

'The old gang. Just like it used to be.' A thought clouded his smile briefly. 'And no Lotus. I know you don't approve.'

Li protested. 'Hey, listen, Yongli, it's not that I disapprove–'

Yongli cut him off. 'Not tonight, pal. Okay?'

The moment of friction between them was past in an instant. An onlooker might barely have been aware of it. Yongli grinned again, warmly. 'We're gonna get you drunk.'

V

To Margaret's surprise, the bar was deserted, except for a balding middle-aged man in the far corner nursing a large Scotch and flipping desultorily through the pages of the *International Herald Tribune*. She felt better for having showered and changed and soaked up a little of the unexpected luxury of the Friendship Hotel. Built in the fifties to house

Russian 'experts', this vast granite edifice was a throwback to the days of uneasy co-operation between China and Stalin's Russia, all polished brass and white marble dragons beneath curling green-tiled eaves supported on rust-red pillars. She had changed into a cool cotton summer dress, and blow-dried her hair. It fell now in natural golden curls across her shoulders. Before leaving the room she had examined her face in the mirror – pale skin dotted with freckles – as she applied a little make-up, and had noticed the beginnings of lines around her eyes and the deep shadows beneath them. And she remembered with a painful stab the events of the last eighteen months and the devastating effect they had had on her life. In all her fatigue, and in all the strangeness and disorientation of China, they had actually slipped from her conscious mind for the first time. Now they came back like the pungent taste of something not quite right eaten some hours earlier. A drink was required.

A barmaid lounged on the customer side of the bar and two young men hovered behind it. Whatever conversation they'd been having ended abruptly when Margaret entered, and as she eased herself into one of the tall bar stools the barmaid thrust a drinks menu into her hand. Margaret handed it back, unopened. 'Vodka tonic, with ice and lemon.'

The man in the corner looked up, interested for the first time by the sound of her voice. He folded his paper, drained his glass, and headed for the bar. He was short, only a little taller than Margaret, and stockily built. Margaret turned as he approached and saw a man whose face was collapsing, jowls deforming a weak jawline, deep creases running down fleshy cheeks from puffy eyes that were watery and bloodshot. His remaining hair, wiry and unruly, was almost entirely grey and plastered to his head with some kind of scented oil that assaulted Margaret's olfactory senses. He smiled unpleasantly, and even above the scent of his hair oil, Margaret could smell the alcohol on his breath. 'Put that on my bill,' he said in an unmistakably Californian drawl.

'That's quite all right,' Margaret said coolly.

'No, I insist.' He tossed a glance at one of the barmen. 'And gimme another Scotch.' Then he refocused on Margaret. 'Makes a change to hear a voice from the old country.'

'Really? I thought this was where the international set hung out.' It was what she'd read, and one of the reasons she had chosen to stay there. After relations between Russia and China had become less than warm and the Russian 'experts' had departed, the Friendship Hotel had become a haven for 'experts' of all nationalities, and more recently a gathering place for expats who preferred English to Chinese.

'Used to be,' he said with a hint of bitterness in his voice. 'But you know how it is. One place is popular this year, another the next. And the beautiful people move on.' Margaret was aware of an increasing rancour in his tone now. 'Still, I can't say I miss them. The aesthetic can become somewhat tedious, don't you think?' But he wasn't really interested in what she thought. He went on without pausing, 'A steady supply of whisky's all a man really needs. And from a quiet corner in here the solitary drinker can always watch the ridiculous spectacle of the Chinese *nouveaux riches* in search of status. My name's McCord, by the way. J. D. McCord.' He held out his hand, and she felt compelled to shake it. She had expected it to be limp and damp. Instead, it held her a little too firmly, and there was something almost reptilian in its cold, dry touch. 'And you are?'

'Margaret Campbell.' She felt trapped by his politeness. And the arrival of her vodka tonic, on his bill, slammed the door on immediate escape.

'Well, Margaret Campbell, what brings you to Beijing?'

There was nothing else for it. She took a long sip of her vodka and almost immediately felt its effect. 'I'm lecturing for six weeks at the People's University of Public Security.'

'Are you indeed?' McCord seemed impressed. 'And what's your subject?'

'Forensic pathology.'

'Jeez! You mean you cut people open for a living?'

'Only when they're dead.'

He grinned. 'I'm safe for a while, then.' And for one malicious, wishful moment, she visualised taking a circular saw round the top of his skull and watching his addled, alcoholic brain plop out into a shiny stainless-steel dish. His Scotch arrived and he took a long slug. 'So . . . you just got here?' She nodded and sucked in more vodka. 'You'll be needing someone to show you the ropes, then.'

'Someone like you?'

'Sure. I've been here nearly six years. Know all the wrinkles.'

'You've stayed *here* for six years?' She was astonished at the thought of anyone staying in a hotel for that long.

'Hell, no, I don't stay at the Friendship. I only drink here. My company's got me staying at the Jingtan on the other side of town. Goddamn place is full of Japs. Can't stomach 'em. But that's only the last two years. Before that I was in the south.' He shook his head, remembering personal horrors. 'Coming here was like dying and going to heaven.' He put his hand out quickly. 'But don't go reaching for that scalpel just yet. I ain't really dead. That was just a metaphor.'

'Simile,' she corrected him.

'Whatever.' He drained his glass. 'So. Can I buy you dinner?'

'Afraid not.'

He grinned, unabashed. 'Hey, I don't mind a woman playing hard to get. I enjoy the chase.'

Margaret finished her vodka, its heady warmth making her bold. 'I'm not playing hard to get. I'm just not available.'

'Is that tonight? Or ever?'

'Both.'

He chewed that over for a moment, then pushed his empty glass towards the barman. 'Fill her up. You want another?' She shook her head. 'So, where are you eating tonight – if I may be so bold?'

'She go eat banquet.' Lily had entered unnoticed. 'And we late,' she said to Margaret. For once Margaret was almost relieved to see her.

'Banquet, huh? Quanjude Beijing Duck, by any chance?'

Margaret was taken aback. 'How did you know that?'

'Because everyone from the President of the United States to even a humble forensic pathologist gets the Beijing Duck treatment. Enjoy.' He raised his glass then took a long pull at it as Lily steered Margaret down the hall.

'You know him? 'she asked disapprovingly.

'No, I don't know him. I just met him. Who is he?'

'McCord. Everyone in Beijing know McCord. He work for Chinese government, got *guanxi*, big connection. And he like pay Chinese girl for . . .' She broke off. Suddenly, uncharacteristically, self-conscious. 'For . . . something no one else want give him.'

'Prostitutes? He goes with prostitutes?' Margaret was disgusted.

Lily pursed her lips. 'And we no can touch him.'

VI

The Quanjude Beijing Duck restaurant stood on Qianmen Dajie just south of Tiananmen Square. This was a busy commercial centre, bustling with all manner of shops still open for business. The streets were thick with early evening shoppers, and workers nipping in on their way home for sit-in or carry-out meals in the dozens of Western and Chinese fast-food joints. Off the main street ran a jumble of *hutongs*, choking with market stands and food stalls hanging with red lanterns, neon-lit Chinese characters projecting from every shopfront. Their BMW edged its way through the traffic, past the fast-food section of the Quanjude – duck-burgers a speciality – and turned into a tunnel lined by glass-framed poster-sized photographs of world leaders stuffing their faces with roast duck.

In the carpark, Bob stood anxiously underneath the lanterns at the door, glancing at his watch. He took Margaret's arm as she emerged from the back of the BMW and guided her hastily in through the revolving door.

'You're late,' he hissed.

'Well, that's hardly my fault. The car picks me up, the car drops me off.'

'Okay, okay.' He glanced around self-consciously. The ground floor of the restaurant was packed, dozens of tables stretching off to infinity, steaming roast ducks on trolleys being wheeled to tables for carving by chefs in tall hats. 'Now, listen, before we go up, there's a few things you should know.'

'Oh, I'm sure there are.' Although still tired, she was getting her second wind now, and the vodka was having its effect.

He ignored her tone and steered her away from the door. 'You'll be placed on the right hand of your host – that's Professor Jiang. Don't sit until he indicates where. He'll propose a toast welcoming you to Beijing. You reply with a toast thanking the generosity of your host.' Margaret felt like a naughty child being admonished for earlier indiscretions and briefed to prevent further *faux pas*. Her attention wandered to a panoramic window giving on to the kitchens, where dripping ducks hung roasting inside great wood-burning ovens. 'The meal usually comes in four courses. You let him serve you the first couple times then tell him you can manage fine from now on. You *can* use chopsticks, can't you?'

She sighed. 'Yes.'

'Good. Well, turn them round and use the other end to

serve yourself from communal plates. Oh, and it's not considered good form for women to drink too much. So just take a sip for the toasts and then leave the rest, okay?'

Margaret nodded, but she wasn't really listening. She was looking in a large glass case mounted on the wall at a signed photograph of George Bush with a mouthful of duck. Asked for his autograph, he had obviously scrawled his name and as an afterthought reckoned he should make some polite comment about the restaurant. 'A superb meal. Many thanks,' he had written. Inspirational as always, Margaret thought.

'Another thing. Don't talk shop unless they raise the subject. And don't be surprised if they ask you . . . well, personal questions.'

She frowned her consternation. 'What kind of personal questions?'

'Oh, about how much you earn, how much you paid for your apartment in Chicago.'

'None of their damned business!'

'Jesus, Margaret, don't tell them that. If you really don't want to answer something, try and make a joke of it. Say something like . . . "I've promised my father to keep it a secret".'

'Well, that'll have them rolling in the aisles.' She had a peculiar sense of floating now. There was a strange air of unreality about everything.

'We'd better go up.'

As he led her to the stairs, Margaret noticed a group of seven or eight young men sitting around a table with large half-litre glasses of beer and two ducks being carved simultaneously.

There was a great deal of raucous laughter rising with clouds of cigarette smoke from the table. Oddly, Margaret thought she recognised one of the faces. An ugly square-jawed face with a flat-top crew cut. She caught the man's eye and then remembered. It was the bad-tempered cyclist they'd had the collision with that afternoon. To her astonishment, he smiled and waved. Bob waved back, and she realised the wave hadn't been meant for her. 'You know him?' she asked as they climbed the stairs.

'Sure. He's a graduate of the university. Way before my time. But he comes back to give occasional lectures. Li Yan. One of the bright upcoming detectives in Section One.'

'Section One? What is that?'

'Oh, it's a kind of serious crime squad. Part of the Municipal Police, but it deals with the big stuff – homicides, armed robberies, that kind of thing.' He paused. 'Why, do you know him?'

'No. Not really. We sort of bumped into him when we were picking you up earlier.' She glanced back from the top of the stairs, but Li Yan was engrossed in a story being recounted loudly by a big, round-faced young man sitting next to him. There was an eruption of laughter from the table.

The upstairs of the restaurant formed a gallery overlooking the dining area below. Long green lamps dripped like tears from a high ceiling. At the far side their hosts awaited them by a large circular table. Professors Jiang, Tian and Bai, Dr Mu, Mr Cao and their respective partners, as well as Veronica, wearing the same dress she had worn in the afternoon. They went through the formal and tedious process of introduction and reintroduction. Dr Mu's husband had long hair swept back over his collar and a wispy beard trained to a point, and seemed out of place in this gathering of clean-cut, clean-shaven faces. He gave Margaret a warm smile and produced a pack of cigarettes. He offered her one.

'I don't, thanks,' she told him.

He shrugged. 'You don't mind if I do?'

Bob looked tense. Margaret smiled. 'Your funeral.'

'I am sorry?'

'I've seen first hand what it does to the lungs.'

He looked slightly puzzled, but lit up anyway. Professor Jiang spoke and Veronica translated. 'Professor Jiang say we should sit.'

The professor stood at his place and indicated the seat on his right to Margaret. She sat, he sat, and then the rest sat. So far it was all going to plan. A waitress arrived with small porcelain cups filled with a clear, evil-smelling liquor and placed one by each person. '*Mao tai*,' Bob told her from the other side of the table. 'Made from sorghum. It's one hundred twenty proof, so take it easy.'

Professor Jiang raised his cup and proposed a lengthy toast which the laconic Veronica translated as, 'Welcome to Beijing, welcome to the People's University of Public Security.' They all raised their cups and muttered, '*Gan bei*,' and sipped at the liquor which was as evil-tasting as it smelled. Margaret had difficulty forcing it over, and felt it burning all the way down. Then she remembered that it was her turn, and told them that she was honoured to be there and would like to drink a toast to the generosity of their host, Professor Jiang. Veronica translated, Professor Jiang nodded, clearly satisfied, and they raised their cups again. '*Gan bei.*' This time, she saw, the men drained their cups in a single draught, while the women barely wet their lips. Hell, she thought, it was easier to get it over in a oner than to sip and taste the damn stuff. She tipped her head back and poured it over, banging her cup back down on the table. She thought she was going to faint. Then she thought she was going to die of asphyxiation. Her lungs refused to draw breath. All eyes were on her, her face, she was certain, bright puce, before finally she managed to suck in a breath and smile as if everything were normal. The temptation to give expression to the pain that burned all the way down to her stomach was almost, but not quite, irresistible. Dr Mu's husband grinned wickedly and clapped his hands. 'Bravo,' he said. 'Your funeral.' Which made her laugh. And everyone else round the table laughed, too. Except for Bob, whose glare she assiduously avoided.

Now that the pain had subsided, the effects of the *mao tai*, on top of the vodka, on top of the twenty-four hours without sleep, were inducing a positive sense of euphoria. When the drinks order came, she asked for beer, and then the food started to arrive, culminating in the carving of three ducks, pieces of which they dipped in *hoi sin* before wrapping them in very thin pancakes with strips of spring onion, cucumber and minced raw garlic. It was delicious.

They asked her politely about her journey, her hotel. She

asked them about their families, their homes. The more beer and wine they drank, the more informal the proceedings and, eventually, the more personal the questions. Mr Cao leaned across the table and said, 'Forensic pathologists are quite well paid in the USA, I believe.'

Veronica translated for the others, and Margaret replied, 'Everything is relative, Mr Cao. I'm sure in terms of Chinese salaries you would think so. But you must remember, the cost of living is so much higher in the United States.'

Mr Cao nodded. 'And how much do you earn, Dr Campbell?' In spite of Bob's warning, Margaret was still taken aback by the direct and personal nature of the question.

Dr Mu passed some comment and everyone around the table laughed. Veronica translated, 'Dr Mu say, when the wine is in, the truth is out.'

Well, thought Margaret, if they want to know . . . 'I make around eighty-five thousand dollars a year,' she said.

In the silence that followed, she could almost hear the computations going on in their heads. Eyes widened, jaws dropped, and there was no doubting that they were genuinely shocked by the extreme wealth of the *yangguizi* whose dinner they were paying for. Margaret began to wish she'd told them she'd promised her father to keep it a secret.

A tasty consommé arrived, boiled up from the carcasses of their ducks, and then a huge platter of fried rice. Margaret finished her beer and helped herself to some rice as Dr Mu's husband asked, 'So, Dr Campbell, you are forensic pathologist?'

'That's right.'

'And do you have any, ah, special area, ah, expertise?'

'Sure. Burn victims.' She looked around their expectant faces. They were waiting for her to continue. 'People who die in fires. I was just training at the time, but I was an assistant to one of the pathologists they called in to Waco, Texas, to help identify the corpses – you know, all those victims of the fire. That's where my interest started, I guess. Funny thing is, the first few times you do an autopsy on a burn victim, the smell of charred human flesh stays with you for days. Now I don't even notice it.' She took a mouthful of rice and saw that everyone else around the table was putting their chopsticks down.

Veronica, who had been translating, had turned very pale. She rose quickly. 'Excuse me,' she said, and hurried away in the direction of the toilets.

'Could I have another beer?' Margaret asked the waitress.

'And I'll have a large Scotch.' Heads turned as McCord pulled a chair from another table and drew it into theirs. He was quite unsteady on his feet and very flushed. 'Fancy meeting you here,' he grinned lecherously at Margaret and sat down. 'You good folks don't mind if I join you for a dee-jest-eef?'

Stony faces greeted him around the table. Mr Cao leaned over and whispered something to Professor Jiang, who contained his anger with a curt nod. Bob gave Margaret a long, hard look. She shrugged. McCord leaned towards her. 'So, Margaret Campbell . . . how was your Beijing Duck?'

Mr Cao rounded the table and stooped to whisper in McCord's ear, eliciting an indignant outburst. 'Well, hell! That's not very hospitable!'

Bob stood up and took one of his arms. 'I think maybe you've had a little too much to drink, Dr McCord.'

McCord pulled his arm free. 'How the hell would you know how much I've had to drink?'

Margaret tugged at Bob's sleeve. 'Who is he?' she whispered.

'I thought you knew,' he said coldly. 'He seems to know you.'

She shook her head. 'He tried to pick me up at the hotel.'

'I'll tell you who I am.' McCord pushed his snout between them. 'I'm the man that's feeding this goddamn country.'

Mr Cao shrugged helplessly towards Professor Jiang, who nodded and waved at him to sit down. Bob said, 'Dr McCord was responsible for developing China's super-rice. You've probably heard about it. They introduced it as a crop about three years ago. Since when production has increased by . . . what . . . fifty per cent?'

'A hundred,' McCord corrected him. 'Indestructible, you see. Disease-resistant, herbicide-resistant, insect-resistant. You name it. I made it that way.'

'And no doubt it tastes as good as it always did.' Margaret couldn't conceal her scepticism.

'You tell me. You're eating it.' McCord grinned as Margaret took in the bowl of rice in front of her.

'Perhaps you should have some of it yourself, then – to soak up the alcohol.'

He laughed. 'Never touch the stuff.'

The waitress arrived with his whisky and Margaret's beer. She watched him guzzle thirstily and, through her fatigue and a haze of alcohol, a vague and distant memory was beginning to surface, attached to other things she would rather forget. 'McCord,' she said. 'Dr James McCord.'

'That's me.'

'You got kicked out of ... where was it ... the Boyce Thompson Institute at Cornell University? About six years ago?'

McCord's complexion darkened. 'Those fucking people!'

'Field-testing genetically engineered plants without a permit from the EPA. Something like that, wasn't it?'

McCord hammered a clenched fist on the table and everyone jumped. 'Fucking regulations! They got our people so tied up in them they can't move. Paperwork, bureaucracy, everything takes so goddamn long, by the time we get permission for a field test, the rest of the world's growing the stuff.' He grabbed a bowl of rice. 'This. *We* could have been growing this. Or wheat. Or corn. Feeding the planet. Instead, it takes a third world country like China to have the vision.'

Those Chinese around the table who understood English bristled at his description of their country as 'third world'.

'So it was the Chinese who financed your research?' Margaret was curious.

'Hell, no. They just facilitated it. It was my employers, Grogan Industries, put up the money. Good old-fashioned capitalist high-risk investment. They did the deal with China. Strange bedfellows, huh? But, boy, did they both hit the jackpot.'

'How?'

'Well, it's obvious, isn't it? The Chinese got a quarter of the world's population. And for the first time in their history they can feed themselves. Hell, they're growing so much rice now they're exporting the stuff.'

'And Grogan Industries?'

'They got the patent on all my work. They're going to be launching my rice all over Asia and India next year.'

Margaret had heard of Grogan, a multinational US-based biotech company with an unsavoury reputation for ruthlessly exploiting the pharmaceutical market in the third world.

'And no doubt the poorest countries – those with the greatest need – will be the last to get it. Because I'll bet your technology doesn't come cheap, does it, Dr McCord?'

'Hey!' He threw his hands up in self-defence. 'Don't blame me. The sole purpose of the scientist is to work for the benefit of mankind.' He grinned. 'Or something. But it's money that makes the world go round.'

'Yeah, and it's money and vested interests that persuade politicians and governments not to put sensible constraints on the work of people like you.' Margaret's passion was born of years of argument and discussion, and it was resurfacing now in a blur of painful memories.

McCord seemed taken aback by her vehemence. Others around the table sat in fascinated silence, initial offence overcome by curiosity at the spectacle of these two *yangguizi* battling it out. As a puzzled Veronica returned to the table, Bob slipped inconspicuously away.

'Sensible constraints? What's sensible about them?'

'What's sensible about them is that they stop arrogant scientists with God complexes releasing genetically altered materials into the environment without the least idea of what the long-term effects are likely to be.'

'I'd have thought the effects were obvious. Long-term or otherwise. A lot of hungry people are getting fed.'

'But at what cost? How did you develop this "super-rice", Dr McCord? Built-in insecticide, antifungal, antiviral genes?'

He was genuinely taken aback by the extent of her knowledge. Then he remembered. 'Of course, you're a doctor, aren't you? Well, I'm glad you're interested.' He relaxed again. 'Naturally, I realise genetics isn't your speciality, so let me explain it to you – in terms that you'll understand.' He made a fist and extended his little finger. 'Think of my little finger as being like a virus,' he said. Then he smiled salaciously. 'Or perhaps you'd be more comfortable thinking of the virus as being like something more familiar to you – like a penis.' Veronica blushed deeply, and Mr Cao and Dr Wu's husband turned their eyes down to the table.

'No, let's stick with your little finger,' Margaret said, 'since your penis probably isn't any bigger.'

He grinned. 'Bear with me. My little finger represents a penis, representing a virus I'm going to put into the rice. Okay? Now imagine I slip a rubber over my penis.' And he ran his forefinger and thumb down the length of his little finger. 'And this represents the protein overcoat of the virus. Because, after all, what is a virus except a gene with a protein overcoat?'

Margaret nodded. 'Okay.'

McCord said, 'So, to this overcoat I attach the gene fragments I want to introduce to the rice – the stuff that's going to make it disease and insect-resistant. We insert the virus into the rice, like the penis into the vagina. Only, once inside the rubber slips off and sends my gene fragments to all the right places, like sperm to the egg.' He sat back, pleased with himself, and drained his glass.

Margaret was incensed. 'So, effectively, you've contaminated the entire rice crop of China with a virus.'

McCord nodded happily. 'Sure. But it's a harmless plant virus. Hell, we eat the damned things all the time. And a virus is *the* best carrier for the genes. 'Cos, you see, a virus only has one aim in life, and that's to reproduce. So it carries the genes into every cell, and bingo! We just helped Mother Nature do a better job.'

Margaret shook her head. 'I can't believe you've actually gone into production with this stuff, that you actually think you're somewhere up there with "Mother Nature". Jesus Christ, McCord, you're tinkering at the edges of a billion years of evolution. You can't possibly know what kind of monster you're releasing into the environment.'

'Dr McCord,' a friendly voice boomed out, and a big hand slapped down on his shoulder.

Margaret looked up, startled to see Bob with Li Yan and Li's animated friend from the table downstairs. It was the friend who had greeted McCord with such bonhomie. McCord looked up at him, confused.

'What . . . Who the hell are you?'

'Ma Yongli. Chef at the Jingtan. Don't you remember? Good friend of Lotus. She's waiting for you back at the hotel.' He grinned and winked.

'Is she? I didn't know that.'

'She says you made an arrangement.'

'Really? Jeez, I don't remember.'

Yongli almost lifted him out of his chair. 'Come on. We'll get you a taxi. Don't want keep Lotus waiting, huh?'

'Hell, no.'

And Yongli led him off towards the stairs. Bob shook Li's hand. 'Thanks, Li Yan. Appreciate it.'

Li smiled. 'My pleasure.' He nodded acknowledgement to Professor Jiang and they exchanged a few words. He nodded to the others around the table until his eyes fell on Margaret. The clear contempt they held for her had an almost withering effect and she flushed with embarrassment and lowered her eyes. And she wished with all her heart that she had never come to China. When she looked up again he had gone. A buzz of conversation broke out around the table and Bob pulled up a chair beside her.

'Not the most auspicious of starts,' he said through clenched teeth.

'I didn't invite him,' she said.

'You didn't have to engage him in open warfare.'

'I wouldn't have had to if you people had had the balls to tell him where to go.'

'We couldn't!' Bob was in danger of raising his voice. He stopped himself and lowered it again. 'McCord has connections in this town. His whole rice project had the backing of Pang Xiaosheng, former Minister of Agriculture, now a member of the Politburo – and a national hero. It was Pang who persuaded the leadership to do the deal with Grogan Industries, and it's Pang who's reaped the rewards. He's the bookie's favourite to be the next leader of the People's Republic.' Bob stopped to draw a grim breath. 'And you don't fuck with people like that, Margaret.'

It was dark outside as Li and Yongli escorted the now semi-conscious McCord through the tunnel from the restaurant to the street. A sleepy trishaw driver lingering in the carpark raised a hopeful eye, assessed the situation, and relapsed into a semi-slumber. The traffic had not abated, and the street was still crowded, ablaze with the lights of neons and vehicles. Li waved at an air-conditioned taxi, but it was occupied and sailed past. He turned and whispered to Yongli, 'He's going to be pretty disappointed when he finds out that Lotus isn't waiting for him back at the hotel.'

Yongli shrugged. 'I'll give her a call. She'll take care of him.'

Li looked at his friend with complete incomprehension. 'You'd ask her to do that?'

'Why not? The guy's drunk. It's not as though he'd be any threat. She's dealt with him before.'

Li shook his head. He knew he would never understand his friend's relationship with Lotus. He waved down another taxi, but a black Volvo with darkened windows swung into the space at the kerb and blocked it off. The taxi driver honked his horn furiously, but decided against an argument with the Volvo and screeched away in a temper. A large, uniformed chauffeur stepped out and took McCord's arm from Yongli. 'I'll take Dr McCord,' he said.

'Back to the hotel?' Yongli was puzzled by the sudden appearance of the chauffeur-driven limousine.

'No. He has an appointment elsewhere.' The chauffeur opened the back door and bundled McCord unceremoniously inside.

'Hey, I got a rendezvous with Lotus,' McCord protested, suddenly aware that plans were being changed over his head. The door was slammed shut on him and he disappeared from view behind the tinted windows. The chauffeur slipped behind the wheel, and the car whispered away into the traffic.

'Government car,' Yongli said thoughtfully. 'Wonder where they're taking him?'

Li knew better than even to think of asking.

CHAPTER TWO

I

Tuesday Morning

Buses and bicycles fought for space among the people and traffic that clogged the narrow artery that was Chaoyangmen Nanxiaojie Street. It ran north to south, bisecting the centre-east of the city. Cycling north along it took Li directly into the heart of Dongcheng District, where the Beijing Municipal Police had sited the new operational headquarters of Section One. The final stretch before the intersection with Dongzhimennei Street was heavily shaded by leaning, leafy trees, and was a deliciously cool escape from the early morning heat. Li coasted the last few hundred yards, enjoying the respite, and pulled over at the corner of Dongzhimennei. Mei Yuan greeted him with her usual, 'Hi, have you eaten?'

And he responded with his customary, 'Yes, I have eaten.' And she began preparing his breakfast. The familiar greeting, ritually exchanged between Beijingers, had little to do with food but much to do with friendship.

Li parked his bike and leaned against the wall, watching Mei

Yuan at work. She had a round, unlined face with beautifully slanted almond eyes that sparkled with mischief. Her dark hair, showing only a trace of grey at the temples, was drawn back in a tight bun and wrapped in a green scarf. Dimples in her cheeks became like deep scars when she smiled, which was often. For the moment, her concentration was on the preparation of his *jian bing* on the hot plate in the replica house that stood on the back of her three-wheeled cycle. Its corrugated roof, pitched and pink, had tiny curled eaves, and sat over sliding glass screens that protected the gas hot plate and Mei Yuan's cooking ingredients. She splashed a ladleful of watery batter over the hot plate and it sizzled as it quickly cooked and set. Then she flipped the pancake over and broke an egg on to it, spreading it thinly. Smearing this with *hoi sin* and a little chili, she sprinkled it with chopped spring onion and broke a large piece of deep-fried whipped egg white into its centre. She then folded it in four, wrapped it in brown paper, and handed it to Li in exchange for two yuan. She watched with satisfaction as he bit hungrily into the steaming savoury pancake. 'Wonderful,' he said, wiping a smear of *hoi sin* from the corner of his mouth. 'If I didn't have to share an apartment with my uncle I would marry you.'

She laughed heartily. 'I'm old enough to be your mother.'

'But my mother never made *jian bing* the way you do.'

In truth, his mother had never made *jian bing*. And had the world turned another way, Mei Yuan would not have had to. In another era she might, perhaps, have been a lecturer at the university, or a senior civil servant. Li inclined his head a little to catch the title of the book she had stuffed down the back of her saddle. Descartes' *Meditations*. He looked at her plump little hands, scarred by a thousand tiny burns, and felt the pain of her life in his heart. A generation cursed by the twelve years of madness that was the Cultural Revolution. And yet if she had regrets, there was no hint of them in that dimpled smile and those mischievous eyes.

She had not missed him noticing her book. 'I'll lend it to you when I'm finished. He was an extraordinary man.' She smiled. '*I think, therefore I am.*' It would have taken her a long time to save up enough money to buy the book, so her offer to lend it to him was an extraordinary act of generosity and trust.

'Thank you,' he said. 'I would like that. And I will be sure to return it to you when I have read it.' He filled his mouth with more *jian bing*. 'So. Do you have an answer?'

She grinned. 'The third person in the queue must have been his wife. You tried to make me think it was a man.'

'No, no. I didn't try to make you think anything. You *assumed* it was a man. It was only when you stopped making that assumption that you realised who she was.'

She shook her head, still smiling. 'Not very clever. But effective.'

'So what have you got for me?' He devoured the last of his *jian bing* and threw the wrapper in the bin.

'Two men,' she said. 'And there is no ambiguity here.' She twinkled. 'One of them is the keeper of every book in the world, giving him access to the source of all knowledge. Knowledge is power, so this makes him a very powerful man.

The other possesses only two sticks. Yet this gives him more power than the other. Why?'

Li turned it over quickly in his head, but no solution came immediately to mind. 'It'll have to wait till tomorrow.'

She nodded. 'Of course.'

He winked and glanced at the fob watch he kept in a leather pouch on his belt. 'Got to go. *Zai jian.*' And he flicked his bike stand up with his foot. She watched with affection as the tall figure in short-sleeved white shirt and dark trousers dodged the traffic to cross Dongzhimennei Street. Somewhere in this vast country, she liked to believe, lived the son she had been separated from almost thirty years ago, when Red Guards had dragged her off to the labour camp. He would be about Li's age now. And it was her fervent hope that he might have turned out something like him.

Li cycled up the gentle slope to the corner of Beixinqiao Santiao, where the square, flat-roofed, four-storey brick building that housed Section One sat discreetly behind a screen of trees. Past the traditional revolving sign of a barber shop, the musty smell of damp hair and the snip of scissors as he passed its door, he was still turning over Mei Yuan's riddle in his head. Two sticks. Were they chopsticks? No, why would that give the man power? Were they big sticks with which he could beat the other man to death? If so, why would he require two? Focusing his mind on the problem calmed the butterflies in his stomach reflecting the self-doubts that dogged the start of his first day as Deputy Section Chief. He turned in past the red-roofed garage and parked his bicycle. A uniformed officer came down the steps from the door of Section One. He gave Li a wave. 'Heard the good news, Li Yan. Congratulations.'

Li grinned. 'My ancestors must have been watching over me.' Important to seem confident, not to be taking it too seriously.

He went inside, turned right, and climbed the stairs to the fourth floor. Everyone he met in the corridor – a secretary, another uniformed officer, a rookie detective – offered their congratulations. It was becoming embarrassing. There were only two officers in the detectives' room when he went in, Qu and Gao. Both had been with Section One longer than he, and were now a rank below him. Qu winked. 'Morning, boss.' There was a heavy ironical stress on the word 'boss', but it was fond rather than rancorous. Li was popular with the other detectives.

'Come to get your stuff?' Gao asked. 'Can't wait to move into your new office, eh?'

Strangely, Li realised, he hadn't given that a thought. He had been heading instinctively for his old desk. He glanced, almost with regret, around the cluttered detectives' office with its jumble of desks and filing cabinets, walls plastered with memos and posters and photographs of crime scenes past and present.

'Don't worry about it,' Qu said. 'One of the girls'll put your stuff in a box and take it through. Chief wants to see you.'

Section Chief Chen Anming rose from his desk as Li came into his office and shook his hand. 'Well done, Li Yan. You deserve it.'

'Thanks, Chief. That's what I've been telling everyone.'

But Chen didn't smile. He sat down again, distracted, and shuffled some papers on his desk. He was a lean, silver-headed man in his late fifties from Hunan province. A chain-smoker, years of cigarette smoke had streaked his hair yellow above his right temple. He wore a permanently dour expression, and the girls in the typing pool had been known to run a book on days of the month on which he might smile. 'Busy start for you. Three suspicious deaths overnight. Two of them look pretty much like murder, the third could be a suicide. A charred body in Ritan Park. Still burning when it was discovered. Can of gasoline near by. Looks like he doused himself, squatted among the trees and lit a match. Bizarre stuff. Qian Yi's already there. I've dispatched Wu and Zhao to the suspected murders. You'd better have a look at the suicide, just in case. Then debrief the other two and let me know what you think.'

Several hundred curious onlookers had gathered by the lakeside among the willows. Word had swept like wildfire through the nearby market streets, and rumours of death in the park held the promise of drama; a kind of street theatre, something to break the monotonous repetition of their daily lives. Nearly sixty uniformed officers had been assigned to crowd control. Several plainclothes policemen moved among the spectators, listening to gossip and speculation in the hope of picking up even the smallest piece of information that might prove useful. From across the water, where people were packed in under the shade of the pavilion, from above the babble of voices, came the mournful wail of a single-stringed violin, like a dirge for the dead. The rest of the park was deserted.

Li inched his way through the crowd in a dark blue Jeep, red light flashing on the roof, horn sounding. People were reluctant to get out of the way. Curious faces stared in at him as he squeezed past, but he was oblivious. Confidence had returned. He was back on home territory, doing what he was good at. Finally, at the north side of the lake, he drew into an area that had been cleared and taped off by the uniformed police. Several other vehicles, including an ambulance and a forensics van, were already there. As he got out of the Jeep, a uniformed officer pointed up a dusty slope to the trees beyond.

At the top of the rise, Li stepped over the line of powdered chalk that ringed the potential crime scene and caught his first scent of burnt human flesh. It would linger in his nostrils for hours to come. He curled his upper lip and clenched his teeth firmly to prevent his stomach from heaving. The dead man, or woman, was still squatting in the centre of the clearing, a stiff, blackened figure in the shape of a human. And yet there was something strangely unhuman about the corpse, as if it might have been the abstract creation of a sculptor chiselling roughly in ebony. The charred debris of the victim's clothes was scattered around it. The leaves of nearby trees had been scorched by the intensity of the heat. Lights had been erected, and the corpse was being photographed from various angles. Two forensics officers wearing white gloves were combing the area for anything that might throw some illumination on the events of little over an hour before. A doctor

from the pathology department at the Centre of Criminal
Technological Determination in Pao Jü Hutong, Dr Wang Xing,
also in white gloves, stood talking to Detective Qian on the far
side of the clearing. Qian saw Li arrive, detached himself from
the doctor, and made his way carefully around the perimeter
of the clearing. He shook Li's hand. 'Congratulations on the
promotion, boss.'

Li acknowledged with the faintest nod. 'What's the verdict?'

Qian shrugged. 'Well, all the doc can tell us at this stage is
that it's a male. If he was carrying ID then it's been destroyed.'

'Cause of death?'

'Burning's the obvious choice, but until they get him on
the slab they won't know for sure. Doc says an autopsy on a
body in this state's a bit specialised. They'll probably have to
send it up to the pathology lab at the university. Identification
could be a problem. All we've found so far are the remains of a
Zippo cigarette lighter, a charred signet ring and a belt buckle.
Nothing particularly distinguishing about any of them.'

'The gasoline can?'

'Just an ordinary can. They're dusting it for prints. No sign
of a struggle, but then it would be hard to tell. The ground's
baked hard here. It hasn't rained in weeks. Oh, and we found
this . . .' He removed a clear plastic evidence bag from his
pocket and held it up to let Li see the cigarette end inside.
'Looks like he had a last cigarette before pouring gasoline all
over himself and igniting his lighter.'

Li took the bag and examined the cigarette end closely. It
had been stamped out before burning down to the tip, and

the brand name was still clearly legible. *Marlboro*. 'How come the cigarette end didn't burn up in the fire?'

'It wasn't next to the body. Forensics found it over there.' He pointed to the west side of the clearing.

Li was thoughtful for a moment. 'Anyone see him arriving?'

Qian made a moue with his lips and exhaled sharply through them. 'Nobody's come forward yet. We're trying to get the names of everyone who was in the park from six this morning. A lot of them will be the same people who come every day. Someone might have seen a man carrying a can, but it isn't much of a description to offer them. I've already spoken to the ticket clerk but she has no recollection. Until we know who he is and maybe get a photograph . . .' He shrugged.

'What about the people who found the body?'

'A nanny – a peasant girl from Shanxi province – and a couple of kids. They're down there in the ambulance. The nanny was in a worse state than the kids. I think the paramedics have given her a sedative.'

When Li stepped into the ambulance, he was taken aback to see that the girls were twins. Pretty girls, unspoilt as yet by the approach of adulthood and the loss of innocence – unaware, perhaps, how lucky they were. Since the introduction of the One-Child Policy to control the population explosion, it was rare for any child to have a brother or sister. And a whole new generation would never know the joy of an extended family with uncles and aunts. There was no way of knowing the long-term effects on a society so orientated around the traditional family. But there was a reluctant acceptance by the Chinese that the alternative was worse – a spiralling population growth leading to inevitable starvation and economic chaos.

The girls regarded him solemnly, a strange outward calm concealing the trauma of what they must have witnessed. Their baby-sitter, on the other hand, was still sobbing feebly, clutching a damp handkerchief to her mouth, sucking on a corner of it for comfort.

'Hi.' Li sat down opposite them and spoke directly to the twins. 'Did you girls see the dancers earlier?' They nodded eagerly. 'And those guys that go swinging the swords about? They really scare me.' The girls giggled. 'Do you come to the park every day?'

'No,' one of them said.

'Just sometimes,' the other added. 'Usually with Mommy.'

Qian watched Li from the door, thinking what a good manner he had with the kids. Gentle, positive. And they responded to him.

'But you were with your nanny today?' They nodded again. 'Did you see anyone near the path out there, before you went up to where the fire was?' This time it was a solemn shaking of the heads. 'No one moving away, maybe round the lake?' Again the shaking of heads. 'Good girls. You've done really well. But I don't think you want to hang around here any longer, do you?'

'No,' they said in chorus.

'So my friend here . . .' He nodded towards Qian. '. . . is going to get a nice policeman to buy you some ice cream and then take you home to see your mom. Okay?'

Their faces lit up. 'Yeah.'

'Can we have strawberry?'

'You can have whatever flavour you like, sweetheart.' He ruffled their heads and they scrambled out to be led off by Qian. He turned to the baby-sitter. 'Okay . . . Just relax.' He moved over and sat beside her and took her hand. It was a small, fleshy hand used to toil. He felt the line of calluses on the palm. She was probably no more than sixteen or seventeen. 'This is hard for you, I know. Because you've never seen anything like this before.' He spoke very softly and felt a sob shudder through her body. 'But we really need your help here, and I know that you want to help us all you can.' She nodded vigorously. 'So just take your time and tell me what happened.'

'It was the smoke,' she said, breath catching the back of her throat. 'The children were running to see what it was. I kept shouting at them to stop, but they were in such high spirits.'

'So you followed them up the path.'

'Yes.'

'And the body was still on fire?'

The tears filled her eyes again as she remembered. 'He was still alive. Reaching out to me, like he was asking for help.'

Li found Pathologist Wang squatting down by the lakeside. Having divested himself of his white gloves, he was having a smoke. Li hunkered down beside him and was offered a cigarette. Without a word, he took one and the pathologist lit it. 'So what do you think?' Li asked. He drew deeply on the cigarette and blew the smoke out through his nostrils, trying to get rid of the smell.

'I think there are times I don't much like my job.' He glanced grimly at Li. 'Looks like some kind of weird suicide ritual. On a cursory examination there's no sign of blood or injury prior to the burning. So unless an autopsy tells us otherwise, you can probably assume he burned to death.'

'One of the witnesses says he was still alive when they found him.' *Reaching out, like he was asking for help.* The nanny's interpretation of what she saw had formed a gruesomely indelible image in Li's mind.

'Which pretty much fixes time of death, and rules out foul play prior to burning,' Wang concluded. 'We get him back to Pao Jü Hutong and I'll do a preliminary. Should be able to tell a little more about him then. But if you want a full autopsy . . .'

'I do.'

'Then you're going to have to send him up to the Centre of Material Evidence Determination at the university.' He stood up. 'But first we want to get him into the fridge fast – to stop him cooking.'

After the body had been removed, and the ambulance and various police vehicles had gone, the crowd started to break up, reluctantly drawn back to the relentless humdrum of their everyday lives. Li, however, lingered a little longer. He circled the lake and climbed the rocky outcrop at the far side to find himself looking down on the pavilion, now deserted apart from an old man scratching away on his violin, and a woman who might have been his wife, singing a jagged, haunting melody. To his left was the path that climbed through the trees to the clearing where the body had been found. He was still troubled by the image the peasant girl from Shanxi had conjured in his mind, of the hand reaching out from the flaming mass. *Like he was asking for help.* What an appalling way to die. Li tried to picture the man walking slowly through the park (for if he had had time to smoke a last cigarette he was surely in no hurry), past the early morning dancers, the practitioners of t'ai chi, the old ladies gossiping on park benches, carrying his can of gasoline in his hand, and intent in his heart. What possible horrors could drive a man to such a desperate act? Li imagined him lighting his last cigarette, standing smoking it, almost down to the tip. He lit a cigarette himself and stared down at the still, green water of the lake reflecting the willow trees beyond, and wondered why no one had seen him on that slow walk through the park. Were people so engrossed in their spiritual and physical activities that he had been invisible to them?

Deep in the bowels of the multistorey building of the Centre of Criminal Technological Determination that backs on to Pao Jü Hutong, Pathologist Wang made a preliminary, superficial examination of the body. The charred corpse lay on its side on a metal table, like a toppled Buddha, fixed in its squatting position. Muscle shrinkage had forced the arms up, with fists clenched like those of a bare-knuckled pugilist. Li watched from a distance, the squeak of Wang's rubber sneakers echoing off white-tiled walls as he moved around the table. And still there was the awful smell. Wang wore a face mask, and worked his way quickly and carefully around the body, taking measurements, making notes. He spent some time opening and examining the mouth that had been pulled shut by contracted muscle, the tip of a charred tongue poking from between blackened lips. Then he nodded to his assistant, who wrapped the body in heavy plastic, securing it with a nylon cord, and wheeled it away on a gurney to be bagged and taken across the city to the pathology labs of the Centre of Material Evidence Determination on the campus of the People's University of Public Security. Li followed Wang into his office and they both lit cigarettes. Wang slumped in his chair and took a deep breath.

'I'll give you a written preliminary as soon as possible. But the victim was male, aged around fifty. From what's left to be seen externally, there's nothing physically distinguishing about him. Apart from his teeth. He'd had some pretty expensive professional work done there.'

Li frowned. This was unusual. General dentistry in China was still very basic and high-quality professional work did not come cheap.

As if reading his mind, Wang said, 'This guy wasn't any common labourer. He wasn't short of a yuan or two. A man of some position, I'd guess. Almost certainly a Party member. If you get any idea of who he is, you'll have no trouble confirming his identity from dental records.'

II

It was still only 10 a.m., but the heat was already stultifying. A hot wind blew the dust about the streets, coating leaves, grass, cars, buildings. And people. It got in their eyes and their mouths and their lungs and made them hack and spit.

Li's new office was airless and stifling, and the window would not open properly. His personal belongings had been left on his desk, in two cardboard boxes. The room itself had been stripped of any vestige of its previous occupant, scarred walls divested of their paper history. All that remained of Li's predecessor were the cigarette burns along the edge of his desk. Even his memory had faded in Li's mind; a colourless and pedantic man who had always remained tight, like a closed fist, enigmatic. For all the years his colleagues had worked with him they knew very little of his private life. A wife, a daughter at Sun Yat Sen University in Guangzhou, a heart condition. In the last months his face had been putty grey. Li fished an ashtray out from one of the boxes and lit his last cigarette. He looked out of the window through the trees at the All China Federation of Returned Overseas Chinese, gold characters on pale brown marble, and wondered what private thoughts had passed through the mind of this man who had preceded him as he looked down through the same trees at the same buildings. Had he once had the same hopes and aspirations for the future as Li? What cruel spins of fate had spawned his disillusion, reducing him to the grey and secretive man who had sweated out his last weeks in this office when he should have been at home with his family? A knock at the door disturbed his thoughts. Wu poked his head into the office. 'They're ready for you, boss.' And Li felt a flutter of fear. *They're ready for you.* Now that he was their boss, his colleagues would have expectations of him. It was possible to be ambitious beyond your ability. Now that this particular ambition had been realised, he would have to prove his ability, not just to those with expectations, but to himself. He slipped a pen into his breast pocket and took a fresh notebook from one of the boxes on his desk.

There were nearly a dozen officers sitting around the big table in the meeting room on the top floor. And nearly all of them were smoking cigarettes, smoke wallowing about in the downdraught from the ceiling fan that swung lazily overhead. Papers and notebooks and rapidly filling ashtrays cluttered the table. There was a brief, spontaneous round of applause as Li walked into the room. He flushed and grinned, waved his hand dismissively and told them to shut up. He pulled up a chair and looked around the expectant faces. 'Anyone got a smoke?' he asked. Nearly a dozen cigarettes got tossed across the table. He smiled and shook his head. 'Crawlers.' He lit one and took a deep draw. 'Okay,' he said. 'I've just been out to Ritan Park. I've already had initial reports from Detective Qian and Pathologist Wang. It's almost certainly a suicide, but the body's so badly burned we might have a problem identifying it. And it could take some time. We're going to have to match incoming missing-persons reports with what we know here. Pathologist Wang tells me the victim's male, aged around fifty, with some pretty expensive dental work. Detective Qian will co-ordinate attempts to identify him ASAP. We can't consider this case cleared until we know who he is and, if possible, why he killed himself. And we need witnesses, anyone who might have seen him making his way through the park. Any joy on that front, Qian Yi?'

Qian shook his head. 'Not yet. We're still compiling the names of everyone who was there, but nothing so far.'

'Anyone else got any thoughts?' No one had. 'All right. Let's move on for the moment to the stabbing in Haidan District. Detective Wu's been out there.' He raised his eyebrows in Wu's direction.

Wu leaned to one side in his chair and chewed reflectively on a piece of gum that had long since lost any flavour. He was a lean man in his forties, thinning hair brushed back, a wispy moustache on his upper lip designed to disguise over-prominent front teeth. His skin was unusually dark, and he liked to wear sunglasses, whatever the weather. Right now they were dangling from the thumb and forefinger of his left hand, a cigarette burning between the fingers of his right. He habitually wore blue jeans and white trainers and a short denim butt-freezer jacket. Image was important to Wu. He liked being a cop, and Li suspected that he modelled himself on the undercover cops he'd seen in American movies. 'It's a murder, all right,' Wu said. 'No doubt about that. His name was Mao Mao. Known to us. A petty drug dealer in his mid-twenties. Did time as a juvenile for theft and hooliganism. Reform through labour. Only whatever labour they put him through didn't reform him.'

'What was it, a fight?' Li asked.

Wu cocked his head doubtfully. 'Well, he was stabbed in the heart, up through the lower ribcage. But there were no signs of a struggle, no bruising or cuts on his hands or face. The pathologist thinks he may have been attacked from behind. Autopsy should confirm. Looks like it might have been some kind of gangland killing. He was lying face down in his own blood on a stretch of waste ground near Kunminghunan Road. A factory worker found him on his way to work this morning. The ground out there's hard as concrete. No footprints in soil, or blood. In fact nothing for us to really go on at all. Forensics are doing fingernail and fibre tests, but I get a feeling about this, Li Yan. I don't think they're going to find anything. In fact, the only thing we picked up at all at the scene was a cigarette end, which is probably entirely unrelated.'

Li was suddenly interested, instincts aroused. 'Just one? I mean, there weren't any others lying around near by?'

'Not that we found.'

'What brand was it?'

'American. Marlboro, I think. Why?'

Detective Zhao said, 'That's odd. We found a Marlboro cigarette end close to the body out at Di'anmen.'

Qian leaned into the table. 'It was a Marlboro brand cigarette end we found out at Ritan, wasn't it, boss?'

Li nodded slowly, his interest fully ignited now. It was a remarkable coincidence, if, indeed, that was what it was. But he knew better than to go jumping to premature conclusions.

There was a speculative buzz around the table. He asked Zhao to give them a rundown on the body found at Di'anmen.

Zhao was the baby of the section, a good-looking young man of around twenty-five. What he lacked in flair he made up for in sheer hard work and attention to detail. He was always self-conscious at these meetings, finding it difficult to give coherent expression to his thoughts in the group situation. He was much better dealing with people one to one. Colour flushed high on his cheekbones as he spoke. 'He was carrying an ID card, so we know he was a building worker from Shanghai. Probably an itinerant. He may well have just arrived in Beijing looking for work, but there's no known address for him here, no known associates. I've already faxed Public Security in Shanghai asking for his details.'

'How was he killed?'

'A broken neck.'

'He couldn't just have fallen? An accident of some kind?'

'No. There's absolutely no sign of trauma. He was found in a condemned *siheyuan* in a *hutong* that was cleared about a month ago. But the crime scene is so clean I think he was killed somewhere else and dumped there.'

'So what makes you think the cigarette end is connected to it?'

'It was fresh. It was the only one there, and it was about three feet from the body.'

Li lit another cigarette, leaned back in his chair, and blew smoke thoughtfully at the blades of the overhead fan.

'Do *you* believe there's a connection?' The section chief watched his new deputy carefully. But Li wasn't being drawn into anything rash – not just yet. He stood by the window smoking one of his chief's cigarettes. When he'd asked for it, Chen had raised a wry eyebrow and told him dryly, 'You know, Li, someone in your elevated position really should start buying his own.' Now he regarded Li with professional interest. While there was no denying his flair, and his record of success, there was an impetuous quality in him, an impatient streak that Chen had hoped would mellow with age. But until now there had been no sign of it. Perhaps responsibility would temper impulsiveness. As long as it didn't dull a keen instinct.

'The thing is,' Li said seriously, 'we have no reason to believe the man at Ritan Park was anything other than a suicide. If we can establish that the time of death of the two murders was prior to his, and that he smoked this brand of Marlboro cigarette, then it's conceivable – just conceivable – that he killed the other two before doing away with himself.' But he couldn't keep his face straight any longer, and a mischievous smile crept across it.

Chen laughed. Not just a smile. A deep, throaty, smoker's laugh. Li wished the girls in the typing pool could see it. 'First day on the job,' Chen said, still chuckling. 'A suicide and two murders, and you've solved the lot already.'

Li's smile turned rueful. 'I wish it was that easy. But there's something wrong here, Chief. These two murders. There's not a shred of evidence at either scene. Except for the cigarette ends. Would somebody who obviously took so much care to leave no other evidence be careless enough to leave a cigarette end?'

'Maybe the killer, or killers, weren't that clever with the evidence, or lack of it. Maybe they just got lucky.'

'Hmmm.' Li wasn't convinced. 'Something doesn't feel right. If there *is* a connection, it's . . . well, very strange.' He sighed and flicked his ash out of the open window. 'The first thing we need to do is ID the guy in the park, but it could be some time before we can match the body with a missing person. And the municipal pathologist's not interested in doing the autopsy. Burn victims aren't his speciality, he says. Personally I think he's just queasy about it.'

'So who's doing the autopsy?'

'They've sent the body over to the Centre of Material Evidence Determination at the Public Security University.'

Chen looked thoughtful for a moment, then rummaged through some papers in an overflowing tray on his desk. Finally he drew out a sheet of paper, a circular from the Public Security Bureau visa section, and reread it with interest. He looked at Li. 'The doctor of forensic pathology in Chicago who took my course on criminal investigation when I was at UIC last year? Just happens to be in Beijing at the moment – lecturing to students at the Public Security University.'

Li shrugged, not making a connection. 'So?'

'The good doctor's speciality is burn victims.'

III

Margaret's nightmare had begun early. It started with a hangover about 2 a.m. She had fallen into a dead sleep after the banquet, but slept for only around four hours. At two she was wide awake with a headache the size of Lake Michigan. Back in Chicago it was early afternoon. She swallowed a couple of Advil and tried to get back to sleep. But two hours later, visions of Michael's face at their last meeting swimming relentlessly into her consciousness, she was sitting up, fully dressed, watching Hong Kong kung fu flicks on satellite *Star Movies*. She had already watched an hour of repeat bulletins on CNN and was ready to throw the television set out of the window. How was it possible, she wondered, to be so tired and yet incapable of sleep? If this was how it felt to be an insomniac, it was a condition to which she fervently hoped never to succumb. At five she had gone down to the twenty-four-hour café and washed down another couple of Advil with stewed black coffee, and by six felt woolly-headed and exhausted.

By then it was time to pick up her hire bike and attempt the long and difficult journey to the University of Public Security. Whatever fears her observation of Beijing traffic the previous day had conjured up were as nothing compared to the reality. The roads were sheer and utter chaos. And if she had hoped an early start would avoid the worst of the traffic, then she was wrong again. The whole of Beijing, it seemed, was on the move. And no one, apparently, had priority – at junctions, at traffic lights, between lanes. It was survival of the boldest. Just go, and hope that the bus bearing down on you would give way rather than kill you. Strangely enough, it worked. And in the sticky hour it took Margaret to cycle to the university, she learned the golden rule of biking in Beijing – that there were no rules. Expect the unexpected and you would never be surprised. And for all the honking of horns (she soon realised their purpose was to alert you to a vehicle's presence, or its impending manoeuvre), and the cutting between lanes, everyone on the road seemed remarkably even-tempered. Road rage had not reached China. It occurred to Margaret that all these drivers were so recently cyclists themselves, used to jockeying patiently for position in overcrowded cycle lanes, they did not automatically assume that they had priority simply because they were behind the wheel of a car, or bus, or lorry. These were Chinese exercising that most enduring of Chinese qualities – patience.

When finally she reached the university at around 7 a.m., there had been loud martial music blaring from speakers all around campus. Bob had found her in her office, window closed, elbows on the desk, fingers pressed to her temples.

'Got a bit of a hangover?' he asked. His tone made her glance up at him sharply, but there was no hint in his expression of the sarcasm she had detected in his voice.

'What is that goddamned music?'

'I wouldn't go around calling it "that goddamned music" if I were you,' he said. 'It's the Chinese national anthem. They play it every morning.'

'Then thank God I didn't take an apartment here,' she said.

'Tried Advil?' he asked.

She glared at him. 'I just bought shares in the company.' She leaned over to lift her rucksack on to the desk. 'Listen, you said yesterday that after two years you still hadn't managed to photocopy your lecture notes. I take it that was a joke?'

He shrugged. 'Well . . . sort of. It was a kind of metaphor to illustrate that things here don't always work like you would want them to. I did actually get my notes photocopied. Eventually.'

'Good.' She lifted a book out of her rucksack. 'I want to photocopy a description of an autopsy.' She dropped the book on her desk. Bob turned it round to face him. *EVIDENCE DISMISSED: The Inside Story of the Police Investigation of O. J. Simpson.* 'I take it they've heard of O.J. Simpson in China?' she said.

'Oh, yes,' Bob said. 'They've made quite a study of the case here. They use it to demonstrate the failings of the American justice system.' She flicked him another glance to see if he was being facetious. 'They may just have a point,' he added.

She railed protectively, 'It wasn't the system that failed. It was sloppy police work and incompetent prosecution. Theirs was the burden of proof. Theirs was the failure. Better that ten guilty men go free than that one innocent man is wrongly convicted. The presumption of innocence is still paramount.'

'Yeah, well, the Chinese have only just introduced that concept into their legal system. I don't think they've quite got used to the idea yet.'

'What?' Margaret looked horrified.

'What you've still not grasped, Margaret' – Bob had become

smug again – 'is that culturally, historically, American and Chinese societies are a million miles apart. You can't just come here and expect to apply American values to Chinese society. Or vice versa. The Chinese have always, since the days of Confucius, emphasised the need for the individual to suppress personal ambition in favour of social harmony. The rights of society are given greater emphasis than the rights of the individual. "The nail that sticks up gets hammered down." And that idea, and the practice of it, was around three thousand years before the communists ever came on the scene.'

'So what about the rights of the individual in law?'

'The accused, in the Chinese constitution, has plenty of rights. The trouble is that in China individual rights go hand in hand with a responsibility to society. There is no right without duty. So there's built-in conflict.'

In spite of her increasing antipathy towards Bob, Margaret found her interest being engaged. 'Like what? I mean, give me an example.'

'Okay.' Bob waved a hand vaguely towards the ceiling. 'According to Chinese law a defendant has the right to defend himself. But he also has a duty to co-operate with the police and the court in uncovering the truth about his case. You might think that right to defend himself would lead automatically to a right to silence under interrogation, to protect himself, like Americans take the Fifth. Only he also has a duty – to the state, to society – to answer all questions faithfully and truthfully, even if that incriminates him.'

'Well, that's crazy!'

'Is it?' Bob sat on the edge of her desk. 'I mean, in America we're so obsessed with protecting the rights of the individual, we sometimes forget about the rights of society. At least the Chinese are trying to accommodate both.' He sighed and shook his head. 'The real problem with China is that while the defendant's rights are pretty well protected in the constitution, they're often neglected, or even abused, in practice. But there's a lot of bright people in this country working hard to change that. And not without success. Things *are* improving.'

After her lecture from Bob had come her meeting with Mr Cao. He had been very polite and smiled a lot, and told her that while they usually had access to a 35mm slide projector it was not currently available. In that case, she had told him, smiling fixedly in return, the substance of her lectures would be necessarily limited, since they were all based around the visual presentation of real-life material. Perhaps he would like to see if they could *borrow* a slide projector. He doubted if that would be possible, but said he would see what he could do. And yes, he agreed, it would be an excellent idea if it could be arranged for her students to witness an actual autopsy. Unfortunately, he thought, this might be a little difficult to arrange. He told her he had timetabled three lectures a week, and she had shaken her head sadly and told him that, unfortunately, she had only brought material for twelve lectures. However, if he could arrange access to an autopsy, then she was sure she could *fill in* the other six hours without any difficulty. There was a further exchange of frozen smiles. He said he would see what he could do.

There had followed a brief period of relative calm before the nightmare resumed with the arrival of Lily Ping. She presented her unsmiling face at the door of Margaret's office shortly after 9 a.m. 'You got everything you need?' she had made the mistake of asking.

'Well, no, actually,' Margaret said. 'I don't have a slide projector, so most of my lecture material is redundant. I can't find the photocopier anywhere . . .'

'You want something photocopy?' She held out her hand. 'I arrange for you.'

'Oh.' Margaret was taken aback. This was new. Co-operation. 'Sure.' She picked up the O. J. book. 'I need about twenty copies.' Lily snatched the book from her and was halfway out of the door before Margaret could call after her, 'Pages 108 to 111.' She crossed the office hurriedly and called down the corridor, 'Before ten. I've got a class at ten.'

'Sure,' Lily said, without turning, as she disappeared into the bowels of the building.

At a quarter to ten Margaret went looking for her, eventually spotting her ten minutes later crossing campus towards the auditorium. Margaret chased after her, the glare and heat of the sun bouncing back at her off the tarmac. 'Lily! Lily!' She was breathless and red-faced by the time she caught up with her. 'Lily, where are my photocopies? I've got class in five minutes.'

'Oh, photocopy take time. Girl busy right now,' Lily said, and resumed her progress towards the auditorium.

Margaret chased after her. 'That's not good enough. I want them now. And I need that book back.'

'This afternoon,' Lily said without breaking stride.

Margaret stopped, fists clenched at her sides. 'All right. I'll do it myself. Where's the photocopier?'

'No need you do it yourself. That what secretary there for.' And Lily disappeared into the auditorium. Margaret stood, stock still, the sun beating down on her like a physical blow, and felt the most powerful urge to scream at the top of her lungs.

The bleep on the hour from her digital watch had come as a sickening reminder that she should be somewhere else. She had hurried back to the office to collect her stuff and then literally run across campus to the red-brick building that housed the lecture rooms. It had taken her fully another five minutes to find *her* lecture room. Fifteen students, twelve male and three female, sat in patient and curious silence as the puce-faced and perspiring pathologist made her breathless entrance for her debut lecture.

Her attempt at composure, which consisted of a deep breath and a big smile, was met with blank faces. 'Hi,' she said, confidence dissolving fast. 'I'm Dr Margaret Campbell. I'm a forensic pathologist from the Cook County Examiner's Office in Chicago, Illinois. And over the next six weeks it *had* been my intention to take you through twelve real-life murder cases from the US. Unfortunately, a lot of the material I have is visual. Photographic slides. And, sadly, it seems the university is unable to provide me with a projector to . . .' Her voice trailed off as she saw a 35mm slide projector on a table at the back of the room – at the same time as most of the students turned to look at it. 'Ah,' she said. 'Looks like they've been able to lay their hands on one after all.' A tense pause. 'If they'd told me, I'd have brought my slides with me.' Her cheek muscles were beginning to ache with the effort of holding, for hours it seemed, a smile on her face. 'I'll just go and get them. Back in five minutes.'

That, she had reflected, as she hurried back to her office, was what the Chinese would have described as extreme loss of face. But she wasn't going to be fazed by it. These were simply teething troubles and she was going to deal with them calmly and coolly. She passed Bob in the corridor. He smiled cheerily.

'Hey, I hear Mr Cao managed to get you a slide projector after all.'

'Well, he might have damn well told me!' she snapped, and slammed the door of her office.

Later, as she sat in the gloom of the darkened lecture room, running through slides of burn victims from Waco, it occurred to her that Bob – and everyone else at the university – must wonder what kind of premenstrual maniac the OICJ had dumped on them. From somewhere in the depths of the depression that had descended upon her, a voice told her that one day she would be able to smile about it all. But at that moment, she doubted it very much.

When she had drawn the blinds she noticed that the fifteen faces in her classroom had gone quite pale. One of the girls asked to be excused and hurried out to the toilet holding a hand over her mouth. Margaret had smiled grimly. 'These are just photographs. If any of you ever become real cops you're going to see a hell of a lot worse in the flesh.' She had thrown the class open for discussion. But not a single student ventured a question or a view. And now, as they filed silently out at the end of the hour, she slumped back in her chair and let out a deep and heartfelt sigh of relief. A knock at the door made her turn her head. Her heart sank at the sight of Bob.

'How'd it go?'

'Don't ask.'

He grinned. 'Don't take it personally. They're like that with everyone at first.'

'What do you mean?' She sat up.

'Well, let me guess. You found them unresponsive, reluctant to answer questions, even more reluctant to ask them or discuss a point?' She nodded dumbly. 'Chinese students aren't used to the kind of interactive classes we have in the US. Here, they tend to be lectured to.'

I know the feeling, Margaret thought bitterly.

Bob continued, unaware of her growing desire to stuff her trainers down his throat. 'The voice of the teacher is the voice of authority. Most students believe there is only one right answer to any question. So they just memorise stuff. They're not used to discussing, or debating, or expressing a view. But I'm sure you'll win them round.'

Margaret searched his face for that sarcasm she heard in his voice again. But again there was no sign of it.

'Anyway,' he said, 'you'd better get back over to Administration. There's an old friend waiting to see you in your office.'

*

Section Chief Chen Anming rose from one of Margaret's plastic seats and gave her one of his rare, and warm, smiles. 'Dr Campbell. What a very great pleasure it is to meet you again.' He pumped her hand enthusiastically.

Margaret might have been hard pushed to place him had it not been for the yellow nicotine streak in his hair, and the fact that Bob had explained to her who he was. 'Mr Chen.' She inclined her head towards him. 'The pleasure is all mine.'

'Perhaps you will not remember me?' he said.

She had only the vaguest recollection of him. So many students on short courses over the last three years. 'Of course, I remember you well.' Then suddenly she did remember – a painting mounted on a scroll that hung on her study wall at home. He had presented it to her, almost ceremonially, on his last day. It was something she looked at often and appreciated, something that had nothing to do with her and Michael, but with her alone. An old man with a wicked grin and bristling beard, squatting on the ground dangling a pair of sandals in one hand. 'You gave me the painting of the Chinese ghost.'

'Not a ghost, exactly. A good Chinese spirit.'

'I've never been able to remember his name.'

'*Zhong Kui*. He is a legendary figure.'

So many hours in his company, and only now did she know his name. 'I had no idea when you gave me it how much pleasure it would give me.' She thought of those long, dark nights when *Zhong Kui*'s roguish smile was the only thing that seemed to keep her sane, when his presence in her home was the only company she could bear. It seemed extraordinary that she should now be reacquainted with her benefactor in this unusual circumstance. And she flushed with guilt at having almost forgotten who he was and, indeed, how the picture had come into her possession. 'I am sure I must have thanked you at the time. But I am very pleased to be able to thank you again, this time with the knowledge of hindsight.'

'Forgive me, Doctor.' He seemed suddenly embarrassed. 'I know you have only just arrived, and you must be very busy . . .' He hesitated. 'I was wondering . . . could I, perhaps, ask you for a very special personal favour?'

'Of course.' She couldn't imagine what it might be. 'Anything.'

'This is not official, you understand. Just personal,' he stressed again, and it dawned on Margaret that she was witnessing *guanxi* in practice. He had presented her with a gift in Chicago. Now he was asking for something in return.

'We have a suspected suicide, but there are problems with identification. The victim set fire to himself, and the autopsy is, I think, a little specialised. He is very badly burned.'

'And you want me to do an autopsy,' she realised. 'Well, of course. I'd be only too happy to help.'

He relaxed immediately and beamed again. But she was already thinking how she might turn this to her advantage. *You're going to have to start getting yourself a little* guanxi *in the bank*, Bob had said. A window of opportunity was opening up for her students to observe an autopsy – without the help of Mr Cao. Not the burn victim, perhaps. But that particular corpse would put some *guanxi* in the bank for later.

Mr Chen took her arm and ushered her out into the corridor. 'I am so very pleased you agree to do me this favour,' he said.

She was a little taken aback. 'What, you want me to do it now?'

'No, no. I want you to come and meet my deputy. He is with Professor Jiang. I have, of course, already asked Professor Jiang for permission to ask you.'

And the professor, Margaret thought, was probably glad to get her out of his hair for a while. In fact, when Professor Jiang rose from behind his desk as they knocked and entered his office, she felt that his smile lacked a little in warmth. He looked at Chen. 'Well?'

'Dr Campbell has agreed, of course.'

Jiang seemed relieved, and Chen turned to a younger man who had been sitting by the window. 'My deputy, Li Yan,' he said. 'He is in charge of the case.' And as Li stood up Margaret realised who he was.

Li hurried to keep up as Chen strode across campus to where they'd parked their car in the shade of some trees. Chen was furious. 'What do you mean "not necessary"?' he barked.

Li tried to be reasonable. 'The pathologist at the Centre of Material Evidence Determination will not be pleased. It will be a loss of face for some American to be brought in.'

'You didn't think so when I first suggested it.'

'I didn't know who it was then.'

'And just what do you have against this woman? She is a recognised expert in her field.'

'I realise that, Chief. It's just . . .'

But Chen cut him off. 'And do you not think *I* will lose face if suddenly I turn around and tell her we've changed our minds? It's out of the question. I have asked. She has agreed. And that's an end to it.' He climbed into the driver's seat, slammed the door shut, started the engine and drove off with an impetuous squeal of tyres.

IV

The sky was lost in a dazzling wash of haze and dust. The diffused glare of the sun reflected back from every surface, and the world seemed burned out, like an overexposed photograph. Margaret slipped sunglasses over her eyes to bring back definition, and hurried to keep pace with Lily on the long walk from the administration block, past the playing fields, to the squat, four-storey concrete building at the far end which housed the Centre of Material Evidence Determination. Her spirits were high for the first time since her arrival in China, lifted in large part by the look on Deputy Section Chief Li's face when she had walked into Professor Jiang's office with Mr Chen. All his irritated superiority of the previous day had been replaced first by astonishment, and then dismay. His handshake had been cursory, his eyes distant. He had said almost nothing. Enough, and no more, to remain polite. And now he would be waiting for her impatiently in an autopsy room, the stink of disinfectant and formaldehyde wrinkling his nose. They were the perfumes of her profession, an olfactory sensation so often experienced it no longer registered – except as something familiar, almost comforting. But not to Li, she was sure.

In fact there were five metal autopsy tables in the room, with gutters and reservoirs perfectly placed to collect blood and other fluids draining from the bodies during dissection. Li stood stiffly by the door making desultory conversation with a pathologist in a white gown. Both turned as Margaret entered with Lily.

'Dr Campbell, Professor Xie.' Li made the bleak introduction. There was no warmth in either hand or eye as Professor Xie shook her hand. Margaret understood immediately that the professor had lost face, being made to play second fiddle not only to an American, but to a woman. She was, she realised, beginning to learn something about the psychology of the Chinese. She decided not to indulge in appeasement for the moment. She turned to Lily.

'No need for you to hang around, Lily.'

'No, I stay in case there be anything you need, Doctah Cambo.' Lily was determined not to miss out on this moment between Margaret and Li, especially after what had passed between them yesterday afternoon.

'Actually,' Margaret said acidly, 'there *is* some photocopying I was wanting done.'

'All taken care of, Doctah,' Lily replied, quite unfazed.

Margaret turned to Li. 'So – you have no idea who the victim is?' she asked.

'No,' Li said. 'We will have to wait and match dental records with missing-persons reports as they come in. It could take some weeks.'

'Weeks?' She was astonished.

He took her tone as criticism. 'Time is unimportant. Results are.'

'In the States *both* are.'

'Yes, but in China we pride ourselves on getting things right.'

She bit her tongue. After all, she had no ammunition with which to fight back. The Chinese might make studies of well-known cases in the US, but Americans were profoundly ignorant of headline crimes in China.

'I was once involved in a murder investigation that lasted more than two years,' Li went on, to illustrate his point. 'A family were found slaughtered in their home. A mother, father, grandfather, child. There was a forced entry, a night-time burglary we believed had gone wrong. Blood everywhere. Footprints in blood, fingerprints. But our national fingerprint register is, as yet, limited. We had to trace and interview nearly three thousand migrant workers known to have been in the area at the time.'

Margaret interrupted. 'How did you know it was a migrant worker?'

'In China,' Li said, 'people respect the police. They know it is their duty to help the police. If they have a job, their *danwei* provides their apartment, pays for their medical treatment. Someone on their street committee will know if they are at home or not at home. There is a network of information about people's lives and movements that we can call on. We call it the masses line. The masses line is the single biggest reason for low crime figures in China. People do not commit crime if they know they will be caught. And if they are caught they lose everything – job, house, medical treatment, pension . . .' He shook his head and scuffed his foot on the floor. 'Everyone agrees, economic reform in China is good. Deng Xiaoping said: "To be rich is glorious." But now the iron rice bowl is broken . . .'

'Iron rice bowl?'

He seemed annoyed by the interruption. 'Job for life. We call it the iron rice bowl. Now that the rice bowl is broken, there are many unemployed people. Many workers are itinerant. They move about the country looking for work. They are what we call the floating population. And as the floating population grows, so does the crime rate.'

Margaret nodded, beginning to understand just how such fundamental differences in a society can affect its criminal activity. 'So you went after your three thousand itinerant workers.'

'We found eleven had gone missing. One by one they had to be found and eliminated from our inquiry. Finally we got our man.'

'Two years?'

'Two years.'

Margaret shook her head in wonder. 'In the States we wouldn't have had the money, or the manpower, to pursue one case that long. And anyway,' she grinned, 'there'd have been a few hundred other homicides in the meantime.'

'I know,' Li said seriously, and Margaret wondered if this was straight-faced sarcasm. But he gave no indication of it.

Professor Xie glanced pointedly at his watch and sighed audibly.

'Okay,' Li said. 'You want to have a look at the body?'

'Are there any belongings?' she asked.

'Don't you want to see the body first?' Li seemed surprised.

'No. Sometimes you can tell a lot from what a person was wearing, or carrying.'

Professor Xie spoke to one of several hovering assistants, who hurried away, returning a few moments later with a small plastic bag containing the few effects that survived the blaze. He tipped them out on one of the tables and they gathered round to have a look, Lily squeezing in between two assistants to catch a glimpse. If she had been expecting something macabre, then she would have been disappointed by the charred belt buckle, Zippo lighter and signet ring.

Margaret picked up and examined the buckle closely. It was a simple loop with a long, thin tongue. Quite unremarkable. She dropped it with a clatter on the metal table and picked up the Zippo, turning it this way and that with dexterous fingers before flipping open the lid. Inside was a blackened mess, the interior working melded to the exterior sheath, the cotton and wick incinerated in the fire. She asked for a pair of rubber gloves, a piece of cotton cloth and some cleaning fluid. An irked Professor Xie relayed the request to an assistant, who rushed off to comply.

Margaret continued examining the lighter, and Li took the

opportunity to cast a discreet eye over her. She was dressed casually, in sneakers and jeans, a baggy white tee-shirt tucked in at her belt. He marvelled at the colour and texture of her hair, tumbling in golden curls from grey clasps. But her eyes were compelling. He had met many blue-eyed Westerners, but these were startlingly blue, as if lit from within. Her eyes met his for a fleeting moment, and he glanced away self-consciously. When he looked again, she seemed absorbed still in the lighter, scratching at the carbon coating with long, elegant white fingers. It was looking at her hands which drew his attention to her freckles. Her bare forearms were covered in them, beneath a mesh of fine, downy blonde hairs. He noticed, then, the sprinkling of them across her nose and forehead. She wore little or no make-up, a hint of brown on her eyelids, a scraping of red on her lips. His gaze dropped a little, following the smooth line of her neck, and he saw that she was not wearing a bra, breasts moving freely against the cool cotton of her shirt. Unaccountably, and to his intense annoyance, he felt a tiny knot of desire unravel somewhere deep inside his loins.

The assistant returned. Margaret snapped on the rubber gloves, soaked the cloth with fluid, and rubbed the lighter with it, slowly working off the carbon coating along its bottom face. 'There's some kind of engraved lettering here.' She found a pair of half-moon reading glasses in her purse and squinted at the lettering, disappointed to bring into focus the *ZIPPO* registered trademark, and beneath it, *Bradford PA, Made in USA*. 'Well, that's a bit of a let-down.' And as she said it, she wasn't quite sure who she was saying it to. She glanced up self-consciously, then turned back to the lighter, working quickly with the cloth and fluid over its other surfaces. 'Something else.' More, very faint, lettering appeared as the carbon lifted along the bottom edge of the flip-lid. She had to turn it to catch the light to read 'Solid Brass'. She dropped the lighter with a clatter back on the table and lifted the ring. 'Signet ring,' she said, and rubbed at it with the cloth. 'It appears to be set with a flat, engraved, semi-precious stone of some kind.' But no matter how hard she rubbed at the stone it refused to come up anything other than black, even though its metal setting began revealing patches of tarnished silver. 'Could be ebony.' She held it up and turned it to catch the light, screwing her eyes up behind her reading glasses. 'There's a symbol of some kind on it, and some lettering.' As she turned it through the light, and the engraving fell into relief, she suddenly realised what it was, and her heart skipped a beat. She examined the rest of the ring more closely. It had been deformed by the heat, but not entirely melted. Perhaps his ring hand had been resting on the ground, half protected from the upward-licking flames. She squinted at the inner surface of the ring, rubbed it for a few furious seconds with the cloth, and then squinted at it again. Now she removed her glasses. She glanced at her watch and made a quick mental calculation. 'Damn.' And she looked up to find a row of curious faces watching her with affected patience. 'Is there a phone I can use to call the States?'

Li looked at Professor Xie, who nodded. 'In my office.'

While she made the call, Margaret could see, through a

large window, the others waiting in an outer office. Professor Xie was a small man, almost effeminate, in his early forties, Margaret thought. He was dark-complexioned and his jet-black hair was swept back from a remarkable widow's peak that seemed to begin halfway up his forehead. He was perched on the edge of a desk and appeared lost in his own gloomy thoughts.

Li, too, seemed preoccupied. Smoking, she saw with distaste. Lily was babbling away to him, but it was obvious he wasn't listening. Margaret took a good look at him, but saw no reason to reappraise yesterday's assessment. He was ugly, bad-tempered and moody. *And* he was a smoker. The ringing in her ear was suddenly interrupted as someone answered at the other end.

'Twenty-third Precinct,' said a woman's voice.

'Detective Hersh, please.'

Li looked past his reflection in the window and saw Margaret in its shadow. She had been talking animatedly for some time, laughing easily. Someone she knew well at the other end. And now she seemed to be waiting, tapping a pencil on the polished surface of Professor Xie's immaculately tidy desk. He could not imagine the purpose of the phone call, or what she had seen in the ring. She still had it with her, and as she waited on the phone, she kept examining and re-examining it, a girlish excitement apparent in her inability to sit still. He noticed the ring on her wedding finger, and in spite of himself felt curious about the man who had married her.

It was Li's firm belief that he would never marry. The few

relationships he'd had at university had gone nowhere, and since joining Section One there just hadn't been the time. He was still embarrassed by the recollection of half-remembered adolescent fumblings with teenage girls in his home town of Wanxian in Sichuan province. He had been an ugly boy, always tall for his age, and clumsy. The more experienced girls had made fun of him, teasing and taunting.

But there had been one girl, shy, not like the others. Like him she was no beauty, but also like him she was gentle, in body and spirit, strong in character. They had walked by the canal together during long, dusky summer evenings before he left for Beijing and the Public Security University. She had not wanted him to be a policeman. He was made for better things, she had told him. He was a sensitive soul, he had no place among brutish criminals in the big city. His family was pushing him into it, she said, because his uncle was a famous policeman in the capital. But Li knew that wasn't why, at least not entirely. There was an anger in him that seemed to burn on a constant simmer. An anger at all the unfairnesses in life, the inequalities, the triumphs of evil over good.

Once, at his school, it had boiled over. A bully, the biggest boy in his year, was mercilessly baiting one of the juniors, a soft boy with a deformed hand of which he was crushingly self-conscious. He was almost hysterical with shame and embarrassment at the bully's cruelty. A crowd had gathered, the way that crowds do, scared, fascinated, glad that it wasn't them. Li broke through the circle of boys and told the bully to stop. The boy was not used to being challenged. He turned, wild-eyed, and demanded to know who the hell Li thought he was. Li said, 'I am Li Yan. And if you do not stop I will break your skull.' And he meant it. And the bully saw in his eyes that he meant it. But he was trapped by his own weakness. He could not back down without losing face. So Li had to crack his skull. He was in hospital for nearly two weeks and Li was visited by the juvenile delinquency officer and almost expelled from his school. But no one ever bullied the boy with the deformity again, not while Li was around. And Li had never had to fight anyone else again since.

So he knew that this girl was wrong. He was not made for better things. He was made to be a policeman, and to Li that was the very best thing he could be. He had never regretted coming to Beijing, and the last he heard the girl he walked by the canal with had married the bully whose skull he'd cracked. He had smiled, for the bully was weak, and she was strong and would mould him into whatever she wanted.

Margaret, he noticed now, was scribbling in a notebook whatever was being relayed to her across the ether. She nodded and smiled and hung up the phone, tearing the page out of the notebook before coming through. She handed it to Li, a gleam in her eyes. 'Chao Heng,' she said. 'That's the name of your John Doe through there.' She jerked her thumb towards the autopsy room. 'About ninety-nine per cent certain.'

Li looked at the piece of paper. She had scribbled, *Chao Heng, graduated microbial genetics, University of Wisconsin, 1972.*

He looked up at her in astonishment. Professor Xie said, 'How can you possibly know this?'

She held up the ring. 'In the States, there's a tradition among university graduates. To mark the occasion they have special graduation rings made that bear the crest of their university. In this case, the University of Wisconsin.' She handed the ring to Professor Xie. 'You can see the crest carved in the stone. Even if it hadn't actually said *University of Wisconsin* on it, I'd have known the university because . . .' Li saw a cloud, like a cataract, come across her eyes and the skin darken around them '. . . because someone I knew well graduated from there.' The moment was past, and she was back on her roll. 'The thing is, they very often get them engraved on the inside. A name, a date, initials. In this case, if you look carefully, the initials C.H. and the date, 1972.'

Professor Xie peered at the engraving and passed it to Li.

'We're lucky it wasn't completely melted.' She shrugged. 'So fate was kind to us. Anyway, it's half past ten at night over there, so I couldn't call the university. I did the next best thing; spoke to a friend on the Chicago force. He goes on-line to the Internet, pulls up the alumni register for Wisconsin, and checks out the initials on all the graduates from '72. There's only one Chinese name with the initials C. H. Chao Heng. Graduated in microbial genetics.'

Li clenched his fist around the ring, a gleam in his eye which when he turned it on her might have held a hint of admiration, albeit grudging. She felt a flush of pleasure. She remembered reading something somewhere, once, a very long time ago. She knew it was Chinese. 'Women hold up half the sky.' She shrugged it off as if it were nothing.

Li raised an eyebrow, and she saw pure mischief in those dark eyes. 'Ah,' he said. 'You are quoting from Mao Zedong.' She nodded. So that's who had said it. 'Of course,' Li continued, 'he meant the lower half of the sky.'

There was a moment's stand-off, before a wide grin slashed his face. It was irresistibly infectious, and she found herself smiling back when what she really wanted to do was punch him. She turned to Professor Xie. 'Professor, if I may, I would very much like to assist you in the autopsy. I am sure there is much I could learn from an experienced pathologist like yourself.' Credentials established, she had no problem with restoring Professor Xie's *mianzi*.

He responded immediately with a small, dignified bow. 'It is my pleasure,' he said.

V

'There is extensive thermal injury, with fourth- and third-degree burns over greater than ninety per cent of the body surface, with scattered second-degree burns. Portions of the scalp and virtually all of the scalp hair are charred away, with the exception of a small amount of singed, coarse, straight black hair averaging three centimetres in length on the left side of the head. The facial features are not discernible. The nose is absent, as is the right ear. The left ear is shrivelled and charred. The eyes are not recognisable. The teeth are partially charred, but are in excellent repair, with multiple amalgam fillings and porcelain crowns. The maxilla and mandible will be retained for future dental comparison. The skin and soft tissue of the right cheek are charred

away and there is char fracturing of the right zygoma. The tongue is protruding slightly; the tip is charred, and there is a small amount of white froth about the mouth. No facial hair is identified.'

Lily's protestations that she was no longer required had been ignored, and she stood shivering at the back of the autopsy room beside Li, hardly daring to watch as Margaret made her preliminary examination of the body. Margaret measured and weighed, describing her findings as she went for the benefit of an overhead microphone. The recording of the entire proceeding would later be transcribed for the autopsy report.

She and Professor Xie had gone off earlier to change, returning swathed in layers of clothing; green surgeon's pyjamas covered by plastic aprons, in turn covered by long-sleeved cotton gowns. Both wore plastic shoe covers on their feet and shower caps on their heads. Wondering what had drawn her to such a macabre profession, Li had watched with involuntary fascination as Margaret pulled on a pair of gloves, slipping plastic sleeve covers over her freckled forearms to cover the gap between sleeve and glove. She had drawn a steel-mesh glove over her left, non-cutting, hand, and snapped on a second pair of latex gloves over the lot. The post-mortem mutilation of a human being was a messy business.

As both surgeons had pulled up their face masks and lowered goggles over their eyes, two assistants had wheeled in the charred body of Chao Heng on a gurney and transferred it to the autopsy table. Lily had let out a small gasp. His upper body was still frozen in the defensive attitude of the boxer, as if preparing to fight off any attempt to cut him open. The chill air of the room had been suffused immediately with a smell like overcooked steak on a grill, an insidious odour that crept into the soul via the too-sensitive medium of the olfactory nerves.

The assistants had placed covers on the floor beneath and around the table to collect the fine charcoal dust that Margaret had warned would settle all around them and track across the room as they moved back and forth dissecting organs for later microscopic examination. Professor Xie, although nominally the lead pathologist, now that *mianzi* was restored had deferred to Margaret's greater experience and asked her to perform the autopsy while he assisted.

Now, as she examined the feet of the corpse, she found and pulled back a piece of black and stiffened material from the top of the left foot. '*The charred remains of what appears to be a leather shoe and part of a sock are present over the dorsum and the sole of the left foot and the sole of the right foot. There are no remaining identifying features, other than that the left shoe appears to have been of a laced variety. The skin of the dorsum of the left foot is dark red and blistered and there is an apparent needle track in the skin in the area of the saphenous vein and venous arch.*'

Margaret reached up and switched off the microphone, turning towards Li. 'Looks like our man might have been a junkie. The top of the foot is quite a common place to shoot up if you want to hide the needle tracks. We can confirm that by checking for narcotics residue in and around the capillaries of the lungs. Blood tests will tell us what he was shooting up. Probably heroin.'

'Will you get sufficient blood and material for testing? I mean, won't everything be cooked?' Li's distaste at his own question was palpable.

'Superficially, yes. Normally we would draw off fluid from the eyes and blood from the femoral veins at the top of the legs, but that *will* be cooked and solid. Inside, though, should be pretty much protected and preserved. Beyond the accelerant used to set him on fire, there wasn't much else to sustain the blaze, so he wouldn't have burned for that long.'

The assistants turned the body over and Margaret switched on the microphone. *'The posterior trunk shows a symmetrical external contour. The spine is clearly mid-line. There is charring of the skin of the back and multiple small areas of skin splitting over the latissimus dorsi bilaterally. There is no obvious blunt or sharp force trauma of the back.'*

Having placed the body on its back again, the autopsy assistants placed a rubber block around six inches thick beneath the body, in the mid-chest area, to help expose the chest cavity when Margaret made the first Y-shaped incision, starting at each shoulder, meeting at the bottom of the breastbone, and continuing down past the belly button to the pubic bone. She peeled back the skin and musculature of the chest to reveal the cavity.

'There is diffuse drying and fixation of the soft tissues of the thoracic and abdominal walls, with skin splitting. All organs are present and in their appropriate positions.'

Professor Xie cut through the ribcage with what looked like pruning shears. The snapping of the bones made a sickening sound that echoed back at them off the cold tiles. When he had finished, they removed the breastplate to reveal the heart. Margaret snipped open the pericardial sac so that the blood that poured into it out of the heart could be collected by the assistants for testing in toxicology. Professor Xie slipped his hands into the cavity and lifted up the heart, allowing Margaret to sever the major vessels and arteries so that he could remove it for weighing and later dissection.

They worked methodically down the body, removing the lungs, the stomach – looking like a slimy, fluid-filled purse, its foul-smelling contents drained for further examination – the liver, the spleen, the pancreas, the kidneys; weighing everything, removing blood, fluid and bile samples.

'*The stomach contains 125 grams of grey-brown, pasty, partially digested food material. No medication residue is grossly identified. No ethanol odour is noted.*'

Working quickly now, with dexterous hands, Margaret cut the guts free and, starting at the duodenum end, began pulling the gut towards herself, an arm's length at a time, using her scalpel to free its loops from the sheet of fat to which it was attached. When it was straight, she sliced down its length with a pair of scissors, holding them partially open and drawing the intestine along them, as if she were cutting a piece of Christmas wrapping paper. The stink was almost unbearable. Li and Lily moved instinctively away, mouths closed, breathing shallowly. '*The small and large intestines are examined throughout their entire length and are grossly unremarkable.*' The intestine was discarded into a stainless-steel bucket lined with plastic.

Urine samples were drawn from the bladder for toxicology, and Margaret examined the prostate and testes, cutting sections from each for testing, before discarding the remains in the bucket.

She turned to the neck now, pulling the top flap of skin from the Y-shaped incision up over the face. '*The bony and cartilaginous structures of the neck are intact and without evidence of trauma. The musculature of the neck shows marked heat fixation, but there is no evidence of haemorrhage in the strap muscles or soft tissues of the neck.*'

Attention turned, then, to the head, a head-block placed under the neck to raise it from the table. An incision was made at the back running from one ear to the other, and the skin peeled down over the face to reveal the skull. Using a circular saw, one of the assistants cut through the skullcap so that it could be removed, with a sucking and popping sound like feet being withdrawn from mud, to reveal the brain. Margaret had warned everyone to stand back as the saw cut through bone. 'Try not to breathe this stuff,' she said. 'It smells kind of smoky-sweet, but latest thinking is that it might carry HIV and other viruses.'

She examined the skull. '*Reflection of the scalp reveals a 2 x 3.2 centimetre area of subgaleal haemorrhage over the left parietal bone, with a possible contusion of approximately the same dimensions of the scalp – impossible to say for sure because of heat artifact. There is a small amount of subdural haemorrhage deep to the area of subgaleal haemorrhage. On removal of the dura, an irregular-shaped fracture, measuring 2.6 centimetres in length, is clearly visible. There is no charring or eversion of the fracture.*'

She concentrated then on removing the brain from the skull, pulling it gently back towards her, examining its worm-like surface as she did. *'The meninges are slightly dried, but thin and translucent. There is a small contusion of the left parietal lobe, with a trace of haemorrhage.'* She snipped it off at the stem and it plopped out into her hands for weighing. Lily put a hand over her mouth and fled from the room.

Margaret let out a deep breath as she relaxed her concentration. 'Well, apart from breadloafing the organs, there's not much else we can do just now. It'll take some time to prepare permanent paraffin sections for microscopic examination . . .'

Professor Xie interrupted her. 'If you wished, we could examine fresh frozen sections in about fifteen minutes.'

'You've got a cryostat here?' She was unable to hide her surprise.

He smiled. 'This is a very modern facility, Doctor. We are not *so* far behind the Americans.'

The cryostat was about the size of a small washing machine with a crank handle on its right side and a window on top with a view into its icy interior, kept at a chilly minus 22°C. Margaret was happy to let Professor Xie demonstrate his expertise, and watched as he prepared sections of lung tissue and skin from the left foot for freezing. He squeezed globs of a jelly-like support medium into metal chucks that would provide holding bases for the tissue. The tissue samples were then placed on the chucks which were, in turn, set on a rack in the cold working area in the cryostat. Working with prac-tised ease, the professor pressed metal heat sinks against the face of the tissue samples, both to flatten and to freeze them.

Li had attended many autopsies over the years, but this was a procedure that was new to him. He watched, fascinated, as only a few minutes later the professor removed the frozen lung tissue from the freezer and transferred it, in its chuck, to the cutting area. Placing it hard against the blade, he turned the crank handle, drawing the sample across the cutting edge, for all the world like a ham slicer, cutting a wisp-thin section of tissue only microns thick, which was then touched to the surface of a room-temperature glass microscope slide. The sample instantly melted. The professor stained it with hema- toxylin and eosin and handed it to Margaret for examination under the microscope.

'*Microscopic examination of multiple sections of the lungs shows granulomata and multinucleated giant cells containing polarisable material.*'

The process was repeated with the skin samples taken from the areas of needle track on the left foot. Margaret pushed her goggles up on to her forehead. 'Same thing,' she said.

'Meaning what?' Li asked.

'Heroin users often grind up whatever other narcotics they can and inject the powder the way they do heroin. Particles of the pill residue get trapped in the tiny capillaries of the lungs and the surrounding lung tissue. Where the particles remain they get engulfed by inflammatory cells. There is clear evidence of that in this man's lungs, as well as in the tracks in his foot.'

'So what does this tell us?'

'Nothing, except that he was probably a heroin user.'

'And cause of death?'

'As we all thought. Extensive thermal injury. Burning.'

'You said something about contusion, haemorrhaging, a fracture of the skull . . . What does all that mean?'

'It means someone hit him on the head with a blunt instrument. Not enough to kill him, but it would certainly have rendered him at least semiconscious, if not wholly unconscious.'

Li was startled. 'It couldn't have been accidental, or self-inflicted?'

She said dismissively, 'Oh, I don't think so. With an injury like that he'd have been in no condition to go walking around and setting himself up as a bonfire. And, as I understand it, he was found still in the lotus position. So he didn't fall and hit his head on anything once he'd started burning. I believe he was knocked on the head and then sedated.' She paused. 'Are you familiar with the term Special K?' Li frowned, clearly not. She smiled. 'At least, that's what they call it on the streets. A drug called ketamine. They used to use it as an anaesthetic induction agent in the States. Got some pretty nasty hallucinogenic side effects. My guess would be that when we get the blood tests back we'll find he had been injected either with ketamine, or a very high dose of heroin. That would have made him more compliant and easier to handle.'

'You're telling me he didn't kill himself.' Li was stunned.

'Suicide? Good God, no. This man was murdered.'

CHAPTER THREE

I

Tuesday Afternoon

They stood outside blinking in the sunlight – a very different kind of light from the bright lamps that illuminated the subterranean gloom of the autopsy room. Margaret slipped on her sunglasses. Lily had still not reappeared after her dash to the toilet, and Li and Margaret stood uncertainly, unsure how to conclude their business. Each exhibited a strange hesitancy about saying goodbye. To share the experience of something as traumatic and revealing as the dissection of another human being had an almost bonding effect, inducing a shared and heightened sense of mortality.

Margaret looked up and down the street. 'Did you leave your car up at Administration?'

'No, the Chief took it. I'll take the bus back.'

'Bus?' Margaret was shocked. 'Surely police resources would stretch to a taxi.'

He shrugged. 'I don't mind the bus.'

'In this heat? I've seen the buses in this city. They're jammed full. Standing room only. How far is it?'

'Other side of Beijing.'

Lily appeared, looking distinctly pale. Her heightened sense of mortality had clearly manifested itself in an emptying of her stomach. 'Lily,' Margaret said brusquely, 'I need to go back to Section One with Deputy Section Chief Li.' She waved her hand vaguely. 'Administrative detail.' She paused. 'So I won't be needing you any more.'

'That not possible, Doctah Cambo.' Lily puffed up her indignation. 'How you get back to university? I get car and take you there.'

'Thought she might.' Margaret smiled sweetly after her as Lily strutted off in the direction of Administration to find their car. Margaret turned to Li. 'Can I offer you a lift?'

Li returned a wry smile, perfectly well aware of how she had just manipulated Lily. 'There's really no need.'

'Oh, but I insist. I have no further classes today, and I'd be intrigued to see the operational headquarters of Beijing's serious crime squad. I'm sure Section Chief Chen would have no objections.'

On the long drive across the city, Margaret had ample time to regret her impulsiveness. Lily sat up front with the driver, and Margaret sat in the back with Li in uncomfortable silence, a very awkward space between them that could easily have accommodated a third person. After the adrenalin rush of the morning, her body and brain were once again crying out for sleep, and she found herself having to blink frequently to stay awake. She should, she realised, have gone back to her hotel and slept for the rest of the day. After all, it was bedtime back home. But then again, she persuaded herself, if she had done that her body clock would never adjust to Beijing time.

Li was regretting accepting the lift for very different reasons. He was going to have to take her into the office. Already he could see the smirking faces, hear the whispered comments at his expense. And he knew that he would be unable to conceal his embarrassment. He blushed too easily. And yet it was a measure of his growing ambivalence towards her that he almost relished the opportunity to demonstrate his status and authority.

They approached Section One from the west along Beixinqiao Santiao, passing, at number five, an impressive building studded with colourful mosaic patterns beneath traditional upturned eaves. Marble gateposts were guarded by ubiquitous lions. 'What's that place?' Margaret asked as it slid past their window.

'Hotel for Overseas Chinese,' Li said.

Margaret frowned. 'You mean they have their own hotels?'

'Some overseas Chinese think they are better than us poor mainlanders,' Li said. 'They think their money makes them better.' He did not approve of the status awarded these overseas Chinese, some of them second and third generation, who returned from places as diverse as Singapore and the United States to flash their wealth and shower gifts upon poor relatives. It was true that for many years the money they had sent back to relatives in China had made an important contribution to the Chinese economy. But that was changing now. So much so that with the rapidly changing economic and political climate, many of these exiled Chinese were returning for good. China itself was becoming a land of opportunity, a place to make money.

As they passed the red-tiled façade of Noah's Ark Food Room on their right, Li peered in the window, hoping that at this time of day a number of his colleagues would be grabbing a quick lunch – the fewer to snigger at his enforced association with the *yangguizi*. But the place appeared to be empty. He sighed.

If Margaret had been expecting some impressive showpiece building to house the headquarters of Section One, she would have been disappointed by the undistinguished brick block skulking anonymously behind the trees. From the street there was nothing to suggest that this was the nerve centre of Beijing's fight against serious crime. Only a well-informed and observant onlooker would have spotted that the registration numbers of all the unmarked cars parked in the street began with the Chinese character representing the word *Capital*, followed by a zero – the telltale registration mark of all Beijing police vehicles. Li led Margaret, followed by Lily, in through the side entrance and up to the top floor. To his extreme discomfort the detectives' room was full of officers sitting around poking chopsticks into carry-out dishes of noodles and rice, jars of green tea sitting on desks. There was an odd air of expectation as he walked in, and a hush that descended on their conversation, even before Margaret appeared in the doorway. Her appearance served only to heighten an already tense atmosphere. Detectives sat up self-consciously, wondering, clearly, who she was and why she was there. But Li was determined to play it cool.

'Qian,' he said. 'We've made an identification of our burn victim. His name is Chao Heng, graduated from the American University of Wisconsin in 1972 in . . .' He glanced at the piece of paper in his hand, '. . . microbial genetics. Whatever that is. Let's get an address and find out what we can about him ASAP. Okay?'

Qian almost sat to attention. 'I'm on it already, boss.' And he reached for a telephone. But he hesitated before dialling, watching, like everyone else in the room, as Li opened the door to his office. There were some stifled sniggers as he stopped in his tracks, confronted by the bizarre figure of an old man with long, wispy white hair and an equally long silver goatee. He was wearing what could only be described as black pyjamas and was sitting cross-legged on Li's desk. Margaret peered round Li to see what the cause of the hilarity was.

'What the hell . . .' Li looked at the old man in consternation, aware now of some less restrained laughter behind him. Lily had come into the room and was staring open-mouthed at the old man.

'Who is he?' Margaret finally asked, perplexed by the bizarre nature of the scene unfolding before her.

'No idea,' Li said. And in Chinese to the old man, 'Would you like to tell me what you are doing in my office?'

More laughter from the detectives' room as the old man emerged from some deep contemplation and turned on Li a wizened and solemn face. 'Bad *feng shui*,' he said. 'Ve-ery bad *feng shui*.'

'*Feng shui*?' Margaret said, recognising the words. 'I know what that is.'

Li turned to her in astonishment. 'You do?'

'Sure. It's a current passion among middle-class Middle Americans with nothing better to do with their time. A girl-friend dragged me along to a class once. The balance of yin and yang and the flow of *ch'i* and all that kind of stuff. The spirituality of architecture and interior design.' She paused. 'So who's this guy?'

'Evidently, a *feng shui* man,' said Li through gritted teeth.

'And . . . he goes with the job, does he?'

Li glared at her, and was then distracted by more unre-strained laughter from his colleagues. He turned his glare on them, which muted their laughter a little, before turning back to the *feng shui* man. 'What are you doing in my office?' he repeated, although he already knew the answer.

His heart sank as the *feng shui* man confirmed, 'Your Uncle Yifu asked me to fix your *feng shui*. He is very concerned about this place. And he is right to be. Ve-ery bad *feng shui*.'

Detective Wu brushed respectfully past Margaret with a solemn nod and appeared at Li's shoulder. He pushed his dark glasses up on to his forehead. 'Chief wants to see you, boss.'

'What?'

'As soon as you got back, he said. I think maybe he's worried about your . . . *feng shui*.' And he couldn't keep his face straight any longer.

Li's lips pressed together in a resolute line. 'Excuse me,' he said to Margaret, and pushed back out into the corridor.

At the far end he rapped on a door and walked into Chen's office. Chen's face clouded as he looked up from his desk. 'Shut the door,' he said tersely. 'What is that man doing in your office?'

'He's a *feng shui* man,' Li said hopelessly.

'I know what he is.' Chen was struggling to keep his voice down. 'What is he *doing* here?'

Li sighed. 'My Uncle Yifu sent him.'

Chen leaned back in his seat and groaned in frustration. 'I suppose I should have guessed.'

'I'm sorry, Chief, I had no idea . . .'

'You *know* that the practice of *feng shui* is not approved of in official institutions. Just get rid of him. Now.'

'Yes, Chief.' Li turned to the door, but stopped, his hand still on the handle. He turned back. 'By the way. The suicide in the park? It's a murder.'

When he got back to the detectives' office Margaret was engaged in what appeared to be animated conversation with the entire office, Lily acting as interpreter. Li closed his eyes for a moment and wished, fervently, that he was somewhere else. 'Hey, boss,' Wu said, 'this is some smart lady. Lily's been telling us how she figured out the identity of the body in the park.'

Margaret was sitting on one of the desks and swivelled

towards the door. 'This is a really nice bunch of guys you've got working for you, Deputy Section Chief Li.'

'Li Yan,' Li said. 'My name's Li Yan.' And he felt the colour on his cheeks rise involuntarily, blushing to the roots of his hair. He wondered if his day could possibly get any worse, and hurried into his office. The *feng shui* man was standing in the centre of the room taking notes. 'I'm sorry, but you're going to have to go,' Li said.

The old man nodded sagely. 'I know,' he said. 'I shall need to give this much thought.' He pointed towards the filing cabinet on the door wall. 'This cabinet is no good here. It stops the door opening fully. The door must open one hundred eighty degrees. Negative *ch'i* collects in empty spaces behind doors, and you can't see the whole room when you enter.' He shook his head and turned to the window. 'Window is jammed. Restricts the view. Will bring limited opportunities.' He tapped the desk. 'Are you left or right-handed?'

Li sighed. 'Right-handed. Why?'

'We have to move the desk. Light must not come from your writing side. And we need water in here and fresh plants.' He pointed at dead plants in old pots on the sill. They had once belonged to Li's predecessor, but since his death no one had watered them and so they, too, had died. 'This is very bad *feng shui*. And we should think about the colour of the walls . . .'

Li took him gently by the arm. 'I'm quite happy with the colour of the walls. But you really have to go now.'

'Tomorrow I come back with the plan.'

'Oh, I don't think you need to worry about that. I'll speak to my uncle tonight.'

'Your uncle is my very good friend. I owe him many favours.'

'I'm sure.'

The old man took a last look back as Li guided him out into the corridor. 'Bad *feng shui*,' he said. 'Ve-ery bad *feng shui*.'

Li turned back into the detectives' room to find all of them, including Margaret, watching him with ill-concealed smiles.

'Anyway,' Margaret said, 'I think it's time you took me to lunch, don't you?'

'She just asked him to take her to lunch,' Lily translated quickly for the rest of the room, and they all waited with intense interest to see what Li's response would be. He was trapped. She had just performed a huge favour for his boss, and therefore indirectly for him. The etiquette of *guanxi* required him to return the favour. And lunch was a very small price to pay. Except that his colleagues were unlikely to let him forget it in a hurry. He fumbled to remove his fob watch from the small leather pouch looped on to his belt and glanced at the time.

'I don't have much time, and it's a little late,' he said lamely.

Lily whispered a translation. 'Aw, come on, boss,' Wu said. 'The least you can do is buy the lady some lunch.'

Margaret didn't need a translation. 'Something fast. A burger would be fine.'

Li knew there was no way out of it, and a tiny mischievous thought formed itself in his mind. 'Okay. I know a place.'

'I tell the driver to bring car round.' Lily started for the door.

'That won't be necessary,' Li said quickly. 'I'll take a pool car. We'll meet you back here in an hour.' He held the door open for Margaret.

Lily scowled, displeased to be excluded from this outing, but in no position to argue.

'Bye-bye,' Wu called after them, in English.

Margaret stopped by the door, struggling to recapture what seemed like a very distant memory of an hour spent with a phrase book on the plane. '*Zai jian*,' she said eventually, eliciting some laughter and some applause, and a chorus of 'bye-byes' from the other detectives.

II

Li picked up a dark blue Beijing Jeep in the street outside and they turned south and then west along Dongzhimennei Street. They sat in silence for several minutes as he appeared to focus all concentration on negotiating the traffic. Eventually Margaret glanced at him and said, 'Lily said the detectives told her it was your uncle who sent the *feng shui* man.'

'Yes.' Li was not inclined to talk about it, but Margaret persisted.

'So, it's not widely practised in China now? *Feng shui*.'

Li shrugged. 'Perhaps. But not officially. I don't know very much about it.'

'That's a shame. Since it was the Chinese who invented it. It was an American Chinese who took the class I attended. He told us that the whole philosophy arose from the practice of the ancient Chinese religion of Taoism.'

'What does an American Chinese know about Taoism?' Li was scathing.

'More than you, apparently.'

Li gave expression to his annoyance with a blast of his horn at a cyclist. 'Taoism,' he said. 'From the word *tao*, literally meaning "the way". It teaches us we must all find a place for ourselves in the natural way of things that does not disrupt the function of the whole. When we accept our place in the world, we become more concerned for the consequences of our actions, since for every action there is a reaction, and everything we do has a consequence for others.'

Beyond her surprise at this sudden and unexpected articulation of the centuries-old philosophy, Margaret made the connection for the first time with what Bob had been trying to tell her earlier; about Chinese society and the way it is reflected in its legal system; the sublimation of the individual in favour of the collective good; the realisation that none of us is alone in this world, that we are all interdependent.

Almost as if reading her thoughts, Li went on, 'Of course, this is not just a Chinese philosophy. It has expression in much Western thinking. "No man is an island, entire of itself; every man is a piece of the Continent, a part of the main . . ."'

Almost automatically, Margaret recalled the lines from her classes in English Lit. '"Any man's death diminishes me, because I am involved in Mankind; and therefore never send to know for whom the bell tolls; it tolls for thee."'

'Of course, John Donne was writing in seventeenth-century England,' Li said. 'He no doubt drew his inspiration from much older Chinese philosophies.'

Margaret could barely conceal her amazement. 'They didn't teach you John Donne at the University of Public Security.'

Li laughed at the idea. 'No.'

'At school?'

He shook his head. 'My Uncle Yifu. He was educated at the American University in Beijing before the communists came to power in '49. He was offered the chance to do a post-graduate course at Cambridge, in England. But he chose to stay and help build the new China.' A shadow passed almost imperceptibly across his face. 'You might say that my uncle was the embodiment of the philosophy of Taoism.'

'And how did he help to build "the new China"?' Margaret was sceptical.

But Li didn't notice. His mind was transported to another place, another time. 'He became a policeman.'

'What?'

'He was considered to be an "intellectual". And in those days this was not a good thing to be. Free thinkers were dangerous. So he volunteered to join the police force and go to Tibet.'

Margaret blew a jet of air through pursed lips. 'That's a bit of a leap. From Cambridge post-grad to Tibetan cop.'

Li was philosophical. 'It was how the world turned then. He and his wife walked to Tibet from their home in Sichuan.'

'Walked!' Margaret was incredulous.

'There were very few roads in those days over the mountains to the roof of the world. It took them three months.'

This seemed extraordinary to Margaret. The only thing with which she could equate it was the brave trek west across the United States made by pioneers in the early nineteenth century. And yet this had been less than fifty years ago.

'They brought him back to Beijing in 1960,' Li said. 'By the time he retired five years ago, he had become a Senior Commissioner, and was head of the Beijing Municipal Police. I have been staying with him in his apartment since I came here to the Public Security University.'

He wondered if Margaret could possibly divine from this how hard it had been for him to walk in the footsteps of such an uncle. Footsteps that had always been too big, the strides between them too long. If by some miracle he should ever manage to fill them and match the strides, he would be accused of having been given his uncle's shoes. There was no way for him to win.

They were heading south now on North Xidan Avenue, and near its corner with West Chang'an Avenue Li pulled the car into the kerb outside a colourful restaurant with a red-and-green-striped wall and yellow awnings. A raised, double-sided entrance under a green-tiled arching roof led up to a self-service snack bar on the first floor. In a street jammed with bicycles parked side by side, row upon row under the trees, pavement hawkers of every description were selling their wares: face masks with extending and retracting moustaches; nylons that wouldn't rip or ladder even when jabbed with a needle. An old lady sat with a pair of scales on which you could weigh yourself for a handful of *jiao*. The hawkers were attracting large crowds, who paused briefly to take in the blonde-haired, blue-eyed *yangguizi* who got out of the Jeep with the young Chinese. Margaret felt awkward and, not for the first time, noted that the Chinese were not in the least self-conscious about simply staring at her.

'*Tianfu Douhua Zhuang*,' Li said.

'I'm sorry?'

He let her precede him up the steps. 'It is the name of the restaurant. *Tianfu* meaning "land of abundance", signifying my home province of Sichuan. *Douhua Zhuang* means "Tofu Village". The food is excellent.'

The first floor was jammed with late diners cramming communal tables. Round the walls, pre-cooked dishes sat in bowls behind glass counters. People at the door were queuing for carry-out noodles. Li nodded towards the stairs. 'There is a proper restaurant with a full menu on the second floor, but we are too late for lunch today. This is for snacks, but you can eat well. Okay?'

'Sure,' Margaret said, a little overwhelmed by the strangeness of it all. 'But you choose. I wouldn't know where to begin.'

'Okay. You like noodles?' She nodded, and he grabbed a tray and got them each a bowl of noodles. Then they made their way round the glass counters, Li choosing a range of dishes: boiled tofu with sauce, won-ton, skewered meat, pickled vegetable, sweet dumplings. Everything was smothered with spicy sauces. Li got them each a beer, paid and then found them a corner at a busy table, and they sat down. Conversation lulled momentarily at the table, curious faces turning in their direction, and then the pursuits of idle gossip once more took over and Li and Margaret were relegated to happy anonymity.

'So . . .' Margaret was anxious to pick up their conversation from the car. 'You're still living with your aunt and uncle?'

'No. Just my uncle. My aunt died before I came to Beijing. I did not know her. My uncle has never really got over the loss of her.'

Margaret watched Li carefully, and helped herself from the bowls that he had just visited. The food was delicious, but within minutes a mild burning sensation in her mouth had turned into a searing heat. She gasped for breath. 'My God, it's hot!' And she grabbed her beer, draining nearly half the glass in a single draught. She looked up and saw a smile playing about Li's lips.

'Sichuan food,' he said, 'is always spicy. It is good, yes?'

She was having hot flushes now, her face, she was sure, a bright pink, perspiration breaking out across her forehead. Her eyes narrowed. 'You brought me here on purpose, didn't you? You're *trying* to burn the mouth off me.'

Li's smugness infuriated her further. 'This is the cuisine of my home,' he said. 'I thought you would be interested to try it. I did not realise your soft American palate would be so . . . sensitive.'

She glared at him. 'You're a complete bastard, Li Yan, you know that?'

He felt a thrill of pleasure, not only from the sound of his name on her lips, but from the fact that she had remembered it. She took another gulp of beer and he took pity on her. 'No, no.' He took the glass from her. 'Drinking will not help.' He took a sachet of sugar from his pocket and passed it to her. 'This will help.'

'Sugar.'

'Sure. It will stop the burning.'

Still suspicious, she opened the sachet and emptied its contents into her mouth. Miraculously, as it melted, so did the heat in the sweetness. 'It does,' she said with surprise.

Li smiled. 'Spicy and sweet. And therein you have the balance of opposites. Yin and yang. As in *feng shui.*'

'I thought you didn't know anything about *feng shui,*' Margaret said suspiciously.

'Not of its practice. But I understand the principles.' He filled his mouth with more spicy food.

'How can you do that?' Margaret asked. 'Doesn't it burn you, too?'

'I am used to it. And if you will eat some more now, you will find it does not burn so much and you will taste the flavours. And always take some noodles with each mouthful.'

Hesitantly, she followed his advice, and to her amazement the food did not seem quite as hot as it had. But she proceeded more cautiously now, sipping frequently at her beer. 'So where did you learn to speak such good English? At school?'

'No. We did learn English at school, but it was my Uncle Yifu who taught me to speak it properly. He said there are only two languages in the world worth speaking. The first is Chinese, the second is English.'

Margaret couldn't help but notice the warmth in his eyes when he spoke of his uncle, and she realised, almost with a shock, that she had stopped seeing his face as Chinese, or as different in any way. It was just familiar now, a face she knew, a face she had even stopped seeing as ugly, for there was something deep and darkly attractive in his eyes.

'He made me learn ten words every day,' Li said, 'and one verb. And he would test me on them, and make me practise. In Yuyuantan Park there is a place they call the "English Corner". Chinese who speak English meet there just to talk to one another and practise speaking the language. Uncle Yifu used to take me there every Sunday morning and we would talk English until my head hurt. Sometimes there would be some English or American tourist or businessman staying in the city who would hear about the "English Corner" and come and make conversation with us. And that would be very special, because we could ask about slang and colloquialism and cursing that you cannot find in books. Uncle Yifu always says you only fully understand a society when you know which words they debase for swearing.'

Margaret smiled, seeing the truth in this. 'Your uncle should have been a teacher.'

'I think, maybe, he would have liked that. He never had any children of his own, so all the things a father would like to pass on to his son, Uncle Yifu has passed on to me.' Li raised the noodle bowl almost to his lips, and scooped noodles quickly into his mouth with his chopsticks. 'But I didn't learn all my

English from my uncle. I spent six months in Hong Kong after the handover, working with a very experienced English police officer who had decided to stay on. This was very good for my English. And then I was sent for three months to the United States to take a course in criminal investigation at the University of Illinois in Chicago.'

'You're kidding!' Margaret shook her head in wonder. 'I took that course.'

'But you are a forensic pathologist.'

'Sure, that's what I'm experienced in, but I also had fire-arms training with the Chicago PD. Was a pretty good shot, too. And I took the course in criminal investigation because . . . well, because it does no harm to broaden your horizons. A year later I was teaching forensics part-time on the same course. That's where I met your boss. It's amazing we didn't run into each other.'

Li nodded thoughtfully. 'Your employer paid for you to take this course?'

'Hell, no.' Margaret smiled at the thought. 'I took three months out at my own expense. I suppose I could afford to in those days. I had a husband who was working.'

'Ah.' Li couldn't have explained, even to himself, why he was disappointed to be reminded that she was married. His eye flickered down to the ring on her wedding finger. 'You have been married a long time?'

'Foolishly,' she said with a bitterness he had neither seen nor heard in her before, 'since I was twenty-four. Seven years. Must have broken a mirror.'

'I'm sorry? You broke a mirror?' Li was confused.

'It's a silly superstition in the West. They say if you break a mirror it will bring you seven years' bad luck. Anyway, I am no longer married, so perhaps my luck is changing.'

Li was unaccountably relieved. But still intrigued. 'What did he do, your husband?'

'Oh, he lectured in genetics at the Roosevelt University in Chicago. It was his great passion. Or so I used to think.' Li heard great hurt in her voice, but she was trying to disguise it by being flippant. 'He always used to say genetics could be our salvation, or our downfall. We had to make the right choices.'

'Life is always about making the right choices.'

'And some of us always seem to make the wrong ones.' And she suddenly realised she had gone too far, and her eyes flickered downwards with embarrassment. 'I'm sorry, you don't want to know about my sordid private life.' She tried to laugh it off. 'I'm sure you'd much rather know how I became an expert in crispy critters.'

'In what?'

She laughed. 'That's what a pathologist I used to work for called his burn victims. Crispy critters. Sick, isn't it?' Li thought it was. 'I guess it's a kind of self-defence mechanism, that kind of humour. We live in a pretty sick world, and that's our pretty sick way of dealing with it.'

'So how *did* you become an expert in . . . "crispy critters"?' The distasteful sound of it seemed to bring back the smells of the autopsy room, and Li's nose wrinkled in disgust.

Margaret smiled at his squeamishness. 'Oh, I guess I got

interested when I was assisting a pathologist at Waco. And then during my residency at the UIC Medical Centre I got lots of experience dealing with victims in trauma, fire victims from automobile accidents, home fires, airplane accidents, even a couple of cases of self-immolation, like you thought your guy in the park was. Then when I got a job as a pathologist with the Cook County Medical Examiner's Office, I just sort of developed the speciality. I can't say it had ever been an ambition. But then, we don't always end up doing or being what we started out to do or be, do we?' She looked at him. 'Did you always want to be a policeman?'

'Yes,' he said.

She laughed. 'Short conversation.'

'Why did you want to come to China?' he asked, and it was as if, in asking the question, he had flicked a switch and turned out a light somewhere inside her. She lost all vivacity, and her eyes took on a dull cast.

'Oh . . .' She shrugged. 'It was just something that came up, when getting away from Chicago was what I most wanted to do in life. It didn't have to be China. Anywhere would have done.'

A sixth sense told him that he had now entered dangerous territory, and that to venture any further down this particular path would be both fruitless and damaging. He slipped his watch from its pouch on his belt and checked the time.

'May I see?' She leaned across and held out her hand. He passed it to her, the chain fully extended. It was a very plain, hexagonal watch set in a heavy pewter-coloured casing. A bald-eagle badge decorated its leather pouch. 'It's very unusual,' she said. 'Did you get it in the States?'

'Hong Kong.' He slipped it back in its pouch. 'I really must get back to the office.'

'Of course.' She washed down her remaining noodles with the last of her beer, and they headed out into the afternoon heat that beat down so relentlessly from the burned-out sky. 'My mouth is still on fire,' she said.

He took her arm and steered her south along the sidewalk. 'Chinese are very practical people,' he said. 'Which is why when you have a Sichuan restaurant, you have an ice-cream parlour two doors along.' And they stopped outside a small glass-fronted shop with multicoloured plastic strips hanging down over the door. Above it, white letters on blue, was the legend *Charley's Ice Cream Parlour*. And beneath that, *Sino-America Joint Venture*.

Margaret laughed. 'I don't believe it!'

Li said, 'Specially to cool the palates of over-sensitive Americans.'

She flicked him a look, and he grinned. They went in and picked a couple of scoops each from a huge range of flavours displayed in a glass freezer cabinet, and then ran to the car and the cool of its air-conditioning before the ice cream melted.

III

Something happened on the drive back. Something beyond touch, or reason. Something very tiny in the great complexity of human relations. Like a radio whose tuning has slipped fractionally off-station, turning fine music into something scratchy and irritating. They had finished the ice cream long before they reached Section One, and the chill of it seemed to cool the warmth there had been over lunch. Margaret began to wonder if she had imagined that warmth. Perhaps it had been the heat of the food. For now Li seemed aloof, disinclined to talk. On those few occasions he met her eye, his eyes were cold, his demeanour polite, but formal. Where was the man she had listened to speaking fondly of his uncle, of Sunday mornings in the park at the 'English Corner', of the one ambition he had ever had to be a policeman? The transformation during that short drive from the restaurant to the office was both extraordinary and complete. Back again was the surly, resentful, ugly police officer she had encountered the previous day, and again this morning. Margaret's few attempts at conversation elicited little more than a monosyllabic response. Was it something she'd said or done? She found herself growing frustrated and angry.

Li was furious with himself. He should never have taken her for lunch. He had been trapped into it by his own weakness, and it was only now, as they drove back to the office, that he realised the full consequences of it. It wasn't just the ribbing he would receive from his colleagues. That would be embarrassing enough, but he could handle it. What he knew he couldn't handle was any kind of relationship with this woman. And for a time, as they had talked across the table, he had allowed himself to succumb to some unaccountable attraction to her. And in doing so, had lowered his guard and revealed much more of himself than he would ever have wished. It was ridiculous! And even now, as he manoeuvred the Jeep through the frantic afternoon traffic, he could not for the life of him think what it was about her he found attractive. For a start, she was an American, a *yangguizi* with a fast mouth. She was arrogant and superior and steeped in a shallow culture that could hardly have been more different from his own. He glanced at her sitting in the passenger seat, stiff and removed. For a time, over lunch, she had seemed almost human, vulnerable, displaying a hint of some deep hurt. Perhaps, he thought, that explained why on the drive back she had become distant again. She, too, had revealed too much and was regretting it.

Lily Ping was furious with both of them. They were more than forty minutes late. She said nothing, of course. Not in the presence of Li. But she sat in the detectives' office, a brooding presence in the corner, like a black rain-cloud, awaiting their return. Her fury, though, had less to do with their tardiness than the fact that she had been excluded from lunch. She was extremely curious about how it had gone, as were the detectives in the office. But they had other things to occupy them in the interim. A succession of Beijing low lifes had passed through the office – unshaven creatures in dirty tee-shirts and baseball caps, wide boys in cheap suits and oiled hair – before being led down the corridor to the interview room. Pimps and suspected small-time drug dealers who might have known or had some association with the man found stabbed on waste ground out west that morning. The phones had never stopped. Detective Qian must have made twenty calls, and at one stage had sent a police dispatch rider to pick up dental records from somewhere downtown and deliver them to the Centre of Material Evidence Determination. A fax from the Centre had caused some excitement, but no one was sharing any information with Lily. Conversations were cryptic and careful.

She was checking her watch yet again when Li and Margaret finally returned. A few heads lifted to cast curious glances in their direction, but for the moment the work in hand was serious and took precedence. The smart comments they would save for later. Lily's annoyance intensified when Li and Margaret failed even to acknowledge her, and passed straight through into Li's office. Neither was smiling, and they brought in with them a strange, strained atmosphere. Qian followed them through. Li had already picked up the phone.

'That's us, Chief. Any time.' He hung up and turned to Margaret. 'The Chief'll be through in a minute. He wants to say thanks.'

'Does he.' Margaret's voice was flat.

Qian handed Li the fax from the Centre. 'Dental records confirm the identity of the burn victim, boss. As you thought, his name was Chao Heng. Apparently he was the scientific adviser to the Minister of Agriculture before retiring six months ago through ill health. Lived in an apartment in Chongwen District.'

Li read quickly through the report from the Centre and looked up at Margaret. 'You were right on both counts,' he said. 'Identity, and sedation.' He waved the fax. 'That's the test results from the Centre. They show a high level of ketamine in his blood.'

Margaret nodded dully. Had she had a continued involvement in the case, then her interest would have been keener. As it was, she felt deflated, depressed. Others would unravel the crime she had identified. She had nothing further to contribute, or at least she would not be asked to do so. Li's sudden mood change was having a more profound effect on her than she could have imagined. She had only been in China twenty-four hours, but already it seemed like a lifetime, and she was ready to go.

Li risked a couple of quick glances in her direction as she gazed absently past him and out of the window. He found annoyance welling up inside at her apparent lack of interest. She was happy, it seemed, to swan in for a couple of hours, demonstrate her superior knowledge, and swan out again. Well, to hell with her! He returned the fax to Qian. 'Thanks. We'll talk in a minute.'

Qian turned and passed Section Chief Chen on the way in. Chen shook Margaret's hand warmly. 'Dr Campbell, I am so very grateful to you for your help. It has been invaluable, Li Yan, has it not?'

Li nodded solemnly. 'It has.'

'And has my deputy looked after you well?' Chen asked Margaret.

'Oh, very well,' said Margaret. 'He took me to lunch at a Sichuan restaurant. My mouth is still burning.'

'It was my pleasure,' Li said.

Chen laughed heartily, to the amazement of the detectives who could hear him through the open door. He steered Margaret out and into the corridor, followed by a resentful Lily. 'Come, I will see you to your car. And I will phone Professor Jiang this afternoon to thank him personally for letting us borrow you.'

Margaret flicked a backward glance over her shoulder to see Li already involved in discussions with his detectives. In all likelihood she would never see him again.

As she turned to be led down the corridor, Li looked over to the door to see her back for an instant before she disappeared. Apparently, he thought bitterly, he wasn't even worth a backward glance.

Another couple of sullen hoodlums were bundled in to have details taken before being led away for interrogation. 'We took more than fifteen statements this morning,' Wu told Li. 'Anyone and everyone who knew Mao Mao. The scum of the earth. Dope dealers, pimps, prostitutes.' Li wandered through to his office and Wu followed. 'He wasn't a very nice guy, Li Yan. Nobody's shedding any tears for him. Even his family. You'd think a mother would grieve for her son. When we told her, she just spat and said, "Good riddance".'

From his window, Li could see into the street below. Through the foliage he watched as Margaret got into the BMW. *Good riddance*. Mao Mao's mother's words about her son found an echo in his present thoughts. Just before she closed the door, Margaret glanced up. Damn! She'd seen him watching. He took a quick step back, then felt foolish. This was absurd! He focused his mind again on Wu, who was still talking. 'It was definitely drugs he was into, but he wasn't one of the Golden Circle, just one of the flies attracted by the dung.'

The Golden Circle was what they called the ring of dealers at the centre of the Beijing drug trade, the ones whose hands were always clean, who always had an alibi, who never took the rap. They were the ones who made the money, trading death for gold.

'Of course,' Wu said, 'no one knows a thing.' He paused. 'And you know what, boss? You get an instinct for these things. I don't think they're lying.'

Li nodded thoughtfully. 'Sometimes they know more at the top about what's going on at the bottom than the other way around. Take out the file on The Needle for me. Leave it on my desk. I'll have a glance at it tonight.' The Needle was the nickname they all used for the man everyone knew was behind most of the heroin on the streets. But what was known, and what could be proved, were two very different things. A conspiracy of silence surrounded him, a phenomenon almost unknown in Chinese society. The masses line was no competition for the aura of fear that surrounded him.

'Sure, boss. And I'll get those statements to you as soon as we can get them typed up.' Wu headed back to his desk.

From the door Li called after him, 'By the way . . . was he a smoker? Mao Mao.'

Wu looked sheepish. He knew he'd been caught out. 'Don't know, boss.'

'Better find out, then.' Li beckoned to Zhao to follow him into his office. It was stiflingly hot. He tried to open his window more fully, but the *feng shui* man had been right, it was well and truly jammed. Whether or not it restricted the view, it certainly stopped the flow of oxygen. 'Any news on the intinerant?' Li asked.

'Yeah, we got confirmation back from Shanghai on his identity.' Zhao consulted his notebook conscientiously. 'Guo Jingbo, aged thirty-five, divorced. No criminal record. No known criminal associations. He was a builder's labourer. Finished on a building site in Shanghai about six weeks ago and told friends he was going to Beijing in search of work. But he didn't register with Public Security until four weeks ago, so there's a missing two weeks in there.'

'And did he find any?'

'Any what?' Zhao looked mystified.

'Work,' Li snapped irritably.

'Couldn't have looked too hard,' Zhao said. 'No record of him even applying for any job.'

'Associates in Beijing?'

'None that we know of. He was staying in a hostel in the north of the city. Not somewhere you'd want to spend any great length of time. So most people don't. Nobody really knew who he was or what he did.'

'Was he a smoker?'

Zhao nodded. 'Nicotine stains on his fingers, matches and a half-empty pack of cigarettes in his pocket.'

'Brand?'

'Chinese.'

Li grunted. There wasn't a single damned thing in any of this to give them even a start. He sighed. 'I suppose we'd better start rounding up all the itinerants who've registered in the city in the last six weeks.'

Zhao looked pleased with himself. 'It's under way, boss.' Then his face clouded. 'Might take some time to do all the interviews, though.'

'Why?'

'There's more than fifteen hundred of them.'

'So what are you hanging around for?' Li jerked his thumb towards the door. 'Get started.'

As Zhao went out, Wu poked his head in. 'Just spoke to a couple of Mao Mao's pals. He didn't smoke. So that cigarette end wasn't his.'

Li nodded. 'Thanks.' He got up and closed the door and settled back in the tilting wooden chair he had inherited along with the office. It groaned as if objecting to being sat on, and the tilting mechanism squeaked. It had probably never been oiled since new. He put his hands together as if praying, placed the tips of his fingers beneath his nose, and leaned back with his eyes closed. The first image that floated into his consciousness was Margaret laughing across the table from him at the Sichuan snack-house. He blinked her away furiously and found himself standing on the edge of the clearing in Ritan Park looking at the smouldering cross-legged figure beneath the trees. He was able to visualise his thoughts in three dimensions, words and images co-existing. The first of those words, a question, drifted into his peripheral vision. 'Why?' It had all been so elaborate and high-profile. A murder in a public place staged to appear, at least superficially, like some form of ritual self-sacrifice. Li placed himself in the position of the murderer and faced the same difficulties the murderer must have faced. Somewhere, somewhere private, the victim's home perhaps, the murderer had struck Chao Heng on the head, hard enough to induce unconsciousness, but not to kill him. He had then sedated him by injecting ketamine into his foot. If this had all taken place in Chao's apartment, then the murderer faced the problem of transporting the body to the park, unseen, to stage the finale. It would have had to have been dark. And he would have had to have manoeuvred the body into the park before first light, long before it opened. He must then have sat with the semiconscious Chao in the privacy of the clearing until early morning activities in the park were well under way. The clearing was hidden from general view, but the risk of discovery must have been high. Another image drifted into the picture in his head. The cigarette end. If the murderer was a smoker, and he had sat for two or three hours waiting for the park to open, why was there only one cigarette end? Wouldn't he have smoked at least four or five cigarettes, perhaps more in that stressful situation? He put the cigarette end to one side, next to the 'Why?'. The killer had then arranged the still-dazed and compliant Chao into the lotus position, poured gasoline over him and set him alight. The danger of discovery at that moment must have been at its most intense. He must have retreated through the trees, away from the path that the children ran up just minutes later to make their awful discovery. So the killer was still in the park when the body was discovered. *Someone* must have seen him. A Witness. As if in some virtual-reality mind game, he placed the word 'Witness' next to the 'Why?' and the 'Cigarette End' and pulled the 'Why?' back to centre vision. Why? Why would anyone go to such elaborate and dangerous lengths to fake a suicide? And why would someone so meticulous be careless enough to leave a cigarette end at the scene of the crime. He placed the 'Cigarette End' centrally next to the 'Why?' and let his eye wander to the 'Witness' on the periphery. No matter how careful he was, someone *must* have seen him.

He opened his eyes and shouted, 'Qian.'

Qian appeared quickly at the door. 'Boss?'

'How's your list of habitués in the park progressing?'

'Getting there.'

'Well, get there faster. And start interviewing ASAP. Someone saw the murderer. He was still in the park when the kids found the burning body. We want people's memories when they're still fresh. Put as many men on it as are available.'

Qian said, 'Consider it done.' He turned back to the detectives' room.

Li called after him, 'Has anyone been out to Chao's apartment yet?'

'Just the uniforms, to seal the place up.' Qian looked at his watch. 'Forensics should be there within the half-hour.'

Li jumped to his feet. 'Okay, as soon as you've set up the

interviews, you can run me over there. I want to take a look at the place.'

Qian nodded and disappeared. Li stuck his hands deep in his pockets and wandered to the window. Already it seemed like hours since he had watched Margaret get into the back of the car. She seemed remote now, and irrelevant. He focused his mind back on the picture in his head. The 'Why?' was the answer, but not the means of finding it. The cigarette end was what bothered him most. That and the cigarette ends at the other two crime scenes. He had a sudden thought and lifted the phone. He dialled quickly and waited impatiently. Someone picked up at the other end. 'Dr Wang? I want you to do something for me . . .'

IV

Chao Heng had lived in an apartment just off Xihuashi Street in the Chongwen District in the south-east quarter of the inner city. It was a relatively new high-rise block that stood in its own compound behind high walls. Glassed-in balconies, like miniature conservatories, projected from every apart-ment, and were used for everything from growing vegetables and pot plants to drying clothes and bedding. The walls of the block, all the way up to the twelfth floor, were studded with self-contained air-conditioning units that blew cool air through the apartments and belted hot air out into an already overheated atmosphere. Qian parked their Jeep in the compound next to a blue-and-white, and the forensics van which had got there ahead of them. Old women sat in the shade of huge umbrellas watching with dull-eyed curiosity. Some children were kicking a ball about in the heat of the sun, their cries echoing back from the walls of high-rise buildings that loomed over them like the walls of some deep secret canyon. Dozens of bicycles stood parked in neat rows under the shade of a line of trees, but there were no other vehicles in the compound.

The dusty entrance hall seemed gloomy after the sunlight that blasted white off every surface outside. The doors of the elevator stood open. The operator, a skinny man with wizened brown skin, wearing only a pair of old blue shorts and a grubby singlet, squatted on a low stool just inside, smoking cheap, acrid-smelling cigarettes. There was a pile of ends and ash on the floor beside him. The air hummed with the buzz of flies and the distant echo of the kids playing outside. It was hot and airless. He spat on the floor and stood up as Li and Qian approached. 'Who are you going to see?'

Li produced his maroon Public Security ID wallet and opened it to show the operator his photograph. 'Beijing Municipal Police. CID.'

'Oh. You've come to see Chao Heng's place.' He stood to one side to let them in. 'Some of your people are already up there.' He closed the doors and pressed the button for the fifth floor.

The elevator started its slow assent, groaning and complaining as it went. 'Does everyone use the elevator?' Li asked.

The old man shrugged. 'Not always. During the night, when the elevator is switched off, residents use their gate keys.'

'And there are gates on all the stairs?' Li asked. The operator nodded. 'So what about visitors?'

'They have to take the elevator.'

'What about when the elevator is turned off?'

'No one comes visiting at that time.'

'But if they did?'

The old man shrugged again. 'Whoever they were visiting would have to know they were coming, so that they could come down the stairs and unlock the gate to let them in.'

'So you get to see just about everyone who comes and goes.'

'Yep.'

Li and Qian exchanged glances. There was a good chance, then, that this man had seen the murderer. Li said, 'So what about Chao Heng? Has he had many visitors recently?'

The old man's lip curled in distaste. 'Chao Heng always has visitors. Young boys and *yangguizi*.'

'Young boys?' Qian looked puzzled. 'What do you mean, young boys?'

'Young boys!' the old man repeated as if Qian were deaf. 'Fifteen, sixteen, seventeen . . . Such men should be locked up.' Qian looked faintly shocked.

Li said, 'And foreigners, you said. What kind of foreigners?'

'Americans, I think. They never spoke any Chinese.'

'And other Chinese visitors?'

'Oh, some posh-looking people in big cars. Chao was some big shot at the Ministry of Agriculture.'

The lift juddered to a halt on the fifth floor. Li said, 'What about last night? Did he have any visitors last night?'

The old man opened the doors and shook his head. 'Not for a week or two.'

'Then he must have gone out himself some time yesterday, or last night.'

'Not when I was on.' The old man was adamant. 'He's hardly been over the door himself in a month. Chao Heng was not a well man.'

Li and Qian stepped out of the lift. Li said, 'We'll want you to come up to headquarters and make a detailed statement. Can you get someone to stand in for you?'

'Sure. The street committee'll arrange it.'

A uniformed police officer stood outside the door to Chao Heng's apartment. Inside, two forensics officers wearing white gloves and plastic slip-on shoe covers were going over every inch of it. The air-conditioning was switched off, so it was unbreathably hot. Li and Qian took gloves and shoe covers from a bag at the door and slipped them on. The forensics men nodded acknowledgement and one of them said, 'Don't touch anything unless you have to.'

By Chinese standards, this was a large apartment for a single person. Off a central hall were two bedrooms, a bathroom, a kitchenette and dining area and a living room that opened out on to the glassed balcony. It was a measure of Chao Heng's status that he should be given such an apartment.

Li and Qian wandered from room to room, observing, absorbing. Li sniffed. Above the rancid smell of stale cigarette smoke, on a higher, sharper note, there was a strange antiseptic smell in the place, like disinfectant or something medical. It was not pleasant. In the kitchen the smell gave way to the stench of rotting food coming from a bin that needed to be emptied. Dishes lay unwashed in the sink. Worktops were dirty and littered with the debris of food preparation. An ashtray was filled to overflowing. Li lifted one of the cigarette ends and looked for the brand name. Marlboro. He put it back. A small refrigerator had virtually no food in it. Apart from a pack of tofu, there were just half a dozen bottles of beer, and one bottle of Californian red wine. Unusual. A gift, perhaps. Or brought back from a trip abroad. Li looked at the label. Ernst and Julio Gallo, Cabernet Sauvignon. Chao Heng obviously didn't know much about wine, or he wouldn't have kept a bottle of red in his refrigerator. So it was unlikely he had bought it himself. A wall cupboard was full of dried and canned food: noodles, mushrooms, dried fruit and cans of fruit, tinned vegetables, a large jar of flour, smaller jars of crushed lotus seeds and sweet paste for dim sum. On the work surface beneath it, a can-opener and several empty cans that had once contained lychees in syrup, beansprouts, water chestnuts.

'A vegetarian?' Qian suggested.

'Possibly.' Li let his eyes wander over all the different jars and cans and packs of food in the cupboard. There certainly didn't seem to be any meat, or meat products. There was something else missing, something obvious only because of its absence. But it still took him a few moments to identify it. 'No rice either,' he said.

'Maybe he ran out,' Qian said.

'Maybe he did.'

They went into the bathroom. Like the kitchen it was a mess. Old tubes of toothpaste, creams and ointments cluttered the shelf above the sink. The mirror was spattered with soap and shaving foam. A bloodstained safety razor that had been less than safe lay in a sink which had a ring of grime around it. Used towels were draped over the side of the bath which was ringed, too, with filth, like the contour of scum left by polluted seawater when the tide retreats. Li removed a glove and felt the towel. There was still a hint of dampness in it.

Qian opened a small cabinet on the wall, and cardboard boxes and plastic tubs rattled out and on to the floor. He stooped to pick them up, replacing them one by one. Li looked over his shoulder. There were drugs of some kind, commercially packaged Western medicines with strange and exotic names: *Epivir*, *AZT*, *Crixivan*; and a whole range of traditional Chinese and herbal medicines. 'Either he was a health freak or a hypochondriac,' Qian said.

'Or sick,' said Li. 'Like the elevator man said.'

Qian closed the cabinet and they went through to the first bedroom where one of the forensics men had found Chao's needle set. It consisted of a hypodermic, a metal spoon, a length of nylon cord, a small sachet filled with white powder. They were contained within a tarnished and battered metal box, which bore the scars of time and travel. It was significant, Li felt, that it had not been in Chao's possession when they found him.

There were mirrors all around the walls, including one full

length at the foot of the bed. The bed was unmade, and a dresser was covered in jars of cream and powder, lipstick, eye make-up, perfumes, lotions and potions of every kind. Qian surveyed them with distaste. 'It's like a whore's bedroom,' he said. And almost as if to bear him out, when he opened the wardrobe he found it hanging with black and red silk dressing gowns hand-embroidered with dragons and butterflies. In the drawers there were silk pyjamas, exotic male underwear, thongs and g-strings. There were suspenders and stockings, women's shoes, a short leather whip with three tails. 'This guy really was sick.' Qian looked around the room. 'God knows what must have gone on up here with that procession of young boys.'

They left the forensics man dusting for prints and went through to the other bedroom. By comparison it was neat and tidy. The bed was made up with clean sheets. It didn't look as if it had been slept in recently. The wardrobe was hung with rows of dark suits and pressed white shirts. Beneath them a row of polished brown and black shoes on a rack. In the other bedroom they had just seen the private face of Chao Heng. In this one they saw the face he showed in public. Two different faces, two different people. Li wondered which, if either, was the real Chao Heng. And how many people, if any, knew who that was?

Perhaps a third face revealed itself in Chao's living room. Here was a comfortable, stylish room tastefully furnished with items of traditional Chinese lacquered furniture, many of them antiques; low tables inset with mother-of-pearl, hand-painted screens subdividing the room, embroidered silk throws draped over low settees. Three walls were hung with original scroll-mounted paintings, the fourth groaned with books from floor to ceiling. Books of every description in Chinese and English. Classic fiction in both languages: from Cao Xueqin's *A Dream of Red Mansions*, and Ling Li's *Son of Heaven*, to Scott's *Redgauntlet*, and Steinbeck's *The Grapes of Wrath*. A veritable library of scientific textbooks: *Plant DNA Infectious Agents*, *Risk Assessment in Genetic Engineering*, *Plant Virology*, *Genomic Imprinting*. Books on health: *The Classified Dictionary of Traditional Chinese Medicine*, *Chinese Acupuncture and Moxibustion*, *Fighting Drug Abuse with Acupuncture*.

Qian whistled in amazement. 'Can any one person read that many books in a lifetime?'

Li picked one out at random, *Gene Transfer in the Environment*, and examined the spine. 'Chao Heng apparently,' he said, slipping the book back into the bookcase.

In the far corner of the room there was an illuminated fish tank, multicoloured tropical fish zigzagging through a meticulously recreated seabed, air bubbling constantly up through the water from an oxygen feed. Tins of fish feed were stacked on a small table beside it. Li picked one up. It was half full. He sprinkled some feed on the water and watched the fish peck at it in desultory fashion as it fell slowly to the bottom of the tank. He wandered out on to the glassed balcony. It was north-facing, so no hotter than the rest of the house. There were two comfortable armchairs and a low table with a single, empty bottle of beer on it, an ashtray with half a dozen cigarette ends and a pack of Marlboro cigarettes. Li picked up the pack. There were ten or more cigarettes still in it. He replaced it on the table. With the angle at which the light was striking the bottle, he could see smears of greasy fingerprints all over the dark glass. It was strange, he thought, how dead people left physical traces behind them long after they were gone. This apartment would be filled with vestiges of the oily residue left by Chao Heng's fingers on everything he touched. A touch that was uniquely his. Or hair gathered in the drainer in the sink and the bath, caught on combs and brushes. The fine dust of his dead skin shed over years would lie like a hidden snow among the fibres of the carpet and the bed, and in ledges along undusted surfaces. His scent would linger in the weave of the clothes that hung in the wardrobes. His personality, in all its diversity, reflected in his choice of lifestyle, clothes, furniture, and in the books he read. All of these were clues, not necessarily to the murder, but to the man. And knowing the man was an important step towards knowing his killer.

From the balcony, Li looked down into the compound below. He could see the three police vehicles and the gate in the high wall that led in from the street. He closed his eyes and pictured the killer carrying Chao's prostrate form over his shoulder between the door of the apartment block and the nearest parking point. It was about fifteen feet. He opened his eyes and checked the streetlights. They were few and far between, and the trees would cast dense shadows. But there would be a light over the main entrance and it would have illuminated those fifteen feet, making it the highest risk point of the journey from the apartment to the park. And that after carrying Chao down five flights of stairs, unlocking and then locking the stair gate behind him again. His killer was not only a very determined man, but he was strong and fit.

'Qian,' he called.

Qian came on to the balcony. 'Yes, boss?'

'Go downstairs and see if the light over the front door is working. And check if the stair gate is locked while you're at it.'

Qian hovered for a moment, awaiting an explanation, but when none was forthcoming, nodded and said, 'Sure,' and left the apartment.

Li stood for a long time, thinking, visualising. Eventually he wandered back into the living room and his eyes fell upon the bookcase again. As they drifted back and forth across the rows of multicoloured jackets, he recalled Mei Yuan's riddle: *Two men. One of them is the keeper of every book in the world, giving him access to the source of all knowledge. Knowledge is power, so this makes him a very powerful man. The other possesses only two sticks. Yet this gives him more power than the other. Why?* And suddenly Li knew why. He smiled. How apposite, he thought. How strange. Perhaps Mei Yuan had psychic powers.

A tiny winking red light on the other side of the room caught his eye. He crossed to a small cabinet with an inset shelf. Set back on the shelf was a mini hi-fi stack with tuner, cassette and CD. Li crouched down to look at the array of pinpoint red and green lights, and a digital display of the numeral '9'. 'Either of you guys touched the hi-fi?' he called through to the forensics men.

'No,' one of them called back.

'Me either,' the other one shouted.

Li looked up as Qian came back in, a touch out of breath. 'Someone stole the lamp, boss. At any rate, there's no lamp in the light fitting, and the old boy in the lift says it was working okay when he finished up last night. Oh, and the gate's locked.'

Li nodded. 'Know anything about hi-fi systems?'

'Got better things to spend my money on. In any case, I'd never have time to listen to one. Why?'

'Chao left his on. In fact, he left the CD on pause. The light's still blinking. You want to hear what he was listening to when his killer came calling?'

'How do you know his killer came here?' Qian was curious.

'Educated guess,' Li said, and he pressed the Play button. Immediately the room was filled with the sounds of strange and alien music. He stood up and lifted an empty CD case off the top of the cabinet. 'Western opera,' he said. And reading from the cover, '*Samson and Delilah*. Saint-Saëns.' He took out the inner sleeve. 'Track nine. "*Mon coeur s'ouvre a ta voix*".' And he read, '"Samson, the champion of the Hebrews enslaved by the Philistines, knows that he should resist the approaches of the temptress Delilah. But his determination crumbles when she seduces him with this song of love. He yields completely, enabling Delilah to discover the secret of his strength and cut off his hair, rendering him powerless."'

Was it to the temptation of his drug habit, or his preference for young boys, that Chao Heng had yielded, leaving him powerless in the hands of his murderer? The voice of the female soprano rose in sensuous crescendos.

'So?' Qian was impatient. He had to raise his voice above the music. 'What are you basing this educated guess on?'

'On a number of things,' Li said. 'The first of them being that Chao Heng was almost certainly here last night.'

'How do you know?'

'The bath-towel hanging over the bath is still damp. He'd fed his fish, probably quite late on, because they're still not that hungry. He'd left his cigarettes on the table on the balcony, and his needle kit in the bedroom. And smokers and junkies don't leave those kinds of things behind. Not voluntarily. He didn't leave by the elevator. There was no key among the effects found with his body, so how could he have locked the stair gate behind him?'

Li wandered back across the room to the balcony. 'I think he was sitting here, listening to Delilah seducing Samson, and having himself a bottle of beer from the refrigerator. He had probably been here some time, judging by the number of cigarette ends in the ashtray and the progress of the CD. It was late, long after the lift had been shut down, maybe one or two in the morning, when the rest of the building was asleep. He was watching for a car below. A delivery of heroin, perhaps. The promise of a young boy. Who knows? When he saw the lights of the car, he got up, paused the CD, took his key and went down the stairs to unlock the gate. It would have been darker than usual, because the killer had just removed the lamp from the light over the front door. Maybe that's why Chao didn't recognise immediately that his visitor wasn't who he was expecting.

'Whoever it was probably had a gun and forced him back up to the apartment. Once here, he struck him on the head with a blunt object, maybe even with the gun, and injected him with ketamine. He waited, maybe as long as an hour, to be sure he hadn't been seen, then carried or dragged Chao down the stairs and locked the gate behind them at the bottom. Under cover of the darkness created by the removal of the lamp, he carried him the fifteen feet to where he'd parked the car. Then it was off to Ritan Park, and you can pretty much put the rest together yourself.'

By now Samson had well and truly succumbed to the charms of Delilah. Qian blew air through pursed lips. 'That must be some education you had, boss.' He paused and thought about it. 'How do you know the killer was acting alone?'

'I don't.'

'I mean, it would have been easier with two.'

Li nodded. 'Yes, but there's something very . . .' He struggled to find the right word. '. . . individual, almost eccentric, about this. It just feels to me like a single twisted mind at work.'

One of the forensics team called them through to the hall. He was crouched outside the kitchen door, scraping carefully at the carpet. 'Patch of blood,' he said. 'Looks quite fresh, too. Spectral analysis will tell us just how fresh.'

Qian looked at Li with renewed respect. 'If that's Chao's blood, it looks like you could be right, boss.' Then he grimaced. 'Trouble is, it doesn't really get us any closer to the killer.'

'Everything we know gets us closer to the killer,' Li said evenly. 'Time we talked to the street committee.'

V

Liu Xinxin, chairwoman of the street committee, was a small, nervous, skinny woman of around sixty. She lived in a ground-floor apartment in Chao Heng's block. Her greying hair was drawn back in a tight bun from a delicately featured face, she wore an apron over a grey smock and a pair of black baggy trousers that stopped six inches above her ankles. Her hands were white with flour. 'Come in,' she said when she answered the door. She brushed a rogue strand of hair away from her face and left a smudge of flour on her forehead. She led them into the kitchen where she was preparing dumplings for the family meal. 'You've come at a bad time. My husband will be home soon, and then my son and his wife.'

Li nodded. 'There is never a good time to come about death.'

There was a loud crash from another room, a skitter of giggles, and two boys of pre-school age chased one another, shouting and screaming, through the hall. 'My grandchildren,' Liu Xinxin said. And then she added, quickly, as if they might suspect her family of being politically incorrect, 'The elder boy is my daughter's.' A shadow passed across her face. 'She died in labour and they had to cut the child out of her. My son-in-law couldn't deal with her death, or with the child, so my son and his wife adopted him.'

She wiped her hands on her apron and took it off. 'So . . . Mr Chao,' she said. 'Nobody liked him much. Come through.' And she led them into a cluttered living room, birdcages arrayed along one wall. Pale lemon-and-white birds filled the room with a constant chirruping chorus. The balcony was chock full of plants and drying clothes hanging from a line. Condensation was forming on the glass. Against the opposite wall stood an old upright piano covered with the remains of big character posters which had, at one time, been pasted all over it. 'It's not mine,' Liu Xinxin said, following their eyes to the piano. 'It belongs to the state. I'm a musician really. I don't know how I got mixed up in street politics, except I've been a good member of the Communist Party for nearly forty years. I was only sent for reform two times. Maybe you've heard some of my songs?' She addressed this to Qian, who was nonplussed. He looked to Li for help.

Li said, 'Perhaps if you told us what you'd written . . .'

'Oh,' she said vaguely, 'hundreds. More than I can remember. I've lost more than I've written. In the sixties a collection of my songs was put together in Shanghai. They were all typeset and ready for publication. And then came the Cultural Revolution and my music was condemned as "reactionary". I never did like the official formula for composition – "High, Fast, Hard and Loud".' She parodied stiff marching movements to each word as she said it. 'So they were lost. About fifteen years ago I tried to trace them. But the typesetter was dead, and the publisher knew nothing about the proofs.' She gave a tiny philosophical smile. 'But other songs survived . . . "Let's Build Our World Together" and "That Was Me Then And This Is Me Now" and "Our Country".'

Both Li and Qian had sung 'Our Country' as children, and 'Let's Build Our World Together' had been popular when Li was a teenager in the eighties, and had won a national award. Both were struck by a sense of awe and amazement that this insignificantly tiny and ageing lady should have written such songs.

She saw their surprise and smiled ruefully. 'Today, if I was thirty years younger and writing the same songs, I would have been *gloriously* rich, and very glamorous, and poor Mr Deng, had he still been alive, would have been very pleased with me.'

Liu Xinxin smiled, and her smile was infectious, and Li found himself being drawn to her. 'It could not have been easy for you,' he said. 'A woman writing music in a man's world. My uncle used to often quote an old proverb which he said was still part of the male Chinese mindset, even in communist China: "A woman's virtue is that she has no talent".'

The old lady grinned. 'Ah, yes, but Mao said, "Women hold up half the sky".' And her words brought Margaret sharply, and unexpectedly, back into Li's thoughts.

Qian had wandered over to the piano and lifted the lid to stare at the keys in wonder. Music was a mystery to him. 'Did you write all your songs on this?' he asked.

A sadness clouded her eyes. 'Only the recent ones. The best I wrote on my first piano. It was the love of my life. My passion . . . Long gone.' She paused. 'But you came to ask about Mr Chao.' She grinned bravely. 'So . . . I'll make us some tea and you ask.'

Li and Qian sat on the edge of low chairs as she bustled back and forth from the kitchen, boiling a kettle and making them cups of green tea. The children were somewhere else in the house, drumming incessantly on what sounded like an old tin, competing with the racket of the birds. 'You said nobody liked him much,' Li prompted her above the noise as she poured the tea.

'That was mostly because no one knew him,' Liu Xinxin said. 'The Ministry of Agriculture owns several apartments in this block, but Mr Chao never mixed with those families. And with the rest of us he was . . . how can I explain it? . . . standoffish. Like he was better than us. You would recognise him in the street and say "hi" and he would look the other way. He never smiled or acknowledged anyone. I think he was a very sad man.'

'What makes you say that?' Li slurped his tea. It was good.

'A man who never smiles must be sad,' she said. 'And his eyes, if you ever got a chance to look into his eyes, they were so full of pain, as if he were carrying some unbearable burden. Of course, Mr Dai, the elevator man, knew him best. He is on my committee, so we would often discuss Mr Chao.' She paused to reflect, and then corrected herself. 'When I say Mr Dai "knew" him, what I mean is that Mr Dai saw him most often. Like I said, no one *knew* him.'

Li asked, 'And his family? Do you know anything about his background?'

She shook her head. 'Only the information given when he first came.'

'Which was how long ago?'

'About two years. He had been working near Guilin in Guangxi province in the south for some years before they transferred him back north to Beijing and an apartment here. But he has not worked much in the last six months. He has not been well, I think.' She leaned forward confidentially. 'They said he had been married and divorced, and that he had a young family somewhere in the south.' She dropped her voice. 'He liked young boys, you know.'

Li stifled a smile. He could imagine the conversations that must have taken place between Liu Xinxin and Mr Dai and other members of the committee, about the comings and goings at Chao's flat in the night. But they would have been afraid of his privileged position in Party and state. Perhaps they had reported him to the Public Security Bureau and been told to mind their own business. The scientific adviser to a minister of state would have been a powerful and influential man, a modern-day mandarin. One would have had to have trodden carefully. Li finished his tea and stood up. 'Well, thank you very much, Old Liu. You have been very helpful.' Qian took his boss's cue and got to his feet.

'Won't you stay and have another cup?' She seemed reluctant now to let them go.

'We don't want to keep you back, with your family due home soon.'

'Oh . . .' She waved her hand dismissively. 'They won't be

back for ages yet. Would you like me to play you one of my songs?'

Not wanting to hurt her feelings, Li said, 'We really don't have the time.'

'Just one, then,' she said, and she headed for the piano and drew up a stool. 'You must know "Our Country". They sang it in all the schools.'

Li and Qian exchanged looks. There was no escaping it. 'Just the one, then,' Li said.

She beamed. 'And you must sing it with me.' And as she played a brief introduction, 'I'll sing the verses and you join in the choruses.'

As they stood round the piano singing the words and melody written by this old lady more than thirty years before, Li was glad that there were no witnesses to his embarrassment. He could imagine what comments would be passed in the office. At least he could rely on Qian, who seemed equally ill at ease, to keep silence. Then he noticed Liu Xinxin's two small grandsons standing in the doorway looking at them in astonishment, and, a moment later, their equally astonished parents fresh home from work. Li closed his eyes.

They left the apartment, colour high on their cheeks, thoughts held close, and got into the Jeep. They sat for a long minute in silence before the first sign of a crack appeared in Li's façade. A small explosion of air escaped his nostrils. Qian looked at him in time to see the façade crumble. It was infectious. His face cracked, too. Within moments, both were laughing almost uncontrollably, tears streaming, stomachs aching, like a couple of small boys hearing their first dirty joke. All embarrassment was dissipated. As Li gasped to catch his breath, he wondered for a moment what they were laughing at, before realising it was themselves.

A sharp rap at the driver's window made them turn. It was a young uniformed constable. Qian rolled down the window. 'Yes?'

'Census Constable Wang,' the officer said, peering in disapprovingly at the two grinning faces. 'This is my patch. You should have come to me before interviewing members of this street committee.'

Li leaned over, still with a smile creasing his face. 'Don't worry about it, Wang. We were only here for a singing lesson.' And he and Qian burst into fresh roars of laughter. Wang jumped back, pink-faced and angry, as Qian revved the engine and backed out into the compound with a squeal of tyres. He watched them go with the self-righteous anger of a thwarted petty bureaucrat, the sounds of their laughter still ringing in his ears.

When Li and Qian returned to Section One, there was a constant procession of people arriving to make statements. The street outside was jammed with bicycles and taxis, groups of men and women standing discussing the reason for their summons, children waiting in the care of patient grandparents. These were people from all walks of life: itinerant workers recently arrived in Beijing, small-time crooks, early morning habitués of Ritan Park – civil servants, factory workers, house-wives, an army of pensioners. Additional officers had been drafted in from CID headquarters downtown to help with the interviews.

Qian could barely find space to park the Jeep, and he and Deputy Section Chief Li had to push their way through the bodies to reach the door. Inside was no better. There were queues trailing back down the stairs. Extra interview rooms had been set up on every floor to try to cope. Interviews were being recorded and transcribed, and the girls in the typing pool had been put on shifts to keep the flow of paper-work moving. And as far as Li could see when he entered his office, all that paperwork was moving on to his desk. There was a mountain of it accumulating there. Hundreds of statements had already been taken in all three murder cases – hundreds, maybe thousands, more were still to come. Also on his desk were the pathologist's report from the autopsy on Chao, along with a résumé of his education and career at the Ministry of Agriculture, and various forensics reports from the different crime scenes. And beneath a pile of photocopied statements, he found the file he had asked Wu to take out on The Needle. He scratched his stubbled head and felt crushed already by the weight of it all. It could take weeks just to go through what was already there. A young female administration officer entering with another armful of statements was the final straw. He stood up and raised his hands to stop her. 'Enough! I don't want any more of these statements on my desk.'

The girl, a timid nineteen-year-old, was fazed and looked around helplessly. 'Where'll I put them, then?'

Li glanced round the room. 'There,' he pointed. 'On the floor under the window. Separate the cases and keep three separate piles. I want only stuff I've asked for on my desk, all right?'

She nodded, flustered, and crouched down to start arranging the files on the floor as requested. Another huge pile thumped down beside her. She looked up, startled, as Li said, 'And you can sort that lot out while you're at it.'

Now that he could see his desktop again, Li began sorting out the files he wanted to hand. He glanced at the autopsy report and, quite involuntarily, found himself thinking about Dr Margaret Campbell. They were fragmentary thoughts, bits and pieces of conversation: *'no man is an island'*, *'must have broken a mirror'*, *'you don't want to know about my sordid private life'*. Visual moments: the wedding ring on the third finger of her left hand, the freckles on her arm, the soft thrust of her breasts against the thin white cotton of her tee-shirt.

Annoyed with himself, he put the autopsy report to one side and forced himself to concentrate on the forensics reports. But they told him nothing he didn't already know. The spectral analysis on the blood found in Chao's apartment would, however, be telling. As would the result of the request he had put to Dr Wang. But neither of those would be available until tomorrow. He felt a twinge of irritation at having to wait. Which was unusual, for he was normally a patient man. But there was some instinct at work telling him that somehow speed was important in this, that the usual pedantic sifting of information, the slow building of layer upon layer of carefully gathered evidence, was not the required approach. And yet that was what all his training and experience demanded.

His eyes wandered thoughtfully across the text of the three forensics reports. Still the only real evidence gathered at each scene had been the Marlboro cigarette ends. The fact that Chao smoked, and that Marlboro was his brand, had been troubling Li since he found the cigarette ends and the pack in Chao's apartment. It raised the possibility that the cigarette end found near the body in the park had been smoked by Chao himself, a final wish granted by his killer. In which case there was nothing to connect Chao's murder with the other two, except coincidence. But Li didn't like coincidence. And, in any case, Chao had been sedated, his cigarettes had been left in the apartment, and if he had been capable of smoking, the cigarette would have had to have been provided by his killer, who must also have smoked Marlboro. Another coincidence. Altogether too many. Li drummed his fingers impatiently on the desk. And tomorrow, he thought, seemed far too long to have to wait for answers.

Another batch of statements was carried in and distributed on the piles beneath the window. Through the open door he saw that the detectives' room was still a hive of activity. He lifted the file on Chao and flipped it open. There was precious little detail here. Born 1948, in the town of Nanchang in Jiangxi province, the year before the founding of the People's Republic of China. His father was a professor of English and his mother a Party cadre. He came to Beijing in 1966, the year Li was born, and enrolled at Beijing Agricultural University just as the Cultural Revolution was sweeping the country. Two years into a degree course in agronomy and crop sciences he was denounced by fellow students turned Red Guards and forced to drop out. The phrase *denounced by Red Guards* conjured for Li images of repeated beatings, hours of enforced self-criticism, endless essays confessing to reactionary weaknesses and imperial tendencies. Often it was simply an opportunity for adolescents, freed from the constraints and disciplines of an organised and civilised society, to explore the dark and cruel side of their human nature. Bullies and brutes given the freedom to express themselves in torture and murder without fear of retribution. They were, after all, only cleansing their country of its class enemies, those upholders of the Four Olds. Children were freed to taunt and torment their teachers, forcing them to wear dunce caps and grovel before them in class. Li had witnessed it first hand in his own primary school. Fortunately, by the time he reached middle school, the madness had just about run its course. He imagined that Chao's fellow students had probably picked on him because he was soft, perhaps overtly homosexual, perhaps simply still confused about his sexuality. He was sent to the countryside for re-education.

Here there was a gap in the record of nearly a year. There was no indication of where he had been sent. Either through extraordinary good fortune, or through some influence that his mother had been able to bring to bear, he suddenly turned up in the United States enrolled as a student at the University of Wisconsin. Graduating in 1972 in microbial genetics, he stayed on a further year to complete a postgraduate doctorate in biotechnology. And then he won a research fellowship to the Boyce Thompson Institute at Cornell University, where he remained until 1980, when he returned to China to teach at the very university he had been forced to abandon twelve years earlier.

He had married very quickly then, but was divorced again within three years, during which time he had managed to father a daughter. Li wondered why he had felt the need to marry. Clearly it was always going to be a relationship doomed to sexual failure. Was there really a need to create a veneer of heterosexual respectability? Might he not just have been discreet in his lifestyle?

Whether or not his particular predilections were known, they had not affected his career. He had been influential in the setting up of Beijing Agricultural University's National Key Laboratory of Agricultural Biotechnology, under the auspices of the Ministry of Agriculture, and spent the next ten years directing field projects in Beijing, at the Changping Experiment Station in Hui Long Guan District, Changping County, and then at the agro hi-technology development region in Zhuozhou. He had spent nearly four years working on some unspecified research project near Guilin, then in 1996 he had been brought back to Beijing and appointed senior technical adviser to the Minister of Agriculture before being forced to retire through ill health six months ago.

Li shut the folder. A life summed up in a few scant paragraphs. But it told him nothing about the man, what had driven his ambition, what had led him to heroin and the destruction of his health, what had motivated someone to kill him. Tomorrow, he hoped, he would glean much, much more when he paid a visit to Chao's *danwei* at the Ministry of Agriculture. Tomorrow and tomorrow and tomorrow. Everything was tomorrow! He reached for the file Wu had left for him on The Needle. Somewhere in the drugs connection, he felt sure, he could establish the first concrete link between two of the murders at least.

There was a soft knock at the door and Section Chief Chen came in. He closed the door behind him. 'Chaos out there.' And he took in the piles of statements gathering under the window. 'This could keep us busy for weeks.'

'Or months,' Li said gloomily.

'How is it going?'

'Slowly. I'll be in a better position to brief you on progress tomorrow when we get some tests back from forensics. Until then, we are still sifting through the jigsaw for the first piece.'

Chen nodded. 'Well, I have some good news. In view of the success of the autopsy carried out this morning by Dr Campbell, Professor Jiang has offered us her services for the duration of her stay in Beijing. Provided, of course, that it does not interfere with her lectures.'

Li drew a deep, slow breath. 'That's very good of the professor, Chief, but it's really not necessary.'

'Oh, but I've already accepted on your behalf. I told the

professor she could carry out the other two autopsies in the morning.'

Li clenched his jaw, trying to stay calm. 'Well, you shouldn't have done that, Chief. I've already asked Professor Xie to do the autopsies. This is a Chinese investigation, about which Dr Campbell knows nothing. I have no need of her.'

Chen was about to overrule his junior colleague when their eyes met and he thought better of it. Li was clearly determined, and Chen had already overruled him once on the same subject. Perhaps the younger man should be allowed a little latitude to do things his way. He sighed. 'Oh, well, I'll tell the professor that other arrangements had already been made, and that while we are very grateful for the offer, Dr Campbell's services will not be required.' He paused and added, 'But if this is something personal, Li Yan, then you are very foolish to allow it to cloud your professional judgment.'

He left, and Li stared into space, part of him wishing he had accepted the offer, part of him knowing that if he had, then the danger was that it *would* have become personal – in a way that might well have clouded his professional judgment. She had stirred in him feelings he had spent ten years suppressing, in favour of his career, and did not want to encourage now. He opened the file on The Needle to cast an eye over an old adversary.

VI

The scrape of a door opening was sufficient to penetrate the fragile quality of her sleep. She blinked and lifted her head from a pillow that seemed uncommonly hard and unyielding. One arm had gone to sleep and would take longer to waken than she. Her neck seemed locked in one position. Through fuzzy, unfocused eyes, she saw a man approach the bed. What was a man doing in her bedroom? She raised herself up, blinking hard, heart pounding, and realised she wasn't in bed. For a brief, panic-stricken moment she had not the faintest idea where she was, before suddenly the truth dawned on her. She had fallen asleep at her desk, head resting on her right forearm, in which her blood supply was now painfully re-establishing itself.

'You all right?' Bob asked.

'Yeah. Sorry. I guess I must have fallen asleep. Didn't get much last night.'

Last night? When was that? Her brain couldn't seem to find a context for anything. Like the blood finding its way back into the veins of her arm, memories of the last twenty-four hours leaked back into her consciousness accompanied by a series of pains – behind her eyes, at either temple, at the base of her neck. She remembered the autopsy, the lunch with Li, and her subsequent depression. And then she remembered being called in to see Professor Jiang and asked if she would be prepared to carry out another couple of autopsies and advise Deputy Section Chief Li's murder inquiry in a consultative capacity.

That recollection brightened her again now. She remembered

apologising to Professors Tian and Bai and Dr Mu for having displaced them from their office and, in a grand and magnanimous gesture, offering to let them have it back. After all, she had told them, now that she was assisting Section One with a murder inquiry she would not be spending so much time at the university. She was excited by the prospect.

'But where will you prepare your lectures?' Dr Mu had asked Veronica to ask her.

'In my hotel room,' Margaret had replied. 'There's plenty of space, it's air-conditioned, I have access to a telephone, and downstairs there's a business centre where I can get anything I want photocopied, faxed, e-mailed, you name it.'

They had clearly thought she was mad, but were happy enough to get their office back, and so were not going to argue.

'You should have gone back to your hotel,' Bob told her.

She shook herself to try to clear her head, but only succeeded in producing a pain that felt as if it would crack open her skull. 'Ow.' She rubbed her temples. 'I know. I meant to. I must just have put my head down for a minute, and then . . . well, bang. What time is it?'

'Five thirty. Professor Jiang would like a word.'

'Another one? What, now?'

Professor Jiang smiled uneasily when she came into his office. Veronica sat primly in a chair, hands folded neatly in her lap. She regarded Margaret with some caution. The professor indicated a chair and Margaret sat and listened while he spoke to her earnestly for about two minutes. Then he sat back and allowed Veronica to translate.

'Professor say Section Chief Chen call to say sorry, but his deputy think you are ... how to say? ... superfluous to the inquiry.' She sat back, pleased with her 'superfluous', unaware of its connotations of uselessness and rejection which hit Margaret like a slap on the face.

CHAPTER FOUR

I

Tuesday Evening

Beijingers get their hair cut at all hours of the day and night. And so the ladies in their white coats and peak caps were still doing brisk business outside the gates of Yuyuantan Park on Sanlihi Road at six o'clock. No sooner had one customer vacated a stool than another would replace him. The sidewalk was littered with locks of black hair which the barbers would meticulously sweep up when they finished work. The park, too, was busy, people shifting back and forth in waves beneath the rainbow that arched across its entrance, joining dance groups on their way home from work, or catching some air after long hours in a factory or shop. Early evening traffic, beyond the trees that shaded the cycle lane, was manic.

Li wheeled his bicycle past the barbers at work and lifted it over a low railing into a shaded area of trees and shrubs between flagstone paths that led in various directions down to the river. Here the sound of the traffic seemed remote, the air cooler, shadowed as it had been through the heat of the day, and rising off the water to blow a gentle breeze through the leaves. Birds sang in cages that hung from the trees, their owners – old men mostly – gathered on stools round stone tables playing cards or Chinese chess. A woman had hung large red character posters from a line strung between two trees, and a couple of men, hands behind their backs, stood staring at them without comment. The woman watched their expressions with interest, but they showed no discernible emotion as far as Li could see. In a pergola hanging with creeper an old man played a violin, while a few feet away a dead-eyed young man in army camouflage trousers and skip cap was drinking alcohol from a plastic bottle.

Li found his uncle a little further on, sitting at a low stone table preparing to move in for the kill. The King's Guide had made a fatal error, and Old Yifu was merciless in victory. His Horse jumped the river and the King was trapped. '*Jiang jun!*' he cried, delighted with the pincer movement that had created his checkmate. His opponent scratched his shaven head and shook it in wonder.

'I don't know why I bother playing you, Old Yifu. I'm never going to win.'

Old Yifu smiled. 'You will win,' he said, 'when you stop losing.' He looked up and saw Li approaching. 'Li Yan.' He jumped to his feet and shook his nephew's hand vigorously. 'How was your first day?'

Li smiled ruefully. 'Only three murders, Uncle.'

His uncle's chess opponent lifted a birdcage down from the tree that had been shading their game, hung it from the handlebars of his bicycle and said, 'I'm off for my dinner. All this excitement has given me an appetite.'

'Zai jian.' Old Yifu did not take his eyes off Li. 'You're joking,' he said.

'No.' Li sat down on the stool the defeated chess player had just vacated. 'Three. In different parts of the city. But they're connected.'

Old Yifu sat down opposite him, both excited and concerned by the news. 'You'll give me a game of chess and tell me about it while we play.'

Li took out his watch. 'It's late, Uncle Yifu. We should eat.'

'We can eat after. First you tell me.' He rearranged the chess pieces, simple wooden disks engraved in black or red with Chinese characters, on the board. 'Then we eat.'

Li shook his head fondly. He knew his uncle wanted to hear every detail, and his uncle knew that he wanted to tell him. He watched the old man as he laid out the pieces on either side of the 'river'. He had a thick head of unusually curly hair, highlighted by an occasional strand of silver, and wore square tortoiseshell-rimmed glasses. His eyebrows were raised in a permanently quizzical expression, and more often than not a smile would carve deep creases in his cheeks. He always wore colourfully patterned short-sleeved shirts over baggy trousers that concertinaed around open sandals, and carried a small satchel in which he kept a jar of green tea, his chess set, a pack of cards, a book, and that day's newspaper. 'Your move.' Old Yifu waved a hand at him impatiently, and Li moved one of his Soldiers a single square forward. 'Okay, tell me.'

But Li had other items on his agenda ahead of the murder inquiry. 'There was a strange man in my office today,' he said.

'Oh?' his uncle said casually, apparently focusing attention on his first move.

'A *feng shui* man.'

'Ah.' Old Yifu seemed reassured by this and moved one of his Horses.

'He said he was a friend of yours.'

'Hmm-hmm, hmm-hmm.' Old Yifu feigned indifference. 'Your move. Pay attention.'

'He said you'd sent him.'

'Well, of course he would.'

'Because you did?'

'Why else would he say it?'

Li sighed. 'Uncle Yifu, it's not that I have anything intrinsically against the idea of *feng shui* . . .'

'I should hope not!' Old Yifu was indignant.

'In fact, I'm sure that many of its precepts are based on fundamental truths, and that there is practical value in them.'

'Of course there is. Practical and spiritual. Come on, move!'

Li moved a Horse to protect his Soldier. 'It's just that . . . well, as you know, the authorities are not very keen on it. At least, not officially.'

'Nonsense!' Old Yifu was adamant. 'No builder worth his salt puts up a new building these days without flying the plans past a *feng shui* man. *State* buildings, too.'

'Well, that's as may be . . .' Li took a deep breath. 'But the truth is, Section Chief Chen doesn't want a *feng shui* man in the building and told me as much.'

'Chen?' Old Yifu snorted his derision. 'What does that old fart know? You leave Chen to me. I'll sort him out.'

'It's not just that, Uncle Yifu . . .' There was a hint of desperation creeping into Li's voice now. His trump card had just been dismissed. How could he tell his uncle that it was *embarrassing*? That his colleagues found it a source of great amusement? Besides, he didn't want Old Yifu taking issue with Chen. It would be like a parent berating their child's teacher. It could create bad feeling and rebound on Li. 'I mean, I can take care of Chen. It's just . . .'

Old Yifu moved a Soldier across the river, slapping the piece down on Li's side. 'Just what?'

'Just . . . well, I'm too busy to get involved with that sort of thing just now,' Li said lamely.

'Don't worry,' Old Yifu said. 'I'll make sure the old boy doesn't get in your way. With three murders on your plate, you'll need all the free-flowing *ch'i* you can get.'

Li gave up. He wasn't going to win without giving offence, and he would die before he offended his uncle. Still, sometimes it could be very difficult. He made a careless move, and Old Yifu leapt on his Soldier like a crow on carrion. 'For heaven's sake, Li Yan, you will never beat me at chess if you don't pay attention!'

'How can I pay attention when I've got three murders on my mind?'

'Chess frees the mind and cleanses the intellect. You will

think all the more clearly for it.' His eyes were fixed on the board. He looked up. 'Come on. Your move.'

Li sighed and examined the board. Old Yifu said, 'I got a letter from your father today. Your sister is pregnant.' He paused before adding, ominously, 'Again.'

Li abandoned the game and looked at him in dismay. 'She's not going to have it, is she?' He was horrified by the thought. His sister, Xiao Ling, was even more stubborn than himself. Once she had set her mind to something there was no dissuading her. And she already had a child. A wonderful four-year-old little girl, with a smile that was destined to break hearts. An impudent smile that dimpled her cheeks and lit up her eyes. Li could see her now, grinning at him, challenging him, hair gathered in ribbons on either side of her head swinging free as she cocked it to one side or the other. Xiao Ling was married to a rice farmer near the town of Zigong in Sichuan province. They lived with his parents and made a good living from the land. But they wanted a son – everyone wanted a son, for a son was much more valuable than a daughter, and under the One-Child Policy they could only have one or the other. And if Xiao Ling was pregnant and insisted on having the child, the months ahead would be intolerable. First her village committee would send representatives to try to dissuade her from proceeding with the pregnancy. Then she would be visited by cadres who would exert powerful and increasing pressure on her to have an abortion. She would be subjected to hours of psychological persuasion. It had been known, in cases of particularly intransigent mothers-to-be, for enforced abortion to be applied, usually with the connivance of the family. For if a second child was born, there would be hefty fines to pay, fines that most people could not afford. The families could also be penalised in other ways, with loss of free education, access to medicine, housing, pension. The pressures could be made unbearable.

Old Yifu nodded sadly. 'She's a difficult girl, your sister. She's determined to go ahead.'

'Has my father talked to her?'

'Oh, yes. But, of course, she will not listen.'

'What does her husband say?' Li had never liked him. He thought, like many brothers, that no man was good enough for his sister.

'I think,' Old Yifu said, 'that he would like the chance of a son, so he is sitting on the fence. He will neither support her, nor dissuade her.'

'Bastard!' Li said. He scratched his head. 'She won't listen to me.' He glanced at his uncle. 'The only person she might listen to is you.'

Old Yifu nodded. 'Your father thinks so, too.'

'What will you do?'

'I will go and speak to her. But I will not tell her what to do. The One-Child Policy is a necessary evil. But a woman has a right to bear children. She must make her own decision, based on what is right. Not only for her, not only for China, but for both. And sometimes that is not an easy thing to do.'

They sat in silence for several moments, staring at the chessboard, but their minds were not on chess. Finally, Old

Yifu clapped his hands to break their reverie and said, 'Your move.'

Li blinked at the board and moved his Castle, without thinking, to threaten his uncle's Bishop. Old Yifu frowned, perplexed, unable to see the logic in the move but suspecting a trap. 'So,' he said. 'Tell me about your murders.' And so Li told him – about the burning body in the park, about the small-time drug dealer found on waste ground, about the itinerant lying with a broken neck in a condemned *siheyuan*. 'And the connection?' his uncle asked. Li told him about the cigarette ends. Old Yifu frowned. 'Hmmm. Not much of a connection. Can you prove they were all smoked by the same man?'

'Not yet.'

'Hmmm.'

'What does that mean?'

'It means, hmmm.' Old Yifu took another of Li's Soldiers. 'Perhaps these cigarette ends do indicate a connection. But if you focus too much on that, you may miss other links.'

Li told him about the drugs connection and his intention to 'have a chat' tomorrow with The Needle.

'Hmmm.'

'What this time?'

'The drugs connection links only the body in the park and the stabbing, correct?'

'Correct. But there may well be a drugs connection with the itinerant.'

'But you don't know that.'

'Not yet, no.' Li was becoming exasperated. 'But we're

interviewing every itinerant who has registered in Beijing in the last six weeks. We're pulling in every two-*jiao* drug dealer and junkie. If there's a link, we'll find it.'

'Of course you will.' Old Yifu took Li's Bishop. 'And if there isn't, you won't. And you'll be six months down the line and no further on.'

'So what are you saying? That it's a waste of time interviewing these people?'

'Oh no, you must. There is no substitute for diligence in police work. "Where the tiller is tireless, the land is fertile."'

Li was tiring of his uncle's wisdom. He took a Horse with a Bishop, and banged the wooden disk down on the stone table, the first piece he had taken. '*Jiang!*' he said, having put his uncle's King in check.

'The thing is,' said old Yifu, quite unperturbed, 'as the famous American inventor, Thomas Alva Edison, once said, "Genius is one per cent inspiration, ninety-nine per cent perspiration". All the perspiration in the world will get you nowhere without that one spark of inspiration.' He blocked the check with his Guide and watched as Li manoeuvred his Horse, then slid his Cannon across the board. '*Jiang si le!*'

Li stared at his King in disbelief. There was nowhere it could go. It was indeed checkmate. He sat back and folded his arms. Of course, he hadn't been concentrating. 'So where do I look for this inspiration?' he asked.

'From within,' Old Yifu said. 'From what you know.' He paused thoughtfully. 'Tell me again about the way Chao Heng's killer went about his business. In the apartment, and in the park.'

Li went through it all, replaying his thoughts, all the tiny clues, the moments of discovery and illumination. The CD still paused in the player. The blood on the carpet. His vision of the killer carrying the body downstairs and out into the darkness created by the removal of the lamp. The daring murder in broad daylight, Li's vision of the killer walking nonchalantly from the park even as the blazing body of his victim was being discovered.

'And what does this tell us about the killer?' his uncle said. Li shrugged. 'It tells us that he is a clever man who planned and executed this murder with a professional precision. In the normal course of events, you would never have discovered that his victim had not committed suicide. He could not have known that a visiting American pathologist, expert in the post-mortem examinations of burn victims, would be invited to perform the autopsy. For all our growing expertise in China, we still have a long way to go. Not many of our pathologists would have identified the fracture of the skull as anything other than a heat fracture. Very few of our pathologists have the experience of drugs that would have led them to guess at the use of a sedative – this . . . ketamine – on top of a heroin habit.' He stopped, mobile eyebrows pushed high on his forehead, looking for an acknowledgement from Li.

'You're saying the killer was a professional?' Professional killers in China were a very rare breed of animal. 'In Beijing?'

'Oh, he would have come from Hong Kong probably. "One country, two systems."' His smile reflected a certain irony. 'Some Triad hit-man.' Old Yifu jabbed a finger in Li's direction.

'These other two killings. No clues left at the scene. One is killed by a single thrust of a knife up through the ribcage and into the heart. The other by a clean break of the neck. These were no casual killings, Li Yan.'

Li's breathing had become shallow. More rapid. He fought to make sense of it. 'If they were professional killings, then that establishes a link beyond the cigarette ends.' He shook his head, still perplexed. 'But why? Why would someone employ a hit-man to kill a retired adviser in agriculture, a nobody drug dealer, and an unemployed labourer from Shanghai?'

'Okay.' Old Yifu waggled a finger at him. 'Now you are asking the right question. The big question. But before you know the answer to that, there are many smaller questions to be answered. And this brings you back to the cigarette ends. Because without them you would never have made any connection. But then, why would a professional be so careless in this, when he had been so careful in everything else? This is not right. This is something to focus on.'

Li knew that all of this had been somewhere in his head, but it had taken his uncle, with a disinterested perspective, to crystallise it for him. He gazed thoughtfully at the chessboard, a battlefield, the scene of his ignominious defeat. Old Yifu was right. It was all about focus. His uncle started gathering the pieces and placing them in their box.

'So,' he said, 'this American pathologist. She will continue to help?'

'No!' Li realised immediately he had been too quick, too definitive, in his response.

Old Yifu missed nothing. 'She does not want to help?'

'No . . . Yes . . . I don't know. Professor Jiang at the university offered to make her available.'

'And you said . . . ?'

Li looked at his hands. 'I said I didn't need her.'

'Then you are a fool.'

Li flared angrily. 'We do not need some American showing us how it should be done!'

'No. But you need an edge. You always need an edge. And the experience that this American has will give you an edge.' Old Yifu slipped the box of pieces and his chessboard into his satchel and stood up stiffly. 'Time to eat.'

II

All of Ma Yongli's knives – for paring, scraping, chopping, slicing – were laid out on the stainless-steel worktop, reflecting in its shiny surface. One by one he ran them through the sharpener, three, four, five times, until they offered little or no resistance and their blades gleamed, sharp as razors. He glanced at the figure of his friend sitting on the worktop opposite, legs dangling. 'Cheer up, Big Li. It might never happen.'

'It'll happen,' Li said disconsolately. 'Unless I die between now and tomorrow morning.'

'Sounds like a good excuse for going out and drinking ourselves to death, then. At least we'll die happy.' Yongli paused and scratched his head, then smiled wickedly. 'Mind you – happy? It'd be a first for you.'

Li made a face at him. He had arrived at the end of Yongli's shift. Dinners at the hotel had been cooked, served and eaten. The duty chef, who would provide for the few patrons who made use of the twenty-four-hour café in the small hours, was out back smoking a cigarette. The kitchens were otherwise deserted and in darkness, lit only where Yongli was sharpening his knives.

'So let me take a guess,' Yongli said. 'Would your mood have anything to do with your Uncle Yifu?'

'Do I need to answer that?'

'For God's sake, man, get yourself out of there. Get a woman, get a life! Old Yifu's a lovely old guy, but you can't spend the rest of your days living with your uncle.' This was not what Li needed to hear. 'I'm surprised he hasn't got you tucked up in bed by now.'

'I should be,' Li said grimly.

'You see! You see!' Yongli danced round the worktop towards him. 'He's got you *thinking* like him now. Bed? Shit, man, it's only ten thirty. The night is young. And you are turning into an old man.'

'I'm up at six tomorrow. I've got three murders on the go.' Li drew a deep breath and sighed. 'Only I know I wouldn't sleep.'

'Ah. So you've come to consult with Dr Ma Yongli, that well-known dispenser of sound advice for insomniacs.'

The nearest thing to hand was a pot, so Li threw it at him. Yongli caught it easily and grinned. 'That's more like it. A bit of spirit. A bit of life left in the old dog.' He swung himself up to sit on the worktop beside him. 'So what's he done now?'

'My first day, in my new job, in my new office, and I walk in to find a *feng shui* man sitting cross-legged on my desk.'

Yongli looked at him in astonishment. 'You're kidding!' But it was clear he wasn't. 'And Uncle Yifu sent him?'

'To balance my Yin and my Yang and get my *ch'i* flowing freely,' Li said gloomily.

Yongli roared with laughter, slapping his thighs and then drumming his palms on the worktop.

'Yes, yes, thank you, thank you,' Li said sarcastically. 'That's exactly the reaction it got from the rest of the office.'

'Are you surprised?'

'No, I'm not. But when it happens to you, and your boss calls you in and tells you to get rid of him, and your uncle says he'll fix your boss, believe me, it's not funny.'

Yongli, still chuckling, dug an elbow into Li's ribs. 'Of course it is. Hey, lighten up, Big Li. You're taking life far too seriously.'

'When your life is dealing with death, then you take it seriously,' Li said firmly.

Yongli looked at him and shook his head sadly. 'What are we going to do with you?'

But Li was lost in his own thoughts. 'And then there's my sister. Pregnant again, and determined to go through with it. And then I've got to go in tomorrow morning and lose face to my boss, and to some jumped-up American pathologist who thinks she's better than us.'

'Woah, woah. You're going way too fast for me. What's all *this* about?'

'My boss gets this American pathologist to do an autopsy

for me. She's lecturing at the Public Security University. He met her on a course in Chicago. It's a personal favour.'

'So far so good.'

'It goes well. The university offers her services for the rest of her stay. I turn them down.'

'Why?'

'It's complicated.'

'I thought she did a good job?'

'She did.'

'So what's the problem?'

'God, now you're beginning to sound like my uncle!'

'Ah.' Yongli nodded sagely. 'Now we're getting to the root of it. Your uncle thinks you should take up the offer.'

'Which I've already knocked back.'

'So if you go back and say you've changed your mind . . .'

'I'll lose face.'

'And if you don't?'

'My uncle will be offended.'

'And God forbid you should offend your uncle.'

Li turned on his friend, angry now. 'My uncle's been good to me. I owe just about everything I've achieved in life to Uncle Yifu. I'd never, *never* do anything to hurt him.'

Yongli raised his hands defensively. 'Okay, okay. So you love the old guy. It doesn't stop him driving you crazy.'

Li's anger diminished as quickly as it had flared up. 'No,' he said. 'No, it doesn't.'

They sat in thoughtful silence for a full minute. Then Yongli said, 'So, this American pathologist . . . An old battle-axe, is she?'

Li was evasive. 'Not exactly.'

'But she's old, right?'

Li shrugged. 'Not exactly.'

A worm of suspicion started to wriggle its way into Yongli's head. 'Well, if she's not exactly a battle-axe, and she's not exactly old . . . would you say she was young? Attractive?'

'I guess. Sort of.'

'Sort of young? Or sort of attractive?'

'Sort of . . . both. She was the *yangguizi* at the banquet McCord gatecrashed last night at the Quanjude.'

'Ah.'

'What do you mean, "Ah"?'

Yongli waggled a finger at him. 'It's beginning to fall into place.'

'What is?'

'Your little head started expressing an interest and your big head put a stop to it.'

'Oh, crap!'

'Is it? I know you, Li Yan. I've known you for years. You're scared of having a relationship, even if it was just sex, in case it interfered with your big career plan. First it was the university, now it's your job.' Yongli jumped down off the worktop. 'You know what you need?'

'I'm sure you're going to tell me.'

'You need to get yourself laid a little more often.' Yongli tossed his tall white hat across the worktop and started untying his chef's apron. 'Come on,' he said. 'You're coming with me.'

'Where?'

'The Xanadu Karaoke Club.'

'What?' Li looked at him incredulously. 'You're winding me up.'

'No, I'm not. It's a new place, off Xidan. Open from eight at night till eight in the morning. The booze is cheap, the women are plentiful, and it's not all karaoke. There's live music, too.' He hesitated. 'Lotus is singing there now.' And he saw Li's face darken immediately. 'And don't start preaching at me, all right?'

'For heaven's sake, Ma Yongli, she's a prostitute! A whore!'

Yongli looked at him dangerously. 'I'll take your fucking head off.' His voice was barely a whisper.

Li softened his tone. 'I just don't understand how you can go with her when you know she's been with other men.'

'I love her, all right? Is that such a crime?' Yongli looked away, clenching his jaw. 'Anyway, she's giving all that up. She's making a career for herself as a singer.'

'Yeah, sure.' Li slipped down off the worktop. 'I think I'll pass, though. Wouldn't exactly do me any favours to be seen consorting with a known prostitute.'

Yongli turned on him. 'Can't you stop being a cop for two minutes?'

'No. I can't ever stop being a cop. Because it's what I am.'

'Yeah?' Yongli pushed his face into Li's. 'But you can stop being my friend, right? When it suits you. When you don't like my girl. That how it goes? Well, fuck you!' And he turned and stormed towards the door.

Li stood staring after him, his heart battering his ribcage. 'Ma Yongli,' he shouted. Yongli kept going. 'Ma Yongli!' This time he positively bellowed.

Yongli stopped at the door and turned, his face livid. 'What?'

They stared at each other for fully a quarter of a minute. Then Li said, 'I think it's your round.'

By the time they reached the Xanadu, their spat at the hotel was forgotten. Or, at least, each kept up that pretence for the other's benefit. It was about the last place in the world Li wanted to be right now, but he was trying to be a full-time friend as much as he was a full-time cop. Sometimes it wasn't easy being either.

There was a queue to get in, and they stood for nearly twenty minutes, smoking and watching life drift by on the streets, talking about nothing very much. Groups of sullen youths stared lasciviously at groups of giggling girls in mini-skirts and Wonderbras who flaunted their sexuality with a carelessness that, in the West, would quickly have led to trouble. They made Li feel old, disconnected somehow from their world, as if it were so much different to his. And, of course, it was. In thirteen years the world had turned and was no longer the same place he had inhabited as a twenty-year-old. He didn't recognise the kids of today as being like he had been. They belonged to a new age. Everything – values, expectations, earnings – was different. He was still linked to a troubled past that owed more to the excesses of the Red Guards and the Smashing of the Four Olds.

Eventually Yongli caught the eye of a bouncer he knew, and they were waved in. There was a ten-yuan entrance fee and the first drink was free. A circular red symbol, impossible to read, was stamped on the back of their right hands, and they passed on through a cloakroom area to the bar, which stretched the length of one wall. A large floor area was crowded with tables and chairs, all filled by animated youths drinking and smoking. At the far end was a raised platform with microphone and speakers and a karaoke screen. A spotty boy with a shock of thick, coarse hair that fell across his eyes was singing some unrecognisable Taiwanese pop song. No one was listening to him. Wooden stairs led up to a gallery that ran around three walls, overlooking the floor below. It, too, was crowded. The noise was deafening.

They made their way to the bar and Yongli waved their tickets at the barman, and they got two half-litre glasses of Tsing Tao beer. Li looked around as he sipped his. Where did all these kids get the money? This was not a cheap night out. 'You want to try and find a table?' Yongli bellowed in his ear.

Li nodded, and followed as Yongli climbed the stairs to the gallery two at a time. At the top Yongli spoke to a waitress. Whatever he said, she laughed loudly, and from the way her eyes were fixed on him it was clear that she found him attractive. He grinned back at her and squeezed her around the waist and winked, and she flushed red. He had such an easy way with him. Li wondered, as he had often done in the past, what it was that women found attractive about him. He was far from conventionally good-looking. But there was something about his eyes, and his smile. Something roguish. He could have had almost any woman he wanted. And yet he had fallen for Lotus.

The waitress weaved her way to the far side of the gallery and bent over a table to speak to the group of kids that sat around it. They glanced over towards Yongli, then shrugged and reluctantly moved away, taking their drinks with them, in search of standing room somewhere else. The waitress beckoned Yongli across, and Li followed him to the table. She gave him a big smile, wiped their table clean and placed a fresh ashtray in the centre. 'You give me a shout when you need a refill,' she said.

'You bet.' Yongli grinned and winked again, and she flushed with pleasure, hurrying away through the tables. He flicked a cigarette across at Li. 'Helps when they know you,' he said.

Li laughed. 'It's got nothing to do with knowing you. All you've got to do is smile and you've got half the women in Beijing fawning at your feet.' He lit both their cigarettes.

'True,' Yongli said modestly. 'But it doesn't do any harm that Lotus is a regular on-stage here.'

The music stopped then, and the sense of relief Li felt was enormous, like stopping banging his head against a wall. They no longer had to shout at each other to make themselves heard.

'So, when is she on?' Li asked.

Yongli checked the time. 'About half an hour. There's a guy plays keyboard, and another on guitar. And they've got one of these computerised drum things. They sound like a fifty-piece orchestra. They're good.'

Li had never had much time for music, and he couldn't imagine what Yongli's idea of 'good' was. It was a measure of how far they had grown apart in recent years that a club like this was a familiar part of Yongli's life, and completely alien to Li. He drank his beer and watched the faces all around him, high on alcohol and who knew what else, talking animatedly. Young men and women, drawn to this place in search of different things: romance, sex, a partner, an end to loneliness, an escape from the banality of their daylight lives. The ritualistic search of a boy for a girl, a girl for a boy, and perhaps for a few something in between. But there was a sad quality, desperate and slightly shabby, about it all. Painted and unreal. A gloss for the night on dull lives, which would have worn off by morning, when the veneer of partners picked up in this ersatz twilight world would not have quite the same sheen as the night before. Li felt only relief that he had missed out on this, was no part of it. And yet, was his world any better? he wondered. A world of murderers, pimps and drug dealers. A world in which, only a few hours before, he had stood watching a poor burned man being clinically dissected, had traced his last hours of life from a bloodstained carpet in an apartment to a fiery and agonising death in a park.

'Hi.' Li was startled out of his thoughts by a woman's voice. He turned as Yongli's chair scraped back and the big chef got up and put his arms around Lotus's slender frame. His body seemed to envelop hers, and she looked up at him, smiling with clear affection, before he lowered his head to kiss her. He took her hand and stepped back.

'You remember Li Yan.'

Li stood up and shook her hand awkwardly. 'Of course,' she said, smiling as if they were old friends and Yongli had asked a stupid question. A full-length green silk dress clung to every contour of her body, split on either side from ankle to waist, bare arms exposed by a sleeveless top, her shoulders and neck, by contrast, modestly hidden by a high choker neckline. Beneath her heavy make-up it was clear she was actually very beautiful. She was quick to notice Li's appraisal and, as if by way of apology, said, 'My stage outfit.'

Yongli seemed almost nervous in her company. Gone was the easy self-confidence and the twinkling smile. 'I'll get you a drink,' he said, and he pulled up a chair for her.

'Something soft,' she said as she sat down. 'Don't want to be slurring my words when I'm singing.' She smiled warmly at Li.

Yongli was looking around for the waitress from earlier, but she was nowhere to be seen. He seemed uncommonly agitated. 'Where's that damn girl gone?' He tutted with irritation. 'I'll be back in a minute.'

'No hurry,' Lotus said. 'I'm in good hands.' She did not take her eyes from Li. Yongli hurried away across the gallery towards the stairs. 'You got a cigarette?' she asked. Li was aware of her strong Beijing accent, tongue curled back in the mouth to create the distinctive 'R' sound that formed almost in the throat. He held a pack open for her. She took one and he lit it. She drew deeply on it, threw her head back and blew a jet of smoke towards the ceiling. Then she levelled her gaze again and said, 'You don't like me much, do you?'

Li was taken aback by her directness. He had only met her a couple of times previously. He had always been polite, keeping, he had thought, his disapproval to himself. Perhaps Yongli had spoken to her of his friend's feelings, or maybe she simply knew, by instinct, how a policeman might regard her. There seemed little point in denying it. 'No,' he said bluntly.

No sign of emotion rippled her exterior calm. She maintained a steady eye contact. 'You don't even know me.'

'I know what you do. And I know what you are. That's enough.'

When Yongli met her she had been working the joint-venture tourist hotels, raking in a high dollar income from wealthy businessmen with a taste for Asian girls. She had been based at the Jingtan when he started there as a chef the previous year, and he fell for her immediately.

'What I *was*,' she said evenly. 'What I *did*.'

'I see,' Li said coldly. 'So what you earn here as a singer allows you to maintain the same income and lifestyle as before? That what you tell Ma Yongli, is it?'

She suddenly leaned forward and stubbed out her cigarette. 'Don't you dare judge me!' she snapped. 'You know nothing about me. You don't know what kind of life I've had, what kind of shit I've been through. I do what I have to do to survive. I don't always like me. But Yongli does. He always has. And he's never judged me. He treats me like no one's ever treated me before. Like a princess. And there's not many girls get to feel like that in their lives.' She leaned back in her chair, breathing deeply to regain her composure. Then she said, quietly, 'So if you think I'm bad for him, or that I don't love him, you're wrong. I've never loved anyone so much in my life. And I'd *never* do anything to hurt him.'

With a tiny jab of remorse, Li heard an echo of himself in this, how he felt about his uncle, the passion with which he'd defended him to Yongli just an hour earlier. He heard the same passion in Lotus, and couldn't doubt the sincerity in her eyes. He nodded and said, 'I don't want to see him hurt either.'

'Fresh orange juice and ice, is that all right?' Yongli put the glass on the table in front of her and sat down. 'Sorry it took so long.'

Lotus smiled at him. 'Fresh orange is fine,' she said. She took a long draught, then put it down again, half finished. 'But I'm sorry, lover, I've got to go get ready.'

'Hey, that's okay.' He leaned over to brush her lips with his. 'Good luck.'

'Thanks.' She stood up and smiled at Li. 'See you later?'

Li shrugged. 'Maybe not. I've got an early start.'

'Next time, then.' She touched Yongli's face lightly with her fingers and moved away, gliding elegantly between the tables towards the stair. Yongli watched her go, doe-eyed and smitten, before becoming suddenly self-conscious and turning back to Li.

'So what were you two talking about?' There was a hint of anxiety in his voice.

'You.'

'Pretty boring topic of conversation.'

'That's what we decided, so we stopped.'

Yongli grinned. 'You're not really going to bail out early, are you?'

Li smiled and nodded. 'I really am.'

Yongli shook his head. 'You know, what you *really* need is to get yourself laid.'

'You already told me.'

'No, but *really*. I mean, what about this "young", "attractive" American pathologist of yours? Sounds to me like she could get your juices flowing.'

Li laughed. 'Gimme a break! She's a *yangguizi*.'

'So what?' Yongli punched him mock-playfully on the arm. 'You could turn on the charm if you wanted to. And she'd fall in a dead faint at your feet.'

III

Margaret cursed Li roundly. He was an arrogant, charmless, chauvinistic bastard! The doors of the elevator slid shut and she pressed the button for the ground floor. She saw herself reflected in the polished brass and realised she hadn't even bothered putting on any make-up. She had simply changed into her jeans and a tee-shirt, a pair of open-toed sandals, grabbed her keycard and headed for the elevator. A couple of young attendants sitting playing cards cast curious glances at her through the open door of a utility room as she stalked past. She had noticed before that there always seemed to be cleaners or attendants around on her floor when she came and went. Always nodding and smiling and saying, '*Ni hao*.' If she had thought about it at all, she might have been faintly surprised that they were still there at midnight. But her brain was otherwise engaged, and she needed a drink.

She couldn't get Li Yan out of her head: his initial hostility, then his grudging acceptance of her professional expertise, followed by his warmth over lunch, and then his coldness after it, crowned by his refusal to accept her further help. She was glad, she told herself. She certainly had no desire to be where she wasn't wanted. And she had no time for the mood swings and preconceptions of some precious Chinese policeman with a thing against foreigners. What was the word Bob had used . . . ? *Yangguizi*. That was it. Foreign devil! It was sheer bloody-minded xenophobia!

Her mind had been full of such thoughts all evening. Anger, revenge, the things she would say if she ever got the chance. And then she would remember a moment over lunch when he had smiled at her, dark eyes full of mischief, the soft-spoken quality of his voice, his gently accented English with its errant emphasis on odd syllables. And it would infuriate her that there was something about him she found attractive, and then she would recall the humiliation she felt when summoned to Professor Jiang's office for the second time that day. And the anger would flood back.

The hotel lobby was deserted as she strode through the south wing past reception and down steps to the bar beyond. There were still a dozen or more people sitting at tables in

twos and threes, downing nightcaps and indulging in loqua-
cious post-dinner conversation. Margaret paid them little
attention, hoisting herself on to a bar stool and demanding
a vodka tonic with ice and lemon, then deciding to make
it a large one. The barman responded quickly, pouring her
drink, and then laying out a square of white paper napkin, a
small bowl of raw peanuts, and a tall glass that was misting
already from the chill of the ice. She flashed her keycard at
him, and as he opened an account, she took a long pull at the
vodka and felt the alcohol flooding almost immediately into
her bloodstream and into her brain, like a long, cool wave
of relief. She started to relax, took a handful of nuts, and
looked around the bar. There was a young Chinese couple
smooching at a table against the far wall. A noisy group
of three Japanese businessmen quaffing large tumblers of
whisky. A short, middle-aged man who . . . Her heart took a
jolt as she realised it was McCord. He was slumped in a seat
at a corner table looking considerably dishevelled. Strands of
greasy grey hair had broken free of the oil he used to plaster
it to his scalp, and fell in loops across a forehead beaded
with perspiration. His face was the colour and texture of
putty, bloodshot eyes rolling drunkenly. A half-empty glass
of Scotch was held in his hand at a precarious angle, and
he appeared to be muttering to himself. She turned to the
barman, flicking her head in McCord's direction. 'Has he
been here long?'

'*Long* time,' the barman said solemnly.

She took another stiff pull at the vodka, warmed up her

indignation, and headed across the bar to McCord's table. 'Mind if I join you?' she asked, and sat down without waiting for an answer.

His head jerked up from some alcoholic reverie and he looked at her, startled, and for a moment, she thought, almost scared. 'What d'you want?' he barked, screwing up his eyes and peering at her in the gloom of the bar. It was obvious he didn't recognise her.

'Margaret Campbell?' she said, trying to awaken some recollection in him. 'Dr Margaret Campbell? You ruined my welcome banquet, remember?' He glared at her. 'I just wanted to say, thanks a million.'

He curled a lip and drained his glass. 'Why don't you fuck off?' he slurred. And he got unsteadily to his feet and lurched out of the bar.

She sat for a moment in suspended animation. Handled that well, Margaret, she told herself, and then slumped back in her seat feeling suddenly very tired indeed. As she took the remaining few gulps of her vodka, she glanced at the English-language *China Daily* lying on the seat next to where McCord had been sitting. The headlines washed over her. Something about the House of Representatives approving the US President's decision to continue China's Most Favoured Nation trading status. An item about the completion of the laying of a three-thousand-kilometre fibre optic cable to Tibet. A piece about a 20 per cent increase in the export of rice from China to the rest of the world. None of it held her interest. To bed, she thought. To sleep, perchance to dream . . . She crossed to the bar to sign her bill.

When she got back to her room, Margaret kicked off her sandals and undressed quickly. She caught sight of herself in the mirror, white skin almost blue in the hard electric light. The frail, skinny girl that looked back at her was almost unrecognisable as herself. She was a hard-bitten, experienced forensic pathologist into her fourth decade. She'd been around, she'd seen a bit. And yet it was a child that stared at her out of the mirror. A child abused by life, hiding behind her job, her anger, whatever other barriers she could raise. But in her nakedness, in a strange hotel room on her own, thousands of miles from home, there were no barriers that could hide her from herself. She remembered why she had come here, and was engulfed by a huge wave of self-pity and loneliness. The air-conditioning raised goose bumps all over her skin. She dropped on to the bed, wrapping the sheets around her, curling up into the fetal position. The first teardrop splashed on the pillow, and she cried herself to sleep.

IV

Zhengyi Road was dark and deserted as Li wheeled his bicycle past the shuttered fruit-and-vegetable shop at the entrance to the apartment complex. The slightest breeze stirred the sticky humid night air and rattled the leaves overhead. Li nodded to the night sentry in the guard box as he passed. Row after row of twelve-storey apartment blocks rose up into the murky black sky. Beyond the glow of the streetlights there were no stars visible through the layers of dust and mist in the upper atmosphere.

Li parked and locked his bike and entered the block where he lived with his uncle – superior apartments, behind high Ministry walls, reserved for top Ministry officials and senior police officers. It was late and the elevator was turned off for the night. Li unlocked the stair gate and climbed the two flights to their apartment. There was still a singing in his ears from the music in the club and his hearing felt woolly and dull, but even as he opened the door, he could hear the deep rumble of Old Yifu's snoring coming from the further bedroom. He went first into the kitchen, where he took a bottle of chilled water from the refrigerator and drank deeply, washing away the bad taste of cigarettes and beer, and then into his bedroom, where he sat on the bed for fifteen minutes or more, thinking, about the day that had just passed, about the day that lay ahead. He was tired, but not remotely sleepy. There was an ache at the back of his head, and acid burned his stomach.

He tipped forward and slid open the top drawer of a darkwood utility dresser. Under an assortment of clean underwear, he found the collection of leather strapping he was looking for and pulled it out. He had never worn it beyond the first time he had tried it on. He had adjusted the buckles then so that it still fitted neatly to his shoulder, soft tan leather straps holding the holster firmly in place. It had been a gift from his lecturer in Chicago, a full-time cop, part-time lecturer, who had taken a shine to him and arranged for him to sit in the back of a squad car over several night shifts. It had been an extraordinary experience, frightening, sometimes bloody, often intimidating. It had opened his eyes to a crime culture and the means of combating it that was unknown in China. These cops were as hard and ruthless as the petty criminals, muggers and pimps, junkies and prostitutes they had to deal with. It was a world, Li reflected now, almost shocked by the thought, with which Margaret must be only too familiar. He wondered how it was possible to endure prolonged exposure to it without suffering lasting damage. He saw the soft, freckled skin of her forearm, the unfettered breasts pushing against the thin cotton of her tee-shirt, a recurring vision that somehow emphasised her soft, vulnerable femininity. How long could that survive in the dark, creepy-crawly world she inhabited beneath the rock of civilised Chicago society? How long before the shell she would make to protect herself from it enveloped her completely, making her, like the cops he had shared the night shift with, cynical and hard beyond redemption?

Quietly he slipped down the hall and carefully opened the door to Old Yifu's bedroom. The snoring rumbled on, undisturbed. It would take something approaching ten on the Richter scale to waken his uncle once asleep. Li looked at his face, lying at a slight angle on the pillow, mouth open, and felt a wave of love and affection for him. Those bushy eyebrows were still pushed up quizzically on his forehead. For all his experience of life, of tragedy and struggle, there was still an innocence about him, emphasised somehow by the repose of sleep. His face was remarkably unlined, almost childlike. And for a moment, Li had second thoughts. Then he steeled himself. Uncle Yifu would never know, and what he did not know could not hurt him. He crouched down and opened the bottom drawer of the dresser. At the right hand side, at the back, was the shoe box Old Yifu had kept there for years. Li lifted it out and took off the lid. Inside, on a bed of carefully arranged tissue, lay his old service revolver from Tibet and a box of cartridges. Somehow he had succeeded in hanging on to them over the years, and kept them now as a souvenir. He had only ever fired the revolver in practice, he told Li once, and had never ever pointed it at another human being. Whatever else he might have inherited from his uncle, Li knew that he did not possess his even temperament, his sense of compassion. There was anger and a latent violence in Li, which he strove always to control. But tomorrow, he knew, he was going to ease back a little on that control and take a short cut of which neither his uncle, nor the author-ities, would approve.

He lifted the revolver out of its box and slipped it into the holster. It fitted like a glove, almost as if the two had been designed one for the other. He counted out six rounds and dropped them in his pocket. Quietly, he replaced the lid of the box and returned it to its place at the back of the drawer and slid the drawer shut. As he stood up, his uncle turned over, and the snoring stopped. Li held his breath. But a deep grunt signalled its restart, and Old Yifu rumbled on in blissful ignorance of his nephew's presence. Li drifted silently out of the room, gently closing the door behind him.

CHAPTER FIVE

I

Wednesday Morning

At first it was just a distant glow. But as he drew nearer, he saw that the glow was flickering, flames licking upward in the dark. He continued to close in, peering through the heat, focusing on the dark mass at its centre. Suddenly a hand reached out towards him, shrivelled by the heat, claw-like and blackened, and the face moved out of the flames, mouth open in a silent scream, melting eyes appealing for help. And he realised, in a moment of supreme horror, that he was looking at himself.

He sat up with a start, blinking in the darkness, sweat gathered across his forehead, glistening on his chest, a trickle of it turning cold as it ran down to his belly. He was breathing hard. A red digital display on his bedside table showed 2 a.m. He lay back on the pillow and tried to excise the image from his mind. *Reaching out like he was asking for help*, the baby-sitter had said. But what strange distortions of his subconscious had turned the burning figure of his dream into himself? He forced himself to breathe more slowly and gradually felt the pace of his heart slow, too. He closed his eyes and consciously wiped his mind clean.

Li barely slept the rest of the night, drifting through a dreamlike semiconsciousness until his alarm went off at five, and he rose almost with a sense of relief. The sky was light, but the sun had not yet penetrated the early morning mist, and so it was grey and deliciously fresh as he cycled east then north through the city into Dongcheng District. It was too early for Mei Yuan, who was not at her usual corner at Dongzhimennei, and so he had no breakfast.

The first interviewees of the day were already gathering in the street outside the headquarters of Section One as officers on night shift drifted off to get something to eat before going home to bed, just as their families were getting out of theirs.

'Hey, Li Yan, you're looking very smart today,' an officer greeted him in the corridor. 'Going for an interview?'

Li was wearing a dark blue cotton suit, trousers gathered in fashionable pleats at the waist, a fresh white shirt open at the neck, and a pair of polished black shoes. He grinned. 'Just dressing up for the job.'

'Pity the Chief never thought of that,' the officer said, safe in the knowledge that Section Chief Chen had not yet arrived for work. Chen always wore a pair of baggy grey pants, shiny at the seat, a blue or light grey shirt, and a cream-coloured polyester jerkin that had seen better days. He had been described by one of his bosses early in his career as a sartorial disaster. But it had done him no harm whatsoever.

In his office, Li brewed himself a jar of green tea and sat at his desk to begin sifting through the files that had gathered on it during the night. The piles of transcriptions under the window had grown, and a selection had been pulled out by the lead detectives in each murder for his attention. He lit a cigarette and began the weary process of wading through the statements and testimony of drug dealers and small-time crooks, building workers from all over China, early morning habitués of Ritan Park. By seven o'clock he was on his third jar of green tea, his fifth cigarette, and was none the wiser. The air in his office was thick with smoke, the temperature rising as the sun sneaked in his window at an angle to lay long slabs of pale yellow light across the floor. The day shift detectives next door already had the business of the day well in hand. The third one to knock on his door with some fresh piece of information, and a comment on his suit, got his head bitten off, and Li had not been disturbed for the past half-hour. He liked this time in the early morning, to think, and consider, and sometimes reconsider his thoughts of the previous day. A fresh day often gave distance and perspective to events.

At seven he phoned the Centre of Material Evidence Determination to be told that his test results would be some hours yet.

At seven fifteen there was another knock at his door. Li raised his head, ready to bark at whoever had the audacity to disturb his thinking time. But he closed his mouth again before speaking when he saw that it was Section Chief Chen, carrying with him his habitual cloud of gloom. 'Morning, Li

Yan.' He stopped as he took in Li's suit and frowned. 'You haven't got an interview for another job already, have you?'

'No, Chief. Just thought I'd better tidy up my act, given my new position.'

Chen grunted, unimpressed. 'Anything overnight?' he asked.

Li shook his head. 'Nobody knows anything. Nobody saw anything. Nobody heard anything.' He shrugged. 'I'll let you know as soon as we get those results back from forensics.' Chen opened the door to go out. Li said, 'Oh, by the way . . .' Chen waited. 'I've reconsidered the university's offer to lend us the American pathologist.' He tried to make it sound as casual as possible.

'Oh, have you?' Chen said. He looked at Li thoughtfully. 'Have you been talking to Old Yifu about it, by any chance?'

'I . . . might have mentioned it.'

'Hmm-hmm. And he thought it was a good idea, did he?'

'He, ah . . . he did think her experience could be valuable.'

'Ye-es. It's a pity you're more inclined to listen to your uncle's advice than mine.'

Li was indignant. 'If it had been your advice, Chief, I wouldn't have ignored it.'

Chen grunted. He had allowed Li to have his way yesterday only to have that decision thrown back at him today by Old Yifu. It rankled. 'First we tell her we want her, then we tell her we don't. Then we tell her we've changed our minds and want her after all. She may very well not want to do it now.'

'We can live in hope,' Li muttered under his breath.

'What was that?'

'I said we can only hope she will,' Li said.

Chen grunted again and started out the door. Then stopped. He turned back. 'Almost forgot. Deputy Procurator General Zeng wants to see you.'

'Me?' Li was taken aback.

'Yes, you.'

'What about?'

'I've absolutely no idea. But when a high-ranking procurator says jump, you jump. Nine o'clock, at the Municipal Procuratorate.' And he was gone. But the door opened a second later and he poked his head back in. 'If I didn't know better, I'd suspect you already knew – all togged up like that.' He shut the door again.

Li sat wondering what a Deputy Procurator General could possibly want with him. Procurators were among the most powerful people in Chinese law enforcement. It was the People's Procuratorate who issued warrants for arrest at the request of the police. The Procuratorate also reviewed evidence collected by police and determined whether there was sufficient merit in pursuing a case through the courts. They would then fulfil the role of prosecutors. In particularly sensitive cases, regarding matters of state, corruption, fraud or police malpractice, the People's Procuratorate was empowered to pursue its own investigations. It was sufficiently unusual for a detective to be summoned to the presence of a Deputy Procurator General, outside the specifics of a case in hand, for Li to feel faintly uneasy about it.

*

Two uniformed officers, gun belts strapped around khaki-green shirts, stood to attention in the shade of large umbrellas on either side of the main entrance to the Municipal People's Procuratorate. Li parked his Jeep in the street and walked in through the gates with a sense of trepidation.

The Procuratorate was housed in a modern three-storey building backing on to the High Court, not far from the Municipal Police Headquarters in the old legation quarter. Windows up and down and along the length of the grey-brick building stood open, like so many mouths gasping for air. A detachment of the Armed Police responsible for guarding public buildings was exercising in a compound in front of a huge mural depicting a traditional scene of ancient rural China. Li walked briskly past in the rising heat of the morning and went inside, where he was asked to wait.

Although his appointment was at nine, it was nearly twenty past before a secretary came to fetch him, leading him upstairs and along corridors, through an outer office and eventually knocking on the imposing door of the office of Deputy Procurator General Zeng. 'Come,' Zeng called, and the secretary opened the door for Li to enter. Zeng rose from his desk, a tall, thin man with steel-grey hair swept straight back from a long face punctuated by round spectacles in metal frames. He was in shirtsleeves, with a jacket draped over the back of his seat. He held out a hand. 'Congratulations on your promotion, Deputy Section Chief Li.'

Li shook his hand. 'I am honoured to meet you, Deputy Procurator General Zeng.'

The formalities over, Zeng waved at a chair. 'Have a seat, Li.' He wandered round the desk and perched on a corner of it, one foot still on the floor. Li sat uncomfortably in a deep leather chair. A fan swinging lazily overhead blew hot air from one part of the office to another. 'Second day on the job, hmm?' Li nodded. 'An eventful first day.'

'It was.'

'Three murders in one night. More like New York than Beijing.' Li was uncertain how he was expected to respond, so he said nothing. Zeng stood up and walked to the window, lowering Venetian blinds to stop the sun from streaming in. 'That's better. Can't stand to have it too bright in here. Autumn's a better season in Beijing, don't you think? Not so hot, and the light has a softer quality about it.'

'Yes.'

'You're from Sichuan.' Again, Li was unsure if this was a statement or a question. 'A lovely province. Can't stand the food, though. Too hot for my taste. What do you say?'

This was a good question. Li hadn't a clue. 'I wouldn't know.'

'Wouldn't know what?'

'About your taste, Deputy Procurator General.'

'No, I meant your taste, Li. Do you like all that spicy food?'

'Very much.'

'Well, I suppose you grew up with it. Must be tough.'

Again, Li was lost. Zeng seemed to switch subject without any obvious rationale. It was almost as if he were trying to trip Li up. 'What must be tough?'

'Following in the footsteps of someone as famous in the

police department as your uncle was. Lot to live up to. Given you problems, has it?' He watched Li carefully.

'No, it hasn't. Following in my uncle's footsteps has been an honour and a privilege.' Li was deeply ill at ease. What *was* this all about?

Zeng moved back to his chair, leaning on one elbow and regarding Li speculatively. 'Can't say I approve particularly of using an American pathologist to perform autopsies on Beijing murder victims. Apart from anything else, she's not going to be around when we're prosecuting the case in court.'

So that's what this was about. It occurred to Li briefly to wonder how Zeng already knew that the Chao Heng case was a murder and not a suicide, but then it wasn't exactly a secret, and he was a Deputy Procurator General. 'Her expertise was invaluable in determining that what appeared to be a suicide was, in fact, murder. And since Professor Xie was the lead pathologist, he will be available to give evidence when, hopefully, we bring the case to court.' He saw that Zeng was about to pass some further comment, and added quickly, 'Of course, her offer of assistance was entirely unofficial, a personal favour to Section Chief Chen.'

'Yes, so I understand. I also understand that the Public Security University offered her services for the rest of the investigation – and that you turned them down.'

He *was* up to date, Li thought. 'That's correct,' he said.

'Good. I don't think it would have been politic to have some American thinking they can show us how it's done.'

'That's a pity.' Li was starting to find his feet. 'Because I changed my mind this morning and took them up on the offer after all.'

Zeng's face darkened. 'Why?'

'After discussing it with my uncle . . . I realised that to turn down the chance of such expert assistance simply because she was an American would have been small-minded and petty. At least, that was my uncle's view. But if you disagree . . .'

'Good God, who am I to take issue with *your* uncle?' Zeng was visibly annoyed. It was clearly on his mind to go further, but he thought better of it. He cast a more appraising look in Li's direction. 'I think, perhaps, I can see now why you haven't found it such a problem following in your uncle's footsteps.'

'They are big footsteps, Deputy Procurator General. I still have some way to go before I can fill them.'

Zeng rocked gently back and forth in his chair and stared thoughtfully at the ceiling. He pulled out a pack of cigarettes and lit up, without offering one to Li. Suddenly he leaned forward, elbows on the desk, a decision having been made. 'I'd like a daily written report from you on this case. Chao Heng was a very senior scientist and government adviser. We take his murder very seriously. I want you to write up the report yourself, every night, so that it is on my desk first thing every morning. Is that clear?' Li nodded. 'That'll be all.' Zeng drew a file towards him and opened it. Li realised he had just been dismissed.

II

It was as well, Bob thought, that this was a very long corridor. Otherwise, he was sure, Margaret would simply turn around when she reached the end of it and stride back along its length. She seemed to need to burn up her anger in long, quick strides, and he was having trouble keeping up with her.

'First they say they want my help. Then Mr Smartass Deputy Section Chief Li decides I'm *superfluous* to requirements. "Superfluous", no less!'

'I'm sure that's probably lost – or gained – something in the translation, Margaret. Li wouldn't mean it like that.'

'Oh, wouldn't he? Well, whatever he meant last night, he's changed his mind this morning. Maybe he woke up and realised what an inadequate he really was. Now, it seems, I'm not "superfluous" after all, and they'd be "very pleased" to accept my help. I mean, as if I was offering! *They* asked *me*, then told me I was *superfluous*. Talk about losing face! Jesus!'

'Superfluous' had been an unfortunate choice of word, Bob thought. Almost certainly a result of Veronica expanding the breadth of her vocabulary at the expense of its nuance. Tactless, at the very least. He must have a word with her about it. Unfortunately, where Margaret was concerned, the damage was already done. Clearly it had got right under her skin. 'What are you going to do?'

'I don't know. I know what I'd like to do. I'd like to tell them to stick it.'

'That would hardly help the cause of Sino-American relations.'

'Fuck Sino-American relations!'

'You know,' Bob said, starting to get breathless now, 'most pathologists in the US would give their right arm to be asked to assist in a murder investigation in Beijing.'

'For heaven's sake, Bob, whoever heard of a one-armed pathologist?'

'You know what I mean,' he said, irritated, and she flashed him a wicked half-smile, to his further irritation. 'The thing is, it's going to look pretty damned good on your résumé. Don't you think?'

She stopped suddenly, taking him by surprise, and he was a pace and a half beyond her before he could pull up. He wheeled round. 'For God's sake, Margaret!'

But her eyes were burning with some fresh inspiration. 'Well, if I do it,' she said, 'there'll be a price to be paid. I must have accumulated a little bit of *guanxi* in the bank by now, don't you think?'

III

For the last two hours Li had been locked in conference with the detectives working on the three murders. A pall of depression and cigarette smoke hung over the meeting. From all the interviews, statements, witness accounts, not a single shred of evidence had emerged to shed any light whatsoever on any of the murders. Detectives had been circulating in Ritan Park since six that morning, talking to everyone who came through the gates, trying to jog memories, elicit some – any – piece of information, no matter how small. Still nothing. They knew who all three victims were, but had established no motives for their killings, and no link between them, except for a very tenuous drugs connection between Chao Heng and Mao Mao. But, as yet, they had been unable to determine that the two men even knew one another.

Detective Wu suggested they pull in The Needle for questioning. He knew that Li was interested in The Needle and had asked for the file. But he was not expecting the laughter that came from around the table, and was embarrassed by it. 'What the hell's funny about that?' he demanded.

'The Needle's not going to tell us anything,' Detective Zhao said, indignation overcoming his group shyness. 'Because if he confessed to knowing anything about Chao Heng's habit or Mao Mao's drugs connection, he'd be implicating himself in the drugs scene.'

'And since *we've* been unable to do that in the last five years,' Detective Qian added, 'he's not likely to hand it to us on a plate now, is he?'

'Especially when we've got nothing on him,' said Zhao. 'No leverage.'

Wu looked at Li, chastened by the derision of his colleagues. Fighting to recover face, he said, 'I just thought, since the boss had asked for the file . . .' He waited for Li to bail him out.

'I agree with the consensus,' Li said. 'There would be little point in bringing The Needle here. But if Mohammed won't go to the mountain . . .' He smiled at the consternation around the table. Muslim mythology had not been on the school curriculum, and none of them had Old Yifu for an uncle. 'I understand he hangs out at the Hard Rock Café during the day, that it's his . . . unofficial office.'

'You're going to see him?' Qian asked, surprised.

Li nodded. 'If he could be persuaded to talk to us – off the record . . . it could save us a lot of time and effort.'

'Why would he talk to us off the record?' Wu asked.

'Because I ask him to,' Li said evenly.

And there was a silence around the table as each of them considered what exactly that might mean. They all knew there was a history between Li and The Needle. Li had managed to obtain a warrant for his arrest three years ago. And then the only witness in the case had turned his bicycle under the wheels of a No. 4 trolley bus on Wangfujing Street. It had been impossible to prove it was anything other than an accident, and The Needle had walked.

There had been a time when men like The Needle would have been 'persuaded' to confess to their crimes, and punished accordingly. But times had changed. Police practice, and the whole justice system, was under close scrutiny. And conventional means of applying social pressures on an individual, through his work unit, did not apply to entrepreneurs like The Needle, who would claim that his income came from the covered market stalls he ran in Liulichangxi Street.

The meeting ended in the same gloomy mood in which it had begun. Beyond continuing the interviews and taking statements from potential witnesses, no one had any fresh ideas. But as they drifted out of the meeting room, there was a buzz among the detectives, a sense of anticipation about Li's intention to beard The Needle in his own den.

IV

Li parked at the door of the Centre of Material Evidence Determination and went inside. In Professor Xie's outer office he found Lily Peng sitting with a face like sour cream, flipping agitatedly through a science magazine. 'Is Dr Campbell here?' he asked.

She flicked a thumb towards the autopsy suite. 'In there. For *hours*.'

'Not watching today?' he asked, with a flicker of a smile.

She glared at him. 'No room,' she said.

He frowned, puzzled. 'What do you mean?'

'See for yourself.' And she turned back to her magazine.

Li pushed through two sets of swing-doors into the autopsy suite, and found it crowded with fifteen students in green coats and face masks gathered round the gaping body of the itinerant worker from Shanghai. The chest cavity was still exposed, the scalp peeled down over the face, and the brain had been removed from the skull. Some of the faces of the students were the same colour as their coats. Two autopsy assistants were in the process of tidying up the corpse. Margaret was giving a running commentary.

'The organs from the bucket get put back into the chest

cavity . . . as you see. The breastplate is then reapproximated, and the assistants will sew up my incision with some coarse waxed twine. The skullcap gets replaced, the scalp pulled back into place and sewn closed as well. Then the body will be scrubbed, hosed off, blotted dry and put in a body-bag for return to the refrigerator. I don't know about here, but in the States a mortician would collect the body, pump it full of preservative, dress it up and apply facial make-up so that it can be displayed in the coffin for family and friends at the funeral.'

'In this case,' Professor Xie intervened, 'the body will be returned to the family in Shanghai and there will be a straight-forward cremation. Most people in China could not afford the services of a mortician.'

Margaret turned to the students. 'It's a great pity you weren't here yesterday for the autopsy we carried out on a burn victim. It was an extremely interesting case. Professor Xie employed a useful piece of technology called a cryostat to enable us to speed up our findings. Anyone know what a cryostat is?' No one did. 'Basically it's a refrigerator that allows us to freeze tissue samples for sectioning and microscopic examination almost immediately. It is more commonly used during surgical operations to allow surgeons to have on-the-spot diagnoses made before continuing with the operation.' She turned and indicated the samples she had cut from various organs. 'These samples will take six hours or more to prepare for microscopic examination, using the more traditional method of setting them in paraffin or wax. That allows them to be cut into ultra-thin, but permanent, sections. Using the cryostat the sections melt almost immediately and are corrupted by the process.'

She looked beyond the students and acknowledged Li for the first time. 'Ah. I see we've been joined by Deputy Section Chief Li. Nicely timed, Detective Li.' She turned to her students and told them, as if in confidence, 'He's a little squeamish about these things.'

There were a couple of giggles and a few smirks and Li, to his intense annoyance, felt his face reddening. She turned back to him. 'I took the opportunity of asking the professor if he would mind my class sitting in on this morning's second autopsy. Of course, he was entirely agreeable. I think it's very important that they gain this kind of experience during training, don't you?'

'Of course,' he said stiffly. 'And while demonstrating your skills to your students, did you happen to notice what the victim died of?'

There were some more stifled laughs among the students, and a collective intake of breath. Despite the fact that English was their second language, they had been aware immediately of the atmosphere between the pathologist and the policeman.

Margaret was quite unruffled. 'This victim died from a separation of the skull from the first vertebra of the neck. It's known as an Atlanto-occipital disarticulation. The first vertebra, the one on which the head rests, is called the atlas.' She smiled sweetly. 'Those anatomists were cute with names, don't you think?' This failed to raise a smile. She shrugged. 'Anyway, it is jointed in two places to the occipital bone at the base of the skull. When the separation of one from the other occurs, probably with a double "pop", much like the cracking of your knuckles, the spinal column is severed by the edge of the *foramen magnum* through which it passes into the skull. Death would have been instantaneous, a very rare thing. Most deaths – including our previous autopsy, the single knife strike to the heart – take a minute or two.' She removed the goggles which she had pushed high up on her head and pulled and stretched the elastic as she spoke. 'This particular injury is very common in automobile accidents, but a lack of any other major trauma in this case means he probably wasn't in a car at the time.'

Again she smiled, and again found that no one else shared her sense of humour. She sighed. 'From the absence of any finger bruising on the victim's neck or face, I would suggest that his assailant grasped the victim with the arms, one around the forehead, the other at the base of the back of the head, twisting while forcing upwards and forwards, causing the *foramen magnum* to slide across the top of the spinal column and sever the spinal cord. Such a clean and fatal break, in the absence of other major trauma, suggests to me a substantial degree of expertise.'

The imagery conjured up by Margaret's description left everyone in the room uneasy.

'In our previous autopsy . . .' She checked her watch. 'Goodness, how time flies when you're enjoying yourself.' The faces around the room stared back at her with a serious intensity. Didn't they realise, she wondered, that humour was the only thing that kept you sane in this job? 'In our previous autopsy, the victim was killed by a single stab wound to the heart. My guess would be that he was approached from the rear, held around the neck by an arm, and the knife driven inwards and upwards by the assailant with his free hand. The blade was about nine inches long. It entered at the base of the breastbone, severing parts of both the left and right ventricles. The direction from which the stab came is unreliable. So I can't tell you if the killer was left- or right-handed. That's just for the movies. But I can tell you that the delivery of a single, fatal wound of this nature would require considerable skill.'

She paused for effect. 'In my view these were execution-style killings, Detective, carried out by a very experienced professional.' Her words had a sobering effect on everyone in the room.

Li stood very still. *You're saying the killer was a professional?* he had said to Old Yifu. *Some Triad hit-man*, his uncle had responded. *These were no casual killings, Li Yan.*

'Can I ask a question?' Margaret said.

'Go ahead.'

'What makes you think the burn victim from yesterday and the two we've looked at today are linked?'

'Why do you think I do?'

'Because you wouldn't have asked me to perform these autopsies today if you hadn't thought they were connected.'

Li nodded. There was logic in that. The students waited with bated breath. He said, 'I don't think these are matters we should be discussing in front of your students.' And there was a collective groan.

'Perhaps not,' Margaret conceded. She turned to the disappointed students, who were just beginning to get involved. 'Leave your gowns and your masks with Professor Xie's assistants, and I'll see you in class in the morning.'

As the students filed out, Li and Margaret and Professor Xie moved away from the autopsy table. Li said, 'There was a single cigarette end found at each crime scene. The same brand.'

'One I might know?'

'Marlboro.'

'Oh, yes,' she said. 'Marlboro Country. Where the cowboys ride around with oxygen tanks on their backs to help them breathe.' She paused. 'You know, there seem to be a hell of a lot of people who smoke in this country. Don't you know it's bad for you?'

'The American tobacco companies must have forgotten to tell us that,' Li said.

'Well, they would, wouldn't they?' she said. 'I mean, it's a big market. If they flood China with cigarettes they'll put big bucks in the pockets of the shareholders back home. You know, the ones who gave up smoking years ago because it was damaging their health.'

Professor Xie asked, 'There was only a single cigarette end at each scene?' Li nodded.

Margaret snorted. 'And you think that it might be the same killer, smoking the same brand of cigarette, who smoked one at each crime scene and left the butt there for us to find?' She clearly thought this stretched the bounds of credibility. 'The same man who was so professionally meticulous in the execution of these crimes? You think he'd be careless enough to leave a cigarette end behind?' She shook her head. 'It seems pretty unlikely to me.'

Li shrugged. 'Perhaps so. But it does not change the fact that the cigarette ends were there.'

Margaret turned to Professor Xie. 'Do you have facilities for DNA testing here?'

'Of course.'

She looked at Li. 'Then, if there's any trace saliva on the cigarette butts, you can match the DNA, and tell immediately if they were smoked by the same man.'

Li said, 'I sent the cigarette ends for testing yesterday. We should have the results this afternoon.'

Margaret looked at him for a moment, then smiled wryly. 'Okay, so I think we're into grandmother and eggs territory here.' And she laughed at his look of complete incomprehension and shook her head. 'I'm sorry, forget it. I was being a smartass and you caught me.' An awkward silence descended on them. Margaret's smile faded. 'So . . . these cigarette butts are the only connection?'

'No,' Li said. 'There's the style of the murders. All professional – execution-style killings, as you call them. This is very unusual in China. There is also a drugs connection. As you know, Chao Heng was a heroin addict. The first of your autopsies today, the man known as Mao Mao, dealt drugs on the street.'

'He was also a user,' Professor Xie interrupted.

'Needle tracks on the left arm,' Margaret said.

'Anything else I should know?' Li asked.

Margaret shrugged. 'Nothing that'll make a difference. You'll get the report tomorrow when we've done the sections.' She looked to Professor Xie for confirmation. He nodded.

She started untying her gown. 'I'd better get washed and changed.'

'Excuse me,' Professor Xie said, and moved off to talk to his assistants.

Li said, 'I'm heading across town, following up on the drugs connection.' He hesitated, slight colour rising on his cheeks again. 'Perhaps you would like to come with me.'

Margaret was taken aback, and slightly suspicious. 'Why?'

'The man I am going to see is known to control the drugs traffic in Beijing. His nickname is The Needle.'

Margaret looked at him in astonishment. 'Well, if you know who he is, why's he not behind bars, or six foot under with a bullet in his head? That's how you do it here, isn't it?'

'If we have the evidence,' Li said, controlling his annoyance. 'Contrary to popular belief we don't shoot people just because we suspect they are guilty. But at least when they are convicted, a bullet in the head is better than ten years on Death Row, destroying their hope and their health before frying them in an electric chair anyway. That sounds like an Amnesty International definition of torture to me.'

'Lethal injection seems to be the current vogue,' Margaret said, neatly sidestepping a fight. She did not want to get involved in an argument about capital punishment. 'So I guess that means you don't have anything on this guy – The Needle.'

'No, we don't,' Li acknowledged.

'So what do you want me along for?' Margaret was desperate to go, but she wasn't going to let Li know that.

'I don't . . . particularly,' Li said casually. He didn't want to seem over-anxious to have her join him. But at the same time, he didn't want to put her off. 'I thought you might learn something.'

'Oh, did you?' She snapped off her outer gloves. 'Like how it can take two years to solve a murder?'

CHAPTER SIX

I

Wednesday Afternoon

Lily's anger at being told again that she was not required was palpable, and she watched with grim dislike as Li and Margaret pulled out of the university compound in Li's Jeep. She strutted off towards the administration block plotting her revenge.

Following their exchange in the autopsy room, Li had been cold and distant. Margaret wondered if this was a response to her jibe about taking two years to solve a murder, or whether it was a repeat performance of his mood swing of yesterday. Despite the fact that *he* had asked *her* along, she had the strong feeling that he resented her presence. They drove east in uncomfortable silence through the late morning traffic along West Xuanwumen Avenue, a huge loop of six-lane freeway that marked the outer boundary of the inner city. Bamboo scaffolding scaled concrete towers. High among the structures, tiny figures in blue, with yellow hard hats, moved easily around the skeleton blocks. Giant cranes swung back and forth overhead, like prehistoric monsters stalking a concrete landscape. Margaret's growing resentment at Li's silence finally found voice. 'Look, if you don't want me around, just say so. Stop the car now and I'll get a taxi back to the university.'

'What are you talking about?' He seemed perplexed, but made no move to pull over.

'I'm talking about you resenting every minute you have to spend in my company. This may be news to you, but it wasn't my idea to get involved in any of this. I didn't offer my help. You asked for it.'

'No.' He shook his head. 'My chief asked for it.'

'And don't you just hate the fact that your chief thought you could use the help of some foreigner.'

'I don't need your help.' He flashed an angry glance at her across the Jeep.

'No? And how long would it have taken you to identify Chao Heng without me?'

'We would have identified Chao Heng in time.' His voice was steady and controlled.

'Yeah, six weeks from now. And you'd probably still be looking at a suicide. Are you going to let me out or not?'

Li kept driving. 'You know, what I don't understand is why you ever came here in the first place.' He knew that some-where in this area she was vulnerable.

'That's none of your business!'

But he was not going to be deflected. 'I mean, when I went to the States I spent months reading up on it. Constitution, law enforcement, culture . . . Hah.' He laughed out loud. 'If it's possible to use the words *American* and *culture* in the same breath.' She glared at him. 'You decide to come to China, and what do you do? Nothing. You prepare nothing, you know nothing. About our law enforcement, our history, our culture. You're in the country five minutes and you're shouting the odds in the street about male attitudes to women drivers. You pick a fight in a restaurant and offend your hosts who've gone to great expense to welcome you.'

'Welcome me?' Margaret spluttered her indignation. 'From the moment I arrived in this goddamn country people have been telling me what not to do, what not to say, in case I stepped on your precious Chinese sensibilities. You know, you people ought to lighten up and join the rest of us in what will very shortly be the twenty-first century.' She immediately raised a hand. 'And don't tell me about your five-thousand-year history. I've already had that lecture. How you invented paper and the printing press.'

'And the crossbow, and the umbrella, and the seismograph, and the steam engine – about a thousand years before the Europeans thought of it,' Li said.

'Jesus,' Margaret gasped. 'Spare me. Please.'

But Li was on a roll. 'And what has America given the world? The hamburger and the hot dog?'

Margaret was stung. 'We invented the light bulb, the means of generating electricity on a commercial scale, the gramo-phone, the motion picture. We put the first men on the moon, invented the microchip, the personal computer, developed technologies that allow people to communicate around the world in nanoseconds, and send pictures from Mars with better definition than Chinese television. Jesus, everything you people did was in the past. All you can do is look back. We're doing it *now*.'

Li flushed with anger, his knuckles white on the steering wheel. 'Oh yes? And just what exactly is it you are *doing* now?' He raised a hand to stop her answering. 'No, no, let me tell you. You stomp around the world like overbearing school bullies, self-appointed world policemen telling the rest of us how to live and how to behave. And if we don't knuckle down and conform to your moral code, you're just as likely to give us a bloody nose. You preach about freedom and democracy, and practise racial and political discrimination.'

'That's rich, coming from someone with your country's human rights record!'

Li swung the Jeep hard left, honking his horn and driving like a man possessed. They swept past Mao's mausoleum on their left, and the great expanse of Tiananmen Square opened up before them, the orange-tiled roof of the Gate of Heavenly Peace shimmering in the hazy middle distance. 'Don't start,' he said. Hours of listening to his uncle debating world politics with his cronies had given him a good grasp of events over the past thirty years. 'You'll be telling me next how the United States had no part in supporting the murderous regime of the Shah of Iran, or in the downfall of the democratically elected president of Chile. That the United States was justified in dropping Agent Orange and napalm on innocent women and children in Vietnam, or in supporting tinpot dictators who were bleeding their people dry, because it suited US strategic policy.'

'What about the thousands of political prisoners held in Chinese jails without trial?'

'That's history. Myth.'

'Oh yes?' She waved her hand out of the window at the square. 'And I suppose it's a myth that your government sent armed soldiers and tanks into this very square to mow down hundreds of unarmed students engaged in peaceful demonstration. Or is that just "history" as well?'

'It's as much history as the National Guardsmen who gunned down protesting students on campus at Kent State University in Ohio, in '70. The only difference is one of scale.' He breathed deeply in frustration and banged his open hands down on top of the steering wheel. 'Dammit, I'm not trying to justify Tiananmen, but the Western view of it is a romantic fiction. Peace-loving students demonstrating for freedom and democracy? Hah! Your cameras never covered the gangs of armed youths roaming the suburbs, attacking and murdering soldiers and police who were under orders not to harm them, and then stealing their weapons. What would your government have done if it had seen its very existence threatened by a million ranting students in the streets of Washington demanding that the President and the Congress explain their policies to them in person, and then abusing and humiliating them on live TV? If gangs of thugs were beating police officers to death, and the seeds of insurrection were being sown throughout the fifty states, do you think they would just have stood by and done nothing?'

Beads of perspiration stood out on Li's forehead. His eyes burned with a curious fervour. 'It was a nightmare. I know, I was there.' And the bloody images swam before his eyes, like the tears he had spilled during those four fateful June days, for the dead, for his country, for the devastating, wasteful futility of it all. 'But I can look at China today,' he said, 'and I see people with money in their pockets, roofs over the heads, food in their bellies, education for their children, an economy growing at ten per cent a year. And I look at what is happening in the former Soviet Union, or in Yugoslavia, in the name of freedom, and democracy. I see economic ruin, people going hungry, children dying of disease; I see war and rising crime and death and destruction in the streets. I don't believe there are many Chinese who would swap what they have for that. You may not like communism, because you've been indoctrinated in the West by prejudice and preconception. But in China, for all its faults, it has brought stability and peace, and a population that is healthier, wealthier and better fed than at any time in its history.'

They had turned now into East Chang'an Avenue, Tiananmen Square receding behind them. Margaret glanced back, and tried to imagine the tanks rolling down the streets, the square jammed with a hundred thousand students. She recalled vividly the images that had flashed around the world of the student standing before a tank, refusing to let it past, and the tank driver's attempts to get around him without hurting him. What bitter tears must have been spilled with the blood. She had heard the passion in Li's voice, and understood perhaps for the first time the dreadful dichotomy inherent in those images. The wounds clearly still ran deep, and she wondered how it might have been if similar circumstances had presented themselves in the US. There had been rioting in the sixties and seventies over civil rights and Vietnam, divisions that had split the country down the middle. Only now, thirty years on, were some of those scars beginning to heal. Others were still raw.

She shook her head. 'This is stupid,' she said. 'We're doing what people do that makes them go to war – arguing over their differences. When it's our differences that make us . . .' She searched for the right words. '. . . human, unique.' He said nothing, and they drove in silence along the length of Jianguomennei Avenue past the CITIC building and the World Trade Centre and up the ramp on to the third ring road. Eventually she said, 'Where are we going?' She needed a response from him. Any kind of response, to anything.

He said, 'The Hard Rock Café.' But that was all. The atmosphere between them remained sour.

The Hard Rock Café was attached to the Beijing Landmark Towers off Dongsanhuanbei Road. A red soft-top Chevvy with fifties fins projected from a first-floor roof, for all the world as if it had fallen from the top of the adjacent fourteen-storey tower block and lodged there. A blue globe, with the Hard Rock Café logo, sat atop an elaborately roofed mock-Greek-pillared entrance. Out front, on the sidewalk, stood a ten-foot-high red Les Paul guitar. Margaret followed Li up black-and-red steps, scared to touch and smear the polished brass handrail supported on black-and-gold Les Pauls. They passed beneath a large five-point red star over the legend NO DRUGS AND NUCLEAR WEAPONS ALLOWED. They had not spoken for more than fifteen minutes.

Inside, the restaurant was doing brisk business. Staff wearing emerald shirts and black jeans were serving early lunches to Beijing's new young jet set and a scattering of curious tourists and foreign residents.

A pretty young waitress approached Li and they had a brief conversation. She nodded towards a stall in the far corner, and Li headed off towards it. Margaret followed, depressed and annoyed with him, and wondering why she was here. As they approached the stall, she saw that there were four young men seated in it. They were all immaculately and expensively dressed, with beautifully cut hair and manicured hands. They were unlike any other Chinese she had seen since she arrived. They reeked of wealth. A hush fell over their conversation as Li arrived at the table, and one of them aborted the call he'd been making on his cellphone. The man in the far right-hand corner smiled to show beautiful predatory teeth, and Margaret saw that he was not as young as he had first appeared. Mid-thirties, perhaps. His confidence, and the way the other three at the table deferred to him, immediately marked him out as the man Li had called The Needle. He might sell drugs, but he didn't look like a man who used them.

'Well, well,' he said, still smiling. 'If it isn't Mr Li Yan, our friendly neighbourhood cop. Heard you got yourself promoted, Mr Li. Congratulations.' He held out his hand, but Li ignored it.

'I want a word,' he said.

'Oh, do you?' The Needle glanced at Margaret. 'And who's this? Your girlfriend?'

'She's an American observer.'

'An observer?' He exaggerated a look of surprise. 'And what's she come to observe? How Beijing cops harass innocent citizens?'

'No,' Li said evenly. 'She's here to observe how innocent citizens are willing to co-operate with the police and spare them the trouble of getting a warrant.'

'She speak Chinese?' The Needle glanced at her suspiciously.

'No.'

'Hey, lady, you want to fuck?' The Needle directed this at Margaret in Chinese.

Margaret looked at Li, confused. 'Was he speaking to me?'

'Sure,' The Needle said in English. 'I just say, how you doing?'

'I need to talk for a few minutes,' Li said, ignoring this exchange.

'Talk, then.'

'In private.'

'Where?' The Needle grew cautious.

'In the Jeep. I'm just round the corner in the carpark.' The Needle hesitated. Li said, 'You've got nothing to hide, right? So you've got nothing to worry about. It's just a little information I need.'

The Needle was pensive for a moment, then wiped his mouth with his napkin and stood up. 'You've got ten minutes. I'm a busy man.'

His adjutant, on his left, moved quickly to let him out, and he followed Li and Margaret to the door.

'What's going on?' Margaret whispered to Li.

'We're just going to have a little chat,' Li said. But there was something in his tone that set Margaret's nerves on edge. And there was something cold and hard in his eyes that she hadn't seen there before.

The Jeep was in the carpark of the Landmark Towers Hotel. Li told Margaret to get in the back. The Needle got in the front passenger seat. Li started the engine. 'Hey!' The Needle barked, startled. 'You didn't say anything about going anywhere.'

'Just a short drive,' Li said, unperturbed. 'It'll give us a chance to talk.' But he said nothing as they drove south, and then west on Gongren Tiyuchang Road. The Needle grew increasingly uneasy.

'Where are we going?'

'Just somewhere quiet and discreet, so we won't be disturbed. I know how important your street cred is. You don't want to be seen hanging around with a cop, do you?'

'Stop, right now, and let me out!' The Needle was starting to panic. 'This isn't what I agreed to.'

Li turned south on Dongdoqiao Road. 'You're not making a very good show of co-operating with the police,' Li said. 'You don't want to give our American observer the wrong idea, do you?'

'Fuck your American observer! Let me out!' He tried to open the door but it was locked.

'What's going on?' Margaret asked from the back, becoming concerned.

'Oh, nothing much,' Li said. 'Just a routine breach of human rights.'

He turned the Jeep hard right, through open gates, and into a vast concourse, the giant circular Beijing Workers' Stadium looming ahead of them. Soldiers on exercise, dressed in green camouflage, were piling into covered lorries and sweeping through the concourse in a wide arc towards the gates as Li drove in. He steered a course between them and slid the Jeep to a stop outside one of the exit ramps from the stadium. He killed the engine, flicked off the central locking and turned to The Needle. 'Get out,' he said.

Through a crack in the vast doors that opened on to the stadium at the top of the ramp, there was a glimpse of green grass and concrete terrace. The Needle jumped out of the Jeep. 'What the hell are you up to, Li?'

Li rounded the bonnet and with one hand grabbed The Needle by his lapel. There was a sound of tearing cloth and stitching. Margaret was right behind them. 'What are you doing?' She was alarmed now.

Li dragged the unwilling Needle up the ramp behind him, the drug dealer's physical resistance feeble in the face of Li's size and strength. He searched around desperately for some sign of life – a face, a figure, a witness. But there was no one. No one but Margaret, chasing after them up the ramp, shouting at Li, demanding to know what the hell he thought he was up to.

Li ignored them both, pulling the door open a fraction and jerking The Needle through the gap. Margaret stood for a moment, panting, then squeezed through in their wake, in time to see Li push the other man down the slope, across the running track and on to the grass pitch. Terraces of empty seats rose up all around them. On days when China's national soccer team played here, it was filled with sixty thousand cheering, screaming fans. Now it was eerily quiet, the voices of the two men on the grass echoing around the acoustic bowl of the stadium. Margaret heard the creak of the door they had entered, and turned in time to see it shutting behind them. A sensation, like ice-cold fingers, touched the back of her neck. 'Li!' she screamed. But Li's attention was elsewhere. His left hand was holding The Needle by his shirt collar, twisting it, pushing it hard into his throat.

Gone was the cool confidence of this untouchable trafficker in drugs and misery. He seemed very small beside Li, childlike and whimpering. His feet almost left the ground. With his free hand, Li drew a large revolver from a shoulder holster beneath his jacket, and pushed the nozzle-end into The Needle's fore- head. His face was pale and grim, his eyes black. Margaret ran on to the grass. 'Stop this,' she said quietly. The Needle flicked a panicked glance in her direction. She might be an ally, the witness he needed to stop Li.

Li ignored her. 'I want you to tell me about Chao Heng and Mao Mao,' he said, his focus totally on The Needle.

For a moment, consternation replaced fear on the face of the drugs baron. 'What do you mean?'

'We both know,' Li said, 'that anything you tell me now is just between us. She doesn't speak Chinese, and I can't use information extracted at gunpoint against you. So do us both a favour and tell me what I want to know.'

'I don't know what you're talking about!'

Li sighed deeply. 'Okay, we'll do it the hard way.'

'What?' The Needle was panicking again. Li turned him round and forced him to his knees. 'What the hell do you think you're playing at? You won't get away with this!' The Needle tried to get up and Li pushed him back down. 'Help me!' The Needle screamed at Margaret in English.

She stood several feet away, breathing hard, eyes wild with fear and anger; fear of what was going to happen, anger that Li had dragged her here. 'I won't be any part of this,' she said.

'Don't be,' Li said.

She looked around. There didn't appear to be any way out, and the door they'd come in through was shut. 'If you harm that man I will give evidence against you.'

'Will you?' Li glanced at her. '*He* trades in misery and death. *He* has ruined thousands, maybe tens of thousands, of lives, and you would give evidence against *me*?'

'Why did you bring me here?'

He gazed at her steadily. 'To watch,' he said.

The Needle was sprawled on the grass now, trying to edge away as Li turned his attention back to him. 'Stay where you are,' he snapped. 'I'll give you a chance. Maybe several. But the odds'll get shorter.' He flipped the barrel out from the main body of the revolver and took out the bullets one by one, leaving only a single round. 'A game invented by our neighbours in Russia.' He snapped the barrel back in place.

'For God's sake!' Margaret said, and she walked away, out towards the centre of the pitch, her back turned towards them. She put her hands on her hips and stared up to the heavens. Physically, she knew, there was nothing she could do to stop it. But she was damned if she was going to watch.

The Needle followed her with his eyes, a sense of hopelessness growing like nausea in his belly. She wasn't going to do anything. Li hauled him back to his knees and placed the revolver at the base of his skull. The tip of it was cold and hard against his skin and pulled at his hair. 'Okay, so I'll ask you again,' Li said softly.

'I told you, I don't know what you're talking about.' The Needle had had a sudden revelation. Li wasn't going to pull that trigger. Not with the American there. It was obvious there was friction between them. Then he felt, more than heard, the squeezing of the trigger mechanism raising the hammer, and the smack of it against an empty chamber. He lost control of his bladder and felt a rush of hot urine on his thigh.

Margaret heard the sound of the hammer on the empty chamber echo around the terracing, and swivelled to stare at Li in disbelief. Somehow, somewhere deep inside, she hadn't believed he would actually do it. 'Jesus!' And she listened to her voice whispering round the stadium, as if it belonged to someone else.

'Tell me about Chao Heng,' Li insisted.

'I told you . . .' The Needle started to weep.

Crack! The hammer smacked down on another empty chamber.

'Li! For God's sake!' Margaret screamed at him.

'Tell me,' Li said, his voice tight and controlled. He blinked and flicked his head as a trickle of sweat ran into one eye.

The Needle felt the grate of the trigger mechanism again. 'Okay, okay, okay!' he screamed.

'I'm listening,' Li said.

'Chao Heng was well known,' The Needle gasped. 'He used to hang around the clubs downtown trying to pick up boys. The younger the better. Everyone knew what he was like.' The Needle was babbling like a baby now, words and all inhibition loosened, like the muscles of his bladder, by naked fear. 'I didn't know him personally, but I knew him by sight. He got his stuff off a guy called Liang Daozu.'

'One of your people?'

'I don't have any people,' he shouted, and felt the muzzle of the gun push harder into his neck. 'Okay, yeah, he was one of my guys.'

'What about Mao Mao?'

'What about him?'

'What was his connection with Chao Heng?'

'I've no idea.' Again the muzzle pushed hard into the base of his skull. 'For God's sake, I didn't even know they knew one another! Mao Mao was low life, street scum. He didn't move in the same circles as someone like Chao Heng.'

'Or you?'

'Or me. Shit, I don't trade stuff on the streets. Never have. That's for users and losers like Mao Mao.'

'Maybe Mao Mao was into little boys, like Chao?'

The Needle shook his head. 'Not that I knew of.'

Not that anyone else knew of either. Li had read the statements of Mao Mao's family and friends. He'd had a wife and a kid somewhere, and a string of mistresses. Li's adrenalin rush was slowly giving way to disappointment. He had The Needle on his knees in front of him, confessing to anything and everything. But not only would it be impossible to use any of it against him, none of it helped in the investigation. He pulled the trigger anyway. Crack!

The Needle yelped. 'Shit, man, what are you doing! I told you what you wanted to know.'

Li pushed him over on to his back, and The Needle lay staring up at him in disbelief, paralysed by fear. Li extended his arm downwards and pointed the revolver straight at the centre of The Needle's face.

'Li?' Margaret took a step towards him. She had thought it was over. The Needle had talked rapidly for nearly a minute, telling Li, it had seemed, what he wanted to know. Now Li was going to kill him in cold blood.

Li pulled the trigger once, twice, three times. The Needle screamed, a long scream of anguish, the pain of knowing he was going to die, almost worse than death itself.

Margaret's heart stood still. 'That's six,' she said.

The Needle looked up at Li in breathless disbelief. Li

extended his left hand towards Margaret and opened his fist. Six bullets nestled in his palm. 'The speed of the hand deceives the eye,' he said grimly.

Margaret closed her eyes. She wanted to strike him with her fists, with her feet, to bite him, inflict pain on him in any way she could. 'You bastard,' she said.

Li ignored her, holstering the gun and slipping the bullets into his pocket. He stooped and dragged the hapless Needle to his feet and pushed his face into his. 'Maybe you think you've lost a bit of face here today.' The Needle said nothing. 'I just hope the next time you go visiting a stadium, it's to get a bullet in your head for real. And with a bit of luck they'll blow your face clean off.' He let go of him, and The Needle dropped back to his knees. Li looked in disgust at the black urine patch on his trousers. 'I was going to give you a lift back, but I don't want you fouling up my Jeep. And maybe you'd rather change before you drop back in on the boys.'

The Needle stared up at him with hatred in his eyes and murder in his heart.

II

'Just take me straight back to the university.' Margaret sat tight-lipped and furious in the passenger seat.

'Sure.' Li nodded and they drove in silence for some way.

But she was unable to contain her anger for long. 'You had that all planned, didn't you?' He shrugged. 'And someone at the stadium knew we were coming.'

'I've got my contacts,' he said.

'It was moronic,' she said. 'Absolutely moronic. I've never seen anything like it.'

'Funny,' he said. 'I learned it from a couple of cops in Chicago. I think, maybe, they did it for my benefit. Back seat of the squad car, up a blind alley. A small-time pusher with dirt on someone higher up the chain. They sure as hell scared the kid. He told them everything they wanted to know.'

She flashed him a look that might have turned him to stone had he met her eye. 'That doesn't justify it. For them, or you.'

'At least I saved a dozen of my detectives maybe six weeks' work chasing a connection that doesn't exist.'

'How can you know that?'

'Because if there was a drugs connection between Chao Heng and Mao Mao, The Needle would have known about it. And, somehow, I believed him when he said he didn't.' He glanced over at her. 'I wouldn't spill any tears over The Needle. He'll get over it.'

'I don't give a shit about The Needle,' she said. 'It's what you put *me* through in that stadium. If I'd known there were no bullets . . .'

'You would have approved?'

'No, of course not.'

'Which is why I did not tell you. I was not sure I would even take you into the stadium.'

'Oh, I'm supposed to feel honoured now, am I? Jesus!' She slapped her palms on the dashboard. 'Why *did* you take me in?'

'You were so ready to believe in human rights violations in China, I thought maybe you should see some for yourself, first hand, as inspired by Americans.'

'Well, first off, let's not confuse human rights and civil rights. What you saw those cops in America do was a breach of that kid's civil rights. They also broke the law. And I can assure you it's not common practice.'

'Nor is it in China.'

'Oh yeah? Like there are no violations of civil or human rights in China?'

'Not on *my* watch.'

'Oh, so today was the first time you've ever done anything like this, right?'

'It was.'

'Sure.'

He turned to meet her disbelief face on. 'It was.' And the sincerity in his eyes disconcerted her. 'For myself, I would happily have killed that man. As a policeman, it is against everything I believe. My uncle would be ashamed of me. He would tell me that the measure of any civilisation is the strength and balance of its system of justice. And he would be right. And he would not listen when I told him that I had a feeling, an instinct, that we could not afford to spend weeks, months, maybe years finding this killer. He would tell me that I should employ good police work to back up that instinct.'

In spite of herself, she was interested. 'What instinct?'

'If I knew what it was, maybe today would never have been necessary. There is something . . . bizarre about these killings.

Something in what we already know that I am missing. Something that troubles my unconscious mind, but that my conscious mind has not grasped. So I have taken a short cut that I should not have taken, because somehow I know there is no time.'

'You think he's going to kill again?'

He shrugged. 'I don't know.' They had stopped at traffic lights, and he turned and examined her face, and thought he saw the shadow of doubt in it. 'Have you never had an instinct about something? Something you can't explain, you just feel?'

There was a catch in her throat, and she didn't dare to speak, as she remembered how she had fought her instincts, committing to an act of faith in Michael that went beyond all reasonable expectation. She found it hard, now, to understand why. She should have known better. She dragged her eyes away from Li's and nodded. 'Yes,' she said finally. 'And I didn't follow it.' Her hands were clasped in her lap, and Li saw her knuckles go white. 'And I should have.'

They drove past the top of Wangfujing Street and into Wusi Street, which took them into Jingshanquan Street and past the rear gate of the Forbidden City. The car in front of them braked suddenly to avoid a child on the road, careening sideways into a trolley bus amidst a shower of sparks, before spinning across two lanes of oncoming traffic and ploughing into the cycle lane. Vehicles travelling nose to tail slithered into one another, locking fenders. All traffic ground to a halt, horns blaring, a trail of devastation across the road. The child who had caused the accident ran away, unharmed, down the far sidewalk. Several cyclists picked themselves off the dusty street, and started examining buckled wheels and twisted frames, shouting oaths at drivers, remonstrating with one another. Some were bleeding from grazes on arms and foreheads, others had torn trousers at the knee and shirts at the elbow. Above the noise of horns and raised voices and revving engines was a woman's single, repeating scream.

Li had swung the Jeep side-on across the middle of the road and planted a flashing red lamp on the roof, and was now making an urgent call on the police radio. Margaret was shaken, but unhurt. She could hear the woman screaming, but couldn't see her. She got out of the Jeep and started running between the vehicles and the people standing arguing in the road. There was a crowd gathering around the car that had slewed across the street in the first place. It had half mounted the sidewalk and buried its nose in the trunk of a locust tree. The dazed driver was staggering from the vehicle. Margaret grabbed him and looked at the wound on his forehead. He would live. The woman was still screaming, a babble of hysterical voices rising from the crowd around the front of the car. As she rounded the bonnet, Margaret saw the buckled remains of a bicycle under the front wheel and a woman trapped beneath the bicycle, gouts of blood spouting from a wound high on her left leg. She was screaming more in fear than pain as she saw the life flooding out of her. Li appeared at Margaret's shoulder. 'She's going to die if we don't stop that bleeding fast,' Margaret said. 'We've got to get her out of there.'

Li's voice boomed out above the racket, insistent, commanding, and seven or eight men immediately detached themselves from the crowd. Li waved them to either side of the vehicle and they all found what handholds they could. As they lifted, there was a groan of metal, and a jet of steam escaped from the broken radiator. Margaret grabbed the woman under each armpit and pulled. She was aware of others beside her. The bicycle was torn away. The woman was drawn free. The intensity of her screams was fading along with her life. There was blood everywhere, still pumping from her leg as her heart fought vainly against the rapid drain of the wound.

Li said, 'Emergency services are on their way.'

'No time!' Margaret shouted. 'Hold her down.' And to Li's and everyone else's amazement, this fair-haired, blue-eyed *yangguizi* kicked off her trainers and stood on top of the injured woman's thigh, pressing her full body weight down on to the wound. She grabbed one of the men who had lifted the car, and held him for balance. He froze, like a rabbit caught in headlights. The woman lurched and screamed, and tried to buck Margaret off. 'For Christ's sake hold her still,' Margaret said. 'Her femoral artery's been severed. This is the only way I can get enough pressure on it to stop the bleeding.'

Li sat in the road by the woman's head, gently taking her flailing arms and folding them in, raising her head on to his lap, restraining her fight and her fear, talking rapidly, gently, reassuringly. Her resistance subsided and she relaxed and started weeping. There were several hundred people in the street now, pressing around them in silent amazement.

Margaret looked down at the blood oozing slowly through her toes. She had staunched the bleeding for the moment, but the woman had lost a great deal of blood. She was in her mid-forties, stockily built, with the flattened features of a peasant Chinese. Her blue print dress was soaked in red. The ribbon that tied her hair back had come free, and long black strands of it sprayed out across Li's legs. She gazed up at him as he continued softly speaking, stroking her face. Margaret had no idea what he was saying, but she found it almost impossible to equate this gentle, genuinely caring man with the cold, ruthless individual she had witnessed in the stadium just fifteen minutes earlier.

In the distance they heard the sound of sirens. Minutes later paramedics were pushing their way through the crowd with stretchers, and Margaret was relieved of the burden of standing on the wound. The injured woman held Li's hand all the way to the ambulance. He returned to find Margaret retrieving her shoes, still an object of intense curiosity for the crowd. They were dispersing reluctantly on the orders of uniformed traffic cops who were trying to clear the road. Li's hand slipped gently round Margaret's upper arm and he led her back to the Jeep, her bare feet leaving a trail of bloody footprints in their wake. There was blood drying on her hands, on her tee-shirt, on the bottoms of her jeans. 'I'm going to need to change,' she said.

'I'll take you back to your hotel.' Li started the Jeep, turned it around and headed back for the previous junction before swinging north.

III

'I'll wait for you here.' Li had parked in the forecourt at the foot of the steps to the main entrance.

'Don't be silly. Come up. You need to wash. You've got blood on your hands and your face.' She jumped out of the Jeep, forgetting, as it was so easy to do, that they had been cocooned in air-conditioned unreality. The heat bounced back at her from the white concrete, dusty and hot, almost violent in its intensity, and she felt her knees weaken.

Li looked and saw the crusty rust colour of dried blood on his hands, aware of it for the first time. In the rear-view mirror he saw a smear of it on his cheek. He could see the dark stains of it on his trousers and jacket, and vivid spatters on the white of his shirt. He got reluctantly out of the Jeep and followed Margaret up the steps, passing between pillars the same colour as the blood on his hands, and into the chilled atmosphere of the lobby. On the third floor, the attendants regarded them with amazement, watching open-mouthed as they walked the length of the corridor.

Her room was soft and luxurious, palely seductive, slashed by the blood-red silk of the headboard on her bed. He never ceased to be astonished by the degree of luxury demanded by foreigners. And yet it was without character or personality, like any hotel room in any city around the world.

She threw her bag on the bed. 'I'll take a quick shower and change, then you can get in and wash.' She grabbed the remote control for the television and switched it on. 'To stop you from getting bored.' She smiled. It was tuned to CNN, a news report about freak flooding in northern California. He heard the rush of water in the shower and wandered to the dressing table. There were make-up items and creams, a map and a guidebook. He picked up and flipped through a small red Chinese phrase book, stopping at random. A page on dealing with money. *I'm completely broke. Can I use this credit card?* He shook his head in wonder at the things foreigners thought important. Another page on 'entertainment'. *Do you want to come out with me tonight? Which is the best disco round here?* Li smiled. Somehow he didn't think that either phrase would trip off Margaret's tongue.

He lifted a hairbrush and teased some of the shiny golden hair free of its bristles. It was very soft and fine. He put it to his nose and smelled her scent. On an impulse he could not have explained if asked to, he wound the hair around his index finger to make a curl of it, and slipped it carefully into his breast pocket between the pages of a small notebook.

The rush of the shower stopped abruptly, and the bathroom door creaked slightly ajar. In the mirror above the dresser he could see, reflected through the crack in the door, the pale lemon of a towel draped across the shower screen. Suddenly it slid from view, and he saw Margaret's naked form, still standing in the bath, legs apart, body glistening in the light; slim and white and tempting. Her breasts were firm and erect, juddering as she briskly towelled herself down. He glanced quickly away, reddening with shame, feeling guilt for having looked. But in a moment, his eyes were drawn back, and he saw her step out of the bath, water still clinging in droplets to the pale triangle of curled pubic hair between her legs. She swivelled on the ball of one foot and he caught a glimpse of the pink half-peach rounds of her buttocks and the firm muscle that tapered in from the tops of her thighs. He followed the arch of her back up to beautifully squared shoulders and saw that her head was turned, and that she was watching his reflection watching hers.

He dropped his eyes immediately, crushingly embarrassed, like a small boy caught peeking at his sister undressing. His heart was hammering against his ribs and his hands were shaking. What could he say to her? How could he apologise? He glanced up and saw that she had moved out of his line of vision. But she had not closed the door. And it occurred to him that she had enjoyed him watching her. That she had known he could see her all along, perhaps wanted him to. He moved away to the window and tried to analyse his feelings towards her. They were completely ambiguous. She was irritating, arrogant . . . and unaccountably attractive. She both angered and challenged him. There were times when he had wanted to slap her face, and others when he had wanted to touch her and feel the softness of her porcelain-white skin, run his hands through her hair, feel her lips push against his. But more than anything, he was drawn by the provocation in those pale blue eyes, challenging him to a battle of intellect, of culture, of race. He decided to say nothing, behave as if he had never seen her, nor she him.

When she stepped out of the bathroom she was wearing a

pale yellow sleeveless cotton dress, cut square across the neck and flaring out from a narrow waist to a line just above her knees. On her feet she wore cream open-toed sandals with a small heel that served to emphasise the gentle curve of her calf. Her skin glowed pink, and her freckles seemed darker somehow, more prominent. She was towel-drying her hair, head cocked at an angle so that it hung down in wet strands. In that moment, without a trace of make-up, her hair still wet from the shower, the simplicity of the pale lemon dress, he thought she looked quite beautiful. His throat was thick, and he could think of nothing to say.

'All yours,' she said, nodding towards the bathroom as if nothing had happened. 'What are you going to do about your clothes?'

'I'll have to stop by the apartment and change.' He brushed past her, smelling her perfume, and went in to wash his hands and face.

On the drive to his apartment he asked if she had a class that afternoon.

'No,' she said, 'just prep for tomorrow. Although I don't even need that. It's a lecture I've done dozens of times.' She hesitated. 'Why?'

He seemed embarrassed. 'I thought, perhaps, you might want to come back to the office. The results of the DNA tests on the cigarette ends should be in. And a spectral analysis of blood found on the carpet in Chao Heng's apartment yesterday.'

'*His* blood?' she asked, curiosity aroused.

'That's what we'll find out,' he said.

She was silent for a moment, thoughtful, then said, 'Yes. I'd like that.' She paused. 'Tell me about the blood in the apartment.'

And so he told her. About the CD on pause, the empty bottle on the table on the balcony, the cigarette ends in the ashtray, the lamp missing from the light over the front door. He painted for her his picture of what he believed happened that night: Chao Heng forced back to his apartment at gunpoint then knocked on the head and sedated; the patch of blood left on the carpet which, he felt sure, would be Chao's, and which spectral analysis would show to be around twelve to fourteen hours old; the killer carrying the prostrate body of the agricultural adviser down the staircase, locking the stair gate behind them; the drive to the park, the long wait among the trees, and then the immolation and the killer's escape to anonymity seconds before the blazing body was found.

She sat listening in silence. 'I hadn't thought through the planning that must have gone into it. Not in that kind of detail. In my job you are so preoccupied with the details of death that you don't think much about motivation, or premeditation.' She fell silent again, thinking about it some more. 'It's extraordinary, when you examine it. Why would somebody go to such lengths? I mean, it wasn't even as though it was a particularly convincing suicide.' She turned it over again in her mind. 'Are you sure these three killings are connected?'

'No, I am not sure.'

'I mean, they were all professionally executed, but the other two were simple, uncomplicated, almost casual. Chao Heng's killing was . . . bizarre and ritualistic and, if you are right in your assumptions, minutely plotted and planned.' She turned to look at him. 'You've eliminated a drugs connection, right?' He nodded. 'So all that's left to connect them are the cigarette ends.' He nodded again. 'And, God knows, that's pretty damned weird.' She frowned. 'Something not right. Something *really* not right.' And for a fleeting moment she understood his obsession, was touched by a feeling both ephemeral and elusive, which he might have called instinct. A feeling that left her uneasy and uncertain, but intrigued. 'Tell me about Chao Heng.'

As he drove along Chang'an Avenue, he recapped for her the details from the file he had been given on Chao Heng. 'Retired due to ill health?' she mused. 'What was wrong with him?'

'I've no idea. His bathroom cabinet was full of medicines.' He turned into Zhengyi Road and parked in the street outside the police apartments. 'I'll be five minutes,' he said.

She watched him go, noticing for the first time how narrow his hips were in contrast to his broad shoulders, the pleasing square set of his head. She knew he was fit from the way he moved, muscles toned and taut. A man's body was usually the last thing she found attractive. Normally it was the eyes that would first appeal. Windows on the soul. You could tell so much about someone's personality from the eyes; their humour, warmth, or the lack of either. She liked a man to be cerebral, to have a sense of humour. Masculinity was important, but 'macho' was a turn-off. Li was moody and defensive and prickly, but there was something in his eyes that told her she would like him if only she could get near him. There was no doubting his masculinity, but he had a sensitive – perhaps over-sensitive – quality, betrayed by the ease with which he blushed. No doubt it embarrassed him, but she found it endearing. His guilt, when she had caught him looking at her reflection in the mirror, had been amusing. But for a long moment it had been more, a strange feeling of desire flipping over in her stomach. That feeling returned now, and she felt herself grow hot and flushed. She drew a deep breath and closed her eyes. This was not going to happen. She had not escaped from Chicago, from the person she had been, the life she had left in ruins, just to fall for some damned Chinese policeman with a chip on his shoulder and a severe case of xenophobia.

She forced herself to focus on the murders, recreating in her mind the picture of Chao's apartment that Li had painted for her. If Chao was the key to the three murders, then there must be clues in his life and lifestyle, in his work, his apartment. But her thoughts were interrupted by the opening of the driver's door. Li was wearing a fresh white short-sleeved shirt open at the neck, and neatly pressed black trousers over gleaming brown shoes. 'Very smart,' she said. 'Who does your ironing for you? Your uncle?'

'I do it myself,' he said, and blushed, covering his embarrassment by making a meal of pulling on his seat belt and starting the engine. Margaret looked at him with mixed feelings. In the last couple of hours he had taken her through the entire emotional spectrum, from anger verging on hatred to stirrings of lust and affection. He was an infuriating man.

IV

The headquarters of Section One were still besieged by people who had been summoned to make statements. The offices and hallways of the building were baking in the afternoon heat. Corridors were lined with people on chairs, or squatting with their backs to the wall. Cigarette smoke hung heavy in the still air, in long horizontal strands, like mist. Officers and interviewees alike were crotchety and tired. Even the cheap standard-issue stationery slipped into typewriters by secretaries had gone limp. The temperature rose as Li and Margaret climbed the stairs to the top floor, and by the time they had reached the detectives' office Li's shirt was sticking to him in a tapering line down his back, turned sheer by perspiration. Margaret could see clearly the sculptured lines of muscle interwoven across his shoulders and upper back. She knew the names of every one, memorised during hours spent studying for anatomy exams: *trapezius*, *hood*, *latissimus dorsi*, *erector spinae*. She knew the way they were layered and overlapped, and what they looked like beneath the skin. She had never regarded them as anything other than anatomical. Until now. There was something animal, sexual and attractive, about the way they pressed against the wet, semi-transparent cotton of Li's shirt. She cursed herself under her breath. What in God's name was happening to her? She forced her eyes away.

Li's heart sank as he turned into the detectives' room and saw heads lift and faces light in expectation. The door to his office stood ajar, and beyond it the room seemed to glow, as if filled with sunlight, and yet his windows, he knew, faced north-east and only caught the sun obliquely in the early morning. Necks craned to catch his expression as he pushed the door open. His office was unrecognisable. All the furniture had been moved. A large fish tank filled with golden carp stood on a table in one corner. Flowers bloomed in pots all along the windowsill. A small tree in a porcelain pot spread large fleshy leaves into the office from another corner. His desk now faced the door, side-on to the window on its left. The filing cabinet that had stood behind the door had been moved to the far corner. The floor was covered with paint-spattered blankets, and a painter in overalls stood on a stepladder spreading bright yellow paint over cream walls that had gone grey with age and smoke. The previously jammed window stood wide open – no doubt, Li thought furiously, to let the paint fumes escape.

The *feng shui* man from the previous day was sitting cross-legged again among the files on Li's desk, examining a large sheet of paper held open in front of him. He looked up at Li and smiled. '*Much* better. You like it?' He held out the sheet of paper. 'My plan. Ve-ery good *feng shui*.' He smiled at the walls. 'Yellow. The colour of the sun. The colour of life. This will uplift your spirit and stimulate your *ch'i*. You feel good, you work better.' He grinned, revealing his bad teeth. 'Your men are very good. They move furniture ve-ery quickly.'

Li was incredulous. 'You used my detectives to move the furniture?' Behind him, he heard the unrestrained mirth of his detectives. He looked at the fish tank, and the array of plants. 'Who's paying for all this?'

'Your uncle tells me, spare no expense. I think he is very fond of you.'

Li grew hot with anger. He looked at the painter, who was listening in with interest. 'You,' he said. 'Out.'

'But I haven't finished yet,' the painter protested.

'I don't care. Get your blankets off my floor, take your paint and your ladders, and go. This is a working office, and I am in the middle of a murder investigation.'

'But once it's dried, I'll never be able to match the joins.' The painter saw Li's eyes widen with fury. 'Okay, okay. I'm out of here.' He scrambled down the ladder and began clearing his stuff.

Li took the old man by the arm and invited him to get down off his desk. 'Tell my uncle thank you very much,' he said, struggling to keep his anger under control. 'But I have to work now, so you'll have to go.'

'I'll send the painter back on the weekend,' said the *feng shui* man.

Li drew breath sharply and clenched his fists at his side. 'Just go.'

'Okay,' the *feng shui* man said. He looked around the office, and nodded, satisfied. 'You feel mu-uch better now.'

And the crowd of detectives at the door parted, like the Red Sea, to let him through. Margaret stood smiling just inside the office. She might not have understood a single word, but she knew exactly what had transpired. The painter rattled his ladders, lifted his paint pot, and hurried out after the *feng shui* man. Li glared at the faces gathered round the door. 'What are you lot looking at?'

Wu said, 'Nothing, boss.' He cast an appraising eye around the room, nodding his approval. 'Bi-ig improvement.' There was a splutter of laughter among the others.

'Get out,' Li said, shaking his head and restraining a smile, able finally, if reluctantly, to see a funny side to it. He called after them, 'And if I get any more crap from you guys, I'm going to give that *feng shui* man every one of your addresses.' He pushed the door shut.

Margaret said, 'It *is* much better like this. Or, at least, it would have been if you'd let him finish painting the walls.'

'Don't *you* start.' He looked at the piles of transcripts under the window. They seemed to have doubled in size since the morning. His desk was covered again with folders and papers. 'Would you look at this stuff. I'm going to go blind with paper-work before we're through with this investigation.' There was a knock at the door. 'What!' he shouted.

Qian poked his head in apologetically. 'Sorry, boss. Thought you'd like to see the preliminary reports from forensics. They came in by fax about an hour ago.'

Li grabbed the sheets and ran his eyes over the fax-fuzzy rows of tiny Chinese characters that delivered verdicts on the

DNA tests and the spectral analysis of the blood from Chao's apartment. He looked up at Margaret. 'It *was* Chao's blood on the carpet. And as near as they can determine, it was spilled some time Monday night into Tuesday morning.'

'Which bears out your theory,' she said.

He nodded, and paused to re-examine the fax. Then he met her eye, and there was a muted excitement in his voice. 'The DNA from saliva traces on all three cigarette ends matches.'

'Jesus,' Margaret said. 'So they *were* all murdered by the same guy.'

She sat at his desk, swivelling the chair slowly from side to side. The detectives' office outside was empty. They were all in the meeting room with Li, reviewing progress. She looked at the ragged line on the wall where the fresh yellow paint stopped and the old paint began, and she smiled. His Uncle Yifu was certainly nothing if not persistent. She wondered if he had any idea how much it embarrassed Li, and from all that she knew of him concluded that he probably did. Her eyes fell on the faxes that still lay on Li's desk, and she marvelled at how it was possible for people to read these strange and complex pictograms. She had read somewhere that although different languages were spoken throughout China, the written language, the characters, remained the same. They just had different words for the same pictures. Of course, standard Beijing Mandarin was now taught in all the schools.

From somewhere deep in the building she could hear the

distant sounds of phones ringing, voices raised, the chatter of keyboards. She closed her eyes and started tumbling backward through a dark abyss.

She opened her eyes immediately, or so she thought. She had not realised how tired she was. Her brain was still not keyed to Beijing time. She looked at her watch and realised with a shock that she had just lost twenty minutes. She blinked and tried to make her mind focus on something. The cigarette ends. There was a pack of cigarettes lying on the desk. She picked it up and took one out. The tobacco had a strong, bitter, toasty smell. It made her think of coffee stewing on a hot plate. She examined the pale pattern on the cork-coloured tip, the brand name red on white just above it. A single cigarette end at each crime scene. Smoked by the same man. What was it that was so wrong about that? She knew, of course. No professional would be so careless. And yet they were professional killings. And then suddenly she had a revelation, and sat forward in the chair, heart pounding. It had only been obscure because it was so obvious.

The sound of voices came through from the outer office as the detectives returned from their meeting. Li appeared in the doorway.

'I've just had a revelation,' she said.

'You hungry?' he asked, as if he hadn't heard

She hadn't thought about it, but now that she did she realised that her stomach was growling. 'Sure. Listen, this is important.'

'Good. I haven't eaten all day. We'll get something at the

stall on the corner, and then I'm going to the Ministry of Agriculture. If you want to come . . .'

'Try keeping me away.' She stood up. 'Li Yan . . . Are you going to hear me out or what?'

He held the door open for her. 'Tell me on the way.' But, as he turned, the chain on his fob watch caught on the handle and broke. 'Damn!'

She looked at the chain. 'It's just a broken link. It's fixable.'

'Later.' He slipped it off his belt and dropped it into the top drawer of his desk. He saw she was wearing a wristwatch and tapped his own wrist. 'You can keep me right.'

By the time they were out in the corridor she was having trouble keeping up with him. He seemed infused with a fresh energy and new determination. 'I just put a stop to wasting any further time on trying to make some futile drugs connection. At least it'll cut down on the paperwork.'

'Li Yan . . . The cigarette ends . . .'

'What about them?'

They were on the stairs now. 'I think I know why he left one at each crime scene.'

Li stopped. 'Why?'

'Because he *wanted* you to find them. He *wanted* you to make the connection.'

'Why?' Li asked again.

'I don't know. If we knew that we wouldn't be here. But it makes a hell of a lot more sense than believing that someone so careful and meticulous in every other respect would be so careless in that one.'

Li stood and thought about it. He was on the step below her, and she became aware that her eyes and his were on a level. But he wasn't looking at her. He was staring off into the middle distance, lost in contemplation. It gave her an opportunity to look at him close up. The features she had first taken as ugly she saw now as strong. A forceful nose, a well-defined mouth, prominent brows, beautiful, almond-shaped eyes, a brown so deep and warm it was hard to distinguish the iris from the pupil. He had a strong jaw, dimpled at the chin, and his flat-top crew cut emphasised the squareness of his head. His skin was the colour of pale teak, and was remarkably unlined, except for the traces of laughter around his eyes and mouth.

He became aware of her looking at him, and for a moment they stood staring into each other's eyes. And then he was overcome by embarrassment.

'It's an interesting thought,' he said, almost dismissively. 'But it doesn't take us any further.' He turned and resumed his progress down the stairs.

She chased after him. 'Yes it does. If he wanted you to make the connection, it means he had a motive for doing so.'

'Of course,' Li said. 'But it doesn't help us know what that motive is. We need more information.'

Margaret tutted her irritation. 'Well, thanks for the thought, Margaret, it was really helpful.'

Her sarcastic edge and serrated tongue were becoming familiar to him. He decided to play dumb. 'It was,' he said, as if blissfully unaware of her tone. He smiled to himself as he heard her gasp of exasperation. Perhaps he was finally beginning to get her measure.

Mei Yuan sat on a stool by her *jian bing* 'house' on the corner of Dongzhimennei. Business was slow, but she was not unhappy. It gave her time to read. She had almost finished her copy of *Meditations*, and it was from some cold imagined Dutch medieval landscape that she had to drag herself as a dark blue Beijing Jeep pulled up at the kerb and a pale, blonde Western woman in a lemon dress got out of the passenger side. Then she saw Li coming round the bonnet, and her face broke into a smile. 'Hey, Li Yan, have you eaten?'

'Yes, I have eaten, Mei Yuan. But I am hungry.'

'Good. I will make you a *jian bing*.' She lit the gas under her hot plate and looked at Margaret. 'Two?'

'Two,' said Li. And in English, 'Mei Yuan, this is Dr Margaret Campbell, a forensic pathologist from the United States.'

'Ah.' Mei Yuan held out a plump hand. 'Are you here on holiday or on business?'

Margaret was taken aback by the perfect English that rolled fluently off the tongue of what she had taken to be a peasant street vendor. 'I'm lecturing at the People's University of Public Security,' she said.

'And are you a practising pathologist, or an academic?'

Again Margaret was startled. 'Practising,' she said. 'I only lecture part-time.' And then, 'You speak excellent English.'

'Thank you,' Mei Yuan said. 'I get very little chance to practise it nowadays. So I am what you would call a little rusty.'

'No, not at all.' Margaret glanced at Li for illumination.

'Mei Yuan was a graduate of art and literature at Beijing University in the late fifties,' he said.

Mei Yuan added, without any apparent regret, 'But my life did not follow an academic course. I spent most of it in the countryside in Hunan province. I only returned to Beijing a few years ago when my husband died.' She turned to Li. 'You missed breakfast.'

'I was too early for you.'

'I think, perhaps, my riddle was too difficult for you. You were avoiding me.'

Li laughed. 'No, I wasn't. I figured that out yesterday afternoon.'

'Figured what out?' Margaret asked.

Li shook his head, smiling. 'It's a sort of game we play,' he explained. 'I usually stop for breakfast on the way to work. Mei Yuan will pose me a problem, or a riddle. I've got till the next day to figure it out. If I come up with the right answer, I set her one. Mind games.'

Mei Yuan laughed. 'Mindless games. For people with nothing better to do at that time of the morning.'

'So what was the riddle?' Margaret was intrigued.

'There are two men,' said Li. 'One of them is the keeper of all books, giving him access to all knowledge. Knowledge is power, so he is very powerful. The other has only two sticks. But they give him more power than the other. Why?'

Margaret thought for a moment. 'That's easy,' she said.

Li looked at her sceptically. 'Oh, sure.'

'We have a saying at home about not having two pennies to rub together – meaning you are very poor. But if you have two sticks to rub together, you can make fire. And if you can make fire you can burn books and destroy the knowledge they contain. You take away knowledge, you take away power.'

Mei Yuan clapped her hands in delight. 'Very good.'

Li was astonished, and full of grudging admiration. 'It took me all day to work that out.'

Margaret grinned, and as Mei Yuan prepared their *jian bings* asked her about the book she was reading.

'*Meditations*,' she said.

'Descartes?' Margaret was taken aback.

Mei Yuan nodded. 'Have you read it?'

'No. I suppose I should have. But there are so many books. You can't read them all.'

'If I had one wish in life,' said Mei Yuan, 'it would be that I could spend the rest of it doing nothing else all day but reading.'

Li remembered the books lining the wall in Chao Heng's apartment, and wondered if he had read them all.

Margaret bit into her *jian bing* and crunched it cautiously. 'Hmmm,' she said enthusiastically. 'It's fantastic.' And then quickly, 'It's not going to burn the mouth off me, is it?'

Li laughed. 'Not this time. Just a gentle chili burn.' And she felt the slow warmth and the flavours fill her mouth.

Mei Yuan handed one to Li. 'So,' she said. 'You have something for me today?'

Li's mouth was full of *jian bing*. He shrugged apologetically.

'I haven't had a chance to think of anything, Mei Yuan. I have a big investigation on.'

She waggled a finger at him. 'This is no excuse.'

'Okay,' he said, his mind turning over quickly. 'What about this? A man commits three perfect murders on the same night. There is nothing to connect them to one another, or to him. But he quite deliberately leaves a clue beside each victim which makes it clear that they were all killed by the same man. Why does he do this?'

'That's not fair,' Margaret said.

Mei Yuan looked at her, puzzled. 'You know the answer to this?'

'No, I don't.'

'Then it must be very difficult.' She thought for a moment. 'What sort of clue does he leave?'

'A cigarette end. He is clever enough to know that traces of his saliva will remain on the paper and that the police will discover that the DNA in the saliva from each cigarette end is the same.'

She looked from one to the other. 'Is this real?'

Li nodded grimly. 'I'm afraid it is.'

'Then I will think about it,' said Mei Yuan seriously. 'And if you ask me tomorrow I will tell you what I have thought.'

Li smiled. 'I only hope I will know the answer by then, so that I can tell you if you are right or wrong.'

In the Jeep, as they headed north through the traffic chaos of bicycles and buses in the narrow Chaoyangmen Nanxiaojie

Street, Margaret said, 'Why is a woman like that selling fast food on a street corner?'

Li shrugged. 'The Cultural Revolution ruined many lives in China. Hers was only one.'

Margaret shook her head in exasperation. 'What exactly *was* the Cultural Revolution?' And she was immediately embarrassed by her ignorance. 'I mean, I know I should probably know. But it was a long time ago in a far-off place . . . from America, that is.' She flicked a glance at him. 'Jesus, I never realised how little I knew about the rest of the world until I came here.'

Li glanced at her across the Jeep and thought for a moment. 'You know how it is, as a young person, to feel you have no control over your life, that everything is run by old people? And that by the time you are old enough to change things, you are too old to enjoy them? Well, the Cultural Revolution reversed all that. It gave power to the young, to change things while they were young.' He shivered in the heat as memories of his childhood came flooding back.

'Young people came from all over China to Beijing to become Red Guards and parade in front of Mao in Tiananmen Square. For them, Mao was the "red, red sun in their hearts". But really, they were just children with all discipline removed. They went crazy. They attacked people just because they were "intellectuals". They could come into your house and take over your home. And you would be "criticised", and maybe you would have to write essays criticising yourself, or they would force you through "struggle sessions" or maybe just beat you up for fun. Many people were put in prisons or sent to labour camps. Others were killed – just murdered. And nothing would happen to those who killed them because the legal system had fallen apart, and most policemen were in prison themselves or had been sent to labour in the countryside.'

Margaret tried to imagine how it must have been, to have all the constraints of a civilised society removed, for power to be in the hands of children run riot. But it was unimaginable.

'All the worst and most basic instincts of human nature were given free rein,' Li said. 'And you know how cruel children can be. In my classroom at primary school, my teacher was made by some of the older kids to sit in front of class wearing a dunce's cap and recite over and over, "I am a cow demon". For a short time you think it is funny. But then when your teacher is found kicked to death in the school dining room, you get pretty scared.

'It all got out of control. Even the extremist cadres in the Party, who had set it all in motion, and thought they could control it for their own ends, lost control. Many of the country's leaders had been purged, Deng Xiaoping among them. And eventually the army had to be sent in to restore some kind of order. But we had twelve years of it. Twelve years of madness. I was born the year before it began. I was thirteen when it ended, and my family was destroyed.'

Margaret was shocked. 'What do you mean, destroyed?'

'Both my parents were sent to labour camps. They had been denounced as 'rightists'. They were educated, you see. My mother died there, and my father was a broken man. My

Uncle Yifu was a policeman in Beijing. He was denounced and spent three years in prison.'

Margaret was stunned. 'I had no idea. I really had no idea.'

She thought of all the Chinese she had met since her arrival. Every one of them had lived through the Cultural Revolution. Some of them would have been Red Guards, others their victims. Now, it seemed, they lived and worked together as if nothing had happened. 'How do people do that?' she said. 'I mean, live with each other again. Red Guards, and the people they persecuted.' A society riddled with the forces of guilt and revenge.

Li shrugged. 'I don't know. It just seemed natural. Like being better after being ill. You just got on with your life. People didn't talk much about it at the time. They do now, if you ask. For many people being a Red Guard was the most exciting time of their lives. They travelled all over the country. They didn't have to pay for their train fares or their food. People were scared of them. They had power.

'You know, maybe like old soldiers remembering a war, no matter whether it had been good or bad for them, the experience was so heightened, everything in their lives after it seems dull.'

'And their victims?'

'When the war ends you don't go on fighting,' Li said. 'You get on with the peace.'

Margaret was not convinced she could have been so philosophical. 'What happened to Mei Yuan?'

'She was sent to a labour camp in Hunan where she was

forced to work in the fields along with the peasants. But in some ways she was lucky.'

'Lucky!'

'Her husband was sent to the same camp. They were not separated like so many others.' His face clouded. She saw it immediately.

'What?'

He shrugged. 'In other ways she was not so lucky.' There was a catch in his voice. 'Their baby boy was taken away from them. She never saw him again.'

A towering marble statue of Chairman Mao in greatcoat and peaked cap stood just inside the gate of the Ministry of Agriculture on Hepinglidong Street, an arm outstretched in welcome. The Ministry, set in its sprawling, leafy compound, was housed in a huge concrete edifice behind stone-pillared gates. A stone-faced guard stood outside, glowering at a crowd of several dozen schoolchildren and their teachers, who had set up a long table on the sidewalk. A strip of white linen ran its length, and the children were trying to persuade passers-by to sign it in support of some conservation issue.

Li skirted the schoolchildren and turned past the guard and parked the Jeep in the shade of a large tree inside the compound walls. He said, 'Perhaps you should wait for me here. It might not be politic for me to take you into a government building.'

She nodded. 'Sure.' She watched him head off inside and sat for a long time thinking about the Cultural Revolution, about what it must have meant to have had your parents torn away from you as a child, to grow up in a world where all the norms of civilised behaviour were turned on their head. That was all Li had known until he was thirteen. What would 'normal' have meant to him? She wondered who had raised him when his parents were in labour camp. Did he have any brothers or sisters?

After a time she found herself succumbing again to an over-powering desire to sleep, and she did not want Li returning to find her snoring in the passenger seat. She got out of the Jeep and wandered back through the gates to the street to see what cause the children were espousing. Beneath green Chinese characters on a long white banner was an explanation in English. They were collecting a million signatures in support of an international drive to save the world from desertification.

Almost immediately she was besieged by clamouring teenage girls who took her hands and pulled her towards the table. A teacher on the other side smiled and handed her a red marker pen. What the hell, she thought. It seemed like a reasonable enough cause. She glanced briefly at all the multi-coloured character signatures scrawled across the cloth, before stooping to sign her own name in looping Roman letters. All the children gathered round to watch in amazement, and her signature provoked both astonishment and amusement.

The girls were eager to try out their embryonic English. 'You British?'

'No, American.'

'American! Coca-Cola. Big Mac.'

Margaret smiled wryly. Maybe Li was right. Perhaps that was how the rest of the world saw America's contribution to international culture after all. In a country whose culinary creations included aromatic crispy duck and lamb that 'tastes like honey', fizzy drinks and hamburgers probably seemed pretty crass. But then, she reflected, there were always long queues at the McDonald burger joints she had seen in Beijing.

As she turned back towards the gate, a taxi drew up and a familiar figure emerged. Perspiring profusely, and gasping with the effort of getting out of the car, McCord leaned through the window to pay the driver. As the taxi pulled away, and he turned into the Ministry of Agriculture, Margaret fell into step beside him. 'Well, hello again,' she said.

He turned, startled, with eyes like a frightened rabbit. When he saw who it was his face relaxed into a sneer. 'What the hell are *you* doing here?'

'I was going to ask you the same thing.'

'I work here, remember?'

'Of course.' She paused. 'You were very rude to me in the bar last night.' He looked at her blankly. 'You probably don't even remember.'

'So what *are* you doing here?' he persisted.

'Oh, nothing much. Lending my expertise to the fight against Chinese crime would probably be a good way of putting it.' He frowned. 'I did an autopsy on a murder victim who used to work here.'

McCord stopped in his tracks. '*You* did the autopsy on Chao Heng?'

'Yes. Why? Did you know him?'

McCord brought out a grubby white handkerchief and mopped his face, avoiding her eye. 'Worked with him for five years. A real weirdo.' Then he looked at her very strangely, she thought. 'I heard he committed suicide.'

But her mind was riffling back through the things Li had told her earlier about Chao Heng, making a connection that hadn't occurred to her before. 'Wait a minute. After his post-grad year at Wisconsin, he spent seven years at the Boyce Thompson Institute at Cornell University. Isn't that the place you got kicked out of?'

'I didn't get "kicked out" of anywhere.'

'So you knew him back then?'

'So what? It's not a crime.' He dabbed furiously at his face with his handkerchief. 'You're not suggesting I had anything to do with his murder, are you?'

'Of course not. I doubt if you could hold a match steady long enough to strike it.'

His mouth relapsed into its earlier sneer. 'Why don't you fuck off?'

'Hey,' Margaret said, 'you already asked me that. And you know what? I can't think of a single reason why I should.'

He glared at her for a moment, thoughts flitting through his mind like clouds on a windy day. But he thought better of giving voice to any of them. And suddenly he had that frightened-rabbit look again, and he turned without a word and hurried off towards the main building. He passed Li in the doorway but didn't acknowledge him. Li walked across the compound to where Margaret stood waiting.

'Renewing old friendships?' he asked.

'You know, that man seriously pisses me off,' Margaret said.

'He didn't look too happy about seeing you either.' They walked towards the Jeep. 'You know he and Chao Heng worked on the super-rice project together?'

'He just told me. Well, not in so many words. But I guessed that's what it was.' She glanced at him. 'You learn anything new in there?'

Li sighed. 'Not a lot more than we already knew. Just that Chao was responsible for setting up the research project that led to the development of the super-rice. Apparently he was the one who suggested bringing McCord in. It seems they knew one another in the States.'

'Yes, they were both at the Boyce Thompson Institute. I just put that one together.'

Li climbed into the driver's seat and started the engine. 'Most of the technology for the super-rice was developed at Zhuozhou agro hi-technology development region, just south of Beijing. After that they spent a number of years in the south near Guilin in Guangxi province conducting field trials. That's where Chao was before returning to Beijing to be appointed adviser to the Minister of Agriculture.'

Margaret was thoughtful for a moment. 'Could you show me Chao's flat?' she asked.

'We've already been through it from top to bottom.'

'I know . . . I'd just like to look for myself.' She looked at him very directly. 'Indulge me. Please?'

He looked at the appeal in those palest of blue eyes and knew that he couldn't resist. 'What time is it?' he asked.

She checked her watch. 'Just after four.'

'Okay. I have to go to the railway station first to pick up tickets for my uncle. Then we'll go to Chao's flat.'

CHAPTER SEVEN

Wednesday Evening

The traffic on the second ring road heading south was nose to tail, crawling through a late afternoon haze of humidity and pollution. Li took a pack of cigarettes from the glove compartment. 'Mind if I smoke?'

Margaret looked at the cigarettes with distaste. 'Actually, yes.' Then she relented. 'Well, I guess if you open your window . . .'

'Then the air-conditioning won't work.' He dropped the pack back in the glove compartment. 'In China,' he said, 'it is considered bad manners to refuse someone permission to smoke.'

'Then why did you ask?'

'I was being polite.'

'Well, in the States it's considered impolite to ask somebody else to breathe your smoke.'

He smiled. 'We're never going to agree on very much, are we?'

'Well, there's certainly room for improvement on our record to date.'

He blasted his horn at a yellow taxi and switched lanes to gain a couple of car lengths. 'So what happened that night?' he asked.

'What night?'

'The night of your banquet.'

'What, with McCord?' He nodded. 'The guy's a total creep.'

'So why did you invite him?'

'What?' She was shocked. 'Where in the hell did that story come from?'

'I thought you knew him.'

'He tried to pick me up in the bar of the Friendship. I'd never seen him before then. It was Lily who told him we were going to a welcome banquet, and he just turned up.' She gave vent to her indignation. 'Jesus!'

'But you got into a fight with him.'

'I didn't get into a fight with him. I took issue with the work he does.'

Li was surprised. 'But he's a scientist.'

'He's a biotechnologist. He tampers with the genetic make-up of foods and then expects us to eat them.'

'He was responsible for developing the super-rice. What's wrong with that? It's feeding millions of hungry people.'

'Of course that's the argument scientists use in its favour.' She stopped herself. One step at a time, she thought. 'Do you know what genetic engineering is?'

He shrugged, reluctant to admit his ignorance. 'I suppose not.'

'And do you know why you don't?' He didn't. 'Because a lot

of scientists think that we laymen are too stupid to understand it. In fact it's really very simple. But they don't want to explain, because if we understood it we might just be scared of it.'

He glanced at her across the Jeep. 'You seem to know a lot about it.'

'Oh yes,' she said bitterly. 'I lived with it for nearly seven years.' And she remembered Michael's earnest passion which she had shared, infected by his commitment and enthusiasm. It was strange, she thought now, how that passion lived on in her still, while all feeling for Michael had withered and died.

He recognised the same bitterness he had seen in her at the Sichuan restaurant, and it came back to him that she had told him her husband lectured in genetics. He knew that somehow he had touched on the same raw nerve, then and now. 'So explain it to me,' he said.

'You know what DNA is?'

'Sort of.'

'It's just a code. A sequence of genes that determines the nature of all living things – their substance, their character-istics. So, suppose you grow tomatoes, and all your tomatoes are being destroyed by a certain type of caterpillar. What do you do?'

'I don't know. Spray them with an insecticide, I guess, to kill the caterpillar.'

'That's what people have been doing for years. Trouble is, it contaminates the food, it contaminates the environment, and it costs a lot of money. But now you discover that a certain type of potato you are growing is never attacked by these caterpillars. In fact, they positively avoid it. And you find out that the reason for this is that the potato, in its genetic code, has a gene that creates a substance that is poisonous to the caterpillar. So, says your friendly neighbourhood genetic engineer, here's the solution to your tomato problem. You take the gene that creates the poison in the potato and insert it into the DNA of the tomato. And, bingo, suddenly you've got a tomato that the caterpillars will avoid like the plague.'

'It sounds like a pretty good idea.'

'Of course it does. But hold it in your head for the moment. Because you've got another problem with your tomatoes. They ripen too fast. By the time you've picked them, packed them and shipped them to the shops they're starting to go rotten. So along comes the genetic engineer, by now your very close friend, and says he has identified the gene in the DNA of your tomato that makes it shrivel and rot. He tells you he can remove the gene, modify it, and put it back in so that the tomato will ripen later on the vine and stay fresh for weeks, even months. Problem solved.'

Traffic had ground to a halt. Li leaned on the wheel and looked at her. 'I thought you were trying to sell me the idea that genetic engineering was a bad thing.'

'Oh, I'm not saying that the idea in itself might not have some virtue. I'm saying that the current practice of it could be disastrous.'

'How?'

'Well, you think you've just created the perfect tomato. It is impervious to caterpillars, it's got a long shelf-life in the shops, and you've saved a fortune on pesticides. But then the technology doesn't come cheap. The company which employs the genetic engineer has spent millions on research and development, and they're going to pass these costs on to you. And it's not just a one-off cost, because the genetically engineered DNA is not passed on in the seeds. You have to buy them every year.

'Then you find that the poison that was innocuous to humans in the potato has combined with another substance in the tomato to create something that thousands of people have an allergic reaction to. Some of them die. And modifying that gene to slow down the ripening and rotting? It's ruined the taste. So even if your customers don't have an allergic reaction to your tomatoes, they don't like the taste of them. You're ruined.'

She grinned at the expression on his face. 'But do you know what else? In moving these genes about, the geneticists used another gene that had nothing to do with either the potato or the tomato. They call it a "marker" gene. All it does is allow them to check up quickly and easily on the results of moving the other genes about. But this gene was taken from a bacterium which just happened to be resistant to an antibiotic widely used in the treatment of killer diseases in humans. So what's happening now? The people who eat your tomatoes, who don't die of an allergic reaction, become resistant to certain types of antibiotic and start dying from diseases that have been under control for decades.'

He stared at her in disbelief. 'But surely the tomato would

have been tested first? These problems would have been seen and they would have stopped growing them.' A symphony of horns sounded behind them. The traffic had moved on and Li had not. He slipped the Jeep hurriedly in gear and lurched forward.

'You would think so, wouldn't you?' said Margaret. 'But the companies that put up the cash for research and development want their money back. And the scientists who developed the technology are so arrogant they believe that a technology which is only a dozen or so years old can replace an ecological balance that nature took three billion years to arrive at.

'So they are all prepared to ignore the evidence, or deny it exists. I mean, there's already been one genetically engineered soybean found to cause severe allergic reactions in people who've eaten it. Then there was a bacterium genetically modified to produce large amounts of a food supplement that killed thirty-seven people and permanently disabled another fifteen hundred in the United States.

'Crops that have been genetically modified to resist herbicides and pesticides can pass on that resistance through cross-pollination, creating "super-weeds" that simply beat the original crop hands down in the fight for space in the soil.

'Hey, and do you know what else . . . ?' Her nose wrinkled in disgust as she thought about it. 'They're now taking genes out of animals and fish and putting them into plants. A potato with chicken genes in it to increase resistance to disease. Lovely if you're a vegetarian. Tomatoes with genes from a *flounder* – can you believe it! – to help reduce freezer damage.

In some crops they've even used the gene that creates the poison in scorpions to create built-in insecticide.'

Li nodded. 'It is a great delicacy in China.'

She looked at him, puzzled. 'What is?'

'Scorpion. Deep fried. Eaten for medicinal purposes.'

'You're kidding me.'

'No,' he said very seriously. 'It is true. But I wouldn't recommend them. They taste like shit.'

'Yeah, and I can just imagine how the toxin genes might make my porridge taste.' Her smile faded. 'The thing is, all this is just the tip of the iceberg, Li Yan. Scientists are releasing modified bacteria and viruses into the environment in vast quantities through the introduction of genetically engineered crops. And they haven't a clue what the long-term effects will be. Jesus, in ten years, it's doubtful if there will be a single food left on the planet that hasn't been genetically tampered with, and there's not a damned thing any of us can do about it.' She took a deep breath. 'And do you know why?'

'Why?'

She paused for effect. 'Money. That's what motivates the whole science. Research into biotechnology will be worth around one hundred *billion* dollars by the turn of the millennium. They tell us it's for "the good of mankind", to feed the hungry millions of the world. But there is not a shred of evidence that the technology will be any cheaper, or any more productive in the long term.

'When they ran into trouble with regulators in the States, the big biochemical companies simply started moving their projects to other parts of the world. Like China. Places where there is little or no regulation to govern the commercial intro- duction of genetically modified crops. And do you know what's interesting? When one of these companies comes up with a crop that's resistant to a certain herbicide, guess who also manufactures that herbicide.'

'The same company?'

'You're catching on. And instead of reducing the amount of herbicide we're polluting our planet with, we'll be using even more, because the crop we're growing is resistant to it.'

She slapped her palms on her thighs. 'Jesus, it makes me so mad! And these goddamn scientists! Philanthropists? Like hell. They'll do anything to keep the funding coming in from the biochemical companies so they can carry on playing God. And don't believe the myth about these crops bringing down costs and increasing yield to feed the third world. Remember the guy with the tomatoes – the fact that he has to buy fresh seeds every year? Well, that's what farmers in the third world are going to have to do, too. And who will they have to buy them from? Well, the biochemical companies, of course – who also control the price.'

Li shook his head. 'This is all a bit too much for me. I mean, all I know is that they brought in this super-rice three years ago and they have doubled production. There is no hunger in China. For the first time we are major exporters of food to other countries.'

Margaret shrugged, passion finally spent. And she wondered what point there had ever been in it. There was nothing she could do to change the way things were. 'I guess,' she sighed. 'Like I said, it's not as if the technology might not have some benefits. It's the long term I worry about. The consequences we can't possibly predict that are going to affect our children, or our children's children.'

Li growled and banged the steering wheel. The traffic had ground to yet another halt. 'What's the time?' he asked.

'Nearly half past.'

He shook his head. 'We'll be here all day at this rate.' He opened his window and placed the red light on the roof, flicked it on and activated his siren. 'Hold on,' he said, and started nudging his way out of the gridlock and into the cycle lane, where they picked up speed, bicycles parting in panic ahead of them. He flicked her a glance. 'Now that the window is down anyway, maybe you wouldn't mind if I had a cigarette? After everything you have told me it can't be as bad for me as eating.'

'Don't count on it,' she said. 'You wouldn't believe the genes they've been putting in tobacco plants.'

II

The great paved concourse in front of Beijing railway station was jammed with rush-hour commuters. Modern twin clock towers separated by a gigantic digital display rose above broad steps leading to the main entrance, where baggage was being run through X-ray machines under the watchful eye of armed policemen. Li nosed the Jeep over the sidewalk and on to the concourse, exchanging horn blasts with buses and taxis. By now he had cut the siren and brought the flashing red light back inside. So he was just another anonymous citizen in a Beijing Jeep. A couple of girls sweeping up litter with old-fashioned straw brooms, and clever shovels with mouths that opened and closed like hungry dogs, shouted imprecations at the Jeep for forcing them to move out of the way. They could have been no more than seventeen or eighteen, dressed in baggy blue overalls and white tee-shirts. They had large pale blue bandanas wrapped around their faces to protect them from dust billowing up from the concrete as they swept. Red motorised baggage trolleys weaved their way among the crowds. Groups of travellers sat patiently on the steps in the shade of black umbrellas, luggage piled high all around them. Margaret followed Li into the ticket hall in the station's west wing.

Long queues snaked back across marble tiles from a row of hatches that ran the length of the back wall. Destinations were marked above each window in Chinese characters, and Margaret wondered how the casual foreign traveller would know which one to go to. A woman's strangely disconnected nasal voice droned monotonously over the Tannoy, announcing departures and arrivals. Li joined the back of one of the queues and stood tapping his foot impatiently.

'Where is your uncle going?' she asked, more for something to say than out of any real interest.

'Sichuan,' he said distractedly.

'That's where your family comes from, isn't it?'

'He's going to see my father in Wanxian, and then on to Zigong to talk to my sister.'

There was something in the stress he put on the word 'talk' that aroused her curiosity. 'Is there a problem?'

'She is pregnant.'

'That's a problem?'

'You ask too many questions.'

'I'm a nosy bitch.' She waited.

He sighed. 'She already has a child.' He took in Margaret's frown of puzzlement. 'You have never heard of China's One-child Policy?'

'Ah.' Understanding dawned. Of course she had heard. And she had always wondered how it was possible to enforce such a policy. 'What can they do to you if you do have a second child?'

'When you get married,' he said, 'you are asked to make a public commitment to having only one child. You sign what they call a "letter of determination". In return you receive financial and other privileges – priority in education and medicine for your child, an increase in income, better housing. There is also strong pressure to be sterilised. But if you then go on to have more than one child, you will lose all your benefits, maybe even your house.' He shook his head slowly, clearly concerned. 'And during the second pregnancy there will be other pressures, psychological, sometimes physical, to have an abortion. The consequences can be terrible, either way.'

Margaret tried to imagine the US government trying to tell Americans how many children they could have. She couldn't.

But at the same time she knew what unchecked population growth would do to a country that already comprised a quarter of the world's population. Starvation, economic ruin. It was a dreadful dichotomy. 'Is she going to have the baby?' He nodded. 'But did she and her husband sign this "letter of declaration"?'

'Yes.'

'Then why is she so determined to have another child?'

'Because their first child was a girl.'

Margaret pulled a face. 'So? What's wrong with girls? Some would say they're a lot better than boys.' She grinned. 'And, in my humble opinion, there'd be a lot of merit in that view.'

'Not in China.'

And she saw that he was serious. 'You're kidding. Why not?'

'Oh, it's not easy to explain,' he said, waving an arm in a gesture of futility. 'It has to do with Confucianism, and the ancient Chinese belief in ancestor worship. But perhaps more than all of that, there is one very practical reason. Traditionally, when a son marries he brings his new wife to live with his parents, and as the parents grow aged the younger couple look after them. If all you have is a daughter, she will go to live with her husband's parents, and there will be no one to look after you in your old age.'

'But if everyone only has one child, and every child is a son, there won't be any women to bear the next generation of children.'

He shrugged. 'I can only tell you how it is. The orphanages are full of baby girls who were abandoned on doorsteps.'

'So your uncle is going to talk her out of having the baby?'

'I don't know what my uncle is going to say to her. I'm not sure he knows himself. But whatever he says, she will listen, in the way that she will listen to no one else.' He stretched up to look down the length of the queue. It didn't appear to have moved at all. 'This is no damned good,' he said, and pulled out his Public Security ID wallet from a back pocket and pushed his way up to the head of the queue.

Margaret watched from a distance as several people at the head of the queue began to remonstrate with him. She smiled as he turned and with a few sharp words and a flash of his ID silenced their complaints. *And some were more equal than others*, she thought wryly.

He hurried back across the concourse with the ticket and she followed him outside into the crowded square. 'I'm sorry, I'm going to have to take the ticket to my uncle first,' he said, glancing up at the nearer clock tower. 'His train is in just over three hours.'

'How long will he be away?'

'Oh, he'll be back tomorrow night.'

'Short conversation.'

Li shrugged. 'He'll say what he has to say then go. At the end of the day it is her decision.'

They climbed into the Jeep. 'What do *you* think she should do?' She watched him closely, interested in his reply.

'I think she should not have got pregnant,' he said.

'That's not what I asked.'

He looked at her very seriously. 'It is not my problem. I have enough of my own.' And she realised that a veil was being drawn over a part of him he did not want revealed.

As he shifted into first gear and started to pull away, he had to brake sharply as a woman in her thirties wheeled a pram across their intended path. It was a strange, crude, wooden pram, with two tiny seats facing each other across a small, square table. Home-made, Margaret might have thought, except that she had seen others just like it in the street. But there was only one seat occupied. The other, empty one was a potent symbol of frustrated Chinese parenthood. Li didn't seem to see it as he waited for the mother to pass, glaring at them as she did. Then he slipped back into gear and squeezed the Jeep into the main stream of traffic heading west on Beijingzhanxi Street.

III

Songbirds in bamboo cages hung among the pines, competing with wailing renditions of songs from the Beijing Opera. Their voices raised in Eastern discord, a group of a dozen old men, accompanied by the plucks and whines of age-old Chinese instruments, sang behind trembling wisteria in the pergola where yesterday Li had seen a drunken youth sucking alcohol from a plastic bottle. The same white-coated barber was clip-clipping among the trees, tufts of black hair tumbling to the sun-baked dusty earth. Bicycles leaned against tree trunks, their owners gathered around games of cards or chess. Somewhere in the distance, from the park itself, came the sound of a disco beat, insistent and incongruous.

Li and Margaret walked through the dappled early evening sunlight. Li said, 'In the park there is a lake, Jade Lake, officially designated for swimming. In the winter it freezes over and it is used by skaters. But they cut a hole in the ice at one side for bathers to dip themselves in the freezing water. My uncle does this every morning.'

Margaret shivered at the thought. Li put a hand on her arm to stop her. She glanced at him, then followed his eyes to where an old man with dark, curling hair stood in the shade, legs apart, slowly arcing a sword above his head, before bringing it down in a long slow sweep through 180 degrees to point at the earth. In perfect slow motion, he swivelled on the ball of one foot, folding one leg high to his chest, and turned to swing the sword up and across his body, then out to his right, stamping his raised foot down with a thud, the sword now pointed directly at Li and Margaret. The old man glared at them with fiercely burning eyes and then broke into a broad grin. 'Li Yan,' he said. 'Have you got my ticket?'

Li took the ticket from his pocket and held it out as he approached him. 'It leaves at eight.'

Old Yifu looked beyond him at Margaret. 'And you must be Dr Campbell,' he said, his English almost without accent. He lowered his sword and held out his hand. 'I am very pleased to meet you.'

Margaret shook his hand, bemused to find that Li's legendary Uncle Yifu was this smiling, shrunken old man swinging a sword under the trees.

'My Uncle Yifu,' Li said.

'I've heard a great deal about you . . . Mr . . .' Margaret didn't know how to address him.

'Just call me Old Yifu. When you get to my age people call you "old" as a mark of respect.'

Margaret laughed. 'That won't come easy to me. In the States, to call someone "old" would be dismissive, or derogatory.'

He took her arm and steered her towards the low stone table where his chessmen were laid out on their board. 'Ah, but in China to be old is to be venerated. Age equates with wisdom.' He grinned. 'We have a saying: "Old ginger tastes the best". Sit down, please.' He indicated a folding canvas chair. 'Naturally, at my advanced age, I should be very wise. And, of course, everyone thinks I am.' He laid his sword on the ground and sat opposite her, then leaned confidentially across the table. 'I *would* be very wise if I could remember everything I knew.' He sighed sadly. 'The trouble is, nowadays I've forgotten more than I can remember.' And his eyes twinkled as he added, 'That is why I am still learning my English vocabulary. It helps to fill up all the empty places left in my head by everything I have forgotten.'

'Well, you certainly haven't forgotten how to charm a lady.' She smiled back at him, an immediate rapport established.

'Pah,' he said dismissively. 'Not much use to me now.' He raised an eyebrow and nodded towards Li. 'If only my nephew had inherited a little of it. But he takes after his father. Slow in affairs of the heart.' He looked at Li. 'What age are you now, Li Yan?'

Li was acutely embarrassed. 'You know what age I am, Uncle.'

Old Yifu turned back to Margaret, mischief all over his face. 'Thirty-three years old and still single. Doesn't even have a girlfriend. All work and no play makes Jack a dull boy, I think.'

Margaret stifled her smile, enjoying Li's discomfort.

'I'm glad he at least took my advice,' Old Yifu said.

'Advice on what?'

'Uncle, I think you should be going back to the apartment and getting packed,' Li said.

Old Yifu ignored him. 'On obtaining your help for the investigation.'

Li wished the ground would simply swallow him up. Margaret cocked an eyebrow at him then turned back to Old Yifu. 'Oh, so that was your idea, was it?'

'Well . . . let's just say I encouraged him in that direction.' Old Yifu bared his teeth in a broad smile. 'Now I can see why he didn't take *too* much persuasion. He didn't tell me how attractive you were.'

'Perhaps he doesn't think I am.'

'Oh, I do not think he would be blushing like that if he did not think so.'

Li could barely contain his embarrassment. He sighed and gazed off through the trees, teeth clenched. Margaret was enjoying herself.

Old Yifu asked, 'Do you play chess?'

'You don't have time, Uncle. Your train is at eight. It is nearly five thirty.'

'Of course I have time.'

Margaret said, looking at the board, 'I think the chess you play may be a little different from the version I know.'

'No, no, no. It is very similar. Instead of your representational carvings, we play with these wooden disks. The character on each disk tells us what it is.'

'She's not familiar with Chinese characters, Uncle. Once the pieces are out of position she'll never remember what they are.'

'I don't think that will be a problem,' Margaret said, a tiny edge to her voice. 'I have a pretty well photographic memory.'

'Good, good.' Old Yifu clapped his hands with pleasure and began explaining the board and the rules. Instead of moving pieces into each square, you moved them on to the intersection. There was a King, but no Queen, just two King's Guides. The four-square area at the centre-back at each side was the only area in which the King could move – one space at a time at right angles. The same rule applied to the King's Guides, except that they could only move on the diagonal. The pawns were called Soldiers, the knight was a Horse, and while it moved in the same way as the knight, it could not jump another piece to do so. There were other minor variations in the names of pieces and their movements, but essentially it was the game Margaret knew and played in the States. The board, however, was dissected by a single broad belt representing a river. And you didn't 'take' a piece, you 'ate' it.

Margaret was to play with the red pieces, Old Yifu with the black. Li, resigned to the game going ahead, sighed and leaned back against the trunk of the tree that shaded the board and folded his arms across his chest. 'How is your office?' Old Yifu asked him as Margaret made her first move.

'It's fine,' Li said.

'Fine? Just *fine*? The *feng shui* man showed me his plan. It looked excellent to me. You will work well in this office.'

'Yes, of course. Thank you, Uncle.'

Old Yifu grinned wickedly at Margaret. 'I detect a little scepticism. He thinks his uncle is a superstitious old fool.'

'Then he is the fool,' Margaret said. '*Feng shui* or not, I can see sound reasons for all the changes.'

'Naturally. Superstition grows from the practice of truths. Not the other way around.' He brought his Horse straight into play. 'Your move.' And as she contemplated her next move, he said, 'I have always been a great admirer of the Americans. Like the Chinese, you are a very practical people. But you are also dreamers who try to make your dreams come true. And that is not at all practical.' He shrugged. 'But, then, you have succeeded in turning so many of your dreams into reality. I think it is a good thing to have a dream in life. It is something to aim for, to give you focus.'

'Is that not a bit too much of an "individual" concept for a communist system?' Margaret slid her Castle across the back line.

'You must not give way to that bad American habit, Dr Campbell, of intolerance for other ideas. One must always be pragmatic. I was a committed Marxist myself as a young man. Now I am, I guess, a liberal. We all evolve.'

'Didn't someone once say if you are not a Marxist at twenty you have no heart, and if you are not a conservative at sixty you have no brain?'

He smiled with delight. 'I had not heard that one. It is very clever.'

'Very paraphrased, I think. I don't know where it comes from.'

'The words are unimportant if the meaning is plain. And a truth is a truth no matter who says it.' One of his Soldiers ate one of her Soldiers.

Li sighed theatrically to signal his impatience, but they both ignored him. Margaret slid her Bishop across the diagonal, eating one of Old Yifu's Soldiers and threatening his forward Horse. He was forced into a defensive move, conceding the initiative to her. 'Li Yan told me you were imprisoned during the Cultural Revolution,' she said.

'Did he?'

To her disappointment, Old Yifu seemed disinclined to talk about it. 'For three years, Li Yan said.'

'He says a lot, it seems.'

There was no eye contact during this. Both were focused on the board, contemplating the next move, sliding a piece here, jumping the river there.

'You must have been very bitter.'

He ate her Bishop. 'Why?'

'You lost three years of your life.' She swooped on the offending Horse and left his Castle wide open to attack. Again he was forced on to the defensive.

'No. I learned much about human nature. I learned even more about myself. Sometimes learning can be a difficult, even painful, process. But one should never resent it.' He thought carefully before blocking the line to his Castle with his King's Guide. 'Besides, I was only in prison for one and a half years.'

'You always told me three,' said Li, taken aback.

'I was physically there for three years. But for half that time I slept, and when I slept I dreamed, and when I dreamed they could not keep me there. Because in my dreams I was free. Free to visit my childhood and speak again to my parents, free to go to the places I have loved in my life: the high mountains of Tibet, the Yellow Sea washing on the shores of Jiangsu, the Hong Kong of my boyhood, with the sun setting blood red across the South China Sea. They can never touch those things, or take them away. And as long as you have them, you have your freedom.'

Margaret's eyes flickered up from the board to look at Old Yifu, his attention still focused, apparently, on the game. What horrors must he have endured? And yet he had chosen to take the positive view. Tales of torture and persecution would, perhaps, have been too painful, or too easy. Instead he chose to remember the escape he had made each day, sustaining hope and spirit.

'My only regret,' he said, 'is that I was separated from my wife for that period. We had so little time together afterwards.'

And she saw a moistness in his eyes, and a colour rising on his cheeks. *My uncle has never really got over the loss of her*, Li had told her. She swooped quickly to eat another of his

Soldiers with her Horse, changing the pace of the game and the mood of their conversation. 'So you were brought up in Hong Kong?' she said.

'The family was originally from Canton. But we had been in Hong Kong for nearly two generations, a wealthy family by Chinese standards. Li Yan's father and myself were in middle school when the Japanese invaded and we fled to China as refugees. We ended up in Sichuan, and I finished middle school there before going on to the American University in Beijing.'

He took the bait and made the mistake of eating her Horse. She slid her Castle two-thirds of the way down the board. 'Check.'

'Good God!' Old Yifu seemed genuinely taken aback, then he looked up at her, smiling shrewdly. 'Now I see,' he said. 'All these questions. You were hoping to distract me.'

'Me?' said Margaret innocently, and feigning shock.

Old Yifu brought his remaining Horse into play, blocking her route to the King. It was his only real option, but it left his other Castle exposed and unprotected. He shook his head sadly. 'I can see my demise.'

Margaret ate his Castle quite ruthlessly. 'You must have seen a lot of changes in your lifetime.'

But his concentration was on his move, and he did not reply until he had moved a Bishop to threaten a Soldier. 'Everything has changed,' he said, 'except the character of the Chinese people. I think, maybe, that will remain the one great constant.'

'So what do you think of China today?'

'She is changing again. More rapidly this time. For better or worse I do not know. But people have more money in their pockets and food in their bellies and clothes on their backs. And everyone has a roof over his head. I remember when it was not so.'

Margaret smiled. It was clear to see where Li's influences lay. She moved her Horse into a position that would threaten Old Yifu's King if he took her Soldier, and lose him his Bishop if he didn't. 'I read somewhere that in fifty years, as the West declines and the East develops, China will become the richest and most powerful country on earth.' He was still puzzling over his next move. 'Do you think that's true?'

He took her Soldier, effectively conceding defeat. 'It is difficult to say. China has such a long history, and this period is such a small link in a chain that stretches back five thousand years. Only time will tell. Mao once said, when asked what he thought of the French Revolution, "It is too early to say". So who am I to predict the future for China?' He smiled as she moved her Castle.

'Checkmate,' she said.

He conceded defeat with a small shrug and a nod of his head, and his smile seemed full of genuine pleasure. 'Congratulations. It is the first time I have been beaten in many years. One grows complacent. I look forward to more games with you.'

'It will be a pleasure.'

'If only my nephew could be such a worthy opponent.'

'Perhaps if I'd had a better teacher . . .' Li responded, stung by his uncle's rebuke.

'You can teach anyone the rules,' Old Yifu said. 'But the intelligence to use them you must be born with.' He started packing his chess pieces into their old cardboard box. 'Anyway, I can't afford to hang about here wasting time talking to you. I have a train to catch. And I'm going to be late.' He winked at Margaret.

IV

The uniformed officer unlocked the door and let them into Chao Heng's apartment. There was that same, strange antiseptic smell as before, Li noticed. They walked around the bloodstain on the carpet, now ringed off by strips of white tape, and into the living room. 'What is it you are looking for?' he asked Margaret.

She shook her head. 'I don't really know. Like you, I just get the feeling that this whole case is about Chao Heng. I don't know where the other two tie in, but they seem . . . incidental, somehow. There's got to be something we are missing. Something we already know, or should know about him. Something here in this apartment, maybe. Something in the weird nature of his killing.'

Li had offered to run Old Yifu back to their apartment, but he had had his bike with him and said he had already packed and only needed to collect his bag. He would get a taxi to the station, which was just around the corner anyway.

The two had embraced, a strangely touching moment after all the friction there had been between them. They hardly spoke. 'Tell Xiao Ling I send my love,' Li had said.

On the drive over to Chao's apartment, Li hadn't said a word, his thoughts, she assumed, filled with concern for his sister and the mission his uncle had undertaken at the behest of his father. Now, at Chao's apartment, he seemed moody and unfocused. Margaret knew only too well how difficult it could be sometimes to concentrate on work when personal problems preyed on your mind. She knew she needed to shift his brain back into gear. 'So you think he was sitting out there on the balcony,' she said, 'waiting for his late-night caller?' Li nodded. The bottle of beer and the cigarette ends in the ashtray were still there. 'And the CD is where?'

He crossed the room to the mini hi-fi stack and saw that the forensics boys had forgotten to switch it off.

'Do you want to put on the track that was playing?'

He shrugged and whizzed through the tracks to number nine and pressed play. As the soprano's voice soared through the apartment, Margaret wandered to the bookcase and ran her fingers along a line of books with familiar titles. *Plant DNA Infectious Agents*, *Risk Assessment in Genetic Engineering*, *Plant Virology*. Titles that had lined Michael's bookshelves at home. The same titles that had seemed so alien to Li just twenty-four hours before. She slipped her hands into the neatly tailored pockets of her dress and moved out on to the balcony. She looked at the empty beer bottle, the pack of cigarettes, and wondered what he had lit them with. Then remembered the Zippo lighter among his effects. And something began happening in her mind, something spontaneous, a sequence of electrical sparks making connections that would never have occurred consciously. All that data that the brain holds in limbo, accessed by some pre-programmed instinct. She could taste the *jian bing*, the salty sweetness of the *hoi sin*, the burn of the chilli, the sharpness of the spring onion. And she saw Mei Yuan's round, smiling face. She wheeled round to see where Li was. But he had left the room. She hurried into the hall and called his name. 'In here,' he said, and she went into the kitchen.

'Mei Yuan's riddle,' she said.

He looked at her blankly. 'What about it?'

She shook her head in frustration. 'It's just a thought process. Bear with me.' She fought for the words. 'The man with the two sticks. If he was going to burn the books, he would do it for a reason, right?'

'To destroy them.'

'Exactly. So the keeper of the books couldn't access them. He would have no way of knowing what was in them.'

Li shrugged. 'So?'

'So why set Chao Heng on fire?'

'To make it look like suicide.'

'No. That's incidental. I did an autopsy once on the burned body of a woman pulled from a car wreck. Turned out she had a bullet in her. And that's what killed her. The guy who'd shot her put her in the car, set it on fire and ran it off the road. He was trying to hide the fact that he'd shot her. He thought maybe the evidence would be destroyed in the fire.' She ran her hands back through her hair. 'You see what I'm saying?'

Li thought about it. 'You think the killer was trying to

destroy evidence?' He paused. 'Evidence of what? Chao hadn't been shot, or stabbed, or had his neck broken. He had a bump on his head and sedative in his blood. If the object of the exercise was to try and hide that by burning him, it wasn't very successful, was it?'

Margaret's mind was racing. But it was racing in circles. 'No,' she had to concede. 'No, it wasn't.' She felt as if she had held something precious and elusive in her grasp for just a moment, and then lost it again. And now it was like some half-remembered face that lurks in the memory somewhere just beyond recall. 'Hell, I don't know,' she said, deflated. 'There's something there. Why don't you take me on a guided tour of this place? In fact, why don't we retrace events, just as you think they happened?'

'What for?'

'For another perspective. Something you've already seen that I might see differently. Something you might see differently second time around.'

He was not convinced, but he shrugged and said, 'Okay.'

So they put on *Samson and Delilah* again and went on to the balcony. Margaret sat in Chao's seat, from where she had a view of the compound below. She had been tossing and turning in her hotel bed trying to sleep when Chao had been sitting here, she realised. It had all been less than forty-eight hours ago. He had still been alive when she arrived in China.

'He would have seen the lights of the car coming in,' Li said. 'The elevator was off, so he would have gone downstairs to let his visitor in.'

'Let's do it.'

They crossed the living room and Li put the CD on pause.

'We'll be back up in a few minutes,' he told the officer in the hall.

They went into the stairwell and down five flights. The gate at the foot of the stairs was locked. 'Don't you have the key?' Margaret asked, irritated.

'No. The killer must have taken it to unlock the gate on the way out with Chao.'

'And locked it behind him?' It seemed unlikely, somehow.

'Perhaps. It was locked when we got here yesterday. But it could have been locked by one of the other residents if they found it open in the morning.'

They craned to see round the wall of the lift shaft, but it effectively blocked off their view of the lobby and the main door. 'So Chao wouldn't have seen his visitor until he was right at the gate,' Margaret said. 'Wouldn't have seen him crossing the lobby and got alarmed when it wasn't who he was expecting.'

'Hold on. I think I might have made a mistake there,' Li said suddenly. 'I assumed that Chao was expecting someone else and that his killer was unknown to him. But if it was someone he already knew, a new supplier maybe, or someone he believed might provide him with young boys, there would be no reason for the killer to tip his hand at that stage.'

'And if Chao knew him he would probably have invited him up,' Margaret said.

'So he didn't have to be forced up the stairs at gunpoint.'

Li began to think there might be virtue in this exercise after all. How often had his uncle told him that the answer almost always lay in the detail.

They went back up the stairs and into the apartment, stopping by the bloodstain on the hall carpet. 'The killer wasn't going to hang around making polite conversation,' Margaret said. 'It looks like he hit him on the head as soon as they got in. The size of the contusion and fracture would be consistent with your idea that he might have used the barrel of his gun. And he would have injected him with the ketamine straight away. He couldn't know just how hard he had hit Chao, or how long he would be unconscious. He would have pulled off his left shoe, stripped back the sock and followed Chao's well-worn needle path into the bloodstream. So either he knew him well, or had been very thorough in his research. He pulled the sock back up and replaced the shoe. Then what?'

'He waited,' Li said.

'Why?'

'He would have some time to kill before dawn. Safer to wait here than in the park.'

'Okay. But he needed to be in the park with Chao by sun-up.'

'Is it not true that the darkest hour is just before the dawn?' Li asked.

'I guess it is,' Margaret conceded. 'And I've had plenty of opportunity to put it to the test the last couple of nights.' She thought for a moment. 'So he left, with Chao, some time between three and four a.m. In time to get him into the park under cover of darkness and be there when it opened. How did he get him down the stairs?'

'Probably over his shoulder.'

'Down five flights? This guy must have been pretty fit. But let's not get ahead of ourselves. He could have spent up to two hours in the apartment, right? Would he not have left some trace? Had a coffee, gone for a pee, smoked a cigarette?'

Li shrugged. 'My guess is he would wear gloves. He wouldn't have a coffee or a cigarette, because he's a professional. If he had a pee, it's long gone.'

'I'd still like to look around,' Margaret said.

They spent nearly fifteen minutes going through the apartment room by room, finding nothing, before finally entering the bathroom. It was as dirty as Li remembered it. The creams and ointments in half-squeezed tubes, the bloodstained safety razor, the spattered mirror above the sink. The used towels still lay over the side of the bath, but were dry now. Margaret opened the bathroom cabinet. 'Jesus,' she said, and lifted out the plastic tubs and bottles of pills. She looked at Li. 'Do you know what this stuff is?'

He shook his head. 'The man was sick.'

'He sure was.' She rattled a bottle at him. 'Epivir. Or 3TC as it's known. A reverse transcriptase inhibitor. You know what that is?'

'No idea.'

'Reverse transcriptase is an enzyme that helps replicate DNA.' She shook one of the plastic tubs and the pills inside rattled like dried beans. 'Crixivan. A protease inhibitor, another enzyme involved in replication.' She picked up another bottle. 'And AZT. Well, there's hardly anyone in the West who hasn't heard of that.'

He was still in the dark.

'Taken simultaneously, these three comprise the triple drug therapy that's now being used to combat HIV. They act to prevent the virus from replicating.' She paused. 'Looks like our friend Mr Chao had AIDS.'

The elevator man watched them with the same intense curiosity on the way down as he had on the way up. He was irritated by the fact that they were speaking English and he had no idea what they were saying.

In his mind, Li was warming to Margaret's idea that Chao had been burned to try to hide something. 'Do you think,' he said, 'that Chao could have been set on fire to try and disguise the fact that he had AIDS?'

Margaret didn't. She used the same reasoning Li had earlier to dismiss her initial idea. 'If he was, they didn't do a very good job. He'd need to have been really fried for us not to be able to get blood or tissue samples to test for it. Anyway, you never routinely test for AIDS during autopsy, not without a reason. And they left his medicines in the bathroom cabinet. Bit of a giveaway. But more than any of that, why would they? Why would anyone have any interest in trying to hide the fact that Chao Heng had AIDS?'

He couldn't think of one. He replayed what she had just said and frowned. 'Why do you say "they", when we are pretty sure the killer was acting alone?'

'Because he was a hired gun, right? I mean, we've agreed on that, haven't we? So he had nothing personal against any of his victims. It was someone else who wanted them dead. "They." It would help a lot if we knew why.'

It was one of the fundamental differences, Li thought, between the American approach and the Chinese approach. The Americans placed more stress on motive. The Chinese preferred to build the evidence, piece by tiny piece, until the accumulation of it was overwhelmingly conclusive. The 'why' was not the key to the answer, but the answer itself. Perhaps by working together they could combine the virtues of both systems.

They criss-crossed the lobby, re-examined the lamp over the door, and retraced the killer's footsteps to his car, where Li's Jeep was now parked. Looking up, Margaret could see that the trees along the farther edge of the sidewalk would have blotted out the light from the streetlamps, and with the lamp over the door out of action, the killer would have been able to carry Chao across the fifteen feet to his vehicle in deep shadow. 'Can we go to the park?' she asked. 'Follow this guy's spoor all the way to where he set poor old Chao on fire?'

'Are you beginning to have sympathy for Chao Heng?' he asked, surprised.

Margaret shrugged her shoulders. 'He probably wasn't a very nice man, Li Yan. But he was dying of AIDS, and someone burned him alive. Maybe that was a little more than he deserved.' She paused. 'Are you going to take me to the park?'

'Okay.' He got into the Jeep in time to hear his call sign

on the police radio. He checked in, and as Margaret climbed into the passenger side was frowning at the message he was receiving in response.

'We've got to go back to headquarters,' he said thoughtfully. 'The Chief wants to see me. Urgently.'

'What for?'

He frowned. 'I don't know. They wouldn't say.'

V

The atmosphere on the top floor of Section One was thick with tension and cigarette smoke. Margaret had noticed Lily's driver, Shimei, sitting in the BMW in the street outside. Lily was ensconced in a corner of the detectives' room waiting for her, something smug in her smile.

Li hadn't even noticed her. He was more aware of the atmosphere when he stepped into the detectives' office. It was uneasy, and anxious, and filled with expectation. Detectives lifted grim expressions from their desks to greet him. 'What the hell's up?' he said.

Wu said, 'The Needle and some fancy lawyer are with the Chief.' He allowed a moment for this to sink in. 'Chief wants to see you straight away.'

Li was impassive. He nodded and went out into the corridor and straight down to Chen's office. Margaret looked to Lily for illumination. 'What's going on?'

'Deputy Section Chief Li in bi-ig trouble,' she said happily. 'I come pick you up. Been waiting very long time.'

'Yeah, well, you can just wait a little longer,' Margaret snapped at her.

The Needle and his lawyer sat in soft seats by the window. The lawyer was young, perhaps thirty, one of the new breed of legal eagles cashing in on recent changes in the justice system allowing accused persons legal representation at an earlier stage in proceedings. He was confident and cocky, wearing a sharp suit and an expensive haircut. The Needle eyed Li with a slow-burning hatred. Chen sat behind his desk, his face grey and severe.

Li gave The Needle and his lawyer a friendly nod. 'You wanted to see me, Chief?'

'Serious allegations, Li, have been made against you by this gentleman and his legal representative,' Chen said gravely. He did not invite Li to sit.

Li raised his eyebrows in surprise. 'What allegations are those?'

The lawyer said, 'That you coerced my client into accompanying you to the Beijing Workers' Stadium. That you put a single round in the barrel of a revolver, placed that revolver against my client's head and repeatedly pulled the trigger until he told you what you wanted to know.'

Li laughed. 'You're kidding me. A *revolver*?' He looked at Chen. 'You know we haven't used revolvers since the year dot, Chief. We use semi-automatic pistols that are only issued to officers on your specific authority.' Chen visibly relaxed. 'And what possible information could I coerce from him that as a concerned citizen he wouldn't be perfectly willing to volunteer?'

'You bastard!' The Needle hissed, and his lawyer placed a restraining hand on his arm.

'You did go to the Workers' Stadium, though?' Chen asked.

'Sure. But there was nothing coercive about it. I went to the Hard Rock Café and asked him if I could have a word. Must have been two hundred witnesses in the place saw him walk out with me of his own free will. We went to the stadium for some privacy, because he wasn't too keen on being seen in public talking to a cop.' He turned towards The Needle. 'Something about street cred, you said, wasn't it?'

The Needle glared back at him. His lawyer said, 'There was a witness.'

Li frowned. 'A witness?' Then, 'Oh, you mean "observer". Dr Campbell is an American pathologist helping us with a case.'

'Where is she, Li?' Chen demanded.

'In the office.' For the first time, he seemed uneasy. A close inspection of his veneer of confidence might have shown hairline cracks. Chen picked up the phone and asked for Margaret to be brought in. They waited in tense silence. There was a knock at the door and Margaret made a tentative entrance. She saw The Needle and immediately felt sick.

Chen said, 'Does everyone here speak English?' The Needle's lawyer nodded. Chen turned to Margaret. 'I am very sorry, Dr Campbell, to drag you into this. But these gentlemen here have made a very serious allegation about the conduct of Deputy Section Chief Li. You might be in a position to help us clarify the matter.'

Margaret felt the colour rising on her face. She glanced at

Li. But he was steadfastly avoiding her eye. 'Of course,' she said.

'Do you know this gentleman?' Chen said, indicating The Needle.

'Sure. Deputy Section Chief Li spoke to him this morning.'

'Where?'

'We met him at the Hard Rock Café and . . .' Her hesitation was almost imperceptible, but she felt as if it lasted minutes. '. . . drove to some stadium or other.' She glanced again at Li, but his face was giving nothing away.

'And what happened?'

'We went inside.'

'And?'

'I don't know. They were speaking in Chinese. I didn't know what they were saying.' Until now everything she had said was true.

Chen took a deep breath. 'It is alleged that Li put a revolver, armed with a single bullet, to this man's head and repeatedly pulled the trigger. Is this the case?'

Again, her hesitation seemed to last a lifetime. 'Not that I saw,' she said finally. After all, it was partially true. She had turned away, hadn't she?

There was a long silence. Margaret could hear distant voices on another floor, a far-off rumble of traffic and horns from Dongzhimennei Street. The Needle glanced at his lawyer. His English had not been up to the exchange. But his lawyer sat stiffly, lips tightly pursed. Chen leaned across the desk towards The Needle and said, 'Get the fuck out of here before I charge you with making false allegations against the police.'

Li was shocked. In all the years he had known Chen, he had never before heard him swear. As his lawyer pulled him to his feet, The Needle turned his hate-filled eyes on Margaret before being drawn reluctantly towards the door. The two men left the room.

There was another long silence. Chen looked at Li dangerously, and in Chinese said, 'What's going on, Li?'

Li shrugged. 'Beats me, Chief.'

'It's not how we conduct our business.'

'Of course not.'

Chen turned to Margaret, and in English said, 'Thank you, Dr Campbell. You have been very helpful.'

And again to Li, in Chinese, 'Do it again and I'll have you drummed out of the force.'

In the corridor, Margaret said to Li, 'I want to talk to you.'

He knew what was coming and sighed. 'Can't it wait?'

'Now!'

They walked into the detectives' room, faces turning towards them in eager anticipation. Margaret marched straight through and into Li's office, her face like the thunder rumbling among the storm clouds gathering in the heat outside. Reluctantly, and to the disappointment of the detectives, Li followed her in and closed the door behind him.

'You bastard!' Margaret almost spat at him. 'That's why you took me along this morning. So I would lie for you!'

Li shrugged innocently. 'How could I know you would lie

for me?' Her eyes narrowed angrily and she wanted to punch him and kick him, to hurt him any way she could. 'Why did you?' he asked.

She turned her head away, counting up to five to herself, trying to keep control. 'That's a good question. I've been asking it myself. I think . . .' She tried to keep her breathing slow and steady. 'I think because I didn't want to make your uncle ashamed of you.' A sudden thought made her turn to face him again, eyes blazing. 'Is that why you took me to see him this afternoon? So I would like him, and not want to see him dishonoured by the behaviour of his nephew?'

'Of course not.'

'I can't believe how stupid I was not to realise this morning why you took me to the stadium. You *wanted* a witness. Someone of unimpeachable character. Someone you *knew* wasn't going to rat on you, no matter how much they disapproved of what you did.' She waited for some kind of reaction. None came. 'Are you going to deny it?'

He couldn't think of anything to say. She stood for several moments, glaring at him, and then quite unexpectedly started to laugh. He looked at her in amazement. 'What's so funny?'

'You. No, not you. Me. I actually thought you were shy. And sensitive.'

'I am,' he protested, a smile breaking across his face.

'You' – she jabbed a finger at him – 'are a selfish, insensitive, calculating, cold-blooded bastard. And you'd better buy me dinner, 'cos I'm fucking starving!'

*

It was after seven thirty as the BMW swung south down the west side of Tiananmen Square. Great dark storm clouds were gathering in the evening sky. The light was a strange pink colour, as if the world were covered in a film of it. The air was oppressive, the heat almost unbearable. A hot wind gusted among the crowds in the square, blowing kites high into the blue-grey sky above the Great Hall of the People.

The atmosphere in the car was oppressive, too. Lily was clearly displeased at not being apprised of events in Section Chief Chen's office. She was even less pleased to be excluded from the arrangement that Li and Margaret had made to meet that night. Margaret was getting very tired of Lily Peng, and their last exchanges had been terse and tetchy. She was no longer sure whether Lily had been given some watching brief, or whether she was simply being officious and nosey. A third possibility that Margaret had toyed with was the notion that Lily might be jealous, that she had some secret fantasy about Deputy Section Chief Li. Whatever the truth was, Margaret was just anxious to shake her off.

They turned on to West Qianmen Avenue and headed towards the university to pick up her bicycle. Shimei, the diminutive driver, had assured her that it would fit in the trunk. Lily had insisted that they drive her back to the hotel, and Margaret wasn't about to argue. She also needed to call in at the Centre of Material Evidence Determination and ask Professor Xie to arrange further tests on Chao's blood, to confirm that he actually had been infected with AIDS. Then back to the hotel, another quick shower, a change, and a taxi to meet Li outside the Foreign Languages Bookstore in Wangfujing Street.

She felt a thrill of excitement at the prospect. She was hopelessly confused about her feelings for him now. All she knew was that for the first time in months her mind was being stretched, her emotions engaged, and she felt alive again.

CHAPTER EIGHT

I

Wednesday Night

Above the Foreign Languages Bookstore in Wangfujing Street the sky was ominously dark, the evening light fading prematurely in the shadow of the black clouds congregating overhead. The heat was suffocating. Sweat soaked Li's shirt, his third that day. On the way there from the railway station he had noticed a digital display on a tower block, alternating time and temperature, reading 20.10 and 37°C. Some time tonight, he knew, lightning would illuminate the sky, thunder would crash and rumble across the city, and it would rain. Hot, torrential rain that would swell the gutters and wash away the dust of weeks. And after, it would be fresher, cooler, and possible to breathe again.

After writing his report for the Deputy Procurator General, he had turned up unexpectedly at the railway station to see his uncle off on the train. Old Yifu had been glad to see him. Surprised, but pleased. The old man had been quiet and solemn, and they had shaken hands before he climbed aboard the Sichuan express to take his seat in Hard Class among the smoking, eating, spitting travellers that jammed his compartment. Li had watched the train pull away from the platform, gathering speed into the misty evening. A deep depression had settled on him, an unaccountable sense of foreboding. He had wanted to call the train back and tell his uncle not to go. That his sister and her husband could look after themselves. His uncle seemed so fragile, somehow. Old in a way that Li had never seen him before. *My only regret is that I was separated from my wife for that period. We had so little time together afterwards*, he had told Margaret. Li had never heard him express his loss like that before. It had always been something held close and private.

A red taxi pulled up at the kerbside and Margaret got out of the back. Li's spirits lifted at the sight of her. She had put on a touch of fresh make-up, her lips warm and red, a smudge of brown on her eyelids emphasising somehow the blue of her eyes. She wore a pair of light, baggy cotton pants that hugged her behind and tapered to fine, slim ankles. She had a pair of white tennis shoes on her feet, and wore a short-sleeved silk blouse tucked in at the waist. A dipping neckline revealed a hint of cleavage, and emphasised the fullness of her breasts. Her hair cascaded back over her shoulders in loops and curls. Her smile was wide and affectionate as she ran up to him, and for a moment he thought she was going to reach up and kiss him. He experienced a mixture of fear and pleasure at the prospect. But she didn't. 'Hi,' she said.

'Hi,' Li responded, suddenly self-conscious. He thought she looked beautiful.

Margaret had seen him standing in front of the bookshop as the taxi drew up. He, too, had changed again, and was wearing a red brushed-cotton shirt, and fawn pants pleated at the waist. Red suited him. Strong and vibrant against the jet black of his hair. He had seemed distracted as he stood waiting for her, something sad in his expression. But his face lit up when he saw her, and his smile had made her stomach flip. She'd had to resist the temptation to reach up on tiptoe and kiss him, a natural, instinctive response to the feelings of affection that filled her with warmth and weakness. Instead, she slipped her arm through his and said, 'Where are you taking me?'

'Not far,' he said, and steered her north along the west side of the street.

Wangfujing was *the* shopping street in Beijing, jammed with department stores, boutiques, photographic studios, jewellers. They were all still open, doing brisk business, crowds of evening shoppers thronging the sidewalks, cramming into fast-food restaurants, spending hard-earned yuan on fresh foods and fancy goods. Trolley buses and taxis and private cars and bicycles clogged the road. The east side of the street was in the process of redevelopment along most of its length. Li said, 'They are building an underground street three hundred metres long on three levels under here.'

'What for?' Margaret asked.

'More shops,' Li said. 'Chinese can't spend their money fast enough these days. But then Wangfujing Street has always been a place for the rich. It is named after ten princes' mansions built in the Ming Dynasty, and their sweet-water well.'

Suddenly Margaret became aware of a smoky-sweet aroma filling the sticky night air. 'Hmm,' she said. 'Something smells good.'

He smiled, and they turned west into Dong'anmen Street. Margaret stopped and drank in the scene in amazement. 'Dong'anmen night market,' Li said.

A row of food stalls stretching as far as the eye could see ran the full course of the north side. Hundreds, maybe thousands, of people were crushed along its length, flitting from stall to stall buying a dish here, a bird on a stick there, eggs fried in batter, noodles. From beneath dozens of striped canopies set cheek by jowl under the trees, smoke rose from hot oil in giant woks on open braziers. All manner of foods were being stir-fried or deep-fried. Huge copper kettles on hot plates hissed and issued steam into the night sky, boiling water tipping from long curling spouts to make bowls of thick, sweet almond paste. Li steered Margaret gently through the crowds, past stall after stall groaning with skewered meat and vegetables, whole fish, barbecued baby quails impaled on chopsticks, heads and all. Dozens of chefs in white coats and hats sweated over steaming vats on hot coals, drawing out bamboo racks of steamed buns filled with savoury meats or sweet lotus paste. Rice and noodles and soup were served in bowls, with buckets set at the roadside for the dirty dishes. You bought and ate or drank on the spot. It was a meeting place as well as an eating place, whole families gathering with friends to eat and talk under lights strung from the trees overhead.

Cooks shouted at Li and Margaret as they passed, beckoning

them to try their fare. Three yuan a time, Li told her. Livings were made on the basis of volume sales. It was a feast for the eyes as well as the stomach, and just looking at all the food was making Margaret salivate. 'Have what you want,' Li said. 'Just point and we'll get it.'

They had bowls of rice and barbecued satay with a wonderful spicy peanut sauce, eggs fried in dough, noodles and pickled shredded vegetables. Between each course, they thirstily devoured large chunks of watermelon, skewered on chopsticks, to cleanse the palate. They tried sticks of marinated pork, others of beef, stir-fried with sesame seeds and soy, chunks of pineapple coated in seed and seared over red-hot coals, soup, and almond paste dessert.

'Stop, stop! I can't eat any more,' Margaret said finally, laughing. 'Take me away from here. I'll burst.' It was impossible to look without wanting to taste.

Li grinned. 'Your eyes are bigger than your stomach.'

'My stomach'll be too big to squeeze into any of my clothes if I'm not careful.'

She was holding his upper arm, quite naturally, and without thinking. And as she turned she felt her breasts brush his forearm, a tiny, tingling, thrilling sensation that stirred the seeds of desire somewhere deep inside her. She knew he'd been aware of it, because she felt him tensing. She released his arm and they moved a little apart, self-conscious and awkward, and started walking slowly. She did a quick mental calculation. Li had spent around fifty yuan, just over six dollars, for everything they had eaten. And with a pang of conscience, she remembered how poorly paid the Chinese were compared to affluent Westerners. Fifty yuan was probably a lot of money to him. She determined that the next time, *she* would treat *him*. They sauntered idly through the crowds in the direction of the Forbidden City. She took his arm again, and glanced up at him. Why had she ever thought he was ugly? 'How come you never married?' she said.

His step did not falter, and he kept his eyes straight ahead. 'In China it is policy to encourage people not to marry young.'

She looked at him sceptically. 'And that's why *you* never married?'

He reddened. 'Not really. I guess I just never met anyone I wanted to marry.'

'Cops,' she said. 'The same the world over. It's not a job, is it? It's a way of life.'

Until a matter of hours ago, Li would have believed that to be true for him. His widowed uncle had been his role model. Single, driven, ultimately successful. Li had never met his aunt, never really pictured Old Yifu and his wife together. He had always known, because Yifu would never talk about it, how much he missed her. But today, in the park with Margaret, Old Yifu had revealed more of himself than Li had seen in twelve years. And for the first time, Li realised that it was the loss of his wife that had driven Yifu all these years. His work, his pursuit of success, had all been a means of filling the void left by her death. He would have traded it all for the chance of five more precious minutes with her. It was making Li question now what was driving *him*. If there was a void in *his* life, it had always been there. He had no memories of a life shared with someone he loved. He had no real sense of what love was, separated as a very young child from his parents, his mother torn away from him, never to be returned. His job, he understood now, wasn't a way of life, it was an alternative to one.

Margaret had watched the sadness descend on him in an instant, like a veil, his dark eyes deep and languid, almost mournful. 'A yuan for them,' she said.

'Hmm?' He looked at her distractedly.

'Your thoughts.'

He dragged himself away from them and forced a smile. 'They're not worth half that,' he said. And, quickly, to change the subject, 'Are you thirsty?'

She nodded. 'Very.' All that salty, sweet food.

'We'll go get some tea,' he said. 'I know a place.'

The Sanwei Bookstore was in a small side street off Fuxingmennei Avenue, opposite the Minorities Palace. It was dark here, leafy spreading trees casting shadows from the streetlights, the noise of traffic on the avenue muffled by a bank of trees on the sidewalk side of the cycle lane. Dark *hutongs* ran off into a maze of *siheyuan* courtyards, dusty and crumbling and newly emerged from behind hoardings raised during the construction of a new stretch of Underground. Everywhere, families had left the cramped and unbreathable spaces they occupied in tiny houses and spilled out on to the pavements to sit on walls, drinking jars of tea and chatting idly. Men squatted in groups under the trees playing chess, and children chased up and down the sidewalks, burning up energy and their mothers' patience in the stifling heat of the night.

Li and Margaret had taken a No. 4 bus from the bottom end of Wangfujing. It was an experience for Margaret – standing room only, crushed among the bodies squeezed into the long articulated vehicle, curious faces staring at her with undisguised amazement. *Yangguizi* never travelled on buses. It was unheard of. And this one was particularly strange. Fair-haired and blue-eyed. A tiny child, clutching at her mother's breast for fear the foreign devil would snatch her away, couldn't take her eyes off Margaret for the entire journey.

They missed their stop at Fuxingmen and had to walk back, past Radio Beijing and Beijing Telecom, crossing via a pedestrian underpass to the dark and decaying south side of the street. The Sanwei, which meant 'three flavours', Li explained, had an undistinguished window and a dark entrance behind a bus stop. A board leaning against the wall outside promised a jazz band every Thursday evening. Margaret thought it seemed an unlikely venue. 'Is this it?' she asked. 'A cup of tea in a bookshop? And if we come tomorrow we get jazz thrown in?'

He smiled. 'The tearoom is upstairs.'

He led her into a small entrance lobby. Down a couple of steps, and through glass doors, was the bookshop, row upon row of shelves lined with thousands of books, assistants idly wandering the aisles. It was not doing much business. They turned left through a door and up gloomy stairs into another world.

Here was a room from another age, peaceful and hushed in its dimly lit elegance, cloistered and unreal, an oasis amidst the humid dereliction of the street outside. From its high ceiling, fans swung in lazy unison, stirring paper lanterns hanging over sets of lacquered dark-wood tables and chairs. Along one side ran a narrow passageway behind a low wall and tall columns. Along the other, ornately carved wooden screens were arranged to create private alcoves. Flowers grew in pots on every available space, vases stood on every table. The walls were lined with both modern and traditional Chinese paintings.

A young girl greeted them at the top of the stairs and led them across the tiled floor to a table in an alcove. There was not another soul in the place. The rumble of traffic was a distant memory, and the air-conditioning took the heat out of the night. The girl lit a candle at their table and handed them each a menu. Margaret was afraid to raise her voice, as if in a church. 'This place is amazing,' she said. 'You would never know it was here.'

'It's popular with writers and artists,' he said. 'And musicians. It's very crowded at the weekends, and there is usually music. But in the early week it is quiet.' His eyes reflected the flickering candlelight like shiny black coals. 'What would you like to drink?'

'Just tea.'

He ordered, and the girl brought a tray of delicacies for them to choose from. Margaret picked a small dish of toasted sunflower seeds to nibble on. The tea came in colourfully patterned china cups set in deep saucers and covered with lids. Hot water was poured over a sprinkling of dried green leaves in the bottom of the cups from a heavy, traditionally shaped brass teapot. The girl left it at the table for them to top up their own. The green leaves floated to the tops of their cups, expanding and turning fleshy as they rehydrated. Li replaced the lids. 'Better to wait a few minutes.'

They sat in silence then for some time. Not a difficult silence, not awkward or self-conscious, but comfortable. Words seemed unnecessary somehow. Li looked at her hands, clasped on the table in front of her. He marvelled at how pink the flesh was beneath the nails, how delicate the fingers that wielded the instruments of autopsy, cutting open corpses to unravel the mysteries of death.

'What on earth made you want to be a doctor?' he asked suddenly, almost without meaning to. And immediately he regretted it, fearing she would take offence at his tone.

But she just laughed. 'Why? Is it so awful?'

'I'm sorry,' he said. 'I didn't mean to be ...' He tailed off and shook his head. 'You know, when you told those students I was squeamish about being at autopsies, you were right.'

She looked at him, surprised. 'But you must have been at dozens.'

'I have. And I want to throw up every time.'

Which made her smile. 'You poor soul.'

'I just can't imagine why anyone would want to do it. Cutting up dead bodies. Or living ones. In fact, that's probably worse. Diseases and cancers. People dying all the time.'

'That's what got to *me*,' she said. 'People dying on me. It's much easier dealing with the dead. You don't get attached to them.' She removed the lid from her cup and sipped at the tea. It was still very hot, and wonderfully refreshing. 'I used to think medicine was vocational. You know, something you were born to. But I'm pretty cynical about it now. Most doctors I know are in it for the money. I'd wanted to be a doctor as long as I could remember. To help people, to save their lives, to ease their pain. But it's not like that. There's never enough money, there's never enough time. When you graduate from medical school you think you know it all, then you find out you know nothing. Whatever you can do, it's never enough.

'When I worked in the emergency room at the UIC Medical Centre, I had people in my care dying nearly every day. Stabbings, muggings, poor bastards pulled from car wrecks, kids hit by automobiles, fires, suicides. You name it. They'd come in with arms and legs hanging off. People burned from head to toe, so bad they don't feel a thing. They'll sit talking to you, and you know what they don't – in a couple of hours they're going to die. They talk about patients in trauma. But half the time the doctors are in trauma, too. There's a limit to how much of that you can take, Li Yan, before you start turning into some kind of automaton.

'The dead? They're gone. Where, I don't know. But the body's just a receptacle, and I can be cold and detached and clinical about cutting it up, because whoever that person was is not there now.'

Her tea was cooling, and she took a longer draught of it and nibbled some sunflower seeds.

'I think maybe doctors must be a little like cops,' Li said. 'No home life.'

Margaret flicked him a glance and then looked away again quickly. 'No,' she said. 'No home life worth a damn.'

He took his life in his hands and strayed into that unknown and potentially treacherous territory he had come close to twice before. 'Is that why you and your husband divorced?'

She met his eye head-on. 'Oh, we didn't get divorced,' she said.

He was taken by surprise, confused and disappointed. 'But you said you were no longer . . .'

'He's dead,' she said simply, interrupting.

'Oh.' Li knew he'd just stood on a land-mine. 'I'm sorry.'

'Don't be. I'm not.' But her voice was tight with emotion. She reined it in and kept it to herself for some moments, staring at her hands. Then she said, 'Michael was a good-looking guy. All the girls thought he was gorgeous, and all my friends thought I was so lucky when we got engaged. So did I. But then, what do you know at twenty-four?' She took a deep, trembling breath. 'He was a few years older than me, so I guess I looked up to him. He was so smart, and so passionate about stuff. Especially genetics. And he was always bucking the Establishment, taking the unorthodox view, speaking his mind, even at the expense of his career. That's why he ended up lecturing at the Roosevelt when he was capable of so much better. I admired him for his principles.' There was a sad fondness in her smile as she remembered.

'In the early days we used to sit up talking late into the night, smoking dope and drinking beer and putting the world to rights. Like teenagers. We were big kids, really.

'But then, life started taking over. For me, anyway. You know how it is. You get your first job. You're on the first rung of the ladder. They know it, so they work you every hour God gives. You know it, so you do it 'cos you want to climb the ladder. Michael wanted kids, I didn't. Not then, anyway. There was a lot I still had to achieve in life. I wasn't about to throw it all away for motherhood. There would be time for that, or so I thought.

'So maybe it was my fault he started playing around. But I think maybe he'd always been doing it. I just never knew until it all came out at the trial.' She stopped herself, wondering why she was telling him all this. It was coming so easy, pouring from her like blood from a wound, or maybe pus from an infected sore.

She glanced up and found his eyes fixed on her, deep and dark and sympathetic. Then for a moment she became aware of the girl who had served them shuffling idly between the tables, adjusting a chair she might have adjusted a dozen times before, wiping a speck of dust from a table, her mind lost in thoughts of a life they would never know.

'I should have known from my student days,' Margaret said. 'There was always one lecturer, maybe younger than the rest though not always, that the girls would all find attractive. And for a semester, or maybe even a whole year, one of them would have a passionate affair with him. They had so much in common, she would tell the others. He was so intelligent, so mature, so experienced. By the end of the year she would grow up and move on, and he would have another passionate affair with some kid the next year, some starry-eyed young girl who would think he was so intelligent, so mature, so experienced.' Margaret's smile was bitter and sad. 'Michael was one of those. Every year another student, or maybe two. And he would sit up with them into the small hours, smoking dope and drinking beer, putting the world to rights. While I was working ninety-five-hour weeks as an intern, busting a gut to build a career.' Her eyes started to fill, and for a moment she panicked, thinking she might start to cry. She blinked furiously, and a couple of salty drops splashed on the lacquered surface of the table. She drained her tea, down to the thick green leaves that had sunk to the bottom of the cup. Without a word Li refilled her cup, and then she felt his hand slip over hers, warm and dry and comforting. She blinked at him and smiled bravely. 'I'm sorry, I didn't mean to . . .' She sighed. 'I should never have started this.'

'It is all right,' he said softly. 'Go on if you want to. Stop if you don't.'

She withdrew her hand from his and took a tissue from her purse and dabbed her eyes, taking a couple of deep breaths to calm herself. 'The first I knew anything about it,' she said, 'was when the police came to arrest him.' She remembered vividly how it had been. 'I was with the Cook County Medical Examiner's Office by that time. I'd been working late. Michael was still up when I got home. He'd been smoking a lot of dope and was acting pretty strange. There'd been a murder on campus, in the student residence. One of his students, a nineteen-year-old girl, raped and battered to death. We'd been talking about it the day before. He seemed pretty shocked. I'd fallen asleep on the settee, and the next I knew the police were at the door. Six in the morning. I was still half asleep. I didn't really know what was happening. They read him his Miranda rights, cuffed him and took him away. He just kept saying, "I didn't do it, Mags, I didn't do it".' She glanced up at Li, a hint of what he took to be something close to shame in her eyes. 'And I believed him. Or, at least, I wanted to.'

She shook her head. 'The trial was a nightmare. He pled not guilty, of course. But there was overwhelming forensic and DNA evidence against him. The prosecution said he'd been drinking and that he couldn't take the rejection when the girl said no. They said he was used to getting his way with young girls, attractive, impressionable students falling at his feet year after year. A procession of them came to the witness stand and went through their affairs with him in graphic detail.' She took a moment to control herself. 'The thing is, I knew it was true. Everything they said. It was just Michael. I was so angry – with myself, for not having seen it. I could believe it of him so easily. I just couldn't believe he was a murderer. My family, my friends, everyone thought the same. He'd been a rat. Sure. But kill someone? Michael? No, not Michael. Not dear, sweet, intelligent Michael with all his great liberal ideas and his concern for humankind.

'So I did everything in my power to try to undermine the

scientific evidence against him. The blood, the semen, the fibres collected at the scene. Contaminated. All contaminated. Sloppy police work, I said. His legal team did a good job. But not good enough. He was no O. J. Simpson. He couldn't afford the best. The trial lasted three weeks and it took every penny we had. We lost the apartment, the automobile. I moved in with a friend.' She paused, lost for a long time in private thought. 'The jury found him guilty and he was sentenced to life. And still he was saying, "I didn't do it, Mags. You gotta believe me, I didn't do it." So I started borrowing money to kick off the appeals procedure. But it wasn't going well, and he was more and more depressed every time I went to see him. And then one night I got a phone call. He'd hanged himself in his cell. He was dead. It was over, and I could always believe he was innocent. The victim of a terrible miscarriage of justice. That's what my folks said, and my friends. They were really supportive. I cried for about twelve hours, till I got that I was aching so much I couldn't feel a thing.

'Then the next day I get this letter through the door. It's his handwriting. I knew it right away. It was like he'd come back from the dead, and I still wasn't used to him not being alive. It didn't say much.' She bit her lip as she remembered. '"Dear Mags, I can't begin to tell you how sorry I am. But I just can't go on living with this. I never meant to kill her. I hope you'll believe that. I'll always love you. Mikey."' Big, silent tears ran down Margaret's cheeks. 'He couldn't live with it. But he made damn sure I had to. Like he was passing on all the guilt. He killed that girl. He raped her and then he hit her again and again and again until he had smashed her skull. He had lied to me about everything. Why couldn't he have lied to me one last time?' She put her fist to her mouth and bit down hard on the knuckles. Li stretched over and pulled it gently away and held her hand as she sobbed, and the tears splashed in great heavy drops on the table, glistening in the flickering candlelight.

It was several minutes before she could speak again. Her tissue was sodden, her eyes red and swollen, her cheeks blotched. 'I never told anyone before,' she said. 'About the letter. It was easier to let everyone else go on believing the lie, or at least hold back from giving them a reason not to.'

'Does it help?' he asked gently. 'Having told me?'

'It may not look like it.' She half laughed through the tears. 'But I haven't felt this good in months.'

She didn't know why she had told him. Perhaps because he was a stranger, a long way from her life back home, from her friends and her family; because in a few weeks she would be getting on a plane and flying back across the Pacific and would never see him again; because she felt close to him, drawn by his deep, dark eyes and the sensitivity she knew they reflected. But maybe simply because she had needed to tell someone. Anyone. The burden of guilt and hurt and confusion had just become too much to bear. And already she felt the weight of it lifted from her. But she was glad it was Li, and in those moments she felt as close to him as she had felt to anyone in years.

Li, too, was wondering why she had told him. It was almost

scary to be the recipient of something so personal, to share in so much of someone else's pain. He felt privileged, too. She had made herself supremely vulnerable, demonstrating an enormous trust in him, even if she was getting on a plane in five weeks' time to fly out of his life for ever. He had never, in his thirty-three years, felt so drawn to someone as he was to Margaret now. He was frightened to speak, to do anything that would spoil the moment or bring it to an end. Her hand felt very small in his. He ran his thumb lightly over the Mekong delta of blue veins that ran down the back of it, and felt the pulsing of her blood. He wanted to hold her whole body to him, and feel its life and its warmth and keep it safe. But he did nothing. Said nothing.

After a while she made a little sigh and withdrew her hand from his, searching again for another tissue in her purse. But she couldn't find one. 'Do I look awful?' she said.

'No more than usual.' He smiled.

She returned the smile, but it was watery and wounded. 'I think I could do with a drink,' she said. 'Something a little stronger than tea.'

II

Outside, the dark night was filled with a sense of anticipation. The rain was so close you could almost touch it. Families still filled the spaces on the sidewalk and under the trees, but were subdued now, children curled up on mothers' knees, card games in suspended animation. The men sat and smoked in silence; the hot wind of earlier had stilled, and their cigarette smoke rose in undisturbed columns. Dust and humidity hung in the air, turned blue by floodlights on a building site across the avenue. Great yellow cranes stood silently overhead, waiting for the first drops to come. The road was thick with traffic moving in long, slow columns. Cicadas were screaming in the trees. Everyone and everything, it seemed, was waiting for the rain.

Li and Margaret walked slowly east along the sidewalk past brightly lit barber shops, small stores selling shoes and underwear and throwing great rectangular slabs of light out into the darkness. The sounds of washing-up in restaurant kitchens came from open windows up narrow alleys. Li's hand engulfed hers and she was happy to leave it there, comforted by its warmth and strength. He knew a bar, he said, at Xidan. They could get a drink there. They walked in silence, his mind full of what she had emptied from hers. And she was happy not to think of anything, to have her mind filled by nothing; no regrets, no sadness, no pain. They passed a small shop whose speciality was shoe repair and key-cutting, its window giving on to a workshop where an old man in greasy overalls sweated over a last. Rows of key blanks hung on rods beside the cutting machine.

Margaret stopped, her hand slipping from his. He turned to see her face etched in concentration as she stared in the window. He looked to see what she saw, and saw nothing but the old man at the last and the key blanks on rods. 'What is it?'

The clouds had rolled back from her eyes and they shone

brightly in the light from the shop. 'The key,' she said. 'The key to the stair gate. The killer must have used it to unlock the gate, right? Whether he locked it behind him or not is unimportant. What's important is he didn't leave it in the lock or drop it on the floor. He must have put it in his pocket.'

For Li, this had come straight out of left-field, catching him on the blind-side. 'Hey, wait. Slow down,' he said. 'What are you talking about?'

'Can we go to the park?'

'What, now?'

'Yes.'

'It's pitch dark. And it'll be locked up.'

'That didn't stop the killer getting in.' Her eyes were burning now with a strange intensity. 'Please, Li Yan. This could be important.'

She wouldn't discuss it further as they took a taxi back to Section One to pick up a car and a flashlight. She might be wrong, she said. She wanted to walk him through it at the scene. There, it would either make sense or not. He didn't press her.

They drove through the deserted streets of the Ritan legation area, streetlamps smothered by trees, embassy lights twinkling behind high walls and shut gates. In Guanghua Road, alive in the day with street traders and hawkers of every description, the gates to the park were also closed, locked and forbidding. The park lay brooding in the darkness beyond.

'This is crazy,' Li said. 'Can't it wait till the morning?'

'No.' Margaret jumped out of the Jeep and started climbing

the gate. 'Come on,' she called. 'It's not difficult. And bring the flashlight.'

Li sighed and did as he was told. He wondered if he would have indulged her in this behaviour had it not been for her confession of just an hour before, or if she had not aroused in him such intense feelings of . . . of what? He had no idea. He had never felt like this before.

He climbed the gate easily and dropped down on the other side to join her. A long, straight avenue lined by trees and park benches cut north into the darkness. As they moved further into the park, away from the streetlights, he switched on his flashlight to lead her through the maze of paths that would take them to the lake.

The park, so open and friendly during the day, dappled by sunlight, and filled with the peace of people seeking solitude or relaxation, seemed oddly menacing in the dark – the rustle of night animals in the undergrowth, the eerie call of an owl, the splash of something landing in water as they neared the lake. The sweet scent of pine filled the hot night air, and the willows hung limp and lifeless, trailing their leaves along the edges of the still water. Li's flashlight picked out the bridge to the pavilion, reflected white in the black water. 'This way.' He took her hand and led her round the east side of the lake to the dusty path that led up to the clearing where the twins and their baby-sitter had stumbled upon the blazing body of Chao Heng less than forty-eight hours before. A length of yellow tape was stretched between two stakes to keep the public out. Li stepped over it, and Margaret followed him up to the clearing. A line of chalk still ringed the crime scene, glowing white in the glare of the flashlight. A charred area remained in the centre of the clearing, but the smell of burning had long ago been replaced by the pungent spice of spruce and locust. But there was a desolate and haunted feel about the place, bled of all colour, monochrome in the harsh electric light. There was a sudden and unexpected flash in the sky, followed a few moments later by the not very distant rumble of thunder. The first fat drops of rain started falling, forming tiny craters in the dust.

'Better make it quick,' Li said. 'We're going to get soaked.'

But Margaret was oblivious. She walked carefully around the clearing, pulling at the shrubs around its perimeter, stopping finally, facing the path they had come up on the other side. Li had tracked her round with the beam of the flashlight. 'He was wearing gloves, right?' she said.

Li nodded acquiescence. 'He didn't leave any prints – in the apartment or on the gasoline can. He must have been.'

'Okay. So he got Chao here in the dark. He sat and smoked a single cigarette, and waited for daylight. The kids found the blazing body when . . . ?'

'Around six thirty.'

'So the park had been open for about half an hour?' Li nodded. 'He poured gasoline all over Chao and struck a match. He wanted the body to be found still ablaze. Why? A macabre sense of theatre, perhaps; or maybe to create a diversion in which he could walk away unnoticed.' She turned around. 'He retreats this way, through the undergrowth, right? Because nobody saw him leave by the path the twins came up.' She plunged through the shrubs and bushes, away from the clearing. Li hurried after her. 'He's going to come out on a path somewhere away over there,' she called back, waving her hand vaguely into the darkness. The rain was still falling in single fat drops that they could have counted had they so desired. Another flash, the thunder nearer this time. 'But he's not going to walk away unnoticed wearing a pair of gloves, is he? Not on a sticky hot summer morning. He could have put them in his pockets, but suppose something went wrong and he got stopped.' She pushed on through the undergrowth. Li followed. 'Some quirk of fate. The alarm gets raised sooner than he thought. There's a cop at the gate who stops anyone leaving. The killer doesn't want to be found with a pair of gloves in his pocket, a pair of gloves stained with gasoline, maybe blood. So he throws them away, somewhere far away into the undergrowth.' She mimicked the action. 'What does it matter if they get found. There's no way to trace them back to him. Then he remembers something. Damn! He's still got the key to the stair gate at Chao's apartment in his pocket. Now, that *could* tie him to his victim if he got stopped. It's a long shot, but this guy doesn't take any chances. He'll have left his gun hidden in his vehicle. He's meticulous. He's a professional. And here's a loose end. So he hurls the key away into the undergrowth after the gloves. Nobody's ever going to find it. Hell, nobody's even going to look. And nobody would know what it was anyway. Just a key. So he doesn't worry about the fact that he's not wearing gloves, and that his fingerprints are going to be on it.'

Her face was gleaming with excitement in the beam of the flashlight. Li's mind was racing, assimilating what she had said. For a moment he closed his eyes to try to visualise what she had described. He saw very vividly the figure of a man retreating through the undergrowth. He was peeling the gloves from his hands as he went. He threw them as far as he could, then stopped suddenly, remembering the key. He took it out of his pocket, looked at it thoughtfully for a moment, then turned and threw it in the opposite direction, before hurrying off, away from the crackle of flame and smoke behind him. Li opened his eyes, and for a moment night turned to day, thunder crashed overhead, and the rain came down like rods, crashing through the leaves, turning dust to mud beneath their feet as they stood. Margaret's face had been caught as if by a photographic flash, and the image of it was burned on to his eyes and remained there as he blinked to regain his night sight.

'I mean, maybe it didn't happen like that at all,' Margaret said. 'But it's possible. Isn't it? And if it did, then those gloves and that key are still here somewhere.' She was having to shout now above the crashing of the rain. 'Worth looking?'

'Was he left- or right-handed?'

She frowned. 'What?'

'The killer. Can you tell? Maybe from the angle of the blow to Chao's head?'

'No.' She shook her head. 'Not for certain. But if you wanted to go by the laws of probability, he would be right-handed. Why?'

'It could affect the direction he threw the gloves and the key.'

'So you think it's possible?'

He nodded. 'I think it's possible.'

She grinned, and he wanted to kiss her right there and then, cup her face in his hands and press his lips to hers. The rain was streaming down her face now, her hair slicked back by the wet. The silk of her blouse clung to the contours of her breasts, nipples puckered and erect, pushing hard against the soft, wet material. She was still not wearing a bra. 'You want to look now?' she asked.

'It's raining!' he laughed, incredulous. 'And I should organise an official search.'

'We're wet already. And before you go calling out half the Beijing police force, it would help to justify it if you'd at least found a glove.' She fumbled in her purse. 'I've got a key-light in here somewhere.' And she laughed. 'Now that's ironic, isn't it? A key-light!' She found it. 'You take the right side, I'll take the left. If we don't find something in ten minutes you can call in the cavalry.'

And before he had time to object, she was off, pushing through the shrubbery, pointing a pencil-beam of light ahead of her. He shook his head. She was in her element. It was as if telling him her story in the tearoom had lifted an enormous burden from her. She hadn't needed alcohol. She was as high as a kite. And he wondered what on earth he was doing there, soaked to the skin, scrabbling about in the bushes in the dark, in pursuit of something that was probably illusory, the creation of two overactive imaginations on an emotionally charged night.

He scrambled through the bushes to his right, scanning the ground with the flashlight. It had been dry for so long and the ground was baked so hard that the rain wasn't draining away immediately. It lay in great pools, filling every dip and hollow. Another flash of sheet lightning lit up the park, reflected off every glistening branch and leaf. For a moment he thought he saw a figure darting through the trees, the briefest flickering movement, like half a dozen frames of an old black-and-white movie. He had lost his bearings. It must have been Margaret. He called out, but the rain was still deafening, and he couldn't hear whether she had replied. He shook his head and wiped the rain from his eyes, and pushed on, swinging the beam of his flashlight from side to side. He went to check the time on his watch, but it wasn't there, and he remembered breaking the chain earlier in the day. He must have been blundering around in the dark and wet for at least ten minutes by now, he thought. He turned, wondering which way it was back to the clearing. As he did, the beam of his flashlight caught the dark shape of something hanging in the branches of a bush. He swung the light back. It looked like a dead bird. He pushed through the undergrowth towards it, and as he reached out it fell to the ground. He crouched down and shone the lamp on it. It was a sodden leather glove. 'Hey!' he called out. 'Margaret! I've found one.' He heard her footsteps approaching from behind and turned as a fist smashed down into his face. The shock of it robbed him of his senses and he keeled over, blinking blood and rain out of his eyes. His flashlight clattered away into the bushes. He saw a dark shadow looming over him. And the fist smashed into his face again. And again. Hard. Brutally hard. His attacker was strong and very fast. He saw the fist draw back again and knew he could do nothing to stop it.

'Li Yan?' He heard Margaret's voice above the drumming of the rain. 'Li Yan, where are you?'

The fist paused and hung uncertainly for a moment, then unravelled into fingers and thumb, flying past him to the ground like some hawk diving on its prey. It retreated again, clutching the glove. Lightning and thunder were almost simultaneous this time, a deafening roar from directly overhead. And for the briefest of moments, Li and his attacker were frozen in the hard blue light, looking straight into each other's eyes. And then darkness, and the man was gone, crashing off through the bushes, his image still burned into Li's eyes, as Margaret's had been earlier.

'For Christ's sake, Li Yan, where are you!' He pulled himself to his knees, and then dragged himself to his feet. Margaret's pencil-beam of light flashed in his face. He heard her gasp. 'Oh my God! What's happened?'

III

The lake and the pavilion were thrown into sharp relief by floodlights raised on stands among the trees. The random cycle of flashing lights on police vehicles and ambulance reflected in rippling patterns on the water. The crackle of police radios filled the night air, competing with the cicadas that had started up again as soon as the rain stopped. Li sat side-on in the driver's seat of the Jeep, the door open wide, as a medic patched up his face: a split lip, a bloody nose – broken, Margaret thought – a bruised and swelling cheek, and an inch-long split on his left brow that required two stitches.

Margaret watched from the lakeside as Detective Qian organised uniformed officers into groups, dividing and sub-dividing the immediate territory into quadrants for searching on hands and knees, inch by inch. She checked the time. It was twenty-five to midnight. It was cooler after the rain, a slight breeze stirring the leaves. Her hair and clothes were virtually dry. The ground, parched after weeks of drought, had soaked up all the rainwater, and it was hard to believe now that there had been a deluge less than an hour before. Margaret glanced at Li and felt another pang of guilt. None of this would have happened if it hadn't been for her, if he hadn't indulged her insistence on searching for the gloves by themselves in the pouring rain.

Qian detached himself from the search groups and crossed to Li as the medic finished up. He looked at his boss's battered face in awe. 'He made some mess of you, boss.'

'You want to see the mess I made of his hand,' Li said grimly.

Qian chuckled. 'Good to see you haven't lost your sense of humour.' Li glared at him and his smiled faded. 'So why do you think he attacked you?'

'Because I'd found one of the gloves,' Li growled.

'And you think that's what he was doing here? He'd come back to look for them?'

Li shook his head. 'I don't know. Maybe. Or maybe he'd followed us. One thing's for sure. When he saw us searching the undergrowth he worked out pretty damn quick what we were up to. And now he's got at least one of the gloves, maybe both of them, and maybe the key as well, if it was ever there.'

'Hell, boss, why didn't you just call in a search when you thought of all this, instead of scratching about in the dark and the rain on your own?' He glanced off towards Margaret. 'Well, almost on your own.' He turned back to Li and saw a warning look in his eyes, and decided to back off. 'I'll just get these guys started,' he said, jerking his head in the direction of the uniforms. And he headed off shouting out instructions.

Li lit a cigarette and looked up as Margaret approached. 'Don't tell me it's bad for my health,' he said. 'It can't do me nearly as much damage as being around you.' He smiled wryly and winced at the pain. 'You should have a health warning stamped on your forehead.'

But his attempt at humour only served to deepen her sense of guilt. 'I'm sorry,' she said. 'I know this is all my fault.'

Li said, 'You didn't murder three people, then come into a park and assault a police officer. How can it be your fault?'

'Because you wouldn't have been in the park in the first place. And you certainly wouldn't have been stumbling about the bushes in the rain trying to find a needle in a haystack.'

'But I found the needle,' he said. 'At least, one of them.'

'And then lost it again.'

He glanced at her anxiously, hesitating for a moment. 'What do you think he was doing here? The man who attacked me.'

'Looking for the same thing as us.'

'Why didn't he do that last night?'

She stopped and thought about it, and then frowned and looked at him, concerned. 'You think he followed us here?' He inclined his head a little to one side and raised an eyebrow. He did not want to commit himself. 'Because if he did, that means he's been watching us.' And a shiver raised goose bumps on her arms. 'That's creepy. Why would he do that?'

Li shrugged. 'I don't know. Maybe he's monitoring our progress. If we get too close to him, or to the truth, he'll intervene. Like he did tonight.'

Margaret felt the hairs rise up on the back of her neck, and she glanced around the dark perimeter beyond the ring of light, wondering if somewhere out there he was still watching. 'Did you see his face at all?' she asked.

'For a moment,' Li said. 'In the lightning flash.' He could still see the face vividly in his mind's eye, pale, tinged with blue like the face of a corpse, contorted with fear and . . . anger. Yes, that was what it had been, anger. But why, Li wondered, had he been angry? With himself, perhaps? For having made the mistake with the gloves in the first place?

'Would you know him again?'

'I don't know. He had the face of a devil. It was like looking at death. He didn't seem human, somehow.' He shook his head. 'It's hard to explain.'

And Margaret realised in that moment that Li had thought he was going to die. He had been caught unawares and beaten to the ground with a fist like steel. Lying dazed and helpless in the mud, his attacker looming over him, he had believed that the man would kill him. What had stopped him? Had it really just been her voice calling through the rain? What could *she* have done? He could just as easily have killed her. But then, she realised, for a professional killer he was behaving uncharacteristically. On impulse. None of it had been planned. He had been responding to the moment, trying to correct or cover up an equally uncharacteristic mistake made nearly forty-eight hours earlier. Perhaps her voice had simply brought him to his senses and he had retreated into the night to lick his wounds. For that was what he was like, she thought. A wounded animal. A professional killer who had made one small mistake, and then compounded it. And that made him extremely dangerous.

A uniformed officer arrived in a police car and got out with a carrier bag of fresh clothes for Li – jeans and trainers and a white shirt, collected from his apartment. Li changed in the back of the Jeep. 'I should take you back to the hotel,' he called to Margaret.

'I'm fine,' she said. 'All dried off now.' She ran her hands back through her hair to untangle the mass of curls. 'Besides,

I wouldn't sleep, wondering if they'd found anything.' She was beginning to doubt that she would ever sleep again. 'How long do you think they will take?'

Li climbed out of the back of the Jeep and glanced up the slope to where police floodlights had turned night into day. Teams of officers were working their way through the bushes, inch by meticulous inch, calling to one another above the thrum of the generator and the screeching of the cicadas. 'It's not such a big space to cover. A couple of hours maybe. If they find nothing, we'll leave armed guards and bring in fresh teams tomorrow to extend the search area.' He was glad she wanted to stay, not just because he wanted to be with her, but because after the events of tonight he was afraid for her. Afraid of unseen eyes watching them, tracking them. The investigation had become dangerous, and he knew that from tomorrow he would have to sever her connection with it.

As he lit another cigarette, there was a shout from the top of the slope. He threw the cigarette away and ran up the path as a young officer emerged from the undergrowth holding up a single glove with a pair of plastic tongs. So the killer hadn't got both gloves. Li derived a momentary satisfaction from that. Qian got the officer to drop the glove in a plastic evidence bag and sealed it. He handed it to Li. 'Look familiar?'

'I don't know. I only saw the other one for a few seconds.' He looked at it closely. It was a plain brown leather glove with a brushed cotton lining, still damp from the rain and stiffening as it dried.

Margaret appeared at his shoulder. 'May I take a look?' He

handed it to her, and she examined it closely through the clear plastic. 'There,' she said, and teased out a maker's label that had curled up at the seam just inside the open end. She squinted at it in the light. '*Made in Hong Kong*,' she read. 'And there, just inside the thumb . . .' She folded out a small, dark stain for him to see. 'Could be blood.' She turned the glove over. 'It hasn't been worn much.'

'How do you know?' Li asked.

'Leather stretches with wear, takes on the shape of your hand. This looks as if it's not long off the peg. See, there's barely been any pull at the stitching. They were probably custom-bought for the job.'

'In Hong Kong?'

'That's where they were made. They're expensive gloves. Probably not widely available in China. If at all. But you'd know more about that than me.'

Li nodded thoughtfully. He took the bag and handed it back to Qian, and they had a brief exchange. Margaret followed him back down the slope to the Jeep. 'What now?'

'The glove'll go straight back to the lab for forensic examination. And we'll wait until they find the key. Or not.' He lit a cigarette and looked at her appraisingly. 'You were right about the gloves. Let's hope you were right about the key as well.'

It was nearly half past midnight when the shout came that they had been waiting for. The key had been nestling in among the roots of a small shrub, about thirty feet from where they had found the glove. Li looked at it excitedly in its small plastic bag, brought to him out of a glare of floodlights by a triumphant Detective Qian. If luck was on their side, it could turn out to be the key to a great deal more than Chao Heng's stair gate. He turned to find Margaret, eyes gleaming, looking at the key as he held it up. He wanted to kiss her. He would never have had the thought that had led them to find it. She used the same thought processes he did. Visualised things, it seemed, in the same way. But she had made a leap of imagination that would not have occurred to him. A wild and unlikely leap in the dark. So unlikely that even if he'd had the thought he would probably have dismissed it. Perhaps she was less afraid of being wrong than he was.

The drive to the Centre of Criminal Technological Determination in Pao Jü Hutong was a revelation to Margaret, an insight into the street life of the real Beijing tucked away behind the façades and advertising hoardings of the new China. Even at this late hour, the streets teemed with night life, the population emerging again from steamy-hot homes into the relative cool of the *hutongs* after the rain. Li's Jeep followed in the wake of a forensics van, two sets of headlights raking the narrow alleyways and *siheyuan*, capturing for brief moments families eating at tables on the sidewalk, a man sprawled in an armchair gazing at the flickering blue light of a television set, food served to card players through open windows whose light spilled across the tarmac, people on bicycles that wobbled in the headlights as the vehicles raced past. Margaret peered from the window on the passenger side, faces flashing past, staring back at her. Some blankly, some with hostility, others with curiosity. Beijingers, Margaret thought, had a preoccupation with getting their hair cut. Barbers everywhere were still doing business. She checked the time. It was almost 1 a.m.

There was an urgency now about Li. His face had swollen around his left eye. It was bruised a deep blue. But the eyes themselves were sharp and alive and burning with a fierce intensity. He was in a hurry to get his man.

They abandoned the Jeep in the street and ran up the ramp through large open gates, past armed guards, into the bowels of the Pao Jü laboratories of forensic pathology. 'A few minutes, Li, that's all,' the lead forensics officer told him. They waited in an office on the ground floor, Li sitting on the edge of a desk swinging his legs impatiently. Margaret recalled Bob's tale about the Three Ps – Patience, Patience and Patience. *The three things you must have to survive in this country*, he had said. Li seemed to have run out of all of them. She examined his face. 'They must have some witch-hazel here.'

'Some what?' he said.

'It'll bring down the swelling and stop your face from going completely black and blue by the morning.'

She spent some time in conversation with a lab assistant before he went off, returning a few minutes later with some clear fluid in a bottle and some large wads of cotton wool. She soaked a wad and told Li to hold it to his face. He didn't argue with her, but with his free hand shook a cigarette from its packet and lit it. He had only taken one pull at it when the lead forensics officer hurried in, pink with exertion and breathing hard. He, it seemed, had also been infected by Li's sense of urgency.

'A single index finger. Smudged. No use.'

'Shit!' Li looked sick.

'Hang on,' the forensics man admonished him. 'We also got a thumb.' He held up a sheet of paper with a blow-up of the print. 'It's not Chao's, and it's just about perfect.'

IV

It was after two when Li and Margaret stepped back out into Pao Jü Hutong. It was cool now, the air fresh and breathable. For the first time since she had arrived, Margaret could see stars in the sky. She was tired, but she wasn't sleepy. She felt an odd sense of exhilaration. The glove and the key had been a major breakthrough. An officer had been sent to Chao's apartment building to check that the key fitted the stair gate. It did. Close forensic examination of the glove had revealed a speck of blood at the top of the interior lining of the middle finger. It might have come from a paper cut, or a damaged cuticle. But there was enough there to enable a DNA comparison with the saliva on the cigarette ends. That test would be done at the Centre of Material Evidence Determination in the morning – along with a comparison of the bloodstain on the outer glove with blood samples taken from Chao Heng. If both tests proved positive, it would conclusively tie the wearer of the glove to the murder of Chao and both the other victims. The thumbprint from the key had been faxed to Hong Kong. It was possible, just possible, that by morning they would know the identity of the killer.

In spite of being on the wrong end of a beating, Li was euphoric. He was still pressing the wad soaked with witch-hazel to his face. 'Let me see,' Margaret said as they reached the Jeep. She took his hand away from his face and stood on tiptoe to look closely at the bruising. Her face was only inches from his. He could feel her breath warm on his cheek. He flicked a glance at her, but she was focused on his injuries. 'The swelling's gone down already,' she said. 'You won't be such a mess in the morning.'

But the mention of the morning only depressed him. He would have to tell her then that she could no longer assist on the case. It was too dangerous. His superiors would forbid it. He knew how she would react. With anger and hurt. After all, he would not have come this close to breaking the case without her. He glanced at her again. Her face was open, eager and happy. She had exorcised ghosts from her past tonight, she had trusted him with her pain. And tomorrow . . . He closed his eyes and sighed. He did not want tonight to end.

She laughed. 'What's the big sigh for? You should be pleased with yourself.'

He forced himself to return her smile. 'I'm pleased with both of us,' he said. 'We make a good team.'

'Yeah,' she said, nodding. 'I do the thinking, you take the punches. You're good at that.'

He grinned and took a mock swipe at her. And when she raised her arm as a shield he grabbed it, pulling her close and pressing her back against the side of the Jeep. They froze in anticipation of a moment they had been flirting with all night. But the moment passed, unconsummated, as she smiled wryly and tipped her head in the direction of the two armed guards watching from the gate. 'I think we're in danger of putting on a show,' she said.

He glanced ruefully at the guards. 'You want me to take you back to the Friendship?'

'You were going to buy me a drink,' she said. 'Before someone had the crazy idea of going gallivanting through Ritan Park in the dark and the rain. Will that bar still be open, do you think?'

He shook his head. 'Not at this hour. But I know somewhere that will.'

There was no queue to get into the Xanadu at this time in the morning. Li had been half afraid that it might be closed. But there was still a steady traffic in and out. Groups of youngsters stood about on the sidewalk outside, smoking and talking. They eyed Li and the *yangguizi* with vague curiosity as they pushed through them and went in past the bouncers. Li took out his wallet to pay, but was waved on through. Inside, the music was still loud, but slow, reflecting the late hour. Margaret took his arm and put her lips to his ear. 'I wouldn't have thought a place like this was your scene,' she shouted.

'It's not,' he shouted back. 'But you wanted a drink. This is about the only place we'll get one.'

He led her through to the bar. Most of the tables on the

main floor were still full, and through the haze of smoke that filled the place, Li could see that there were no free tables up in the gallery. 'What do you want to drink?'

'Vodka tonic with ice and lemon. But I'm paying.' She took out some notes.

He waved them aside. 'No, no.'

'Yes, yes,' she said. 'You bought me dinner, I'm buying the drinks.'

'No.' He still refused to take the money.

'I thought you people believed in equality,' she said. 'Women hold up half the sky in China. Isn't that what Mao said?' And in that moment she thrust the notes into his hand. 'You're buying, I'm paying. And I'm going to get us that table over there that these people are just leaving.' And she breezed off across the floor to lay claim to the table.

She sat down quickly, getting there just ahead of a group of two girls and a sullen youth who had been standing at the foot of the stairs. They glared at her resentfully and moved away. She looked around and realised she was causing a bit of a stir. As far as she could see, she was the only Caucasian in the place, and for all she knew the only one who'd ever been in it. It didn't look like the kind of stop-off that would be on the tourist itinerary. Faces at the tables around her were turned in her direction, gazing with glazed and unselfconscious interest, until she smiled and they became suddenly embarrassed and returned shy smiles like coy children.

On stage a stunning-looking girl in a sexy silk dress with daring splits up either side sang a mournful melody to the accompaniment of a guitarist, and a keyboard player triggering pre-programmed, synthesised computer music. The backing sounded professional. The singer was awful. Margaret watched her with a mixture of horror and embarrassment. She had no talent for it whatsoever. But no one else seemed to notice, or if they did, they didn't care. Li arrived with her vodka and a large brandy and sat down opposite her. She flicked her head towards the stage. 'Pretty face. Shame about the voice.'

Li smiled. 'She's my best friend's girl.'

Margaret almost choked on her vodka. 'You're kidding me.'

He shrugged. 'Don't worry about it. I don't like her much either.'

She looked at him curiously. 'And she's really your best friend's girl?' He nodded. 'So is it her you don't like, or her singing?'

'Both.'

'Why don't you like her?'

'Because she's a prostitute, and he's mad about her, and he's going to end up getting hurt.'

Margaret looked at the girl in astonishment, and with fresh eyes. 'But she's . . . beautiful. Why would she throw herself away on prostitution?'

'You've heard her singing,' Li said. 'And anyway, she's not some street-corner hooker. It's all private deals behind closed bedroom doors in high-class joint-venture hotels. She probably makes a lot of money.' He shrugged. 'A girl like that, she's just making use of the one asset she has – while she still has it.' He looked at her on the stage, eyes closed, living out some sad fantasy, giving her heart and soul to the cheap lyrics of a popular Taiwanese ballad. What arrangement, he wondered, had she arrived at with the manager that allowed her to sing here, escaping for a time from the sordid world of clawing, pawing, sexually frustrated foreign businessmen? He almost felt sorry for her. He had believed her when she told him she loved Ma Yongli. *He treats me like no one's ever treated me before. Like a princess.* What he hated was the effect *she* had on *him*, turning him from a confident, cocky young man with a wicked, if juvenile, sense of humour into a sycophantic and simpering acolyte, all confidence lost in a welter of self-doubt. There was something going on in Yongli's head that told him she was too good for him. He couldn't believe his luck, or that it would last. It was pathetic, and Li hated to see it, and blamed Lotus when perhaps the fault was Yongli's.

'Well, well, well. I see you took my advice and got yourself a woman after all.' Li turned to find himself looking up into Yongli's big, round, smiling face. But the smile vanished almost immediately. 'In the name of God, what happened to you? Don't tell me she's beating you up already?'

Li grinned. 'I got on the losing end of an argument with a villain.'

Yongli shook his head in amazement. 'Must have been a big bastard to put one over on you.'

'Caught me off guard,' Li said ruefully.

Margaret watched the exchange with interest. She could make an educated guess about the topic of conversation. For a moment she had been nonplussed to find that there was something familiar about the face of the big, bluff man who had arrived at their table. And then she had placed him. He had been with Li that first night at the duck restaurant. The affection between the two men was obvious. He turned and grinned at Margaret, and she grinned back, attracted by the infectious quality of his smile and the laughter in his eyes. 'So are you not going to introduce me?' he said to Li in a heavily American-accented English.

'Ma Yongli, this is Dr Margaret Campbell.'

Yongli took her hand and kissed the back of it lightly with full lips. '*Enchanté, madame,*' he said. 'I learned that in Switzerland. It's French.'

'I know,' Margaret said. '*Et moi, je suis enchantée aussi à faire vôtre connaissance, monsieur.*'

'Hey. Woah.' Yongli held up his hands. 'I only know *Je suis enchanté, madame.* No one's ever talked back to me before.' He laughed. 'I'm impressed.' Then he leaned over confidentially. 'Actually, I do know one other phrase, but it's not the sort of thing you would say in polite company. And Li Yan is a bit sensitive. It's way past his bedtime, you know.'

'I know. It's my fault,' Margaret said. 'I'm keeping him out late. But his uncle's away, so he won't get into any trouble.'

'Oh.' Yongli looked at Li knowingly. 'When the mouse is away the cat will play.'

Li said, 'I think that's the other way round, Ma Yongli.'

'Ah,' Yongli said to Margaret, 'I always get my cats mixed up with my mice. What will you have to drink?'

Margaret lifted her glass. It was almost empty. 'Vodka tonic.'

Yongli pointed at Li's glass. 'Brandy,' he said. And to Margaret, 'We have to celebrate. It is so long since I saw Big Li with a woman I was beginning to think he was gay. Back in a minute.' And he headed for the bar.

Li grinned, a little embarrassed. 'Ignore him. He's an idiot.'

'He's nice.'

Li felt a pang of jealousy. 'You probably think he's good-looking. Most women do.'

'No.' She shook her head solemnly. 'But he's attractive. What was he doing in Switzerland?'

'Training as a chef. He spent time in the United States, as well.'

'Oh,' Margaret said, cocking an eyebrow. 'He cooks, too? That makes him *very* attractive.' She had been immediately aware of that defensive look men got when they were jealous, and she enjoyed the fact that Li felt that way about her. If only he knew that Yongli wasn't half as attractive as he was – at least, not in her eyes.

She was beginning to relax, the alcohol easing away some of the tension of the night. It also seemed to be going very quickly to her head. Perhaps it was the tiredness. She had slept for only a handful of hours during the last seventy-two.

Yongli returned with the drinks and sat down at their table with a beer. 'So,' he said to Margaret. 'Cut up anyone interesting recently?'

'Oh, just a burn victim, a stabbing, an Atlanto-occipital disarticulation. Would you like me to go into the gory details?'

Yongli shook his head and said firmly, 'No thanks.'

'That's my trouble,' Margaret said. 'The only interesting people I ever get intimate with are dead. The live ones tend to lose interest in me as soon as they hear what I do for a living. They think I'm only after their bodies.'

Yongli laughed. 'You can play with my organs any time.'

'I'm more interested in a man's brain,' she said. 'Only the sound of the saw cutting through the skull usually puts them off.'

'Hey.' He put up his hands and grinned, shaking his head. 'I'm not going to win this one, am I?'

'Nope.' She raised her glass. 'Cheers.'

They all drank. Li enjoyed the way Margaret had dealt with Yongli. He was usually too quick for most people. And women preferred to laugh at his humour, rather than compete with it. She caught his eye over the glass, and they shared a moment.

There was a scattering of applause around the club as Lotus finished her song and gushed her thanks. She was finished for the night, she said, and stepped down from the stage. Margaret was uncertain whether the applause was for the performance or the fact that it was over. Lotus approached their table, flushed and a little breathless. Yongli was on his feet in an instant, pulling out a chair for her. 'I'll get you a drink. What would you like?'

'Some white wine.' Lotus had learned to affect a taste for wine during the many meals she had sat through in restaurants in joint-venture hotels. She looked at Margaret expectantly, waiting for an introduction.

In English, Yongli said, 'Lotus, this is Li Yan's friend . . .'

'Margaret,' Margaret said.

Lotus shook her hand. 'Ver' pleased meet you,' she said.

'Lotus only speaks a little English,' Yongli told Margaret, almost apologetically.

'A lot more English than I speak Chinese,' Margaret said.

Lotus sat down as Yongli headed for the bar. She was clearly intrigued by Margaret, immediately seeking her approval. 'You like my singing?'

In other circumstances Margaret might have been ambiguous, perhaps ironic, even cruel. But somehow there was such innocence in Lotus's question that she couldn't bring herself to do anything other than lie with great sincerity. 'Very much,' she said.

Lotus beamed with pleasure. 'Thank you.' She reached out and touched Margaret's hair as if it were gold. 'Your hair ver' beautiful.' And she gazed into Margaret's face quite unselfconsciously. 'And your eyes so blue. You ver' beautiful lady.'

'Thank you.'

'*Bukeqi*.' Margaret frowned. It sounded like *boo keh chee*.

Li said, 'It means you are welcome.'

Lotus took Margaret's hand and ran her fingers lightly over the forearm. 'I never see skin so white. So many beauty spot.'

'Freckles,' Margaret laughed. 'I hated them when I was a kid. I thought they were ugly.'

'No, no. They ver' beautiful.' She turned to Li. 'You ver' lucky.'

Li blushed. 'Oh, no, we're not . . . I mean, Margaret's a colleague. From work.'

'What are you saying?' Margaret asked, surprised by Li's sudden lapse into Chinese.

'Just that we only work together.' He blushed again. Lotus's arrival had unsettled him completely.

'You policeman?' Lotus asked Margaret with incredulity.

'No. A doctor.'

'Ah. You fix up his face?'

'Sort of.' She smiled at Li's bruised and battered face.

Yongli returned to the table with two bottles of champagne in an ice bucket, and four glasses. Lotus gasped in delight, forgetting to speak English. 'Champagne! What's this for, lover?'

'A small celebration.'

'What are we celebrating?'

'Oh, the fact that it's three in the morning and Big Li's not tucked up in his bed yet. The fact that he's out on the town with a *woman* . . .'

'Aw, shut up,' Li said.

'She's a doctor,' Lotus protested.

Yongli leaned over confidentially. 'That's what she tells all the boys. Actually she cuts up dead people for a living.'

Lotus looked at Margaret, shocked. Margaret said, 'What's going on? Will somebody speak English?'

'Ma Yongli's just playing the fool,' Li said.

'No I'm not.' He squeezed the cork out of one of the bottles and started filling the glasses, champagne foaming over brims and spilling on the table. 'I'm just proposing a toast.' He pulled his chair in beside Lotus and raised his dripping glass. 'To the two most beautiful women in the Xanadu. Probably in Beijing. Maybe even the whole of China.'

Margaret looked around. 'What table's the other one at?'

Lotus laughed and put a hand on her arm and said, as if to an idiot, 'He mean me *and* you.'

Margaret supposed it was unfair to make judgments on someone's intelligence based on the few words of your language that they knew. She took in Lotus's almost childish delight at having to set her straight. It was quite possible, she supposed, that Lotus was wondering how someone so stupid could possibly be a doctor. 'Oh,' she said, and smiled, raising her glass. 'Well, I'll drink to that.'

And when they had finished the first bottle, Yongli opened the second, and Margaret began to lose track of their conversation. The champagne on top of the vodkas, on top of her lack of sleep, had resulted in the club starting to make slow revolutions around her. They all seemed to be laughing a lot, even Li, who in her experience was not given to laughing easily. She had no real idea of what she was saying. Answering, it seemed, endless silly questions about America, about money, about . . . she wasn't sure what. Every time she lifted her glass it seemed to have miraculously refilled itself. Was there a third bottle on the table?

It seemed like a long time later, and Lotus had her by the arm, and she thought they must be going to the little girls' room. There was a very large step up, and she almost fell. Somewhere in the distance she heard Li's voice. He seemed to be calling her name. He didn't think she should be doing this, whatever it was she was doing. Perversely, it made her more determined to do it. And suddenly there were a lot of bright lights in her eyes and faces turned up towards her, and a sound like running water. Only it wasn't running water. It just sounded like it. And then she realised it was people clapping. Lotus put something in her hand. It was heavy and tubular with a mesh ball on the end. 'What's this?' she asked, and heard her voice booming around the club. More running water.

Lotus turned her to her left and she saw a blue screen, words frozen on it in white. *Yesterday* . . . The sound of an acoustic guitar. Lotus's voice. 'You sing.' But she couldn't, and missed the first line, and Lotus leaned close and sang instead. *Now it look a though they hee to stay* . . . All she could see now was Michael's face. All she could hear was his voice. *I didn't do it, Mags.* And she felt the tears running hot down her face as Lotus's grotesque parody of the Beatles' original forced its way into her consciousness, each word stinging like a slap in the face. She had thought the pain would be all gone now. But Michael seemed to want to go on hurting her for the rest of her life. He took her in his arms now, saying something softly in her ear, but she couldn't make out what it was. He led her back down the high step, past the running water. She felt fresh cool air in her face. She turned to look at him, with the weary anticipation of more earnest protestations of innocence. But it wasn't Michael after all. Of course, she remembered, she was in China. And Michael was dead. And these people were speaking another language.

'Where are you going to take her, Li?' Yongli wasn't exactly sober himself.

'Back to the apartment.'

'Do you need help with her?' Lotus said.

Li nodded. 'Yes. Please.'

The smell of smoke and coffee was the first thing she was aware of. Very slowly the room began to take shape around her, a room similar in shape and size to Chao Heng's living room. Through the glass panes that boxed in the balcony on the far side of the room, she could see the tops of trees swaying slightly in the wind, leaves reflecting light from the streetlamps. There was very little light in the room itself. A small lamp somewhere in a distant corner. She tried to focus on where she was. On a settee, she realised, half sitting, half lying, her head pitched to one side. She turned it to the other side as she felt a movement beside her, and saw Lotus kneeling there with a steaming mug of black coffee, trying to get her to sip it. But the smell of it was doing unpleasant things to her stomach. 'Bathroom,' she said, and wondered distantly if the urgency she felt was conveyed by her voice. Apparently so, for hands were quickly helping her to her feet. And it wasn't far to stagger, it seemed, to a room filled with bright hard light reflecting from white tiles. The unpleasantness in her stomach rose rapidly into her consciousness, and she pitched forward on to her knees, clutching at the rim of something hard and white, mouth and throat filled with a horrible burning sensation. Then she was on her feet again and someone was splashing cold water on her face, and the lights went out on the world.

Li stood unsteadily by the front door. Yongli winked at him. 'See you, pal. Tell her it was all my fault. I should never have bought that champagne.'

'It made her very sad,' Lotus said. 'I think maybe she has some great tragedy in her life.'

Li nodded. 'Maybe.' Lotus leaned across and gave him a soft kiss on the cheek, and he felt guilty for all the things he had thought and said about her. He didn't know how he would have coped tonight if she hadn't been there. 'Thanks,' he said.

She squeezed his hand. She wanted him so much to like her. 'See you.'

Li closed the door behind them and wandered back up the hallway to his uncle's bedroom. In the reflected half-light from the street, he saw that she had already managed to kick the covers off. Lotus had undressed her and come through to the living room saying, 'She has beautiful breasts. I wish I had beautiful breasts like hers.' They *were* beautiful breasts, full and white, with small dark-red aureolae. One arm was thrown carelessly across her chest. The bed cover had twisted around one leg, fully exposing the other and the triangle of tight blonde curls between them. He remembered seeing her reflected in the mirror in the hotel bedroom. She had wanted him to see her. He felt the same ache of desire now. He sat on the edge of the bed and looked at her face, pale and untroubled, at least for now, by her unhappy past and uncertain future. He ran his fingers softly over its contours.

She had changed so much in him, in such a short time. The way he saw himself, his job, his uncle. It was as if he had been sleeping and she had touched him awake. He had not wanted a life, and now he did. He leaned over and kissed her forehead, and untwisted the sheet so that she was decently covered. As he left the room, he pulled the door gently closed and stood for some minutes in the hall with his eyes shut, breathing steadily. He heard the blood as it coursed through his veins. He heard the crackle of cigarette phlegm in his lungs. He heard the tick, tick of the clock in the living room. He heard his life slipping through his fingers like sand. And he made a fist to stop it. It was too precious to just let go.

CHAPTER NINE

I

Thursday Morning

She was aware of something warm lying across her, like an electric blanket, only it seemed to have no weight. The air was hot and she could hardly breathe. She tried to open her eyes, and light and pain seared through her brain like a white-hot poker. She screwed them shut with a gasp. And then slowly, very slowly, eased them open again, bit by painful bit, until the world came to her in a blur. Her pupils were still dilated and the images were burned out and lacking definition. She struggled against the pain in her head to bring them into focus, and as her pupils shrank belatedly from the light she saw that her 'electric blanket' was a slab of sunlight slanting through the window and falling across the bed, burning her white, naked skin. Her mind was working as slowly as her eyes, and it was several moments before the realisation that she was wearing no clothes had its full impact. She sat up, heart pounding, and pain shot through her temple like a slamming blow from an iron. She pressed fingertips to her head and closed her eyes, pushing hard against the pain. Slowly she opened them again and looked around. She had no idea where she was, or who had undressed her, or where her clothes were.

There were framed photographs on the wall above the dresser. A young man and woman in Mao pyjamas and blue peaked caps grinning at the camera. A family group, including a young boy of about twelve and a girl a little younger. There was something elusively familiar about the boy. Another couple. No, the same couple as in the other photograph, only older. The woman was looking at the man and smiling at him with great fondness. He was grinning at the camera. He wore a green police uniform, and Margaret knew at once it was Old Yifu. Immediately above it was an old-fashioned portrait photograph of the woman. His wife, Margaret assumed. There was the gentlest of smiles on her lips, and her eyes were dark and serene, and there was something beautiful in her plainness that came from somewhere within. Old Yifu's words came back to her. *We had so little time together afterwards.* A depression came over Margaret like a cloud. Why did people have to die?

So she was in Uncle Yifu's room. What had happened last night? She remembered being at the Xanadu. Champagne and laughter. But not much else. Oh God, she thought. It was like being a student again. Only she was ten years older, and ten years less able to handle it. She saw her clothes neatly folded on a chair and got unsteadily to her feet to cross the room and ease herself slowly back into them. From somewhere in the apartment, she heard the sounds of someone moving around. The clatter of a kettle on a stove, the rattle of crockery. She moved out into the hall and saw an open door to a small bath-room. She went in and saw herself in the mirror and wished she hadn't. She had a complexion like putty. Lukewarm water chugged and spluttered from the cold tap as she splashed it on her face to try to bring the blood to the surface and some colour to her cheeks. She swilled some around her mouth to take away the bad taste and stop her tongue sticking to the roof of it.

She wandered blearily into the kitchen and found Li making tea. She was shocked by his appearance. If anything, he looked worse than she did. Dry blood scabbed the splits on his lip and cheek and brow. The witch-hazel had brought the swelling down, and the bruising was turning yellow already. It would be gone in a day or two, but right now it was the wrong shade for a face with all other colour washed out of it. He looked at her sheepishly. 'Tea?'

She nodded, and wished she hadn't as the pain pounded her temples. 'What . . .' She hesitated, almost afraid to ask. 'What happened last night?'

'We all had too much to drink.'

'I think I've figured that one out already. What else?'

He shrugged. 'You thought it would be a good idea to sing some karaoke.'

She was horrified. 'You're kidding me! I didn't . . . I mean, I didn't actually get up and sing?'

'No. Lotus sang and you got a bit emotional.' She closed her eyes in shame and disbelief. He said, 'So we came back here.'

'We? Who's we?'

'The four of us. Ma Yongli thought some black coffee might make you feel better. Unfortunately, it seemed to have the opposite effect.'

'Oh my God. I wasn't sick?' He nodded, and she wanted to curl up and die of embarrassment. 'I am so sorry.'

He smiled. 'It's all right. Lotus looked after you.'

'Is she still here?'

'No. They left after about an hour.' He handed her a cup of green tea. She sipped the hot, aromatic brew and felt a little better.

She was frightened to meet his eye as she asked, 'Did we . . . ? Did I . . . ?' And she gave up trying to be delicate. 'Who undressed me?'

'Lotus put you to bed before she left.'

Margaret felt an enormous sense of relief. Not because nothing had happened between them. But because it would have been wasted on her if it had. Through her embarrassment and her hangover she still felt the same about him as she had last night. She wanted him to hold her in his arms now, for comfort, for reassurance. But in the cold light of day they were both awkward and uncertain how to express themselves. They had, as yet, none of the easy familiarity of people who have shared a great intimacy, who have admitted not just to themselves but to each other exactly how they feel. She took another sip of her tea and looked around the kitchen, searching for something. He held up her purse. 'Looking for this?'

'Yes.' She opened it and found a pack of Advil and washed

two down with her tea. In fifteen or twenty minutes she might begin to feel a little more human again. She looked at her watch. 'Jesus Christ! Is that the time?' It was nine thirty. 'I've got class at nine!'

'You *had* class at nine,' Li corrected her. 'D'you want me to get you a taxi?'

He watched the taxi pull out into the street below and still felt the burning on his cheek where she had quickly kissed him goodbye. He wondered when he would see her again, *if* he would see her again. He would be in trouble, he knew, for bringing her back here. The duty policeman would have made his report first thing this morning. But he couldn't have left her at the hotel in that state, and he still had a niggling worry about her safety. If the man who attacked him last night had been following them, he would know where she was staying. There was a great deal he probably knew, about both of them. Li looked up and down the street. There were a number of cars parked at an angle on the sidewalk immediately below, under the shade of the trees. Several dozen uniformed officers were emerging from the academy across the road, traffic cops stopping vehicles to let them cross. Women pushing prams strolled along the strip of parkland that divided the street down its centre. Old men sat on benches gazing into space and puffing on cigarettes. He wondered if there were hidden eyes watching him from somewhere out there right now. It was a disconcerting thought.

The rain of the previous night had washed some of the dust

and humidity out of the atmosphere, and the air was fresher as he followed his habitual route to work, cycling north along Chaoyangmen Nanxiaojie Street. Overhead the sky was blue, instead of a burned-out grey, and the sun was hot on his skin. He was still preoccupied with thoughts of Margaret. Had she been disappointed that nothing had happened between them last night? He had thought she seemed relieved. It was strange, he reflected, how she seemed always on the verge of intimacy, as though they had once known each other well, like old lovers. She seemed often about to touch him, or kiss him, but held back at the last as if realising that she didn't, after all, know him. Or perhaps it was simply that the habit of casual intimacy, born of years living with the man she had married, was hard to break, and that, really, it had nothing to do with Li at all.

At the corner of Dongzhimennei he waved at Mei Yuan as he passed, and called out, 'Sorry, I have no time this morning.' She stood up to wave him over, a sense of urgency in her signalling. But he was already out into the stream of traffic crossing the main road. 'Later,' he shouted back at her.

The corridors of Section One were still crowded with citizens awaiting interrogation about the itinerant from Shanghai, or about what they had seen or not seen in Ritan Park two mornings previously. The detectives' room was empty except for Detective Qian, who was still writing up his report on events in the park the night before. He seemed agitated and tipped his head towards Li's office. 'Chief's waiting for you in there.'

Li braced himself and strode confidently through the door. 'Morning, Chief. Big breakthrough last night.'

Chen was sitting at Li's desk flicking idly through a number of reports awaiting Li's attention. He looked up and said, grimly, 'Is that in your personal or your professional life?'

'What do you mean?'

'Oh, come off it, Li!' Chen slammed the flat of his hand down on the desk. 'We both know that Dr Campbell stayed at your apartment last night. What in God's name did you think you were playing at?'

'She'd had too much to drink, Chief. She wasn't feeling well, so I let her stay over. There wasn't any more to it than that. She slept in Old Yifu's room.'

'Damn you, Li. She's a *foreigner*. You are an official of the state!'

'My relationship with Dr Campbell is strictly work, Chief,' Li protested.

'Then it's time you stopped taking your work home.' Chen stood up in a temper. 'Have you any idea the repercussions this could have? I've already had a call from the university and they are considering sending Dr Campbell home forthwith. I feel entirely responsible. After all, it was me who asked for her help in the first place. And it's you I blame, not her. You're the one who should have known better.'

Li's head dropped, his resistance wilting. 'I'm sorry, Chief. I thought I was doing the right thing. Especially after the attack on me last night. I thought there was a possibility she could be in danger.'

But Chen's anger did not abate. 'We'll come to last night in a moment,' he snapped. 'The fact is, Li, I'm going to have to consider taking disciplinary action against you. Particularly since this comes right on the heels of an official complaint against you yesterday.'

'If you're talking about The Needle . . .'

'Don't insult me by denying it,' Chen warned. 'And as for last night, had you followed proper procedure you would never have been attacked in the first place, and you would not have exposed Dr Campbell to the danger that you did.' He turned towards the window, waving his hands in exasperation. 'For God's sake, Li, you've not even been in this job three days. I thought you understood. We work as a team here. Your job is to lead that team. It is not a licence for you to go off on some individual crusade, firing off like a loose cannon, like some . . . American cop. And if you can't understand that, I'll personally see to it that you spend the rest of your career directing traffic on Tiananmen Square.' He glared at Li. 'Well?'

'Chief?'

'*Do you understand?*'

'Yes, Chief.'

Chen took a deep breath and let a little of the tension seep out of him. He sat down again in Li's chair. 'Notwithstanding anything I've said, that was a damn smart piece of work yesterday. The glove and the key, and the thumbprint.'

'I'm afraid I can't take much credit for that, Chief,' Li said. 'It was Dr Campbell's idea.' Chen flicked him a look. 'She also had the idea that Chao might have had AIDS – because of the drugs found in his apartment. We ordered further blood tests yesterday to confirm. Results should be available later today.'

'Dr Campbell seems to have been *very* busy,' Chen said with an edge to his voice, and added, 'She also seems to have been very right.' He sighed and lifted a folder from the desk and held it out to Li. 'This came in by fax from the Hong Kong police about ten minutes ago.'

Li opened the folder and found himself staring at a black-and-white image of the man who had done so much damage to his face the night before. He felt a chill run through him.

II

Margaret stepped from the taxi outside the university administration block. She had long since stopped hurrying. There was little point. The lecture she should have taken was due to have finished more than an hour ago. She had taken the taxi from Li's back to her hotel, showered and changed, and collected some notes before getting another taxi to the university. Her hair was just about dry, and she was wearing more make-up than usual to mask the ravages of the night before. Her head still hurt, and her stomach was distinctly wobbly. As she ran up the marble steps inside, she heard the clip, clip of footsteps descending. She looked up to see Lily Peng.

'Hi,' Margaret said, a little breathless. 'You don't know where Bob is . . . ?' But Lily failed even to meet her eye as she went past. She disappeared through the doors without a word. Margaret was taken aback. Even when being short with you, the Chinese were usually courteous.

She carried on up, and along the corridor to the office she

had returned yesterday to Professors Tian, Bai and Dr Mu. Only Dr Mu was there. 'Hi,' Margaret said again. 'Do you know where Bob is?' Dr Mu looked at her as if she had two heads. Of course, Margaret remembered, she didn't speak English. 'B-o-b,' she said again, slowly, with emphasis on both 'b's. It sounded ridiculous. 'Forget it.' She headed on down the corridor towards Professor Jiang's office. She was about to knock on the door of the outer office when it opened and Veronica very nearly walked into her. 'Oh, hi,' Margaret said. 'I'm looking for Bob.'

Veronica regarded her very coldly and said, 'He taking lecture.' And then she brushed past without another word.

Margaret was starting to get a bad feeling about this. The pain in her head was making it feel heavy, and the weight of it was beginning to make her neck ache. She sighed and went back downstairs and across campus to the lecture rooms. She found Bob tidying up his notes after class. He glanced up as she came in, then turned back to his notes. 'I'm surprised you bothered turning up at all,' he said, and looked pointedly at his watch. 'I mean, you're only two hours late for your lecture.'

'Shit, I'm sorry, Bob. I slept in.'

'Was that "I" singular or "we" plural?'

Margaret flushed. 'I'm sorry?'

'Well, I'm assuming you didn't go back to your hotel to sleep in after spending the night at Detective Li's apartment. I mean, would it be fair to say that you *both* slept in? Together? At his place?'

Margaret's initial embarrassment was turning very quickly to anger. How in God's name did he know where she'd spent the night? 'I think it would be fair to say that's none of your business,' she said.

He dropped his notes on the desk with a bang and turned to face her, eyes livid. 'Well, I think it would be very *un*fair to say that. Considering I had to take your class at the last minute, and then spend the next half-hour in Professor Jiang's office trying to make excuses for you.'

'What – *everyone* knows where I spent the night?'

'Yes. They do.'

'How?' She was incredulous.

'Lily Peng.'

'What? You mean that little bitch was spying on us?'

'Don't blame Lily,' Bob said abruptly. 'She's only doing her job.'

'Jesus Christ, what is it, a crime to spend the night at someone's apartment in this country?'

'Well, actually, yes it is,' Bob said, knocking all the wind from her sails. 'Everywhere you go in China, every time you change your address, it is a legal requirement to report to Public Security. For legal purposes, checking into a hotel is regarded as the same thing. You didn't stay at your hotel last night. Technically you broke the law. Lily reported your whereabouts to Public Security, they reported to your *danwei* here at the university. Professor Jiang and everyone else in this department feels dishonoured by your conduct. They consider your behaviour to have been outrageous, and I agree.'

'Fuck!' Margaret stood with her hands on her hips, staring up at the ceiling in disbelief. 'This is unreal.'

'No,' Bob said angrily. 'This is China. And it's very real. I thought you'd read your briefing material from the OICJ.'

She couldn't meet his eye. 'I said I'd got it. I didn't say I'd read it.' She heard his gasp of frustration. 'Look, I'm sorry, okay? I only came here to teach a few classes and get away from a lot of shit back home. I didn't know I was going to have to take Big Brother along for the ride.'

'It's not Big Brother who keeps an eye on you here,' Bob snapped. 'It's everyone. Your neighbour, your bellhop, the elevator man. The street committee, the census cop, the work unit. It's a self-policing society. Of course, you'd know all that if . . .'

'Yeah, yeah, I know,' she cut in. 'If I'd read my briefing material.'

'Well, I'm glad *you* can treat it so lightly. I can assure you the OICJ will not. They have spent a great many years building good relations here in China, and you could have ruined that in one night.'

'One night of passion, right?' she said bitterly. 'I mean, that's what you all think, isn't it? Well, it might interest you to know that it wasn't like that. Nothing happened. I slept in one room, he slept in another.'

'I couldn't care less,' Bob said. 'And if you think that's the issue here, then you're missing the point.'

'And just what is the point, Bob?' She was keeping her short temper on a tight leash.

'The point is you are a guest who has abused the hospitality of your hosts.' He stabbed his finger at her across the lecture room. 'You've shown not the slightest interest in this country or its culture since you got here. I'd thought that helping out with Detective Li's investigation would be a good bridge-builder. It's been a goddamn disaster.'

He was clearly unaware of just how much she had contributed to that investigation. She wondered if it would make any difference if he knew, but concluded that in his present frame of mind it probably wouldn't.

'I suggest,' he continued, 'that for the next five weeks you stay well away from Deputy Section Chief Li and his investigation. And you'd also be well advised to stay out of Professor Jiang's way. It was all I could do to dissuade him from putting you on the first plane home.'

'Oh, was it?' said Margaret. 'Well, I'll tell you what. You needn't have bothered. I'll be booking a seat on it myself.' She tossed her notes in his direction and they fluttered gently down through the still air. 'I quit.'

III

Further details had come in from Hong Kong. The man who had repeatedly driven his fist into Li's face in the dark and wet the night before, the man whose face now stared up at him from the fax on his desk, was known as Johnny Ren. He had a long record of juvenile offences from the age of twelve, ranging from theft to rape and assault. A nice kid,

Li thought. He was now thirty and hadn't been arrested for more than eight years. The Hong Kong police, however, did not believe he had suddenly seen the error of his ways. Their information suggested he had been taken under the wing of a Triad gang operating out of Kowloon, and they suspected his involvement in at least half a dozen gang killings in the early nineties. Intelligence from underworld sources led them to believe that he was now operating as a freelance 'mechanic', or hit-man. But they had no evidence to back this up. His legitimate income came from a chain of restaurants in which he was a partner. He lived well, had an expensive apartment near the racecourse on Hong Kong Island, and kept a boat at the marina. He drove a Mercedes Sports and owned a Toyota Landcruiser. He wore Versace suits and smoked American cigarettes. Li didn't need to be told which brand. Someone in the Hong Kong police had done their homework on Johnny Ren. But he wasn't home right now, and nobody had seen him for several weeks.

There was a knock at Li's door, and Qian looked in. 'Everyone's here, boss.'

'Did you get all that stuff copied?'

'Yeah. It's being handed out in the meeting room now.'

'Good. Be right there.' Li gathered his papers and stood up. He closed his eyes for a moment, breathing deeply, and saw Johnny Ren's face as it had been last night in the park. It was burned into his brain. A face contorted by anger and intent, leaning over him, only inches away, the smell of his rank smoker's breath in Li's nostrils. Whatever cool, professional control Johnny Ren had learned over the years had eluded him in the park. He had been going to kill Li. He had been going to drive his fist into the detective's face again and again until the bone splintered and gave way and the soft brain behind it turned to mush. Li had seen it in his eyes. Johnny Ren had made a mistake and Li was going to die for it.

Li opened his eyes and realised he had broken out in a sweat. He had never encountered such brutal and unfettered evil, and he wanted to catch it and stamp it out of existence. He turned towards the door and saw Yongli hurrying into the detectives' office. There was a strange, forlorn look about his friend, almost haunted. Li was surprised to see him. He had never come to the office before. Li went through. 'Hey, pal, what are you doing here?' He saw now that Yongli's face was a dreadful pasty colour, and there were deep, dark rings below his eyes.

'I need your help, Big Li.' He sounded pathetic. Like a small boy who knows that the favour he's about to ask of a parent will be denied.

'What is it? Are you in some kind of trouble?' Li had never seen Yongli like this before.

'It's Lotus.'

And Li's heart sank. He should have guessed. Yongli, he knew, could cope with just about anything life threw at him. But Lotus . . . 'What's she done?'

'She's been arrested.'

Qian appeared at the door, a little breathless. He made a face and nodded down the corridor. 'The Chief's decided to sit in on this one, boss. I think he's getting a bit impatient.'

'I'm on my way,' Li said. He turned to Yongli. 'Listen, it'll have to wait. I've got a meeting.'

But Yongli behaved as if he hadn't heard. He said, 'When we left your apartment this morning we went back to the Xanadu. The cops raided the place just before five. Some kind of vice sweep. We all got taken downtown.'

'Ma Yongli, I don't have time just now.' Li started for the door and Yongli followed him.

'They found drugs in her bag. Heroin. She says she has no idea how it got there.'

'They always do,' Li said, losing patience. It bore out all his worst fears about Lotus. He turned down the corridor, Yongli trailing in his wake.

'I believe her, Li Yan. She's not into drugs. Never has been. But they've arrested her. She could get sent down for years. Hell, they shoot people for less!'

Li stopped outside the door of the meeting room and turned on his friend. 'Look, I told you she was trouble. Right from the start. I mean, what do you expect me to do? I've got a triple murder on my hands, a room full of detectives waiting on me. And you want me to drop everything and bale out some whore with a bagful of smack?' He regretted it as soon as it was out of his mouth.

Colour rose on Yongli's pale cheeks and his eyes turned cold. 'Whatever you think of Lotus, it's me who's asking for help. I thought we were friends, Li Yan. Or was that just some silly delusion I had?'

'Look, don't do this to me,' Li pleaded. 'You know as well

as I do that she'll have been pulled in by another section. I wouldn't have any influence . . .'

'So you won't do anything?'

The door of the meeting room opened and Chen stood there looking at them. 'Deputy Section Chief Li,' he said very deliberately. 'I have a meeting in thirty minutes.'

'On my way in, Chief,' Li said. 'Two seconds.'

'Will that be earth seconds?' Chen asked, and he let the door swing shut without waiting for an answer.

Li drew a deep breath and turned back to Yongli. 'Look, I'll see what I can do, okay?'

Yongli looked at him sceptically. 'Yeah, well, you would say that, wouldn't you? Anything to get me off your back.'

'Aw, come on,' Li snapped. 'Give me a break. I said I'd do what I could.'

There was contempt mixed with the hurt now in Yongli's eyes. 'I won't be holding my breath.' He turned and walked briskly away down the corridor. Li felt like a complete shit. He screwed up his eyes and exhaled through his teeth. Yongli deserved better than that. And he thought about how good Lotus had been last night with Margaret. He would make some enquiries. First chance he got. He wheeled around and walked into the meeting room.

A dozen detectives and Section Chief Chen sat around the table waiting for him. A veil of smoke hung over the group like a cloud, reflecting Chen's mood. 'Sorry to keep you,' Li said. He sat down and lit up. 'You've all got copies of the stuff from Hong Kong.' He pulled out the facsimile image of Johnny Ren.

'Take a good look at this face,' he said. 'He's our killer. I expect to have full forensic confirmation by lunch-time. But I have no doubts that he is our man. He's very good, and he's very dangerous. And he's still here in Beijing. Or, at least, he was last night.' He rubbed his bruising ruefully. 'I want this face on the front page of every newspaper in China by tomorrow morning. I want it on every news bulletin on every TV station. I want his face faxed to every police station, railway station, border post. This man is armed and dangerous. I want us to brief the armed police, the border police, the transport police, *and* the army. I don't want him to be able to move from A to B without someone recognising him. I want us to check every hotel and hostel and guest-house in the city. He's got to be sleeping somewhere. Someone's seen him. Someone knows where he is. It can only be a matter of time. Detective Qian, I want you to co-ordinate this.'

Wu leaned back in his seat, cigarette hand dangling from the arm of his chair. His sunglasses were pushed up on his forehead and he was chewing reflectively on a ubiquitous piece of gum. 'We still haven't established motive on this one, boss, have we?'

'Money,' Li said. 'He's a professional. Probably thinks of himself as a poor boy made good. The truth is, he's a bad boy made worse. What we don't know is who hired him, or why. And when we get him I doubt if he's going to tell us.'

'So meantime we carry on trying to find the connection between our three victims?' Wu asked.

'Unless you've got a better idea.' Wu hadn't. 'So, anything

new on that front?' Heads were shaken around the table. 'Okay, we carry on interviewing. But there is one new piece of potentially important evidence. Chao may have had AIDS. I expect the result of a blood test to confirm that today. We know he had a penchant for teenage boys. Until yesterday afternoon we'd been concentrating on trying to make a drugs connection between Chao and Mao Mao. Thanks to our good friend, The Needle, we've been able to eliminate that possibility from our inquiry.' Detectives around the table glanced at Chen, but he remained impassive. 'Maybe there's a gay link somewhere in all this. Someone with AIDS looking for revenge. I know there's been no suggestion of homosexuality with either our drug dealer or the itinerant. But then, we haven't been looking for it. So, I'm going to have AIDS tests done on blood samples taken from both of them. Zhao' – he turned towards the young detective – 'we need to start digging up the boys who were making regular visits to Chao's apartment. And if someone was supplying them, then we need to know who, and we want to talk to him pretty damn quick.'

'I'm on it straight away, boss.' Zhao scribbled quickly in his notebook.

'Okay.' Li sat back. 'Any thoughts, questions, ideas?'

Wu blew a jet of smoke lazily at the overhead fan and watched it scatter in the breeze. 'Yeah, I got a question,' he said. 'Is that attractive American pathologist still working on the case with us?' His colleagues choked back laughs of disbelief. 'Because, I mean, you know, boss, it's not fair you keeping her all to yourself. Some of us feel we could also benefit from her experience.' He remained deadpan, for all the world as if it had been a serious question.

Chen had a face like sour milk. Li said, 'Actually, Detective, I think you would probably benefit more from a couple of years' experience on traffic duty in Tiananmen Square.' Which allowed the others to release their pent-up laughter. 'You and I can take shift about.' More laughter. Li glanced at Chen, on whose face had appeared the faintest glimmer of a smile. 'And in answer to your question, Wu, Dr Campbell will no longer be assisting us with the inquiry.' He closed his folder. 'That's all just now, unless there's anything else?' There wasn't. 'Okay, let's go catch Johnny Ren.'

As chairs scraped on the floor, and cigarettes were stubbed out in ashtrays, Li said, 'Just one more thing. Keep the paperwork coming into my office down to a bare minimum, guys. Essential stuff only, please. I've got enough already in there to keep me fully occupied for the next five years.'

The detectives drifted out. Chen wandered up the table to Li and touched his shoulder lightly. 'Keep me in touch with developments.'

Li sat for a moment after they had all gone, and found himself filled with a strange, aching melancholy. He picked up his folder and forced himself to stand up. He seemed to have lost all energy. Perhaps, he told himself, it was simply his hangover. He walked slowly back down the corridor. Although he had made light of Wu's reference to Margaret, it had forced him to face the truth – that without her involvement in the investigation he had no real reason for seeing her. At least, not professionally. And the demands of the job were such that he wasn't likely to have much free time in the foreseeable future. In less than five weeks she would be gone and he would be unlikely ever to see her again. So it would be pointless trying to pursue any kind of relationship in the few hours they might have together between now and then. And without the case to discuss, what would they talk about? It wasn't as if they had much in common. In fact, it was insane for him ever to have considered that there might be something between them that could form the basis of a relationship. It was as well that an end had been put to it now. But however convincingly he told himself this, he remained resolutely unconvinced. He was deeply depressed at the thought that she might already have slipped out of his life for ever.

The corridor was buzzing with activity – detectives and secretaries and witnesses, phones ringing; somewhere the sound of a photocopier on a large print run, the whine of a fax machine spewing out images from the ether. As Li approached the door of the detectives' office a man bumped into him, knocking the file from his hand. He walked quickly on without an apology. Li cursed and stooped to pick up the papers that had spilled from the folder. He had caught the briefest glimpse of the man's face, pale and tense and intent on avoiding Li's eye. From his crouching position, he turned and looked back down the corridor at the retreating figure, and a face swam into his consciousness: a face contorted with anger and intent; a face in black and white on the page of a fax; a face that was staring up at him now from a sheet of paper on the floor of the corridor; the face of the man who had just bumped into him.

'Hey!' he yelled. 'Stop! Stop that man!'

Several people turned to stare at him in amazement. But not the man at the end of the corridor. He started running and had reached the stairs even before Li stood up. Li took off like a sprinter from starting blocks, papers from his folder flying in his wake. Someone got in his way, and with a bone-crunching collision went spinning into the wall. 'Get out of the way!' Li shouted. 'Get out of the fucking way!' Bodies scattered left and right. Detectives appeared in office doorways.

'What the hell's going on?' someone shouted.

Li reached the stairs and could hear Johnny Ren's footsteps on the flight below. He saw a flap of Versace suit, caught a glimpse of an expensive haircut, the flash of a face turned briefly upward. He took the stairs two at a time, screaming at people to get out of his way. Above him he heard a voice shouting, 'What the hell's going on, Li!' It might have been Chen. But he wasn't about to stop and explain. He reached the foot of the stairs gasping for breath, and the heat of the day punched through the doorway and struck him like a blow. The contrast between the dark interior of Section One and the white heat of the morning sun momentarily blinded him. He raised an arm to shield his eyes and glanced right and left.

There was no sign of Johnny Ren. Somewhere off to the right came the clatter of a bin. Li followed the noise, past the red-roofed police garage, into a narrow lane behind the shops in Chaoyangmen Nanxiaojie. At the far end he saw the running figure of the Marlboro man. A bin still rocked in the dirt where it had spilled its stinking contents into the sunlight. Li vaulted the bin and pounded down the lane after Johnny Ren, brushing the sweat from his eyes with his sleeve. At the end of the lane he saw Ren turn right. Left would have taken him out on to Chaoyangmen Nanxiaojie. Right took him into a maze of *hutongs* that turned and twisted through a jumble of crumbling brick courtyards and even narrower alleyways. He was already gone from sight by the time Li reached the turn. But he could hear his footsteps echoing off the walls. His lungs tore at his chest in a frantic attempt to suck in more oxygen, and for the first time in his life he regretted being a smoker. His only consolation was that Johnny Ren was one too, and would be sharing in Li's pain. He was running with less conviction now, the excesses of the night before beginning to tell. His head was pounding. He turned a corner and crashed into a meandering cyclist lost in a world of adolescent fantasy. Li's legs became somehow inextricably tied up in the front wheel and he twisted and fell, landing on top of the young cyclist. Just a boy, no more than twelve or thirteen, he yelled with pain and wriggled frantically to get out from under this big, heavy man who seemed to have dropped on him from the sky. Li cursed and staggered to his feet. Blood was oozing from a graze on his elbow, and his pants were torn at the knee. The boy was still yelling. Li grabbed his shoulders. 'Are you all right, son?'

But the boy's only concern was his bicycle. 'Look at my bike! Look what you've done to my bike, you moron!' The front wheel was badly buckled.

Li breathed a sigh of relief. Wheels could be fixed or replaced. 'I'm a police officer,' he gasped. 'Go to the police station round the corner and wait for me there.' And he started running again.

'A likely fucking story!' the boy shouted at his back. 'You're a fucking moron!'

Li reached a junction fifty yards further on. He stopped, fighting for breath, and looked right and left. Nothing. Trees stirring lightly in the breeze. All that he could hear, apart from his own rasping breath, was the distant rumble of traffic on Dongzhimennei Street. He went right, walking past arched gateways to decaying *siheyuan* on both sides, peering in as he went. In the entrance to one, an old woman was sweeping up with a straw broom. He held out his Public Security wallet. 'Police,' he said. 'Did you see a man in a dark suit? He must have passed you.'

She shook her head. 'I saw no one,' she said. 'Except for some small boys about ten minutes ago.'

He turned immediately and started jogging back the way he had come, passing the junction where he had taken the right turn, and carrying on down to Dongzhimennei. The street was thick with traffic, a blur of bicycles in the cycle lane, the sidewalk crowded with pedestrians, a couple of street cleaners, some vegetable sellers. No one even gave him a second glance as he stood breathing hard, his face shining with sweat, looking one way, then the other. Johnny Ren was gone.

'Are you people blind!' he raged at his detectives when he got back. 'You walk out of a meeting where this guy is the main topic of discussion. You all have a photograph of him in your folders. You come back in here and you don't notice him walking out of my office?'

They all stood in stunned silence. The whole building was buzzing with rumour and speculation. Li's first stop had been Chen's office, where he had demanded armed guards on all entrances to the building, and that everyone coming in and out have their IDs checked. 'I can't believe this man's audacity, Chief. We're in the meeting room talking about how we're going to catch him, and he walks into the building, cool as you like, and has all the time in the world to go through anything he wants to in my office.'

'Is there anything missing?' Chen asked.

'I don't know. I'm going to have to go through everything on my desk.'

None of his detectives could say whether Ren had been carrying anything when he left Li's office. 'We just thought he was someone from downstairs in Administration,' Wu said. 'No one paid him any attention.'

Li slammed the door of his office shut and stood seething. He looked around the room and felt sick. It was tainted somehow, dirty, violated. Johnny Ren was either supremely confident, or he was insane. Probably both. He clearly had complete contempt for the police.

Li sat down and searched through the papers on his desk. As far as he could see nothing was missing, but so much had been dumped on it during the last two days he wasn't sure himself exactly what was there. He looked around. Everything in the room seemed in its usual place. The dozens of transcripts piled under the window looked just as they had earlier. He went through the drawers. Pens, notepads, an address book, paper-clips, a stapler, old reports from his predecessor which he had meant to clear out, a pack of chewing gum, some letters. Nothing seemed to have been disturbed. What on earth had Johnny Ren been after? And why would he risk walking into the lion's den? What possible motive could he have had?

There was a tentative knock on the door and Zhao appeared nervously. 'Sorry to disturb you, boss. While you were out there was a call from the Deputy Procurator General's office. Apparently the DPG is concerned that the report he received this morning didn't include the events of last night – in Ritan Park.'

Li closed his eyes. 'Shit!' How the hell had Deputy Procurator General Zeng got to hear about that already? Li hadn't felt inclined to revise his report of yesterday's developments at one in the morning. Now he was paying for it. He strode to the door. Zhao backed out of his way. 'Qian,' he barked. 'You written up last night's report?'

Qian said, 'Just finished, boss.'

'All right, get it copied and have a courier standing by to get it down to the Municipal Procuratorate. I'll do a cover piece for it now.'

He cursed to himself, banged the door shut and dropped into his chair. He reached for his notebook, then hesitated. If he called the Centre of Material Evidence Determination now he might get the results of the AIDS test. If that went with the report it might mollify Zeng a little to be in receipt of the day's most recent developments. He picked up the phone and asked the operator to get him Professor Xie. As he waited he ran through in his mind a summary of where they were at, for his report to Zeng: they had ruled out a drugs connection between the three murders, but with the possibility that Chao had AIDS they were running the rule over a possible homosexual link; they had, almost certainly, identified the killer, a freelance Triad hit-man from Hong Kong known as Johnny Ren, who was still at large in Beijing and, apparently, anxious to establish just how close the police were getting to him. 'This is Professor Xie.' The voice in his ear tore him away from his thoughts.

'Professor, it's Deputy Section Chief Li. Can you give me any idea when we might expect the result of the AIDS test?'

'What AIDS test is that, Deputy Section Chief?'

Li frowned. 'On Chao's blood. Dr Campbell requested it yesterday.'

'Not from me.'

'I don't understand.' Li was caught off balance. 'She told me she spoke to you some time after seven yesterday evening.'

'I'm afraid not. And, unfortunately, such a test is no longer possible. Chao's remains were incinerated this morning, along with all the samples.'

'What?' Li could not believe what he was hearing. 'That body was evidence. You don't go around destroying evidence in a murder investigation.'

There was a long hesitation on the other end of the line. When he eventually spoke, there was a strange quality to the professor's voice. 'I understand his family did not wish to be in receipt of the remains.'

'That's got nothing to do with it. Chao's body was the property of the Chinese people until we decided otherwise.'

'My department had authorisation to release the body for disposal.'

'From who?'

'I'm sorry, Deputy Section Chief, I'll have to go. I'm in the middle of an autopsy.' The professor hung up.

Li sat holding the receiver for fully half a minute before eventually replacing it. Something was very, very wrong here. His hand went instinctively to his belt, searching for the leather pouch that held his watch. It wasn't there. 'Damn.' He remembered breaking the chain yesterday. Where had he put it? Top right-hand drawer. He opened it. There was no sign of the watch. He reached right into the back of the drawer. It definitely wasn't there. He ran quickly through the other drawers. Still no watch. He hadn't noticed its absence when he was searching the drawers earlier, because he hadn't remembered it was there. Now he felt all the hairs stand up on the back of his neck. For some unfathomable reason Johnny Ren must have taken it.

IV

Margaret cycled without thinking, grim and determined, letting the city wash over her as she headed north through meandering, chaotic streets. She was hot and tired and angry and hurt, and thinking was a painful process. If she kept her mind empty, her feelings remained at bay, and she was able to effect a temporary escape from the world. But she could not escape China. At least, not yet. Her flight did not leave until the morning.

As she had crossed campus to get a taxi back to her hotel after her face-down with Bob, she had spotted Lily and taken a minor diversion. Lily had seen her coming, her face reddening, in spite of herself. Margaret kept it short and sweet, an exotic blend of profanities which would have made her mother blush. Even her father, an expert in the use of colourful language, would have been shocked. But whatever satisfaction Margaret had gained from her verbal castigation of the self-important former Red Guard, it was short-lived. She had lain down on the bed when she got back to her hotel and wept for nearly an hour. A hot shower had failed to ease her tension headache. A phone call to the airline office had achieved a rescheduled return flight for the following morning. There would be a considerable additional charge, the girl had told her. She didn't care, Margaret had told her back.

Now, with a map and a guidebook in the basket of her bicycle, she was seeking an escape from the city, the opportunity for some solitude, time to sort out her feelings away from the chance of interruption. She passed the Beijing offices of Apple Computers, choking on the fumes that belched from the back of a diesel truck. She had been cycling for almost three-quarters of an hour, and didn't appear to have made much impression on the route she had planned on the map. The streets always seemed so much longer in reality than they did on paper.

After another twenty minutes, negotiating busy street markets and crowds of lunch-time cyclists, she came to a major north–south–east–west intersection and saw, diagonally across the street, the gates of Yuanmingyuan Park, the Park of Perfection and Brightness. But there was nothing very perfect about the park. It was dusty and neglected, a shabby shadow of the royal playground it had once been during the middle years of the Qing Dynasty. Then, its rolling parkland had been filled with gilded halls, towers and pavilions, its centrepiece a collection of European-style marble palaces modelled on the French Sun King's Palace of Versailles – an early experiment in the art of the joint venture. Sacked twice within forty years by British and French troops at the end of the nineteenth century, all that remained of it now were a few white marble skeletons and some weed-choked lily ponds.

Margaret left her bike at the gates and followed the paths that the municipal authorities had carved through the parkland. Past a boating lake, where forlorn red-dragon pedaloes bobbed at the water's edge. Past stalls where painted girls chatted idly behind high counters of cheap mementos. Battered loudspeakers hung from lampposts and wooden poles at every turn, scratching out sad Chinese dirges performed on plucked stringed instruments. The historic sites were crowded, and with the aid of the map on the back of her admission ticket, Margaret navigated herself away from the beaten tourist track along a narrow tree-lined lane that cut into the farmland heart of the park. Away, at last, from people, the sound of sad music drifting distantly on the breeze, she finally slowed and lingered in the shade of some spindly birches, squatting at the edge of a brackish pond that was alive with frogs. Paddy fields, shimmering in the haze, stretched into the distance on either side. Green shoots of rice pushed up through the still brown water. It made her think of McCord and his super-rice feeding the hungry millions. She snorted her derision. What did people like McCord really care about those hungry millions? Perhaps she was just cynical, but she couldn't help believing that the diseased, the dying and the hungry were simply convenient meal tickets for scientists anxious to grab as big a slice of the research cake as they could get their hands on. She thought of Chao and his association with McCord going back to their time together at the Boyce Thompson Institute. How that chance meeting had brought McCord to China, leading to the development of the super-rice and Chao's elevation to adviser to the Minister of Agriculture. And Chao's death had led her here, to the Park of Perfection and Brightness, to gaze sadly upon their genetically modified rice pushing its green shoots up through the still brown water.

All these thoughts filled her mind, blotting out the one thing she didn't want to think about. Li Yan. If she had been on the receiving end of a dressing-down for spending the night at his apartment, what kind of wrath had rained down upon him from on high? He must have known there would be consequences. Much more serious for him than for her. After all, she was just some stupid American who didn't know the rules. He was Chinese and a keeper of the rules. So why had he taken her back to his apartment when he could easily have dropped her off at the Friendship Hotel? She was frightened to think why. Frightened to believe that he might feel the same way about her as she felt about him. But then, what *did* she feel about him? What *could* she feel about him so soon after Michael's death? Wasn't there a danger of her throwing herself at the first man who showed any interest, of simply trying to fill the empty space that Michael had left?

She didn't know any more. She was tired of trying to analyse her feelings, of attempting to find a context for them. She only knew what she felt, and she felt sick at the thought that she would never see Li again. When she got back to the hotel she would have time to pack, eat and sleep. And tomorrow she would be gone. Back to Chicago and the sham of a life she had left there four days ago. Was it only four days? It seemed like four lifetimes. She felt as though she had known Li all her life. Had she really thought him ugly and brutish and unattractive that first day when their car had knocked him off his bicycle? He had been furious. Angry as she had not seen him since. She thought of all the hours she had spent in his company in that time, how often she had caught herself wanting to touch him or kiss him, lightly, affectionately. No big deal. It had seemed so natural she had had difficulty stopping herself. She remembered catching a glimpse of his face reflected in the mirror through the bathroom door in her hotel room, knowing that he could see her as she stepped out of the shower. It had sent a tiny thrill of sexual desire through her loins.

But they were all over now, those little mind games and fantasies. What possible future could there have been in any of it? A few stolen nights of passion, a release of sexual frustrations. And then goodbye. She had no future in China. He had no future outside it. So what was the point? All this angst over a relationship that neither existed now nor ever could.

She picked up a pebble and lobbed it into the centre of the pond, sending frogs diving from leafy platforms into stagnant water. All that had happened was that she had made a mess of things. She had come to China to escape. But she had been totally unprepared for the demands it would make of her and hadn't had the will to bridge the gap. She had met a man she found attractive, but it was the wrong place and the wrong time. And, in any case, she wasn't ready for another relationship. It was the advice she would have given her sister or her best friend. Don't go rushing into another relationship. You'd only be compensating. Give yourself a break from men for a while. Get out and enjoy life again. She smiled ruefully. How often it was that the advice you gave to others was the advice you would find hardest to follow yourself. Easy to give. Hard to take. She stood up. Just don't think about it, she told herself. Take a taxi to the airport in the morning and get on the plane. Once you're in the air you can start thinking about the rest of your life. Just don't look back. At least, not until you're far enough away to get a perspective on it. Like the rice paddies she had seen as her plane came into land, reflecting sunlight, she remembered, in a fractured mosaic like the pieces of a shattered mirror. How different from the view she had of them from here – green shoots poking through muddy water. Everything in life, it seemed, was about perspective. And she wondered what kind of perspective she would ever have on Michael.

But she felt better already for the perspective Yuanmingyuan had given her of the events of the last few days. Slowly she got to her feet. The secret was simply not to think about it. The most daunting thing ahead of her, she assured herself, was the cycle ride back to the Friendship Hotel.

CHAPTER TEN

I

Thursday Afternoon

She concentrated on the pumping of her legs, on watching the cyclists who whizzed by her on either side with curious passing glances, on the motorists who seemed intent on tipping her on to the tarmac or bursting her eardrums with their horns. And she absorbed the sights and sounds of this strange city like scenes in a movie shot from a passing car. With a pang of regret, Margaret realised she would miss Beijing. It was a place, she felt, that would have got under her skin had she spent any length of time here. It was so alive. *Don't even think about it!* The words came into her head like a reprimand from a higher authority. But it was, she knew, her own counsel. And she took it.

She approached the hotel from the north, passing the Friendship Palace and its shady gardens where birds sang in cages, and wheeled her bicycle into the carpark, hot and uncomfortable in the scorching afternoon. A car horn sounded, but she paid it no attention. Motorists used their horns incessantly. It sounded again. Two short, insistent blasts and a longer one. She turned as a dark blue Beijing Jeep pulled in behind her and drew alongside. Her stomach flipped over as she recognised Li behind the wheel. The driver's window wound down and he switched off the engine. He looked at her apprehensively. His battered face didn't seem as bruised as it had earlier. 'I tried to get you at the university,' he said. 'They told me you'd quit.'

She nodded confirmation. 'My flight's at nine thirty tomorrow morning.'

He thought she seemed cold and distant. He wanted to ask why she had quit, why she was leaving, but he didn't have the courage. 'I just wanted to check with you,' he said. 'About the AIDS test.'

Her disappointment manifested itself as anger. 'Actually, I'm not interested. I'm no longer involved in your investigation, and I couldn't care less if Chao tested positive or not.'

Li responded in kind, hurt by her tone. 'And I couldn't tell you, even if I wanted to . . . since you never requested the test.'

'What?' She glared at him, full of indignation.

'According to Professor Xie.'

'Well, that's ridiculous. I spoke to him last night, on the way back here to change.'

'And asked him to test a sample of Chao's blood for AIDS?'

'Of course.'

'He says you didn't.'

'Then he's a damn liar!'

'You want to tell *him* that?'

'Try stopping me.' She kicked down her bike stand, slipped the lock through the back wheel and rounded the Jeep to the passenger side. As she slipped into the seat she slammed the door shut and glared at Li. 'And you believe him, do you?'

'No,' he said simply.

She stared at him for some moments. 'What's going on, Li Yan?'

'Someone doesn't want us testing Chao Heng for AIDS.'

'Professor Xie?' Margaret was incredulous.

'Only on instruction from someone else.'

'Who?'

'I've no idea.'

'But . . . why?'

'I don't know that either.'

She shook her head. 'This is absurd. You're the police. How can anyone stop you having a simple blood test done?'

'By destroying the body and all the blood and tissue samples.'

'You're kidding!'

'This morning. They incinerated everything.'

Margaret simply couldn't believe it. 'That's not possible. I mean, in most US states *all* toxicology specimens are held frozen for one year. Five in homicide cases.'

'It's not common practice to destroy evidence in China either,' Li said. 'In this case, it seems, authorisation to destroy the remains came as the result of an "administrative error".' It had taken him all morning to track that one down. They had even shown him the form. A clerk had typed in the wrong name, they said.

She shook her head. 'And you believe that?'

'No.' He closed his eyes and breathed deeply, keeping his anger in check. 'Someone's gone to a lot of trouble to cover their tracks. But there is one loose end.' He paused. 'You.'

'Me?'

'You requested the AIDS test from Professor Xie last night – long before he received instructions to destroy the body and the samples.'

'But if he's denying that . . .'

'That's why I'd like a sworn statement from you before you leave. I know it's only your word against his . . .'

'But it's not,' Margaret said. 'There was a witness.'

Li frowned. 'Who?'

'Lily Peng. She insisted on coming in with me when I went to talk to Professor Xie.'

Li processed his thoughts rapidly. 'Well, there's no way he can get around that one, is there?' He ran it through again in his mind. 'And that means I can use you and Lily to frighten him. Sometimes when rats are scared they squeal. Do you still want to go and see him?'

Margaret hesitated. It would be too easy to say yes, to get involved again, let all that emotion back in when she'd just spent the last three hours building resolute defences against it. 'I don't think the university would approve,' she said feebly.

'This has nothing to do with the university. You're a material witness.'

'So . . . I don't have any choice. Is that what you're telling me?'

'That's what I'm telling you.'

'Then I don't have any choice, do I?' There was just the hint of a smile about her eyes.

He grinned. 'No,' he said. 'You don't.'

It took less than fifteen minutes to drive to the Centre of Material Evidence Determination. For the first five neither of them spoke.

Margaret was having immediate regrets. She knew perfectly well that she could have refused to get involved, and Li would not have forced her. She had been foolish. What could possibly come of this but trouble and heartache? Nothing had changed. She was still leaving on the nine thirty flight in the morning. She would never see Li again. She would never return to China. What did she care about the murder of Chao Heng and some drug dealer and an unemployed labourer from Shanghai? What did it matter to her that someone was trying to block Li's investigation? Who cared?

Li said, 'We've identified the killer from that thumbprint.'

And she knew that *she* cared. She couldn't have said why, only that she did. 'Who is he?'

'A Triad hit-man, like my uncle suggested right at the outset. DNA on the blood inside the glove matches the DNA in the saliva on the cigarette ends. So there's no doubt. He's called Johnny Ren. And he walked into the headquarters of Section One this morning and stole my fob watch from my desk drawer.'

Margaret looked at him in astonishment. 'How . . . ? Why?'

'I don't know why.' Li was clearly agitated by it. 'He's been following us – you and me. Following our progress. He nearly killed me last night. And today he delivered a message. That he can do what he damn well likes and we can't do anything about it.'

'You think that's why he took your watch? To make a statement?'

Li shrugged. 'Maybe. I don't know. Maybe he's just a mad bastard. But if he thinks we won't get him, he's wrong. By tomorrow morning his face will be as famous in China as Mao Zedong's.'

They sat in silence for a moment, Margaret thinking quickly. 'But he couldn't have been responsible for blocking the AIDS test. Could he?'

Li shook his head. 'No. That must either have been his employer or another employee.'

'Someone with a lot of clout, anyway,' Margaret said. 'To subvert a pathologist and contrive to have the medical evidence destroyed.'

Li nodded solemnly, then turned to look at her. They had stopped at traffic lights. 'I am beginning to have a bad feeling about it,' he said. 'It is starting to look like your idea that Chao was burned to try to hide something might be closer to the truth after all. They just misjudged how much damage would be done by the fire.'

When they arrived at the Centre Professor Xie was in mid-autopsy. He looked up as the doors swung open, and Margaret saw colour rise on his face behind the mask. There was something close to panic in his eyes. But he remained outwardly cool, slipping off the mask and turning to his assistants, asking them to leave for a few minutes. Li waited until the door had closed behind them. 'Do you still maintain, Professor, that Dr Campbell did not ask you last night to arrange for a sample of Chao Heng's blood to be AIDS-tested?'

The professor smiled nervously and glanced at Margaret. 'No, of course not,' he said. 'I'm sure Dr Campbell did ask. But, you know, my English is not, perhaps, what it might be . . .'

'We never had any trouble with your English through three autopsies, Professor,' Margaret said. 'And I didn't have the impression last night that you in any way misunderstood my request. I'm sure Constable Lily Peng will bear me out.'

The colour drained from the professor's face. Li said, 'You are in deep trouble, Professor Xie. Attempting to destroy or cover up evidence would make you an accessory to murder.'

The professor held himself very stiffly, and he spoke softly, rapidly, in Chinese. 'I am not involved in this, Deputy Section Chief Li. I do what I am told. No more, no less. I have no idea what is going on. But if you try to implicate me, then I can assure you, you are the one who will be in trouble.' Margaret watched his scalpel hand tremble as he spoke.

'Are you threatening me, Professor?' Li's voice was level and steady.

'No. I am telling you how things are. And they are things over which neither of us has any control.'

'We'll see,' Li said, and he turned abruptly and headed for

the door, catching Margaret by surprise. She had no idea what had been said, but the tone was unmistakably hostile. Her brow furrowed in a question to Professor Xie that was formulated entirely in body language. After all, they had performed three autopsies together. There had been an element of bonding in that. The professor responded with an almost imperceptible shrug that carried the hint of an apology. Margaret sighed and followed Li out. She caught him up as he stepped from the cool of the building into the blaze of mid-afternoon sunshine.

'What was all that about?' she asked.

'He was warning me off.'

'What, you mean threatening you?'

'No.' Li smiled grimly. 'Warning me.'

Margaret shook her head. 'I don't understand. I mean, can't you just arrest him for obstructing a police investigation?'

'We have no such law.'

'So, what happens if someone refuses to co-operate with the police?'

Li smiled with genuine amusement at her naïveté. 'No one refuses to co-operate with the police in China.'

Margaret took a moment to fully absorb his meaning. 'But isn't that what Professor Xie just did?' she asked.

Li's smile faded. 'No. He didn't refuse to co-operate. He just lied.'

'Where is she now?' Chen stood behind his desk, eyes blazing with anger as he gathered papers together and slipped them into a briefcase.

'In my office.'

'You're a fool, Li,' Chen raged. 'I told you she was to play no further part in this investigation.'

'She's a witness. I'm taking her statement.'

'Proving what? That Professor Xie's English is less than perfect? For God's sake, Li, what possible reason could the professor have for deliberately destroying evidence or failing to carry out blood tests?'

'None.'

'Well, there you are, then.'

'He was ordered to.'

Chen's laugh was hollow and without humour. 'Oh, what's this? A conspiracy theory now? Dr Campbell is turning out to be the biggest mistake I ever made.' He rounded the desk and unhooked his jacket from a peg on the back of the door.

'It's got nothing to do with Dr Campbell.'

'You're right. It hasn't. This is an investigation by Section One of the Criminal Investigation Department of Beijing Municipal Police.' He pulled his jacket on angrily.

'The point is, someone tried to stop us doing tests on Chao's blood, Chief.'

'Well, if that's true, they succeeded, didn't they?' He looked at his watch. 'Look, I've got a meeting at the Procurator General's office. I'm going to be late.' He paused at the door and cast Li a withering look. 'Perhaps you'd like me to pass on your conspiracy theory to Deputy Procurator General Zeng, since you and he seem very tight on this case.'

Li followed him out into the corridor, ignoring the barb.

'Chief, I think the key to this whole case is in what those blood tests would have shown up.'

'Then find another key. There's always a back door.' Chen checked his watch again without breaking his stride. 'And, for heaven's sake, lose the American. I hear she's quit her job at the university.'

'She's booked a flight home tomorrow morning.'

'Good. Make sure she's on it.'

Li stopped and watched Chen all the way to the end of the corridor, then turned into the detectives' room, ignoring the curious glances of his colleagues and passing straight through into his own office. He slammed the door behind him. Margaret was sitting at his desk, tipping the chair slowly backwards and forwards.

'It's strange to think he was in here,' she said. She lifted a copy of Johnny Ren's photograph from the desk. 'I take it this is him?' Li nodded. 'He doesn't look at all like I imagined him.'

'How did you think he'd look?'

'Not Chinese. I don't know why. I knew he would have to be, but it's not the picture I had in my head.' She examined the photograph again. 'He's got evil eyes, hasn't he? There's no light in them. They're quite dead.' She looked up. 'What did Chen say?'

'He's not buying into a conspiracy.'

'Are you surprised?'

'Not really. He thinks Professor Xie's story sounds quite plausible.'

'So where does that leave us?'

'It leaves *me* trying to catch Johnny Ren. And it leaves you catching a plane home in the morning.' He glanced at her, then quickly averted his eyes, suddenly self-conscious. He wandered to the window, hands pushed in pockets, and there was a silence between them that lingered interminably.

Finally she said, 'Of course, there could be another way of getting access to Chao's medical history.'

He turned, frowning. 'How do you mean?'

'Well, presumably he had a doctor. I mean, where else would he get all those prescription drugs?'

Li shook his head in disbelief. It was so obvious, why had it taken both of them until now to think of it? And then he smiled to himself.

'What's so funny?' she asked.

'Old Chen,' he said. 'He is a prickly old bastard, but he's not stupid. I told him I thought the key to Chao's murder was in his blood. He said,' – and Li was careful to recall the exact words – "then find another key. There's always a back door."'

'As long as you let me help to unlock it.' Margaret raised an appealing eyebrow.

'You've got a plane to catch.'

'A lot can happen in . . .' She checked her watch. '. . . Seventeen and a half hours.'

II

Li turned the Jeep down Beijingzhan Street, and ahead of them rose the twin towers of Beijing railway station, where Old Yifu would arrive back from Sichuan some time that evening. Li had taken a circuitous route to Chongwenmen to avoid the traffic that had ground to its habitual afternoon standstill on the second ring road. He had finally summoned up the courage to ask Margaret what had happened to make her quit the university. And she had told him: about missing her lecture, about the attitude of Jiang and his staff, about her row with Bob. Now he shook his head and said, 'I am so sorry, Margaret.'

'Why? It's not your fault.'

'If I had taken you back to your hotel instead of my apartment none of this would have happened.'

'If I hadn't got drunk . . .' She didn't need to finish. 'Well, anyway, it's that little bitch, Lily Peng, that I blame. It was her that snitched on us.'

Li shrugged. 'If it had not been her it would have been someone else – the duty policeman at the apartments, the staff at the Friendship . . . But there was no reason for you to quit.'

She sighed. 'Yes, there was. I guess maybe Bob's holier-than-thou attitude pushed me over the edge, but the blow-up's been coming since the moment I stepped off the plane. I should never have come here, Li Yan. I came for all the wrong reasons – to escape the mess of my life back home, not because I wanted to come to China. And Bob was absolutely right. I didn't take the interest I should have, I didn't prepare properly. I arrived with all the baggage of popular paranoid American propaganda about China and communism – and a completely closed mind.' She glanced at him across the Jeep and smiled ruefully. 'If I hadn't met you, if you hadn't challenged me

and forced me to open my eyes and my mind, I would probably have gone through my six weeks here like some kind of
automaton, and none of this country would have rubbed off
on me. And I'd have gone home the same person I was when
I arrived. And the same wasted life would have been waiting
for me when I got back. But these four days have changed me.
When I go home tomorrow, it'll be a different me who gets off
the plane in Chicago. And I won't be going back to the same
old wasted life. I'll be starting a new one.' She stared at her
hands. 'I just wish . . .' But she couldn't finish what she had
started and shrugged, a little hopelessly. 'So why *did* you take
me back to your apartment?'

He kept his eyes ahead of him as he circumnavigated the
station, turning east at the junction into Chongwenmen Dong
Street. He wanted to tell her it was because he needed to be close
to her, that he didn't want to leave her, that just her presence,
her scent, in his apartment was worth all the wrath that he
knew would pour down on him from above. He said, 'With
Johnny Ren on the loose I was concerned for your safety.'

'Oh,' she said, somehow disappointed that there wasn't
more to it. 'And is that what you told your boss?'

Li nodded. 'He wasn't impressed.'

Margaret bridled. 'You know, that's what gets me about this
whole disapproval thing. I spent the night in your apartment,
entirely innocently. But they don't believe it. There's something prurient about the whole lot of them.'

Li smiled. 'And when people think you are guilty, you might
as well have had the pleasure of committing the crime.'

Margaret turned and looked at him curiously. 'Pleasure?'

But still he kept his eyes on the road. 'It's a pity we'll never know.' After a moment he glanced across, but she had turned away again and he could not gauge her reaction. In fact, her heart was pounding. Was he really expressing regret that they had not slept together? Certainly, it was characteristically oblique, although paradoxically it was also uncharacteristically direct. She wanted to grab his face and tell him to say what he meant, express what he felt. But she realised that she had done neither herself. Why was it so difficult? But, of course, she knew. It was fear. Her fear of involving herself in a relationship with no future, especially when she was still so raw from the last one. His fear of involving himself in any kind of relationship. She suspected that his career had predominated for so long he had forgotten how to be with a woman.

They turned off Xihuashi Street and into the compound overlooked by the apartment block where Chao had lived. Li parked the Jeep in the shade of the trees and Margaret followed him to the door of Chairwoman Liu Xinxin's ground-floor apartment. Liu Xinxin answered the door cautiously, glaring at Li for a moment until recognition dawned.

'Detective Li,' she said. And then she stared inquisitively at Margaret.

'Chairwoman Liu, this is Dr Campbell, an American pathologist who is helping with our inquiry. Do you speak English?'

Liu Xinxin's face lit up. 'Oh, yes. But I am slow now. I no get much practice.' She held out a hand to Margaret. 'Am very please meet you, Doctah Cambo.'

Margaret shook her hand. 'It is my pleasure.'

'Please to come in.' She led Li and Margaret into her living room. Her two grandsons were squatting on the carpet playing with a toy steam locomotive crudely carved in wood and painted by hand. They gawped at Margaret in awe. 'Tea?' Liu Xinxin asked.

'That's very kind of you,' Li said. 'Unfortunately we have very little time today.' He was anxious not to be drawn into another rousing chorus of 'Our Country' around the piano. 'I wondered if you could tell us which doctor Mr Chao attended.'

'Hah!' Liu Xinxin waved her hand dismissively. 'Very strange man, Mr Chao. He is scientist, educated in West.' She nodded towards Margaret as if to say, 'You should know, you come from the West.' 'Everything modern, modern. Expensive hi-fi. CD player. Mobile telephone. But he no like modern medicine. He like traditional, Chinese herbal medicine. He go Tongrentan.'

Margaret glanced at Li. 'What's that?'

'It's a traditional Chinese medicine store. The kind of place where you pay a year's wages for a piece of fifty-year-old ginseng root.' He turned back to Liu Xinxin. 'What branch?'

'Dazhalan.'

'I don't understand,' Margaret said. 'He went to a medicine store instead of a doctor?'

Li shook his head. 'They have consulting doctors there. Usually retired. It's a way to augment their pensions.'

'And they prescribe herbal medicine?'

'Traditional Chinese medicine,' Liu Xinxin said. 'Very good medicine. Make you well very fast.'

'Well, he certainly didn't get reverse transcriptase and protease inhibitors in a herbal medicine shop,' Margaret said.

Dazhalan was a jumble of street markets and curiosity shops in narrow, medieval *hutongs* just south of Qianmen. Li and Margaret pushed their way through frenetic crowds of shoppers. Tinny music blasted from loudspeakers hanging at every corner. Red and yellow character banners zigzagged above their heads. Shopfronts were fantastic creations of tiled and curling eaves supported on intricate and colourfully painted beams and pillars. 'During the Ming Dynasty,' Li told her, 'there were great wicket gates here that closed off the inner city at night. Dazhalan means, literally, "big stockades". In imperial Beijing, shops and theatres were not permitted in the centre of the city. So they opened up here, just outside the gates. It was the place to come on a dull Beijing night.'

They passed a four-hundred-year-old emporium selling pickle and sauce, a restaurant offering imperial snacks, a shop which had been dealing in silks and wool and furs for more than a hundred years. 'This used to be the red-light district,' Li said. 'Until the communists shut all the brothels down in 1949 and sent the girls to work in factories.' And suddenly he remembered Lotus, and his promise to Yongli. He cursed inwardly, but he was in no position to do anything about it now.

Beneath a colourful and beautifully ornate canopy, white

marble lions in wrought-iron cages guarded the entrance to the Tongrentan Traditional Medicine Shop, purveyor of herbal concoctions since 1669. But they had not prevented several young men from slipping into the shade of the canopy and curling up on the cool marble slabs to sleep away the afternoon. Li and Margaret stepped over an older man who was snoring aggressively and pushed through glass doors into the deliciously cool air-conditioned interior.

It was not what Margaret had been expecting. Somehow the notion of traditional Chinese herbal medicine had conjured in her mind a dark and dingy shop, with daylight slanting in through old wooden shutters, and an old man with a long, wispy white beard serving behind a counter piled high with jars and bottles of exotic pills and lotions. Instead it was large and bright and modern. A gallery on the second floor was supported on red-and-gold pillars and overlooked the first-floor shop where the pills and lotions were displayed in very ordinary cardboard boxes in fluorescently lit glass display cabinets. High above them, huge glass lampshades were painted with scenes of imperial China and hung with long yellow tassels. The medicines themselves, however, surpassed even her wildest expectations: dried seahorses and sea slugs, tiger bone, rhino horn and snake wine, cures for everything from fright to encephalitis – or so they claimed.

Just inside the doors, a long and patiently waiting queue of people snaked across the breadth of the shop. The object of their vigilance was a consultation with an old, pinched-faced man perched in a booth off to the left. This retired doctor of medicine was, apparently, slow in dispensing his sagacity, and Li had no intention of waiting his turn. He pushed his way to the head of the queue, displaying his Ministry ID. Margaret hurried after him, eliciting odd and occasionally resentful stares. But no one voiced any objection. Li and Margaret entered the booth as a girl in her early twenties emerged, pasty-faced and spotty-cheeked, clutching a prescription and looking distinctly worried. The old doctor looked at Li's ID for a long time before examining his face carefully and then inviting them both to sit. He barely gave Margaret a second glance. 'What can I do for you, Detective?' he asked.

'I'm interested in one of your patients, Chao Heng.'

The doctor tipped his head in Margaret's direction. 'Who is she?'

'An American doctor. A pathologist helping us with a case.'

The old man turned to Margaret, eyeing her now with interest. 'Where did you train?' he asked her in perfect English.

She was taken aback. 'The University of Illinois.'

'Ah. I spent some time at the University of California, Davis Medical School. A research project on glandular cancer with my very good friend Dr Hibbard Williams. Endocrinology is his speciality. Perhaps you have heard of him?'

'I'm afraid not.' She frowned. 'I thought you were a practitioner of traditional Chinese medicine.'

'I studied both traditional Chinese and Western medicines. There is much that each can learn from the other. What is your speciality?'

'Burn victims.'

His nose wrinkled in distaste. 'How unpleasant.'

Li interrupted. 'Chao Heng did consult with you? Is that right?'

The doctor nodded. 'Mr Chao, yes.'

'I understand that he was unwell for some time.'

'Has something happened to him?'

'He was murdered.'

'Ah.' The doctor seemed unconcerned. 'How unfortunate. But he was dying anyway.'

'What of?' Margaret asked.

'I have no idea. I treated his symptoms for about six months but nothing worked for him. Eventually I suggested to him that he see a former colleague of mine at the Beijing Hospital in Dahua Lu. He was not very keen. He was a great believer in traditional remedies. But there was nothing more I could do for him.'

'What were his symptoms?' Margaret was curious.

'They were many,' the old doctor said, shaking his head. 'He suffered from exhaustion and diarrhoea, and he had frequent fevers. He had recurrent bouts of thrush and a cough that would not go away. He later developed swollen glands in the groin and the armpits. He was losing a lot of weight latterly. Some of his symptoms responded to treatment, at least for a time. But they always came back.'

Margaret was frowning. 'These are all possible indicators of HIV. Was he ever AIDS-tested?'

'Yes, I believe he was tested for HIV at the Beijing Hospital. That was about the last time I saw him.'

'And?' Margaret asked.

'And what?' the old man responded testily.

'Was the test positive?'

'Oh no.' The old herbalist scratched his chin. 'Mr Chao did not have AIDS.'

III

Li parked the Jeep in the shade of the trees at the east end of Dong Jiaominxiang Lane, a stone's throw away from the back entrance to Municipal Police Headquarters where Li and Margaret had had their first encounter the previous Monday. She gazed along the street towards the redbrick building that housed the headquarters of the Criminal Investigation Department and the arched gateway that led into its compound. Was it really only three days since that first meeting? She said to Li, 'That's where we first bumped into each other, isn't it?' And she grinned. 'Literally.'

'Yes,' he said, smiling and remembering how angry he had been. 'I was going for an interview for this job. Or, at least, that's what I thought. I'd spent all morning ironing my uniform so that I would look my best. And I ended up covered in dirt, with my elbow grazed, and my shirt splashed with water where I tried to wash away the blood.'

Margaret laughed. That's why he had been so annoyed. 'It got you the job, though, didn't it? They must have thought you looked like a man of action.'

'I'd got the job anyway. I'm just lucky they didn't change their minds when they saw the state I was in.'

She touched his arm where he had grazed it, and he felt the heat of her fingers like a burn. 'It's taken a long time to heal,' she said.

'That's a fresh one.'

'Oh.' She sounded surprised. 'Some other girl knock you off your bike?'

He smiled. 'It's a long story.'

'Better not tell me, then. Because we don't have much time left.' She had meant it in fun, but no sooner had she said it than they both felt the truth of it, and there was an unacknowledged pain in the fact of her looming departure.

They walked east in silence then, under the leafy canopy of trees, and turned left into Dahua Lu. It was a long street running north, with mature trees down the east side, shading the entrance to Dongdan Park. The Beijing Hospital, a modern jumble of sprawling white buildings of two and five storeys, ran along the west side behind high white-painted railings. There was a constant traffic of white-uniformed nurses in the street, the occasional ambulance coming or going. An old man in slippers and pale pyjamas, with a face as grey as the ash on his cigarette, shuffled at one of the gates, puffing smoke into the late afternoon sky. They passed the smoker on the way in, and Li asked for directions to the administration block from an armed policeman on sentry duty.

When they got inside, Li spoke for several minutes to a receptionist before they were led upstairs to a waiting room on the third floor and left there to kick their heels. It was a square room, with low, khaki-green settees around the walls and glass-topped tables with lace doilies – standard factory-issue furniture for reception rooms across China. After ten minutes a Reception Officer arrived to shake hands and exchange cards with Li and enquire politely about the purpose of their visit. Margaret watched the ritual exchange in Chinese and tried to exercise all three Ps simultaneously. The dialogue seemed interminable. The Reception Officer left and she asked Li what was happening. 'He has gone to arrange a meeting with the Administration Officer,' he said. 'And to send in some tea.'

'Tea?'

'We might be some time.'

In fact it was several cups and another twenty minutes before the Administration Officer arrived with an entourage of assistants and the Reception Officer, who then made the introductions. More ritual handshaking and exchanging of cards. Then they all sat down, Li and Margaret on one side of the room, the reception committee on the other. They had all cast curious glances in her direction, but otherwise made no comment.

Margaret sat in frustrated ignorance during the subsequent exchange between Li and the Administration Officer. It was a short conversation. She saw Li visibly pale, then the Administration Officer stood up, signalling an end to their meeting. More ritual handshaking, and they were led back down to the ground floor. She was itching to ask Li what had been said, but the Reception Officer was determined to see them out of the door himself, and there was some paperwork to be completed at the reception desk. She contained her impatience.

Li retraced their steps down Dahua Lu in long, loping strides, his hands plunged deep in his pockets. Margaret was struggling to keep up with him, half running to do so. 'But what did they say?' She was almost beside herself with curiosity, and he was being infuriatingly uncommunicative, concentrating on unshared dark thoughts that swam through his head behind deeply furrowed brows. They reached the Jeep and he got in behind the wheel. She got into the passenger side. 'For God's sake, Li Yan!'

He turned towards her. 'Are you hungry?'

'What?'

'I could really go a *jian bing*. I haven't eaten all day.'

'Neither have I, but I'd rather know what they told you in the hospital.'

'Mei Yuan will still be selling *jian bing* at the corner of Dongzhimennei,' he said. He started the Jeep and pulled away from the sidewalk. They had driven north, the length of Dahua Lu, and were turning east on to Jianguomennei Avenue when he said, 'It seems they ran all sorts of tests on Chao.' He replayed in his mind the short conversation he had conducted with the Administration Officer at the hospital. 'But certain results never came back from the laboratory, and the next thing all his medical records were removed from the Beijing Hospital and he was transferred as an in-patient to Military Hospital Number 301.'

Margaret waited. But Li had finished, and the significance of what he had told her somehow escaped her. 'So what's Military Hospital Number 301?' she asked.

'It is a high-security VIP hospital. It treats the top people in government and the bureaucracy. Deng Xiaoping received treatment there during his final illness.'

Margaret frowned. 'But Chao wasn't in that category of VIP, was he?'

'No, he was not.'

'So how come he was being treated there?'

'I don't know. It doesn't make any sense to me.'

Margaret thought for a moment. 'I guess he could only have been admitted to Military Hospital Number 301 if someone very powerful had arranged it, right?' Li nodded. 'Someone high up in government, or the civil service?' Li nodded again, and for the first time Margaret began to understand Li's retreat into himself. 'Are we getting into something here that's starting to get a bit scary?' she asked, a knot like a fist beginning to turn in her stomach.

'I've had a bad feeling about this all day,' Li said. He breathed deeply. 'And it's not going away.'

He sounded his horn more frequently than usual as they weaved through the bicycles and traffic in Chaoyangmen Nanxiaojie Street. He was more used to manoeuvring his way along this street as a cyclist than as a motorist.

'But you will still be able to access his medical records, won't you?'

Li looked uncertain. 'I don't know. Dealing with a place like that is outside my experience, perhaps even my jurisdiction.'

'In the States we'd subpoena the records.'

'But this is China, not the United States.'

'You told me no one in China refused to co-operate with the police.'

'Of course, I will ask for the records,' he said.

'And if they won't give you them?'

'They'll have to have a very good reason.' His words sounded braver than he felt. He felt like a weak swimmer who has strayed further from shore than he intended and is a long way out of his depth.

'Okay,' Margaret said. 'Let's think about this. We're dealing here with someone who has a great deal of power and influence. Someone with enough clout to have Chao admitted to a high-security hospital. Perhaps the same person who hired Johnny Ren to murder him and is now trying to stop you from finding out why. But this is not some all-powerful, or even infallible, individual. He's made mistakes. Like making a mess of getting rid of the evidence, if that's what Chao was. He clearly thought that burning the body would destroy whatever it was in his blood they wanted to hide. It didn't. Then they made a real clumsy job of stopping us doing the AIDS test. Incinerating the body, for Christ's sake, and all the samples! An administrative error? That's not going to hold up for five minutes if you pursue it hard enough.'

'But he didn't have AIDS. We know that. So why were they trying to stop us from testing for it?'

'In case we found something else. Something they didn't want us to find.'

'What?'

Margaret shook her head in frustration. 'I don't know.'

'And what about the other two murders? DNA tests prove that all three were killed by Ren. What's the connection?' Li felt the beginnings of a headache. The deeper they got into this, the muddier the waters were becoming.

'I don't know,' Margaret said again. She was beginning to realise how little they really knew about any of it. 'All I know is that someone must have been watching your investigation every step of the way. Someone with detailed access to your every move, and an understanding of the implications of everything you've done.'

Li frowned. 'What makes you think that?'

'How else would Johnny Ren have known who was leading the case? How would he have known who to follow? How else would anyone know the autopsy results, or that you had asked for an AIDS test? I mean, who else knew about any of it outside the department?'

'No one,' Li said aggressively. He couldn't believe she was suggesting that someone in Section One was implicated. Then he was struck by a thought that turned his blood to ice. 'Except . . .' He didn't even dare to voice the thought.

'Except who?' When he didn't respond, Margaret asked again, 'Except who, Li Yan?'

'Deputy Procurator General Zeng.'

Her brows furrowed in consternation. 'Who?'

'Procurators are a bit like district attorneys. They decide whether to prosecute a case in court. Zeng asked me to provide him with detailed daily reports on the progress of the case. He seemed to know a lot about it already.' He looked at Margaret. 'I mean, it was unusual, but he is a DPG. I never really thought anything about it.'

Margaret whistled softly. 'Well, that tells us something anyway.'

'What?'

'Our man's powerful enough to have the equivalent of a district attorney in his pocket.' She glanced apprehensively at Li. 'That makes him pretty formidable opposition.'

'Thank you for those words of encouragement,' Li said dryly.

She smiled, and thought at least they could still smile. But the smile faded as she remembered that in the morning she would be boarding a plane and Li would be left to face this on his own. She didn't want to leave him. She wished he could get on the plane with her and they could both leave all this behind. The game was no longer a game. It had turned dark and frightening.

Li turned right into Dongzhimennei and drew in at the kerb beside Mei Yuan's *jian bing* house. Mei Yuan rose from her stool as soon as she saw who it was. She gave Margaret a wide smile and said to Li, 'You are a little late for breakfast today.'

Li shook his head. 'No, we are early for breakfast tomorrow.' Margaret checked the time. It was nearly 6 p.m. 'Two *jian bing*,' Li said. 'It has been a long day.'

'It has,' Mei Yuan said, beginning her preparations for the

cooking. 'I have been waiting for you for hours. I have a solution for your riddle.'

Li and Margaret exchanged glances. 'The one about the three murders and the cigarette ends?' Margaret asked.

Mei Yuan nodded. 'You said he deliberately left the cigarette ends beside each of the bodies because he knew that you would find them and match the DNA.'

'That's right,' Li said. 'Why?'

'I think it is so obvious,' Mei Yuan said, 'that maybe I have not understood the question properly.'

Margaret was intrigued. 'So why do you think he did it?'

Mei Yuan shrugged. 'To make you believe these murders are connected – when there is no connection.'

Li frowned. 'But why would he do that?'

'Wait a minute,' Margaret said. 'You once told me that you conducted thousands of interviews to track down a man who murdered a whole family during a burglary. And it took you how long?'

'Two years.'

'So how long was it going to take you to track down all those migrant workers from Shanghai, and all the petty drug dealers and gay boys?'

It dawned on Li. 'Long enough to keep me looking in all the wrong places for months on end, trying to make a connection that doesn't exist. God!' It was so simple. But anyone who understood the *modus operandi* of the Chinese police would know that they would follow a painstaking and pedantic process of information-gathering that could take months, even years. 'The only connection is that there is no connection,' he said. It was a revelation. He gave Mei Yuan a big hug, and Margaret felt a twinge of jealousy. 'How on earth did you think of it, Mei Yuan?'

She glowed with the praise and Li's attention. 'Maybe,' she said, 'because I did not have to.'

CHAPTER ELEVEN

I

Thursday Night

Red light refracting in hot humid air hung over the city like a veil as the sun dipped in the west, and darkness drew like a curtain from the east across the Middle Kingdom. Below them the lights of the city twinkled in the dusk. Red tail-lights of traffic in long lines snaked east and west, north and south, the growling of their engines a distant rumble. Somewhere down there, Margaret thought, people were crowding the stalls at the Dong'anmen night market, taking pleasure in eating, happy and free at the end of a working day. She wished she were among them.

They had entered Jingshan Park by the south gate, almost opposite the place where the woman in the blue print dress had been knocked off her bike and Margaret had stopped the bleeding from her severed femoral artery by standing on her leg. They were entering the park as most people were leaving. It would close in an hour. They had followed a winding path up through the trees to the pavilion that stood on the top of

Prospect Hill. Halfway up, they had stopped briefly to join a crowd of people watching a very old lady in black pyjamas perform incredible contortions. She had laid a mat on the earth and, lying on her back, had wedged both her feet beneath a pole placed behind her neck, effectively folding herself in two. The crowd gasped in amazement, and there was a little burst of applause. The old lady remained impassive, but she was clearly enjoying showing off the suppleness of her joints and muscles. Margaret had guessed she must be in her eighties.

The pavilion was deserted when they got there, orange-tiled curling eaves supported on maroon-and-gold pillars, late evening sunshine throwing warm light on cold marble. Walking round, beneath the eaves, provided a 360-degree panorama of the city below. It took Margaret's breath away.

Li squatted on the steps, looking south, over the symmetrical patchwork of roofs that was the Forbidden City, to the vast open expanse of Tiananmen Square. He liked to come here, he told her, in the late evening, when it was quiet and he could watch the city come to life as darkness fell around him. It was the most peaceful place in Beijing, he said, and it released him to think freely and clearly. She sat down beside him, their arms touching, and she felt the heat of his body and breathed in the musky, earthy smell of him.

For a long time neither of them spoke. Swallows darted and dived around them in the dying light, and below, among the trees, the screech of cicadas rose, pulsing, into the night air.

Eventually he said, 'I'm scared, Margaret.'

She inclined her head towards him and examined his

profile, bold and strongly defined. 'Scared of what?' she asked softly.

'If I knew, I wouldn't be scared,' he said. 'I have a sick feeling in my stomach. I think we are both in danger.'

'In danger of what?'

'Of knowing too much.'

Margaret released a tiny gasp of frustration. 'But we know hardly anything. What do we know?'

'We know that someone with power and privilege and something to hide had Chao Heng killed. We know that a professional hit-man was employed to do it, and that he killed two other, perfectly innocent, people for no other reason than to confuse the investigation. We know, or think we know, that there is a conspiracy to pervert the course of that investigation, involving one of the highest law officers in the land. And we know that the killer is out there, somewhere, watching us getting closer and closer.' He paused. 'We know far too much.'

She shivered, in spite of the heat. For the first time she tasted his fear, and she knew it was real. 'What do you think they will do? Will they try to kill us?' It seemed shocking, somehow, that she was even suggesting such a thing. It had not occurred to her before that they could be in any real danger.

'I don't know,' Li said. 'They will be scared of us, because of what we know, or because of what they think we will find out. And we know they are ruthless people. Whatever they are hiding, they have killed three people to protect it. If it is worth three lives, it is worth three more, or thirty more, or three hundred more. How can you draw a line you have already crossed?'

They sat in silence, each with their own private thoughts, and Margaret slipped her arm through his and held on to him for comfort. Below, the darkness among the trees grew around them, secret and hidden and menacing. Margaret felt surrounded. Isolated. What had seemed peaceful was now threatening. Beyond, among the twinkling city lights, people went about their lives, eating, loving, laughing, sleeping. Families gathering in *hutongs* around flickering blue TV screen light, eating dumplings and drinking beer, giggling at some programme. Normal lives. Something that neither she nor Li could possess. It was all so close, but just out of reach . . . She had seen Bertolucci's film, and understood now the isolation of the Last Emperor, Puyi, shut away from the real world behind the walls of the Forbidden City spread out now beneath her in the dusk. Normality was just a touch away, but untouchable.

Her gaze wandered a little to the west, where the last light in the sky reflected on a long, narrow lake. She frowned, unable to place it. She had not been aware of such a large body of water in the centre of the city. 'What is that place?' she asked. 'I can't remember ever having seen it from the street.'

He followed her eyes. 'Zhongnanhai,' he said. 'The New Forbidden City. It is where our leaders live and work. You have never seen it because it is hidden behind high walls, just like the old Forbidden City.'

She gazed on the dark forbidden lake and wondered if

perhaps somewhere in all the villas nestling among the trees along its banks lay the answers to all their questions. The lights of a car briefly flashed across the water and turned into the drive of a distant villa where light leaked out through slatted blinds. She closed her eyes and let her head rest on his shoulder.

They had been up on Prospect Hill for nearly an hour. The sun finally slid down below the ragged line of distant purple hills, and stars twinkled in a dark blue firmament. Li had smoked several cigarettes, and for the last forty minutes they had not spoken much. Margaret's arm was still through his, her head still resting lightly on his shoulder. The darkness now did not seem so threatening. It wrapped itself around them like a blanket, and she felt safe and hidden. 'There is one other thing that scares me,' Li said finally.

She waited for him to tell her, but he said nothing. 'What?' she asked.

He swallowed and turned to meet her eye. 'Losing you,' he said.

She felt a rush of blood suffuse her with warmth, a trembling inside that was something between fear and pleasure. She understood how big a moment it was for him to have given voice to his emotion. As long as you keep such feelings secret and safe, they cannot hurt you. They cannot be turned against you, or rejected, or laughed at. But the moment you share them you become vulnerable. And once spoken, the words can never be taken back. Her mouth had gone dry, her throat thick. Her voice was husky. 'I don't want to lose you either.' It was almost a whisper. Now she had committed, too. They were equally vulnerable; the genie was out of the bottle.

He put a hand up to touch her face, and tracked his fingers gently down the pale, soft skin of her cheek. Then he ran them back through her golden curls, feeling the shape of her skull through the soft, silken hair. He put his other hand up to cup her face and draw her close. She rested her hands lightly on his arms and closed her eyes as his lips brushed hers once, twice. And she opened her mouth to receive his – soft and warm and smoky. And then their arms were around each other, the first tentative kiss giving way to a fierce, almost desperate passion. They broke apart for a moment, breathless, drinking each other in with restless, hungry eyes. And then they were kissing again. Urgently. Devouring each other. Bodies pressed together. He felt the hardness of her breasts pushing into him. They were on their knees now, his erection pressing hard into her belly. She wanted him inside her. She wanted to suck him in and keep him there. She wanted to consume him.

The crack of a twig snapping under foot cut through the chorus of cicadas from the trees below, and lust was replaced almost instantly by fear. They broke apart, and Li was on his feet. A flashlight shone in his face, and he raised an arm to shield his eyes. 'Who's that?' he called.

The light fell away to the ground, and an old man climbed several tentative steps towards them. He flashed the lamp briefly at Margaret, and said to Li, 'The gates will be locked in five minutes.'

On the steep path down through the trees, Margaret slipped her hand into his. It felt big and protective as it gave hers a small, gentle squeeze. Staff at the gatehouse waited impatiently to lock up, glaring at them as they passed outside to blink in the bright streetlights of Jingshanquan Street. The traffic was heavy, the sidewalks thick with evening strollers and teenagers wandering in aimless, giggling groups. Despite the life in the street, Li and Margaret felt immediately vulnerable, exposed and open to view. He took her arm to hurry her across the road, dodging vehicles to a chorus of horns. They got halfway and were trapped by a seemingly endless stream, standing with a group of others on the centre line, traffic behind them snapping at their heels. They saw a break and made a dash for it. Crossing from the other side, a woman with a bicycle and a bird in a cage lost control of the bike in her panic to cross. The front wheel turned and twisted. She lost her hold on the cage and it fell to the road, its door springing open. There was a screech of brakes and a blasting of horns as the approaching traffic ground to a halt. A large black-and-white bird, a family pet perhaps, worth many weeks' wages, flapped up from the road. The woman wailed and tried to catch it. Her fingers grasped at the feathers but could not hold on, and the bird rose from her outstretched hands and spread its wings, making for the opposite side of the street. Margaret reached up and tried to snatch it from the air as it lifted over her head. With a flutter of feathers beating the air in panic, it eluded her grasp and flew off into the night towards the park. The woman wailed at her loss, still juggling with her bicycle, the shopping from her basket spilling on to the tarmac. Margaret bent to help her, but Li grabbed her hand and pulled her away. 'We must go. We are too exposed.'

Margaret glanced back as they reached the opposite side-walk. The woman was gathering her things from the middle of the road, traffic all around her honking impatiently. Tears streamed down her face. There was something, Margaret thought, inestimably sad in her loss. Both she and Margaret had come so close to plucking the bird from the air. Margaret imagined she had almost felt its heart beat as her fingers brushed its panicked breast. Its instinct had been to escape. And yet, Margaret knew, it would die in the wild.

Li hurried her away along the sidewalk, turning south into the dark, still backwater of Beichang Street, where he had parked the Jeep under the trees. They stopped on the kerb by the car, and without conscious decision by either of them were kissing almost immediately, all the passion and lust of the park returning in a rush. They broke breathlessly and she held his face and gazed anxiously into his eyes. 'What are we going to do, Li Yan?'

It was a big question, a question that was many questions in one. A question he could not answer. His only thought was to make her safe while he tried to decide what he should do next. 'I should get you back to the Friendship Hotel,' he said.

'I don't want to leave you.'

'Just for a few hours.'

'I don't want to leave you,' she insisted, and kissed him, then shook her head and laughed at herself. 'Listen to me. Like some teenage girl.' She took a moment to gather herself. 'I want to love you. I want to make love to you. We don't even have anywhere to go. Not your place or mine.'

Li grinned. 'Not even the back seat of the car?'

Margaret laughed. 'I wouldn't dare. Lily Peng's probably hiding in the trunk.' And then both their smiles faded as they realised that all the jokes in the world could not put off the moment when they would have to face up to reality. They had no future. And she was scared that if they separated now, she might never see him again. Like the bird broken free from the cage, he would slip through her fingers and disappear into the night. He opened the passenger door for her. 'What will you do?' she asked.

'I need some time on my own to think. Then I will ask my uncle's advice. He is due home tonight.'

II

Li watched Margaret run across the forecourt of the Friendship Hotel and up the steps to the main door. He still had the taste of her on his lips. There was a constriction in his throat and his eyes were burning. He knew he would not see her again, and his sense of loss was far greater than he could ever have imagined. But it was important that she remain here, away from him, until her plane took her to safety in the morning. The forces arrayed against him would be happy just to see her go. And they could focus on him, alone – as he intended to focus on them. He had no idea how far or how deep the rot had gone, or from what it had grown, but he knew he could no longer trust anyone, and that a difficult course lay ahead of him. He gunned the engine and pulled away with a squeal of tyres.

Margaret turned at the top of the steps and saw the Jeep drive away at speed. Li's words were still ringing in her ears. *Go straight to your room. Lock the door. Do not answer it to anyone, even room service. Wait for me to call. If I do not call, get a taxi straight to the airport in the morning and get on your plane.* She knew he had no intention of calling, that he believed she would be safe as long as he stayed away from her, as long as she left the country as planned in the morning. But she had no intention of leaving. Her visa was good for nearly five more weeks. What she felt for Li she had not felt for a man in a long time. And she was damned if she was going to throw away the chance of at least a few weeks of happiness after everything that she had been through. After all, she thought, she could be dead tomorrow, or next week, or next year. And she would have played safe for what? For a few more empty days, weeks, months? If she had learned anything from the last year, it was that you had to grab the good things in life when they were there, because they, or you, might be gone tomorrow.

She crossed the polished marble floor to the reception desk to pick up her key.

'Margaret.'

She turned, surprised, to find Bob hurrying across the foyer from where he'd been sitting impatiently reading a paper, waiting for her return. It was not a pleasant surprise. 'What do *you* want?' she said, running up the short flight of steps to the elevators.

He hurried after her. 'I was worried about you. Jesus Christ, Margaret, what have you been up to? Public Security were at the university this afternoon looking for you.'

She stopped and scowled at him. 'What are you talking about?'

'Apparently you're booked on the first flight out of here tomorrow.'

'You don't say,' she said scornfully. 'I brought the booking forward this morning after our little exchange. Only now, I've changed my mind.'

He looked at her in confusion. 'But you can't.'

'I can do what I damn well like,' she said pressing the call button for the elevator.

'Not without a visa.'

'My visa's good for another five weeks.'

'That's the point. It's not. These guys were from the Visa Section. Apparently your visa's only good now till your flight leaves.'

The elevator arrived and the doors slid open. She stared at Bob in disbelief. 'They can't do that.'

'Oh yes they can, Margaret.' He put a comforting hand on her shoulder. 'What's going on?'

She shrugged his hand away. 'None of your fucking

business,' she said, controlling her tears long enough to get into the elevator and press for her floor. As the doors slid shut, the tears came, hot and salty, and a deep sob tore at her chest. It wasn't fair. How could they make her go? What right did they have? But she knew she couldn't fight them, and she saw all her choices dwindling to zero.

She ran, still sobbing, along the landing to her room, past two astonished attendants. Inside, she slipped the chain on the door and sat on the edge of the bed, and let the tears flow freely down her cheeks. Her sense of powerlessness was overwhelming, like that of a child manipulated at the whim of an adult world whose power was absolute. The phone rang and startled her. It couldn't be Li. She let it ring two or three times, fear growing inside her like a tumour, before lifting the receiver.

'Hello.'

'Dr Campbell?' An American accent, the voice oddly familiar.

'Who is this?'

'It's Dr McCord.'

Her relief was almost palpable. 'McCord? What the hell do you want?'

'I need to see you.'

'In your dreams.' Her fear was replaced by anger. 'You're the guy who told me to fuck off twice. Remember? Why would I want to see you?'

'Because I know why Chao Heng was killed. And I think I could be next.'

She caught her breath. There was no doubting the fear in

his voice, an odd desperation. 'I'll meet you downstairs in the bar.'

'No,' he said quickly. 'Too public. Take a taxi to Tiantan Park – the Temple of Heaven. I'll meet you at the east gate.'

Her fear was returning. 'No. Hang on a minute . . .'

But he wasn't listening. 'For God's sake make sure you're not followed. I'll see you there in half an hour.' He hung up, and in the silence of the room she could hear her heart beating.

Li drove with the flow of traffic down Fuxingmennei Avenue towards the Gate of Heavenly Peace. Floodlit buildings on either side illuminated the way ahead. People had taken to the streets again to escape the heat of their homes. The sidewalks were crowded, families gathered beneath the trees on the south side. Li could see the tail-lights of vehicles stretching for miles ahead into the shimmering hazy night. Somewhere in the city Johnny Ren was patiently watching, awaiting further instructions. From whom? Deputy Procurator General Zeng would not be able to sleep for fear that Li had, perhaps, already begun to suspect his involvement. Somewhere, in some dark and secret place wherein power resided, a paymaster or paymasters must be trembling in fear of exposure. But exposure of what? Li's ignorance seemed limitless. Whatever he knew, whatever they thought he knew, he felt a long way away from enlightenment.

How did one begin an investigation of a deputy procurator general without at least some proof? Who would authorise it?

And who else might be involved? Not Chen, surely? But then, he had been so dismissive of the idea that Chao's body had been deliberately destroyed, of the thought that Professor Xie might have been complicit in the incineration of blood and tissue samples. What was it they were so desperate to prevent him from discovering, and who stood to lose most from it?

Li knew he needed his uncle's advice. Old Yifu would listen to everything he had to say without fear or favour. He would trust Li's instincts but have a different perspective. His years of experience, of the police, of the justice system, his ability to calmly rationalise and sift through conflicting evidence, would be invaluable. More than ever before in his life, Li needed his uncle's help now.

He drove past the Gate of Heavenly Peace, Mao's portrait gazing down implacably upon the crowds in Tiananmen Square and his own mausoleum, a stern paternal figure remembered now with affection, his excesses and failures forgiven and forgotten. Past the gates of the Ministry of Public Security, and then right into the shady seclusion of Zhengyi Road. Immediately Li stood on the brakes, bringing his Jeep to a standstill. Near the foot of the road, outside the gates to the Ministry-provided police apartments where he lived with his uncle, were the blue and red flashing lights of several police vehicles and an ambulance. The road was blocked off, several uniformed officers milling on the sidewalk. Li felt a knot of nausea turn in his belly, and a cold sweat broke out across his forehead. He jammed his foot on the accelerator and sent the Jeep careering down the street to screech to a halt behind the ambulance. The uniformed officers turned in surprise as he leapt out of the car. 'What's happened?' he demanded.

'There's been a murder,' said the senior officer.

Li looked up and saw all the lights on in his apartment, the shadows of figures moving around inside. He started running. 'You can't go up there.' The officer tried to stop him, but Li pulled free.

'I live there!'

There was no sign of the duty policeman as he ran to the front door of the apartment block. But inside, the ground-floor landing was swarming with uniformed officers. Li went up the stairs two at a time. Behind him he heard someone say, 'That's Li. Better radio up to the apartment.'

When he got to the second landing it, too, was full of uniformed officers. The door of his apartment stood wide open. Lights were on everywhere. Inside he could see more bodies in uniform and plainclothes, and forensics men in white gloves. He recognised most of the faces. They all stood looking at him, frozen as if in a still frame from a movie. The silence was eerie, broken only by the odd crackle of a walkie-talkie. Li pushed through the figures in uniform and into the apartment. Still no one spoke or moved. He passed down the hall, glancing into the living room. It was a shambles, furniture upturned, the television set smashed. Fear rose like bile in Li's throat. He carried on down to the bathroom where there seemed to be the biggest concentration of plainclothes and forensics officers. Detective Wu, chewing almost manically on a piece of gum, stood in his way. He looked pale and shocked, and his eyes were full of incomprehension.

'What's happened, Wu?' Li's voice was husky, almost a whisper. He cleared his throat.

Wu said nothing. He simply stepped out of the way, and Li saw the red spray of blood across the while tiles, and the body of Old Yifu in the dry bed of the bath, impaled by his own ceremonial sword, driven with such force that it had passed right through him, through the plastic of the bath, and into the floorboards below. The shock brought tears immediately to Li's eyes and he started to shake. He looked at Wu.

'He put up a hell of a fight,' Wu said.

Li wanted to scream. He wanted to smash his fist into faces and walls, lash out with his feet. He wanted to inflict maximum damage on everyone and everything within reach. *He put up a hell of a fight.* But it was Li's fight, not Yifu's. Why had they done this? What possible point could there be in killing his uncle? Wu shifted uncomfortably. 'I've got a warrant for your arrest, Li. Issued by the Municipal Procuratorate.'

Li knew now that this was a dream. A nightmare from which he was certain to wake up. 'A warrant?' It didn't even sound like his own voice.

'For the murder of Li Li Peng.'

Li was almost incapable of taking in this new twist to the nightmare. 'Lily?' he heard himself say.

'Got her head bashed in at her apartment,' Wu said, almost as though it were the most natural thing in the world. 'I'm afraid I'm also going to have to hold you on suspicion of the murder of your uncle and the duty police officer here at the apartments.'

Li looked at the body of his uncle, lifeless eyes staring unseeingly at the ceiling, and then back at Wu. 'You think *I* did this?' His breathing was rapid now, and he felt in danger of losing control. He was holding on to reality by the merest thread. When was he going to wake up?

Wu looked embarrassed. 'To be honest, Li Yan, I don't believe for one minute that you did it. Any of it. None of us do. But we have evidence, and there are procedures to be gone through.'

'What evidence?' His anger almost choked him. He was paralysed now, rooted to the spot.

Wu snapped his fingers in the direction of a forensics officer and was handed a plastic evidence bag containing Li's fob watch, its leather pouch dark with the staining of blood. 'It was found in Lily's apartment beside her body.'

Li looked at it like a man possessed. 'That was stolen from my desk this morning. When we were all in the meeting room, and Johnny Ren was in my office.'

'We only have your word for it that it was Johnny Ren. We all just saw some guy. No one else recognised him. And why would he kill Lily?'

Li already knew the answer to that one. She had been witness to Margaret's request for the blood tests. 'Why would *I* kill Lily?' He couldn't believe he was having to ask the question.

'She snitched to Public Security about the American pathologist spending the night at your apartment.' Wu shrugged uneasily. 'It's what they'll say.'

Li would have laughed if it hadn't all been so grotesque. 'So I killed her? Is that it? Because she got me in trouble with my boss?'

Wu held out his hand and was passed another clear plastic bag. It contained a bloody handkerchief. 'You can see Lily's name embroidered on the corner. I reckon we'll find it's her blood on it. It was found in your bedroom.' And he held his hand up quickly to stop Li's protests. 'And before you say anything more, I'm as uncomfortable with all of this as you are. But I'm still going to have to take you in.'

'Let me see the arrest warrant.'

'What?' Wu was taken aback.

Li held out his hand. 'Just show me the warrant.'

Wu sighed and took it from his pocket. Li unfolded it and looked for the signature. 'Deputy Procurator General Zeng.' He looked at Wu and waved the warrant at him. 'He's your man. He's setting me up.'

'What?' It was Wu's turn to be incredulous, and Li saw immediately how ludicrous it sounded. He realised just how neatly he had been set up. They wanted him out of circulation. They were going to discredit him, and his investigation. They were going to tie up Section One in a scandal and a sordid murder investigation that was going to divert attention away from Chao Heng – even if, in the long run, Li was cleared. He looked around at the officers eyeing him as if he were a madman. He looked at his uncle and wanted to hold him, and tell him he was sorry, and ask for his forgiveness. He felt the tears spring to his eyes again, and he blinked them back.

What was it Old Yifu had always told him? *Action is invariably better than inaction. Lead, do not be led.* He turned and pushed into his uncle's bedroom. 'What the hell are you doing, Li?' Wu shouted after him.

The bottom drawer of the dresser was partially open, as if, perhaps, his uncle had tried in vain to reach his gun. Li had left it fully loaded. He had intended to replace the rounds in the box the previous night, but with Margaret in the apartment he had forgotten. The revolver was still there, wrapped in tissue in the old shoe box at the back. The cold metal fitted snugly in his hand.

Wu was right behind him. 'Come on, Li. I'm taking you back to Section One.'

Li stood and turned, grasping Wu by the collar and pressing the barrel of the revolver into his temple. 'I'm walking out of here, Wu. And you're coming with me.'

'Don't be a damned fool, Li. You and I both know you're not going to shoot me.'

But Li's eyes had taken on a cold, dark intensity. He looked unwaveringly at Wu. 'If you believe I'm capable of any of this, Detective . . . then you must believe I'm capable of blowing your head off. If you want to test me, go ahead.'

Wu thought about it for a very brief moment. 'I take your point,' he said.

'So tell everyone to back off.'

'You heard him. Get the hell out of here,' Wu shouted immediately. No one moved. 'Now!'

Slowly, uniformed, plainclothed and forensics officers

backed out of the apartment on to the landing. Li turned Wu around, pushing the revolver into the back of his neck, and made him follow. They stopped at Li's bedroom and he pulled Wu backwards towards the dresser. 'Get my holster out of the top drawer,' he said. Wu did as he was told. 'Hang on to it.'

Out on the landing, police officers parted to let them pass. 'Don't anyone try anything,' Wu said. 'No heroes, please. I've got a wife and kid who want to see me again.'

'Not what I've heard,' Li said.

Wu smiled grimly. 'Okay, so we're separated. So I lied. That's no reason to kill a man.'

Li pushed him down the stairs one step at a time. 'According to you, I don't need much of a reason.'

'Hey, come on, Li,' Wu said. 'I'm just doing my job. You'd do the same. You know you would. I mean, I don't believe any of this is going to stand up. But you're not doing yourself any favours.'

'Well, I sure as hell can't rely on you to do me any.' And he shoved the barrel harder into the base of Wu's skull.

'Okay, okay,' Wu said. 'Have it your way.'

They passed silent, watching officers on the ground floor as they went through the front doors and out into the hot night, Wu telling everyone quietly and repeatedly to stay calm. The uniformed officers in the street looked on in amazement as Li pushed Wu towards his Jeep. 'All right boys,' Wu said. 'Nothing tricksy, now. We're going to let him go, all right?'

Li grabbed his holster and shoved Wu away, still pointing the revolver at him, and opened the door of the Jeep. He leaned in and started the engine. He looked very directly at Wu. 'I didn't do this.'

Wu raised his hands. 'Hey, I'm not arguing. Just go.'

Li jumped in, threw the revolver and holster on to the passenger seat, banged the gears into reverse, and the Jeep screamed backwards up the street, smoke rising from the wheels in white clouds. A small road cut across the parkland that divided the street down its centre. He passed it, crashed into first gear and spun the Jeep across the road on to the opposite carriageway, and then north towards the bright lights of East Chang'an Avenue. The only thing he could see were the lifeless eyes of Old Yifu staring at the ceiling. *He put up a hell of a fight*, Wu had said. Li could picture it. The old man would not have given his life cheaply. Li's tears for his uncle flowed now without restraint.

And then, with a sudden jolt, he realised that if they had killed Lily just because she had witnessed Margaret's request for the blood tests, then they would have to kill Margaret, too.

III

Margaret's taxi dropped her in Tiantandong Road outside the east gate to the Temple of Heaven. But there was nothing heavenly about Tiantandong Road. It was a wide road in the process of redevelopment, with no streetlights. Piles of rubble and litter lined the sidewalk. Traffic rumbled distantly beyond a deserted cycle lane. Rows of grim apartment blocks opposite cast pale light across the tarmac. In the distance, exotic new buildings based on traditional Chinese designs were floodlit and stood out against the night sky. Another world. Beyond the railings, the park lay in brooding darkness.

In spite of the heat, Margaret shivered. The area was deserted. She felt vulnerable and was already regretting her decision to come. There was no sign of McCord. She walked to the gate and peered through the bars. There was a moon tonight, and as her eyes grew accustomed to its light she saw, beyond a second gate, a long line of cypress trees in an avenue leading towards a distant three-domed temple. The touch of a hot lizard hand on her arm made her squeal with fright. She turned, heart pounding, to find McCord at her elbow. 'Jesus Christ! Did you have to sneak up on me like that?'

'Shhh.' He put his finger to his lips. 'Come on.' He pushed the gate and it swung open. 'Quickly.' She saw the perspiration beading his forehead, smelled the alcohol sour on his breath, could almost touch his fear. He looked back, frightened eyes darting left and right, as he pushed the gate shut behind them. He started scurrying towards the inner gate. She hurried after him.

'Where are we going?'

'Into the park. If we haven't been followed we'll be safe there.'

The small gate by the ticket booth was not locked. He held it open for her, and led her quickly away from the light along the avenue of cypresses. As their pupils dilated, shadows grew out of the wash of moonlight that lay across the park, and the lights of the city receded into the distance.

'For heaven's sake, McCord, whatever you've got to tell me you can tell me now.'

'When we get to the corridor,' he whispered breathlessly. 'It's safer there.'

The corridor was a long, cobbled passageway raised on stone slabs. It dog-legged for several hundred metres towards the distant temple. A steeply pitched tiled roof ran its length, resting on maroon pillars and an understructure of intricately patterned blue, green and yellow beams. Margaret and McCord passed under a brick gate with a pale green roof, through the shadow of a large tree, and up a broad sweep of steps to its east end. McCord seemed relieved. It was dark here, he said, and safe. Through the pillars they could see the park around them in the moonlight, and anyone who might approach. But still he was unable to stay in one place and say his piece. He was driven, nervous and restless, almost on the verge of hysteria, it seemed to Margaret. He continued to walk agitatedly along the corridor, past long lines of shuttered and padlocked counters from which vendors sold cheap mementos to tourists during the day. But his pace had slowed now and he seemed more thoughtful, hands pushed deep into the pockets of his jacket. He glanced nervously in her direction as she kept pace with him along the corridor. He sensed that her patience was wearing thin. 'I need your help,' he said eventually, as if he had had to summon the courage to ask.

'What for?'

'I want you to go with me to the American Embassy. They

won't have anything to do with me.' He chuckled sourly. 'I guess I kind of burned my boats with the good old US of A. But they'll believe you.'

'Believe me about what?'

'That they're trying to kill me.'

Margaret was at a loss. '*Who* is trying to kill you?'

'The same people that killed Chao Heng and those others. They'll do anything to try and cover up.' He pulled a handkerchief from his pocket and wiped his neck and his forehead. His breath was coming now in short asthmatic bursts that wheezed and gurgled in his throat. 'Though God knows what the point of it all is. They're all going to die, the same as everyone else.' There was something chilling in the way he spoke so glibly of death, raising goose bumps on Margaret's arms. He glanced at her again, but couldn't meet her eye for long. 'I didn't know anything about it. That's the God's honest truth. Not until that night at the duck restaurant. They sent a car for me. It was waiting outside. Took me to Zhongnanhai. You know what that is?'

'The New Forbidden City.'

He nodded. 'Where the bigwigs are.' He fumbled a pack of cigarettes from his pocket and lit one, sucking smoke deeply into his lungs through the crackling phlegm in his tubes. 'Gave these things up years ago,' he said. 'But lately I thought what the hell.' He took another draw. 'The thing is, Chao was going to go public. You see, he had nothing to lose.'

Margaret shook her head. McCord was just rambling. 'I don't know what you're talking about,' she said.

'Pang Xiaosheng,' he said, stabbing his cigarette at her. 'You heard of him?'

'Vaguely.' Margaret tried to remember. Something Bob had told her. 'Minister of Agriculture. Sponsored your research into the super-rice.'

'*Ex* Minister of Agriculture,' McCord corrected her. 'Future leader of China.' He smiled grimly. 'Or so he thought.'

Margaret was losing patience. 'You're still not making any sense, McCord.'

'Oh, please,' he said, turning towards her, an unpleasant sneer on his face, 'call me Doctor. Even Mister. I'm not one to stand on ceremony.'

'Look . . .' She stopped and stood her ground. 'Either you tell me what this is all about or I am going. Right now.'

'Hey, cool it.' He tipped his ash on the cobbles. 'I'm coming to it, okay?' They had reached the end of the corridor, and a cobbled slope led up through an arched gate to the temple beyond. A strange smile spread across McCord's face. 'Jeesus,' he said. 'Know where we are?'

'In a park?'

He ignored the sarcasm in her tone. 'Never even thought about it,' he said. 'Kind of ironic really. Come and see.' And he headed up the ramp through the arch. She sighed and stood for a moment before following him, frustration bubbling up inside her. They emerged from the shadow of the gate into planes of shimmering silver marble, rising on three tiers to the blue-and-gold domes that rose, one on the other, more than a hundred and twenty feet into the Beijing sky. McCord wandered out across the paving stones towards the temple, the moon casting his shadow blue in his wake. He flicked his cigarette away, and it showered red sparks across the marble. He had suddenly become diminutive in the scale of things. He raised his arms on either side of himself like a bird and spun round to face her, grinning maniacally. 'I feel washed in the light of heaven,' he said. 'Welcome to the Hall of Prayer for Good Harvests.' And he turned away again to tilt his head back and gaze up at the vast temple that loomed over him. He laughed out loud. 'The Son of Heaven came here twice a year to pray. The first time was on the fifteenth day of the first lunar month to ask for a good harvest.' He turned around again to face her, still grinning like an idiot, and she saw tears brimming in his eyes. 'And then again at the winter solstice to give thanks for blessings received.' And suddenly the grin vanished and he stepped towards her, tears running silently down his cheeks. 'But Pang Xiaosheng didn't have to pray for a good harvest. He had me to engineer one for him.' He shook his head, and with bitterness in his voice said, 'And he won't be giving thanks for blessings received.'

Margaret stood stock still, absorbed by a performance that was both terrifying and sad, a tragedy played out on an ancient stage, a bizarre script performed by a grotesque clown. 'Do you want to tell me what happened, Dr McCord?' she asked quietly, in a voice that whispered back at them from among the terraces.

McCord seemed spent, and very small and insignificant in the shadow of the Hall of Prayer for Good Harvests. 'It was

Chao Heng who set up the super-rice research programme for the Ministry of Agriculture. He was Pang's man. And it was Chao who brought me in. That meant doing a deal with my employers, Grogan Industries. They were happy to put up the money, because Pang was in a hurry and they'd have a free hand. None of the interference they'd have got from government bodies in the States. The chance to put all their theories into practice on a grand scale. If it came off, they got the patent on the super-rice and the chance to sell it world-wide. Worth billions. Billions and billions. The Chinese? Well, they'd just be happy because they could feed themselves, and Pang could sell himself as the man to lead them into the next millennium. And me? I was the man who was going to create the super-rice. And I did.'

He turned away, wandering off across the flagstones, talking at the night. 'Jesus, it was so beautiful. A grain of rice impervious to insects or disease or fungus. Indestructible. Guaranteed one hundred per cent return from planting.'

'How did you do it?' Margaret asked.

He spun round, eyes gleaming. 'How did I do it? It was easy. It was so simple it was perfection. I took a cholera toxin gene – you know, the stuff that makes cholera fucking lethal – and I put it in the rice.'

Margaret looked at him, horrified. 'But that's . . . insane.'

McCord shook his head, almost laughing at her shock. 'No, it's not,' he said. 'The cholera toxin killed everything. Insects, bacteria, viruses, fungi.'

'And people?'

'Well, that was the beauty of it. You cooked it, it was harmless, and the rice tasted every bit as good as it always had. But the really clever bit was getting it in there. Smart stuff, state of the art. But I told you all this.' He waved his little finger at her. 'Remember?'

'Oh, yes,' she said dryly. 'Your little penis.'

He grinned. 'So I took my cholera toxin gene, stuck it on the back of a friendly virus, and sent it in to multiply in the DNA of the rice.'

'A *friendly* virus?' Margaret asked, unable to keep the scepticism from her voice.

He clouded. 'Sure. In this case the cauliflower mosaic virus. Makes all those patterns on the leaves of a cauliflower. We've been eating it for thousands of years and it's never done us any harm.'

'So you thought it would be a good idea to feed people cholera toxin genes and cauliflower viruses when they thought they were eating rice?'

'It worked. And it was perfectly harmless.' McCord was almost aggressive in his defensiveness. 'We had extensive field trials in the south. The research team lived on the stuff for a year before we ever went public with it. The returns were terrific and it tasted great.' It was his turn to be sarcastic. 'And no one died of cholera toxin or mosaic virus.' He lit another cigarette. 'So we launched it three years ago. All over China. The results were phenomenal, Dr Campbell. Phenomenal. Yields increased by up to a hundred per cent. Goodbye hunger.'

'And hello profit.'

'And why the hell not!' McCord turned on her. 'You put up the money, you take the risk, you reap the rewards.'

'Why do I get the feeling there's a "but" somewhere in our future?' Margaret asked.

He gave her a sour look and took a couple of long pulls on his cigarette before he spoke again. 'They never told me about Chao getting ill. Nearly a year ago. At first they thought it was AIDS. He liked boys, you know.' He wrinkled his nose in disgust. 'They were treating him for AIDS, but it wasn't that, and they started getting worried, and Pang had him admitted to Military Hospital Number 301.' He stood staring at the ground, breathing stertorously, as if he had been running. 'It was some new fucking virus no one had seen before. A retrovirus. Lies dormant in the brain for five years or more. You don't even know it's there. Then for no reason it decides it's going to screw you. Starts attacking the white blood cells and ends up completely fucking your immune system. Bit like AIDS, only worse. And harder to pin down, 'cos it mutates faster than you can say "Gotcha".' He dragged his eyes up to meet hers and held them for a long moment before the truth suddenly dawned on her.

'Oh my God,' she said. 'It's in the rice.' And the hair rose upon the back of her neck and along her arms and on her thighs.

His eyes filled up again and he flicked his cigarette vindictively at the night. 'Somehow,' he said, 'somewhere along the line, our innocent little cauliflower mosaic virus recombined with another virus, probably something equally innocuous somewhere out there in the test environment.' He paused to catch his breath, coming now in increasingly short bursts. 'And we got a mutation. A third and, this time, lethal virus. RiceX Virus they're calling it. RXV. Inherent in the genetic make-up of the rice. We never even knew it was there.'

There was a long silence as Margaret absorbed what he had just told her. She was aware of the blood pulsing behind her eyes, in her throat, in the pit of her stomach. She felt sick. 'You mean it's still there in the rice?' she asked eventually. He nodded. 'The stuff that people are growing and eating?' He nodded again. 'And anyone who eats it has got, or is going to get, this virus . . . this RXV?'

He dragged his eyes away from his feet for a moment to stare off into the trees. His voice was trembling. 'Of course, it won't show itself for another couple of years yet. Chao was eating it long before it went into production.'

Margaret simply found herself unable to deal with the scale of what he was saying. 'But that's more than a billion people,' she gasped.

He shrugged. 'More than that. They've been exporting super-rice all over the world. And once the virus is out there, who knows how else it's transmitted? We could be looking at half the world's population or more.'

And in that moment, Margaret was struck by the sickening realisation that she, too, had eaten the rice. For a moment she simply couldn't believe it. There had to be a mistake, some way of undoing it. She couldn't be going to die just because she'd eaten some rice. It was like the moment she had heard that Michael was dead. She couldn't accept it. It just didn't seem possible. She wheeled round on McCord, fear turning to anger turning to rage.

'You fucking people!' she screamed at him, her voice echoing back from every marble surface and rising into the hot pine-scented night. 'You stupid fucking people! What nature took three *billion* years to achieve, you thought you could do in three. You thought you could play fucking God!'

McCord flinched, but he did not speak for a long time. 'Irony is,' he said finally, 'I haven't eaten rice since I was a kid. Got an allergic reaction to the stuff.'

Margaret was riven between despair and anger. She wanted to fly at him, punching and kicking and tearing at his face. But her despair robbed her of strength and she stood helplessly in the night, crushed and burdened by the weight of what she knew – that she had eaten death and there was no way back; that before she died she would see two billion people, maybe more, die ahead of her; that there was nothing she could do about any of it.

Hot, salty tears filled her eyes, blurring and distorting the image of McCord in front her. 'Why are they even bothering to try and cover it up?' she asked hopelessly. 'What's the point?'

'Because they're scared and they're stupid,' he said. 'Grogan figured if they could keep it under wraps, they'd have two years to unearth a cure before they got found out.'

'They're mad!'

'That's what I told them. Jesus Christ, the world's been

searching for a cure for AIDS for nearly two decades, and they think they're going to find a cure for RXV in two years?' He snorted his derision. 'But Pang Xiaosheng went along with it, basically 'cos he'd got no fucking choice. Soon as the Chinese government finds out what he's done he's a dead man. And Chao ... well, Chao was dying already, and he was going to tell the world. So Grogan brought in this pro from Hong Kong. Some Triad hit-man who was going to be invisible in China, they thought. He took care of Chao and reckoned he'd destroyed the evidence by setting him on fire. And then you came along and started cutting him up and asking for blood tests. It was all getting out of hand ...'

Through all her emotions – of self-pity, of horror and shock – her brain was sending tiny alarm signals to her conscious mind. She forced herself to stop and think and focus. She stared at him, and he became discomfited. 'What are you fucking staring at?' he demanded accusingly.

'Those gates into the park shouldn't have been open, should they? This time of night, they should have been all locked up.' Her mind was racing now. She looked around. Great red doors with gold studs closed off all the gates on to the marble terrace, except for the one through which they had come from the corridor. She stabbed a finger towards it. 'That should have been locked, too, shouldn't it?' Maybe she didn't have five years to live. Maybe she didn't even have five minutes. She wheeled round on him. 'You never wanted me to go to the American Embassy with you, did you?' How could she have been so stupid? 'You bastard, you set me up! That's why you've been telling me all this, isn't it? It doesn't matter that I know. Because you're going to kill me.'

He took a step towards her. 'They made me do it,' he said, his jowls trembling, his eyes black and scary now. 'They said just to get you here. It was me or you. And, hey, you're going to die anyway.'

'We're all going to die some time,' she said bitterly.

He took another step towards her.

She stepped back. 'Don't you come fucking near me,' she hissed at him.

'Hey, I'm not going to do it.' He seemed shocked that she should think him capable of such a thing. 'I never hurt anyone in my life.'

'Of course not. You only infected half the world's population with a lethal virus.'

'Hey, come on,' he said, still advancing as she backed away. 'I didn't do that on purpose. It was an accident.' His eyes were darting all around now, in expectation. 'I'm sorry, all right?'

But she wasn't listening any more. She was looking past McCord. She was sure she had seen something move in the shadows beyond the temple.

McCord toppled forward as a dull crack split the night air, pawing at Margaret as he fell, dragging her down and pushing her over so that he landed on top of her. Something hard rattled away across the flagstones and she felt warm, sticky, wet stuff all over her hands. Blood, she realised. She wanted to scream, but she couldn't get the breath. She dragged herself out from beneath McCord's dead-weight and tried to stand, feet slipping on the patch of dark blood oozing across the stone. She fell again and found herself looking into McCord's wide, staring eyes. An expression of complete surprise was frozen on his face in death. This time the scream came, quite involuntarily. But it sounded to her as if it had come from somewhere far away. She scrambled on all fours away from his body and her hand came down on something cold and hard – whatever it was that had rattled across the marble when McCord fell. A small handgun. She grasped it, and got to her knees, and saw a figure coming towards her from the shadows of the Hall of Prayer for Good Harvests. Raising the gun at arm's length and clutching it with both hands, she closed her eyes and fired once, twice, three times in the direction of the approaching figure. But when she opened them again, she could see nothing and no one. She got to her feet, tucked the revolver into the waistband of her jeans, and starting running, slipping as she went, leaving bloody footprints in her wake. Across the marble terrace to the gate they had passed through from the corridor, all the time waiting for the bullet in the back. It didn't come.

In the darkness of the corridor she felt momentarily safer. She stopped, gasping for breath, and looked back. Still she saw nothing, but she had no intention of waiting around. She turned and started running again, on weakening legs that wanted to buckle under her, pillars flashing past, the shadows of trees blurring beyond, dark and sinister. She could hear nothing but the air rasping in her lungs, the smack of her feet on the cobbles. She looked over her shoulder. She thought she saw a figure moving through the shadows, maybe a hundred yards away. She let out a little cry of despair and almost fell down the steps at the end of the corridor.

She staggered through the green-roofed gate and saw the cypress-lined avenue stretching ahead, exposed and bright in the moonlight. Beyond that, the lights of the city. It seemed an eternity away. She knew she would never make it. She heard a clatter from somewhere in the darkness of the corridor behind her, and found the motivation to get her legs moving beneath her again. She staggered more than ran, gasping for breath, a pain in her side. The heady scent of pine in the hot night air was almost intoxicating, like some drug robbing her of the will to fight for life. It would be so easy just to give up, and lie down and wait for death. But something more than fear drove her now, something more than anger. There was a reason to live, a secret to share.

She reached the first gate. But it was locked now. She grabbed the railings and almost collapsed, tears of despair running down her face. The gate was maybe seven or eight feet high. She had no strength in her arms to pull herself up. She was sure she could hear footsteps running down the avenue behind her, but could not bring herself to look. Then she saw the big round hinges at the gateposts. Big enough to provide footholds. Deep sobs tugging at her breast, she got one foot, then the other up on the hinges and pushed herself upwards, flinging an arm over the top and dragging herself over to drop with a clatter to the other side, sprawling on the warm tarmac. Her knee hurt like hell. Her jeans were torn and she was certain there was blood oozing down her shin. She glanced back through the railings and saw a figure jogging towards her between the rows of cypresses. Fifty, maybe sixty yards away.

It was enough to get her back on her feet and limping the thirty or forty feet to the outer gate. It, too, was locked now. She didn't know how she would ever have the strength to get over it. She lunged up and caught hold of the top bar. She could see the blood on her hands in the light from across the street. Her feet slithered and scrambled for a solid hold, but the hinges were smaller. 'Come on, come on, come on!' she shouted at herself. Her right foot got little more than a toehold. But it was enough to give her the leverage to swing her other leg up and over the top. For a moment she hung there, waiting to hear the shot that would signal an end to it all. But still it didn't come, and with one last effort she dragged herself over the gate and fell on to the sidewalk.

This time she didn't linger. She was on her feet and limping across the deserted cycle lane towards the stream of traffic in the road. She saw a flash of yellow. A taxi. One of the crude baby vans they called 'bread cars' because they looked like loaves of bread. She ran into its headlights, waving her arms, and it skidded to a halt, the driver banging on his horn. She ran round the side of it, ignoring his curses, slid the door open and fell in. He looked back at her in astonishment. This blonde-haired, blue-eyed *yangguizi* covered in blood, her face blackened and tear-stained, shouting at him over and over again. 'The Friendship Hotel! The Friendship Hotel!' He saw the gun tucked into her jeans and decided not to argue. He crunched into gear and accelerated north towards the city lights.

IV

By the time the bread car reached the Friendship, Margaret's hysteria had subsided, to be replaced by a deep, black depression. She was physically and emotionally numb. Fear had left her, and she was consumed now by only one thing: a dark, simmering anger. She wanted justice, revenge. She wanted to expose these people: Grogan Industries, Pang Xiaosheng, whoever else was complicit in this madness. She despised their brave new genetically engineered world that had put her under sentence of death, and threatened the very existence of the human race. She despised their greed for money, their hunger for power, the bloody-minded arrogance of the scientists who had used mankind as their guinea-pigs in a world they had turned into a laboratory. And most of all, she despised their cowardice in the face of overwhelming failure. There were, it seemed, no depths to which they would not sink in order to hide their guilt, to squirm away from responsibility. And she knew that since she was now the only bearer of the torch that could illuminate their culpability, they would do everything in their power to eliminate her. But she was not daunted or afraid. For she was already dead. They had done their worst. They could not kill her twice. And the worst that could happen to her was that she would fail.

She made the taxi stop in the street a hundred yards short of the hotel and thrust some notes into the driver's hand. It was far too much, but he was not about to take issue. He was just glad to get her out of his cab so that he could report as quickly as possible to Public Security that he had been forced to pick up a wild-eyed, crazy foreign lady covered in blood and carrying a gun. It was not the sort of thing that happened to you every day in Beijing. He lit up and puffed anxiously on a cigarette as he drove hurriedly away, watching her vanish in his rear-view mirror.

She stood for a moment or two in a pool of darkness between streetlights considering what she was about to do. It was too soon, she hoped, for anyone to be waiting for her at the hotel. However, the moment she walked in covered in blood to ask for her key, she knew that the desk staff would call Public Security – probably about the same time as the taxi driver, who had watched her so carefully in the rear-view mirror all the way across town. But she desperately wanted to change her clothes, and to pick up her passport. When she went hammering on the door of the American Embassy at this hour of the night, she wanted to be able to identify herself without difficulty.

She wondered briefly about Li, what had happened, what his uncle had advised. And she felt sick at the thought that he would only have two years left before the rice virus would start destroying his life. And not just Li. Everyone in this country, and millions more beyond. She could not imagine how the hospitals and doctors would cope. They couldn't. It was a nightmare, beyond visualisation, beyond comprehension. She looked at the traffic, the cyclists passing in the street, lights in the windows of apartment blocks. All these people. They had no idea that they had already eaten the seeds of their own destruction.

The burden of that knowledge weighed almost unbearably on her. She desperately wanted to shed and share it. But who would want to know? She had no words of comfort, could hold out no possibility of hope. The secret she wished to share with others was the intimation of their death.

Bitter tears burned her face as she turned towards the lights of the hotel and walked determinedly in the direction of its floodlit forecourt. As she passed beneath the shadow of the hoardings that marked its boundary, heading for the steps, a figure moved out of the darkness to block her way and whisper her name. She almost fainted with fright. The man stepped forward and his face was caught in the light cast by a distant streetlamp. It was Ma Yongli. He was clearly shocked by her appearance, and looked at her in open-mouthed amazement. 'What has happened to you? Are you all right?'

'I'm fine.' She had difficulty controlling the urge to fall into his arms and weep. 'I have to change and get my passport.' Her brain, it seemed, was only capable of following a single track. Any deviation to left or right might allow other thoughts to crowd in and overwhelm her. Her voice sounded strained and very polite. She was hanging on by a thread and said, absurdly, 'I have to get to the American Embassy. Do you know where it is?'

'You cannot go into the hotel,' Yongli said. 'The police are waiting in there.'

She frowned, confused now. She felt as if she were drunk and the world was spinning out of control. 'How can they be there already?'

'Things have happened,' Yongli whispered. 'Terrible things. Li sent me to find you.' He took her arm. 'I will take you to him.' She allowed him to lead her through the darkness, away from the hotel. They turned down a side street to where a battered old Honda was parked at the kerbside. He opened the door and she slipped into the passenger seat like an automaton pre-programmed to do his bidding. All she could think was that Yongli, too, had the virus in him; that he, too, would have his life taken prematurely. Her tears fell silently in the dark. And there was so much to live for. Perhaps it would be easier for those who went first. Easier than living on while everyone around you was dying, and knowing that your turn would come. The only thing worse than death, surely, was the knowledge that your own was imminent.

'Are you sure you are all right?' Yongli touched her arm.

She nodded. 'Yes.'

He peered at her for a long time in the dark, then started the engine and drove carefully off into the night.

The Honda eased its way gingerly through the maze of crumbling *hutongs*, picking out the life of the back streets in its headlights – card games and family meals, and groups of people just sitting about talking and smoking. Men in singlets stared curiously as the car inched by, their eyes glassy in the lights. They were all dead, Margaret thought. They just didn't know it yet.

They were somewhere in the north of the city. Margaret had no idea where. She hardly cared. They had left the bright lights of the main street behind them more than ten minutes ago. Yongli turned left, and then right, and they found themselves in a long, narrow lane running down a slight slope. Telegraph poles rose into the night, power cables looping from one to the other. But there were no lights here. The surface of the lane was potholed and bumpy. Margaret saw that every few yards the crumbling brick walls had been daubed with large white characters within circles. Her curiosity finally aroused, she asked, 'Where are we? What is this place?'

'Xicheng District,' Yongli said. 'All these *hutongs* are condemned, marked for demolition. They will be pulled down to build new workers' apartments.' Near the foot of the lane, he bumped the car up on to a sliver of sidewalk and told her to get out. He got out himself, took her arm and led her away down another deserted lane, constantly glancing back to make sure they were not seen. But the area had been cleared of people in preparation for demolition. It was completely deserted. They turned through a broken archway into a courtyard littered with rubble. It was very dark, and they had to pick their way carefully to the other side. Windows all around were boarded up, and there was a stench of rotting garbage and old drains. Yongli nudged a broken old pram away with his foot and knocked softly on a wooden door with no handle.

After a moment there was a soft-voiced female response from within. Yongli whispered a reply and the door creaked open. Lotus peered out at them, pale and frightened. Even without a trace of make-up she was still very pretty. She saw the state that Margaret was in and beckoned them inside. 'Quick,' she said. 'Come quick.' Yongli pushed Margaret gently ahead of him and Lotus took her hand, guiding her into the dark interior. 'You okay?' she asked. Margaret nodded, but Lotus could not see it in the dark. With great concern she led her cautiously across a floor strewn with the remnants of someone else's life, and into a tiny back room where a candle burned in the far corner, sending flickering shadows dancing around the walls. Behind them, Margaret heard Yongli shut the door.

Li sat on a cot bed, his back to the wall, knees pulled up to his chest, smoking a cigarette. Margaret saw the tracks of tears on his face. He looked dreadful. His jaw slackened when he saw the blood on her jeans and her blouse, and he threw his cigarette away, unfolding his legs from the bed and reaching her in three easy strides. He held her by the shoulders. 'My God, Margaret, what happened to you?' She looked up into his face and saw the concern in his eyes, felt the heat of his hands on her shoulder.

'It's not my blood,' she said in a dead voice that seemed to belong to someone else. 'It's McCord's. They killed him.' She saw a frown form between his eyes and then his face blurred as tears started to run down her cheeks. Her legs buckled and she felt his arms around her, lifting her, carrying her quickly through the flickering light to the bed and laying her down.

Fingers lightly brushed away her tears and she saw his face very close. Beyond it, Lotus and Yongli looked on, disembodied masks among the shadows.

'Can I get her anything?' she heard Lotus say, but it was in Chinese, and she couldn't understand why the sounds formed no words.

Li shook his head. 'I don't think so. We've got plenty of water. You'd better go.'

Yongli pulled her gently away. 'Come on.'

'I hate to leave her like this.'

'She's in capable hands,' Yongli said. And to Li, 'We'll be back at first light. If not, you'll know we've been picked up.'

Li nodded grimly. 'Thanks,' he said. He turned and the two men made a brief eye contact that forestalled the need for more words.

'I'll bring her some clean clothes,' Lotus said, and let Yongli lead her by the hand away through the outer room and out into the courtyard.

When he heard the door close behind them, Li turned back to Margaret, but her eyes were shut and she was sleeping.

When she emerged from the strange, dark, dreamless chasm into which she had drifted, she was curled up on the cot bed and Li was sitting on the end of it smoking another cigarette. A candle still burned in the corner. He turned as she raised herself on to one elbow. 'How long was I sleeping?'

He shrugged. 'An hour maybe. I don't know what time it is.'

She peered at her watch in the dancing half-light. 'It's just after one.' She swung her legs off the bed and sat up, rubbing her eyes. He moved alongside her and put an arm around her, and she let her head fall against his shoulder. The familiar musky-sweet smell of him was reassuring. 'Why are we here?' she asked. 'What's happened?'

She felt him tense and he drew a deep, tremulous breath. 'They stitched me up, Margaret,' he said. 'I walked right into it. Never even saw it coming.' She lifted her head and pulled away so she could look at him. His eyes were moist and wouldn't meet hers. 'They killed Lily and murdered my uncle . . .'

Margaret uttered a tiny, involuntary cry. 'Oh God, no . . . !' Not that lovely, harmless old man. 'Why? Why would they kill him?'

Silent tears rolled down Li's cheeks. 'To make it look like I had done it.' He gasped in frustration. 'As if I ever would.' He turned towards her, the futility of it etched in the pain on his face. 'I don't know why, Margaret. But I feel like it's my fault, that I got something wrong, that if I'd done something differently my uncle would still be alive. I don't know what it is that would make them want to kill an old man, just to discredit me and stop my investigation. If only I knew what it was we'd got too close to, maybe I'd understand.' His despair was heartbreaking.

She lowered her head and looked at the floor. She no longer wanted to share her secret, for the pain and the horror and the hopelessness it would bring. She wished she could keep it to herself, close and hidden, so that maybe she would just wake up one morning and it would be gone. But she knew it wouldn't. And she knew she had to tell him. She looked up again and wiped the tears from his face. He should save them, she thought, for there were many more to spill. 'I know,' she said. 'Both why, and who.'

CHAPTER TWELVE

I

Friday

Li sat gazing into inky blackness. The candles had all burned out long ago. Just the acrid, waxy smell of them remained. He remembered being afraid of the dark as a small boy, of all the ghosts and monsters that lurked there in his childish imagination. As he grew older, he stopped being afraid, for he knew that the real monsters lurked within; fear and conceit, greed and evil. Only now, someone had let them out, and they were stalking the world, like latter-day dinosaurs, devouring and destroying everything they touched. They were out there somewhere now, looking for him. But they didn't live in the dark, like the monsters of his childhood. They worked in offices and lived in houses. They had wives and husbands, brothers, sisters, children. They controlled and manipulated the lives of those around them, exploited the weak, starved the hungry, reaped rewards from the work of others. And they thought they were gods. Li's hatred of them was tempered only by his sorrow for those he loved. Old Yifu;

dead. His father, his sister, her little girl, her unborn child; their death warrants already signed. Margaret. He could hear her gentle, regular breathing. She slept now, but she, too, was under sentence of death. He thought of his country. All those people, their hopes and aspirations, their lives and their loves. He could see their faces in the dark. The children, happy and innocent, unaware that their future was already lost. Five thousand years of history had brought them to this dead end. He wanted to scream, to pull the house down around them with his bare hands. He wanted to tear those monsters limb from limb. But he did not move. He did not make a sound. Dead men don't fight back. He might have thought that true once. But this dead man was going to fight, with every ounce of strength, every last breath, every final second that he had.

He and Margaret had talked for nearly two hours before she had finally succumbed to utter exhaustion, leaving him to come to terms with the things she had told him. Fear, anger, self-pity, more anger had surged through him in wave after wave, before leaving him, eventually, washed out and despairing. She had convinced him that their only option was to reach the sanctuary of the American Embassy. From there they could tell their story to the world. It was the only way to put an end to it, the only way to stop Grogan Industries and Pang Xiaosheng and all those they had corrupted in their pursuit of silence.

It seemed a hollow victory, somehow, to Li. That he should have to hide away from his fellow countrymen, skulk in the protection of a foreign power, in order to reveal the truth. It made him feel like a traitor. But he could see no other way. He was discredited and disgraced, on the run from his own police, and from a professional killer intent on killing the woman he loved.

The thought stopped him dead. The woman he loved? He struck a match and looked at Margaret as she lay sleeping beside him. She seemed utterly at peace. How could he love her? How could he love a woman he had only known for five days, a woman of another race, another culture? The match burned down to his fingers and he let it fall to the floor. But the image of her face remained imprinted on his retina. He reached out to touch her and saw his own hand in his mind's eye, fingers running lightly over her full lips. He had never been in love before, so he was not sure how it felt, or was supposed to feel. He only knew that he had never felt like this about anyone in his life. He lay down beside her, tucking his knees in behind hers, drawing her back into his chest, gently so as not to wake her, wrapping himself around her like a protective shell. He buried his face in her hair and breathed in the smell of her. He had no idea what it was he felt for her, but love seemed as good a name for it as any. And for the first time in many long hours he felt released from torment. He would happily have died there and then, holding her in his arms. But sleep intervened. Death would have been too easy.

Margaret woke with a start and pushed herself quickly up on one elbow. There was a fine dust suspended in stripes of pale yellow light lying brokenly across the room. Li stood by the window, squinting through the gaps between the boards nailed across it. The blue smoke of his cigarette drifted lazily upwards, turning pale grey in the sunlight that fell through the slats. She felt strangely rested. Bizarrely, it was the best sleep she had had since her arrival in China.

He turned on hearing her stir. She had no idea, he knew, that he had spent the night, or what was left of it, curled around her. He thought how beautiful she looked, sleepy and blurred, not fully awake. She was all he had left now. He must not fail her as he had failed his uncle. He must keep her safe at all costs.

'What is it?' she asked, concerned by the look on his face.

'Yongli and Lotus are here,' he said, and he picked his way through the outer room at the sound of a soft knocking and opened the door to let them in.

Margaret sat up and wiped the sleep from her eyes as Lotus came through from the other room. She was hefting a large suitcase which she dropped flat on the floor, raising a cloud of dust. 'I bring you clothes, and things for you to wash,' she said. She flipped open the lid and brought out a deep metal bowl and a plastic five-litre container. She laid them on the bed beside Margaret and filled the bowl with water from the container, then handed her a plastic toilet bag with soap and a face-cloth, a half-empty tube of toothpaste and a brush. 'You clean up. Then you dress.' She pulled out a pale blue cotton dress with lapels at a V-neck and a belt at the waist, like Margaret had seen many Chinese girls wearing in the street. 'I think this fit. Is too big for me.'

Margaret smiled. It was just as well. Lotus was diminutive. She made Margaret feel like a giant beside her.

Lotus waved a pair of panties at her and grinned. 'These, too. They clean.' She crossed the room and drew the ragged remains of a curtain across the door. 'Men stay outside. I give you help.'

Margaret stripped off her bloodstained clothes. It took several bowlfuls of water to clean the dried, sticky, rust-coloured blood from her hands and arms and neck. Then she sluiced her face with clean water and dried herself off with a small, rough towel. Lotus watched her with admiration. 'You have ver' lovely breast,' she said. 'I have no breast,' she added sadly, cupping what she had and trying to lift them. 'Need wear Wonderbra for cleavage.'

Margaret smiled. 'You are very beautiful just as you are, Lotus,' she told her.

Lotus lowered her eyes self-consciously and blushed with pleasure. '*Xie Xie*,' she said.

'*Bukeqi*,' Margaret responded.

Lotus looked at her and smiled in wide-eyed amazement. 'You speak ver' good Chinese.'

The blue dress fitted Margaret almost perfectly, the belt drawing it in neatly around the waist, the hemline dropping two or three inches below the knee. Lotus had a selection of sandals in the suitcase. 'I borrow from my cousin and her mother,' she said. 'Different size. Hope one fit.'

A pair of cream slingback sandals fitted snugly on her feet, the leather worn and soft and comfortable. There was a matching cream leather purse on a long shoulder strap. Lotus had filled it with make-up and a little spray of eau de Cologne. 'Beautiful lady must look beautiful always,' she said. Margaret laid it on the bed beside her discarded clothes and saw McCord's revolver nestling there among the folds. On impulse she slipped it into the purse and turned back to Lotus. She held her hand and squeezed it gratefully.

'Thank you, Lotus. I don't know how I can ever repay you.'

'Oh, it nothing,' Lotus said. 'You my friend.' And they embraced for several moments, breaking apart only at the sound of raised voices from outside. Li and Yongli were arguing about something. A moment later, Li brushed the curtain aside and stalked in, Yongli at his shoulder.

'Ma Yongli doesn't want to take us to the embassy,' Li said. The colour had risen on his cheeks.

Margaret looked at Yongli, taken aback. 'Why?'

'Because it is too dangerous,' Yongli said. 'Where is the first place they will expect you to go? The American Embassy. They will be everywhere, waiting for you.'

Margaret glanced anxiously at Li. 'He's probably right.'

Li nodded reluctantly. Margaret looked back at Yongli. 'But we've got to try, Ma Yongli. We can't just stay here for ever. If it's not possible to get to the embassy then we will think of something else.'

Lotus turned to Yongli. 'Hey, lover, it's no big deal,' she said. 'Li Yan and Margaret can stay in the car. We will walk past the embassy to see if there are police around. No one will notice us if we go after nine. There are always crowds queuing for visas.'

Li looked at Yongli, who hesitated for only a moment before reluctantly nodding his acquiescence. He could refuse Lotus nothing.

'What's happening?' Margaret asked.

'We'll stay in the car,' Li said. 'They'll check out the street.'

The drive to the Ritan legation area was tense. Li and Margaret sat low in the back of the Honda, wearing straw hats pulled down to shade their faces. Li wore a light jacket over his shirt to hide his shoulder holster and Old Yifu's revolver. Lotus sat in the front with Yongli, talking constantly, trying to calm him. Yongli was agitated and nervous, and drove badly, almost colliding with a bus in full view of a traffic policeman on Jianguomennei Avenue. 'Calm down, lover,' Lotus told him, and put a reassuring hand on his arm. He took a deep breath and tried to relax and managed a half-smile.

Already the heat was stifling, the sun beating in through the windscreen as they drove east. Margaret's hand sought Li's on the back seat and held it tightly. But they said nothing. They crossed the flyover at Dongdanbei Street, past the CITIC building, sitting impatiently at every set of lights, Yongli drumming his fingers on the wheel. There was a high police presence on the main boulevards, pale blue-and-white squad cars cruising frequently by, officers in green, sharp-eyed and watchful. But people in the streets were blissfully unaware, going about their everyday lives, happy in ignorance of the RXV virus that lay dormant within them, or the desperate attempts of a young policeman and an American pathologist to make them aware of it.

Margaret stole a glance at Li. 'Did you tell Yongli?' she whispered.

He shook his head. 'I did not know how.'

It is a dreadful thing to have to tell someone they are going to die. Margaret felt guilty now at the relief she had felt the previous night after she had unburdened herself to Li.

They passed the Friendship Store, and at the junction with Dongdoqiao Road, Yongli turned left, cutting across the flow of traffic and making a U-turn into the westbound cycle lane, where he drew into a parking place. His face was glistening with perspiration as he turned. 'You wait here. We'll approach the embassy from Silk Street and let you know how it looks.'

Li shook his head. 'No. We will be too conspicuous just sitting here in the back of the car.' He leaned across Margaret to look out of the window. 'We'll wait for you in there.' He pointed to a Deli France French-style coffee shop.

Li and Margaret watched for a moment as Lotus and Yongli pushed their way up the bustling length of the Silk Street market, jostling with pushy traders and eastern European tourists in search of big-buck bargains to ship back to Russia by rail. It was a narrow street crowded with stalls up either side. Colourful silk garments embroidered with gold Chinese dragons hung from stands and partitions; great rolls of material were sold by the bundle or the length. Traders smoked and shouted and spat and threw old tea leaves from jars on to the sidewalk. Corrugated plastic overhead shaded them from the sun. It was an ideal approach to the American Embassy, crowded and noisy. At the top end, where the lane emerged into a broader, tree-lined street, would be the tail of the queue that stretched daily up to the embassy's visa department. Li took Margaret's hand and they went into the Deli France café and ordered two cappuccinos. They waited in silence.

It was, perhaps, only twenty minutes before Yongli and Lotus returned. It just seemed longer. They slid into seats beside Li and Margaret and Yongli shook his head. 'The place is crawling with cops, Li Yan. You wouldn't get within a hundred yards of the place.'

Lotus said, 'He's right. They are everywhere, watching for you.'

Margaret didn't need a translation to know what was being said. Although it was what she had expected in her heart of hearts, she was still disappointed. She felt a dread sense of despair creeping over her. 'What are we going to do?'

In English, Yongli said, 'I have been thinking. The nearest international border is Mongolia. There is a train to Datong, and it is not so far from there. It is very remote, and the border is thousands of kilometres long. They cannot guard the whole length of it.'

II

Yongli was gone four hours buying their tickets. When he got back, he was pale and solemn. 'Cops everywhere,' he said to

Li. 'And they got your face pasted up all over the station.' He shrugged hopelessly. It was what they'd expected. There didn't seem anything more to say.

Lotus was boiling up a pot of rice on a single gas ring that screwed into a small gas canister. She had four bowls, but to her surprise, and hurt, Li and Margaret both refused any. Instead, they hungrily devoured some of the fruit that Yongli had bought for their journey. Margaret, in turn, watched in despairing silence as Lotus and Yongli scooped rice from their bowls to their mouths with wooden chopsticks. She glanced at Li, who could not even bring himself to look. There was no point in telling them not to eat it. The damage was done. To Li and Margaret as well. But Margaret could only think of the cholera toxin genes, the cauliflower mosaic and the RXV virus particles, and God knew what else, in the genetic make-up of the small white grains. It made her feel physically sick.

They ate in a tense silence, each with their own private thoughts, and afterwards Yongli took a map he had bought and spread it out on the cot bed. He dropped the train tickets on top. 'Three tickets,' he said. 'The train leaves Beijing just after midnight, gets into Datong at seven fifteen tomorrow morning.' He tracked the route of the train with his finger and jabbed at the dot on the map that represented the city of Datong on the border of Shanxi province and Inner Mongolia. 'You'll have to hide up during the day while I get us some transport. We'll leave as soon as it's dark and drive across Inner Mongolia overnight. We should reach the Mongolian border before sunrise. I'll drop you there, return the vehicle, and then come back to Beijing. No one will know where you've gone.'

Margaret looked at the map with a deep sense of foreboding. Even assuming they managed to cross the border undetected, they would have a long and difficult journey across mountainous territory to Ulaanbaatar. They had no passports, very little money, and if they succeeded in reaching their destination they would then have to try to gatecrash one of the Western embassies. It was a desperate venture. 'We'll never make it to Ulaanbaatar on foot,' she said.

Li said, 'I'd thought we would catch a train.'

'Of course,' Margaret said. 'Why didn't I think of that?' And Li thought her tone carried a little more of the Margaret he had come to know and love. 'And if we get stopped, without passports?'

Li shrugged. 'I guess we'll be arrested. Do you have a better idea?'

She didn't. She glanced at Yongli. 'At least let us do this ourselves, Ma Yongli. There's no need for you to take the risk. We can get to the border on our own.'

Yongli shook his head. 'No you can't. The pictures of Li Yan are posted everywhere. And his face is being broadcast on every television station. It would be almost impossible for him to hire a car without being recognised. Even in Datong. Also, the police will be looking for two people, not three. So it will be safer for you.' He turned and smiled at Lotus. 'Lotus will telephone the hotel and tell them I am sick. I will be back in two days. They will hardly know I have been gone.' He grinned, he, too, a little more like his old self. 'Easy.'

The remainder of the day crawled by, hot and airless in the confined space of the abandoned house. Outside, the sky turned pewtery, the air tinted a strange purple hue, temperature and humidity rising as a hot wind sprang up from the east, rattling the boards at the window. There was a storm brewing, and the atmosphere, already tense, grew oppressive.

Margaret slept off and on in fitful bursts, curled up on the cot bed. One time she woke up to see Lotus and Yongli squatting together in the far corner of the room, whispering to each other. Li stood by the window, keeping eternal, edgy vigilance through the slats of wood. Another time she drifted briefly into consciousness and saw that Lotus had gone. Yongli sat, back against the wall, smoking a cigarette, his eyes closed. Li was still at the window.

She dreamed of her childhood, long summer holidays spent at the home of her grandparents in New England. Home-made lemonade with crushed ice, drunk in the shade of leafy chestnut trees by the lake. She saw herself swinging on her grandfather's arm, the old man strong and brown, his silver whiskers contrasting with his tanned, leathery face. Her brother fishing off the end of the old wooden landing stage. And then he was gone, the sound of his voice calling for help and the frantic splashing in the water. It seemed such a long way away, and no one was paying any attention. She was running around her parents and her grandparents, screaming at them. Jake was in trouble. Jake was drowning. But they were more interested in the contents of a large wicker picnic hamper set out on the lawn. Except for Grandfather, who was sleeping in the deckchair. She shook his arm, the same one she had been swinging on. But he did not stir. She shook and shouted and shrieked, until his head tipped towards her, his old straw hat running away down the slope on its brim. His eyes were open, but there was no life there. A small trickle of blood ran from one nostril.

She opened her mouth to scream, but no sound came. And suddenly it was raining, big heavy drops that stung the skin, and a group of men in black oilskins were pulling Jake from the water. His eyes, too, were open, a trail of green slime oozing from his nostril, where blood had run from her grandfather's. His mouth was open, and a large fish with popping eyes was struggling to escape from it.

Margaret awoke with a start, heart pounding, the sound of rain battering on the broken-tiled roof of the derelict house. It was dark outside. The erratic flame of a candle ducked and dived and threw light randomly among the shadows of the room. Li had abandoned his sentinel position by the window and was sitting on the end of the cot bed. Yongli still sat against the wall, smoking. Lotus was squatting on the floor packing food and clothes into a leather holdall. She looked up as Margaret swung her legs to the floor. 'You okay?' she asked, concerned.

Margaret nodded and wiped a fine film of perspiration from her brow. 'A bad dream,' she said.

Lotus got up and sat on the bed beside her. She had something black and soft and shiny in her hands. 'This is for you,' she said. 'You must wear tonight.' It was a shoulder-length black wig with a club-cut fringe. 'I borrow from friend in theatre. Is good, yes?' Margaret pinned up her hair and pulled the wig on. It was uncomfortably tight. She took a chipped make-up mirror from her purse and squinted at herself in the candlelight. The contrast of the pale, freckled skin and the blue-black hair was startling.

'I look ridiculous,' she said.

'No. We hide your round eye with make-up and cover your freckle with powders. You look like Chinese girl.'

Margaret glanced at Li. He shrugged. 'It'll be dark. The lights on the train will be low.'

Lotus looked at him, hesitated a moment, then said, 'Li Yan . . . I have not had the chance to say thank you.'

He frowned. 'What for? You're the one who's helping us.'

'For getting me out of that police cell,' she said.

He looked at her blankly. 'What police cell?'

Yongli's voice came out of the darkness from across the room. 'She got picked up by Public Security, remember? I came and asked for your help. You said you would see what you could do.' There was a tone, a hint of accusation in his voice.

Li remembered now with a pang of guilt. 'I'm sorry,' he said. 'I never got the chance to do anything.'

Lotus frowned, genuinely puzzled. 'But they let me go. They said there had been a mistake. I thought . . .'

'But it *was* a mistake, wasn't it?' Yongli said.

Lotus looked very directly at Li. It seemed important to her that he believe her. 'They said there was heroin in my bag. But I have never taken heroin in all my life, Li Yan. I swear to the sky.'

Li was uncomfortable, almost embarrassed. 'Then, like Yongli said, they must have made a mistake. Maybe it was someone else's bag.'

'What's going on?' Margaret asked, disconcerted that the conversation had lapsed into Chinese. She sensed a tension in their words.

'It's nothing important,' Li said. 'History. We're only looking forward now, not back.' His words were for Lotus and Yongli more than for Margaret.

A terrific crash from outside startled them all. Li sprang forward and immediately extinguished the candle. The darkness that engulfed them felt almost tangible, as if they could reach out and wrap it around them. All they could hear was the pounding of the rain on the roof and the tug, tug, tug of the wind at the wooden boards on the window. Margaret heard someone shuffle carefully across the floor and into the outer room. Lotus's breathing was quick and close beside her. She reached out and found her hand and held it, and felt Lotus grasp her arm with her other hand, fingers squeezing tightly.

The faintest grey light gave form to the room around them as they heard the front door scrape open. Margaret saw Yongli cross the room to the inner door, where he stooped to pick up a length of wood and hold it like a club. Then the door banged shut and they were plunged again into a darkness that was frightening in its density. The rasp of a match on sandpaper, a tiny explosion and a flare of light burned into the black, and Li came back through shielding the flame from the draught of his movement. 'Tiles off the roof,' he said, and stooped to relight the candle. None of them had realised, until then, just how stretched their nerves all were.

Yongli dropped the chunk of wood he had been clutching and squinted at his watch. 'Anyway, it is time we were going,' he said.

III

Rain continued to fall on the sodden capital. The streets were shiny wet, reflecting all the night colours of the city, like fresh paint that had not yet dried. Thunder rumbled distantly amidst the occasional flash of lightning. The police presence seemed, if anything, greater than it had earlier in the day. Li knew that Public Security expectation of a quick capture and arrest would have been high, and that with political pressure being brought to bear by interested and increasingly desperate parties, the hunt would have been stepped up. He took some grim satisfaction from the fact that their continued success in eluding the police would be creating growing panic in the breasts of Pang and Zeng and the executives of Grogan Industries. But fear of exposure would make them even more dangerous, like wounded tigers. The greatest immediate risk for Li and Yongli and Margaret would be at the station. All points of departure would be under close scrutiny. Li thanked the heavens for weeping on them this night.

He wondered, briefly, where Johnny Ren was. Now that he knew who had employed him, it was no surprise to Li that Ren had been able to move about so freely, evading detection. No doubt he was long gone, safe in some place beyond the reach of the Middle Kingdom.

He stroked the whiskers that adorned his upper lip and chin, a strange, unaccustomed wiry sensation between his fingers, yet another acquisition from Lotus's theatrical friend. He felt guilty now at the way he had treated her in the past, his lack of concern when Yongli had come looking for his help. They could not have got this far without her.

They parked the car a couple of streets away from the station and, huddled in waterproofs under black umbrellas, hurried through the dwindling late night traffic. The concourse was deserted. A few travellers, waiting for taxis, sheltered under bus stands and the awnings of kiosks that during the day would sell fruit and vegetables and cold drinks to thirsty passengers. A queue trailing back into the night had formed at the main entrance to the station, where baggage was being checked through X-ray equipment, and officers of the railway police were randomly scrutinising passengers' papers.

'We'll never get past them,' Yongli whispered as they approached the back of the queue. 'If they check our papers . . .'

But Lotus had more fortitude. 'You said it yourself, Ma Yongli. They are looking for Li Yan and a *yangguizi*. Not two Chinese couples.' She glanced at Margaret. She had a waterproof scarf tied down over her wig. Her make-up was crude, but in the bad light of the station entrance, she would pass for Chinese at a glance. Li Yan's whiskers were convincing. Lotus only hoped that the brim of his hat and his umbrella would shield them from the rain. She had little confidence that the gum would hold in the wet.

More travellers joined the queue behind them as they shuffled forward, making slow progress to the baggage checkpoint. The rain still battered down on them, dampening conversation in the queue. But it was also making the officers checking the queue, after long hours of toing and froing in the wet, less conscientious than they might otherwise have been. They made a cursory check of the documents of a young couple in front of them, and then waved Li and the others through without a second glance. Yongli checked through their holdall and they were into the station. He was pale and trembling, and enormously relieved. They didn't stop to look back, but hurried forward to the gate that opened on to their platform. The train stood huffing and chuffing impatiently, great clouds of steam rising into the night. The platform was heaving with passengers searching for compartments, friends and relatives hugging and kissing them farewell, children waving to aunts and uncles or parents embarking on long journeys, all under the watchful eye of a stern-faced female attendant at the ticket barrier. Li knew her type at a glance. Officious, bureaucratic, unbending. She would slam the gates closed at three minutes past midnight exactly, shutting out all latecomers, even if the train itself were late in departing. She examined their tickets and waved them through brusquely.

On the platform Lotus gave Yongli a long hug and then kissed him and held his face and told him to be careful and come back to her safely. He was choked, almost tearful. 'I'd do anything for you, Lotus,' he whispered. 'Anything. I love you.'

She gave Li a kiss on the cheek and told him to look after her man. Then she embraced Margaret in a long, desperate hug. When they broke apart she said simply, 'Good luck.' She bit her lip as she watched them climb aboard. Yongli leaned down and kissed her again. A whistle sounded, and reluctantly she turned and hurried away into the station before the gate clanged shut. Yongli watched her go with moist eyes. He turned at last, and the three of them made their way into the crowded Hard Class compartment to find their seats among the damp travellers who squeezed into every corner, opening baskets of food and flasks of tea, making themselves comfortable and preparing for the long journey ahead. Margaret heard someone noisily dragging phlegm up from their throat and gobbing it on to the floor. She shivered with disgust, but didn't dare look, keeping her head down, face shielded by the black hair of her wig. She prayed no one would speak to her and was startled when Li whispered, 'If you can sleep, lean against my shoulder.' She nodded and he put an arm around her. He touched his whiskers self-consciously to make certain they were still there, and glanced at Yongli. But Yongli was lost in a world of his own, pressed up against the window, wiping a hole in the condensation to try to see out. There was little to be seen, though, in the dim lights of the empty platform.

Another whistle sounded, somewhere up ahead a light flashed, and the train jerked and then moaned, and started pulling painfully out of the station, creaking and groaning as it gathered speed. As they emerged from the station, trundling and rattling across a great conjunction of lines, Margaret inclined her head a little to see out of the clear patch Yongli had rubbed in the window. Raindrops spattered hard against the glass, running city lights down the pane in wavering, jagged streaks. A flash of lightning threw the skyline into sharp relief for a brief moment. Less than a week ago she had driven into Beijing in the heat of a Monday afternoon, with the hope of an escape for six weeks from a life that had barely seemed worth living. Now, just five days later, she was leaving in the dark and the rain, a fugitive, guarding a life that seemed all the more valuable for the sentence of death that had been placed upon it. She clung tightly to Li. She wasn't even going to try to analyse her feelings for him. All that mattered was that she wanted to be with him. For all that she might have lost, still she had found something precious. Something worth living for – even if that life had only a short time left to run.

CHAPTER THIRTEEN

I

Saturday

A pall of yellow smog hung over a skyline of factory chimneys and tall buildings belching smoke out into the dawn, an early morning mist rising to join with the coal smoke and dust blown in off the desert to make a sulphurous cocktail in the sky.

As their train rumbled and clattered its way into the industrial city of Datong, Margaret awoke from a restless slumber to find herself still nestled into Li's shoulder, his arm holding her safe and secure. Their carriage was a fog of cigarette smoke, people coughing and snorting as they gathered their belongings together. The floor was littered with orange peel and old food wrappings, and was sticky with spit. Yongli still leaned against the window, gazing through the streaked glass, like a blind man, into space. Margaret reached out and touched his arm. He turned and she smiled, and he made a poor attempt at a smile in return. Li got to his feet as the train shuddered to a halt on the platform and flicked his head towards the door. Margaret and Yongli followed him into the corridor and out and down on to the platform where the flow of travellers swept them through the ticket barrier and on to the crowded concourse. Heads down, they hurried past two patrolling police officers and out into the street.

The city was already gearing itself up for the day. The streets were filled with people working in the haze by the roadside, stall-owners sorting vegetables or arranging clothes, tinsmiths wielding hammers, bicycle repairers respoking wheels. Vehicles with their sidelights still on emerged from the mist for a few moments, and then passed into it again. Buildings seemed insubstantial and ghostly, people wandering the sidewalks like spectres. It was cooler than it had been in Beijing, and dry. It also seemed like another country, almost another century. It was how, Margaret imagined, a Chicago of the 1930s might have looked. Even the Chinese-built cars seemed old-fashioned, of another era. Men in dark coats with broad-brimmed hats and carrying tommy-guns would not have seemed out of place.

A work gang in railway colours trotted past. Li tapped Yongli on the shoulder to rouse him from some distant reverie. 'Come on.' He spoke with the authority of a man who had some idea of what he was about.

'Where are we going?' Margaret asked.

'I've no idea,' he said. 'Somewhere out of public view.' And they followed the work gang at a discreet distance, through tall iron gates in a high wall, and out across a great confluence of lines, red and green lights winking in the mist, the occasional grind of metal on metal as rails slid between rails to make connections between lines. They lost sight of the workers and kept on across the lines, towards the dark shadow of a bank of derelict sheds. The rails here were rusted, grass and weeds growing tall between the sleepers. Lines of old carriages lay rotting in front of the sheds.

Li pulled himself up on one and kicked the door open. The inside smelt musty and damp. With Yongli's help, Margaret hauled herself up and followed him down the corridor. It was an old sleeping car, compartments with fold-down beds on two levels, stripped bare and divested of any comfort they might once have had. But the carriage was clean enough, and though it smelled damp, seemed secure against the elements, and dry. Li slid open a door to one of the compartments and looked in. 'This'll do,' he said. With the sheds on one side, and a view out across the junction towards the city on the other, they would be able to see anyone approaching. He threw their holdall on to one of the beds and sat down to light a cigarette and slowly peel off his whiskers. Margaret wandered to the window and looked out through the dusty glass at the sun pushing up above the skyline, dispelling the early morning accumulation of mist and smoke. She pulled off her wig and with relief released her hair to tumble across her shoulders. Yongli remained in the doorway.

'I'll go and try to get us transport,' he said to Li. 'I might be some time.'

Li nodded and chucked him a bundle of notes held with an elastic band. 'See if you can get some cigarettes,' he said.

Yongli turned to go. Li called after him and he turned back. 'I appreciate this, Ma Yongli.' He hesitated. 'And I'm sorry. I was wrong about Lotus.'

There was a pained look in Yongli's eyes, and he looked away, unable to speak for a moment. 'You were,' was all that he said in the end, and he turned away again. They heard his footsteps retreating down the corridor, and then watched his tall, round figure dwindle across the tracks, disappearing finally into the mist without looking back.

'He seems very low,' Margaret said eventually.

Li drew deeply on his cigarette, the tobacco crackling as it burned. 'Ma Yongli is an extrovert. He can be . . . manic, sometimes. He has incredible highs. He also has terrible lows. He'll come out of it.' He stood on his cigarette. 'I must try to sleep. I got none during the night.' He looked at her. 'Will you be okay?'

She nodded, and he curled up on the bed in a foetal position, and within minutes was deeply asleep. She looked at his face in repose, all the tension relaxed out of the muscles. He appeared so innocent, almost childlike, she wanted to hold him and comfort him and mother him. She looked away quickly, tears blurring her vision. She mustn't think about it, she told herself. There was no future in regretting things that had not even happened yet. They were all going to die some time. Dying was not what mattered. Living, and what you did with your life, were the important things. She must try to hold on to that.

She sat down opposite him, and for a long time watched

him sleep, drinking him in, taking simple pleasure in just being with him, at peace and without fear. It seemed to her that she no longer feared death. She was more afraid of losing what life she had left, of wasting even one precious second of it. The worst thing was knowing that in all probability she had longer than Li. She kicked off her sandals and slipped on to the bed beside him, folding herself into his curves, putting her arms around him, holding him tight and feeling his body suffuse hers with its warmth. Ironically, she felt truly happy for the first time in years, almost euphoric. She allowed herself to slip away into a dream-world where anything and everything was possible, where even in the blackest of human moments there would still be light. And she knew she loved him.

He rose slowly, like a diver emerging from the deep, to break the surface of consciousness, soft bubbles foaming around him, the heat and light of the sun strong and bright after the strange underwater gloom of a deep and untroubled sleep. He became slowly aware of her softness enfolding him, and he turned carefully so as not to disturb her, and found his face next to hers. The slow gentle rhythm of her breathing continued, unbroken. She was almost painfully lovely. The fine line of her nose, the arch of her brows, her delicate chin, her full and well-defined lips, the freckles sprinkled randomly across her nose. He brushed a lock of hair gently back from her forehead. Her breath was hot on his skin. He leaned forward to kiss her and saw her eyelids flicker. He closed his eyes as she opened hers.

She saw him lying sleeping, his face only inches from hers, his head tilted slightly as if he were about to kiss her. She felt a strange ache inside as she remembered her final thought before succumbing to sleep. She tipped her head forward to kiss him and saw his eyelids flicker, and closed hers as he opened his.

He smiled when he saw that her eyes were shut. Then, after a moment, they opened again, and she returned his smile. He kissed her softly, feeling the gentle give of her lips against his. She responded, and opened her mouth in a desire to draw him in. They were moved now by something beyond passion or lust. Beyond time. For there seemed no need to rush, and every reason to savour. The sun beat in through the grimy window of the abandoned carriage, bathing their bodies in heat and light as they moved together, joined by love and sadness, affinity and death. Her breasts filled his hands and his mouth, her skin sweet on his tongue. She felt all the fine muscles of his back, firm buttocks that she grasped and pulled towards her, drawing him inside. He was so beautiful she never wanted to let him go. He filled her with himself, moving slowly to the rhythm of their hearts. She gasped, almost sobbing. It was a pleasure close to pain, on the edge of endurance. Her fingers dug into his back, trying to hold him there, to draw him deeper, to finally consume him, until he exploded inside her and she lost all control, wave after wave of ecstasy washing over senses numbed by years of indifference. A convolution of muscles and nerves that robbed the brain of independent thought and immersed them both in unashamed abandon. Nothing mattered now, nor ever would again.

They lay naked, breathless and damp in one another's arms, the sun burning their skin hot through the window. For ten, perhaps fifteen minutes, neither of them spoke. Neither wanted to break the spell, to end the moment, to bring them back from some distant euphoria to their present peril. Eventually Li reached for a cigarette and blew smoke at a ceiling stained brown by nicotine. He said, 'Is there any hope for us?'

She inclined her head to look at him. She could say that maybe a cure would be found in time, that RXV would prove much easier to defeat than AIDS, but it seemed unlikely, and what merit was there in false hope? But then she stopped herself, her heart pounding suddenly. Look for hope, she thought, and you will find it. For there is never any place in the world without light. She had accepted McCord's hopelessness, his dark despair, without thought. But now she replayed the scene they had acted out on moonlit marble and saw light for the first time.

Li saw that light in her eyes. He had asked for hope without hope of it, and witnessed now the unexpected effect it had had on her. 'What is it?'

She sat upright. 'Why did they kill him?'

'Who?'

'McCord. He was on their side. One of them.' She turned bright eyes on him, the light of revelation now illuminating them. 'He was panicking. That's why. He was a loose cannon. He couldn't see what they saw – a point in covering it up. I even asked him why they were bothering. He said they were stupid. But they're not stupid people. They wouldn't be trying so hard to cover up if they thought there was no point. And if they believe there's hope, then there must be.'

Li shook his head. 'I don't understand.'

Her mind raced back over McCord's revelations in the shadow of the Hall of Prayer for Good Harvests. *The research team lived on the stuff for a year before we ever went public with it*, he had said. *And no one died of cholera toxin or mosaic virus.* 'They'd all been eating the rice,' she said. 'Five years ago. And yet only Chao was dying, that we know of.' In all her excitement she was briefly struck by the thought that there was no greater folly than self-delusion. But this was no false hope, she was sure of it. 'Maybe,' she said, 'not everyone who eats the rice gets the virus. Maybe not everyone who gets the virus dies of it. Maybe, with the huge resources Grogan Industries have at their disposal, they genuinely believe that a cure is possible. Why else would they be playing for time?' She felt like the prisoner in the condemned cell who has just had word of a last-minute reprieve. Death had been postponed, maybe temporarily, maybe till it would have come anyway. But the sentence was no longer inevitable.

'You mean you think we won't die?'

'Of course we will die! We all die! But maybe, just maybe, we won't die of RXV.' And with hope came the return of anger. 'That's why the world has got to know about it. We can't just leave it in the hands of Grogan Industries.' She threw her head back and gasped in exasperation. 'And do you know what the real irony is? The profit motive that drove the development of the super-rice in the first place is the same motive that will drive the development of a cure. There is no money to be made from healing obscure or unfashionable illnesses. But imagine what rewards there would be in wiping out a virus that threatens to kill half the world's population!'

She searched his eyes for some sign that he shared her excitement, her hope. But he seemed a long way away. Finally, he returned from that distant place and met her eye. 'They must not be allowed to get away with it,' he said. 'Grogan and Pang and the rest.' He saw his uncle impaled on his own sword.

'No, they mustn't,' Margaret said.

Li gazed up at her for a minute or more. Then he said, 'I love you, American lady.'

Her heart seemed to be in her throat. Her voice came as little more than a whisper. 'I love you, too, Chinese man.'

And they held each other on the fold-down bed in the compartment of a condemned sleeper car in this industrial city in the north of China for a very long time, embracing for the first time the hope of a future together.

II

Yongli returned in the late afternoon. Li and Margaret had eaten some of the fruit that Lotus had packed in the holdall, and they had talked, endlessly. She told him about her childhood in upstate Illinois, summers in New England, the day her grandfather had a stroke and her brother drowned in the lake.

He talked of his boyhood in Sichuan, the horrors of growing up in the Cultural Revolution, the loss of his mother. There was so much they had to tell each other, and neither had any idea of how long they might have to do it.

They saw Yongli hurry across the rusted tracks, glancing cautiously around him, his lengthening shadow following in his wake. They heard him climb aboard and his steps heavy in the corridor. He was breathing hard and perspiring when he reached their compartment. 'That was a lot harder than I thought,' he said. 'But I got us some wheels.' He pulled some packs of cigarettes from his pocket and chucked them on one of the beds. Margaret handed him some bottled water and he drank gratefully. He wiped his mouth with his sleeve and slumped on to the bed. 'Cost me an arm and a leg. It's no great shakes, but it should do the mileage there and back okay. I've to pick it up just after ten tonight.'

Ten o'clock seemed an eternity away. The afternoon dragged by into evening, and still ten o'clock seemed a distant prospect. Yongli's return had put an end to Li and Margaret's conversation. She glanced at him frequently as he sat in the corner smoking. He must have been aware, surely, that his presence had had an inhibiting effect on them? He was surly and withdrawn, so different from the sparkling young man she had met that night in the Xanadu, when he had indulged in a verbal fencing match with her, a battle of wits. But then Li, too, in spite of their revelations of hope, seemed to have descended into the same trough. Perhaps it was infectious. The gloom that settled over Datong as the sun slid down in the west seemed to reflect their collective mood. Two hours earlier they had seen the work gang they had followed that morning, returning from some detail to the north, heading home for a hot meal, a glass of beer, a night relaxing in front of the television. Now darkness fell and they could see only by the dim glow of reflected light from distant streetlamps.

Eventually, shortly after nine thirty, Yongli got to his feet. 'I'll go and get our wheels,' he said. 'Meet me outside the gate in half an hour.' And he was gone without another word, vanishing quickly into the darkness.

Margaret looked at Li with concern. 'Is he all right?'

Li shrugged. 'I don't know.' Usually you couldn't shut Yongli up, or stop him making bad jokes. But there wasn't much to talk about, and not much to laugh at. If they got caught, Yongli could face execution. There was a good chance they would be looking for him in Beijing. It was known the two of them were friends. Still, his friend's mood was puzzling, uncharacteristic. Li looked at Margaret. 'I hate this,' he said. 'I hate doing this to my friend. I hate running away.'

A little after ten they picked their way carefully across the tracks. They heard a train coming in the distance, clouds of steam and smoke rising up in its lights. Its whistle blew several times in the dark. Li took Margaret's arm and led her to a dead area between junctions, and they crouched down to watch the train pass and head on into the station. As soon as it was gone, they sprinted across the remaining tracks and up an asphalt slope to the big iron gate through which they had come that morning. Li peered out into the street. It was quiet, the occasional lorry rumbling by. Haloes of mist were starting to form around the streetlights, and there was a slight chill in the damp air. 'We'll wait in the cover of the wall until he comes,' Li said, and they stood hidden in its shadows with an oblique view through the half-open gate into the street beyond.

By ten thirty, there was still no sign of Yongli, and they were both starting to get nervous. 'Suppose he's been picked up,' Margaret said. 'We wouldn't know. We could be waiting here for hours. And if he talks . . .'

'He won't talk,' Li interrupted firmly, but she could see that he was worried, could hear the tension in his voice.

Another ten minutes went by, and then they saw the lights of a vehicle approaching slowly along the sidewalk. With the curve of the road, its headlights were pointed directly at them. They pressed themselves hard into the shadow of the wall, and as it drew closer and its lights swung away, Li leaned forward to take a look. He pulled back again immediately. 'Police,' he whispered.

The gentle purring of the engine in a low gear drifted slowly past and Li risked another look. It was a uniformed patrol vehicle, and it was heading on down the street.

'Do you think they were looking for us?' Margaret whispered.

He shook his head. 'If they knew we were here to be looked for, they would know where to look.'

Another agonising ten minutes passed before an ancient pick-up truck clattered along the street towards them, pulling up in front of the gates with a squeal of brakes. Yongli leaned across from the driver's side and signalled to them through the open passenger window. Li took Margaret's hand, and they darted out across the sidewalk and up on to the bench seat of the pick-up. Li banged the door shut. 'Where the hell have you been?'

Yongli waved his arms in frustration. 'We had no goddamn gasoline. The guy screwed me for a tankful, and we had a hell of a diversion to get it. I've got more cans in the back. He says if I get caught with his pick-up he'll say it was stolen.' He crunched into first gear and they lurched away from the sidewalk.

'Is everything all right?' Margaret asked anxiously.

Li nodded. 'A fuel problem. But it's okay.'

Yongli withdrew his map from inside his shirt and handed it across Margaret to Li. 'You can navigate.'

Li flicked on the courtesy light and ran his eyes quickly over the large, pristine map of the Middle Kingdom. He snorted. 'There's only one road. To Erhlien.'

'Then just make sure we stay on it.' Yongli's gloom had been replaced by agitation. He seemed excitable, almost hyper. He thrust a pack of cigarettes at Margaret. 'Here, light one for me.' She passed them to Li who lit two and passed one back to Yongli. He dropped the stick into fourth gear and they picked up speed, trundling north parallel with the railway line, heading for the wide open spaces of Inner Mongolia and the northern reaches of the Gobi Desert.

They left the lights of the city behind them with some relief. The road passed among hills that marked the farthest limit of Shanxi province, and through the remains of a huge broken-down wall that stretched to the east and west. 'The Great Wall of China,' Li said. But it wasn't so great here, where it had been allowed to fall into disrepair and was little more than a heap of rubble and stones. For a while the road followed it, before swinging north again, leaving the hills behind, and entering the dark, vast emptiness beyond.

III

It was around three hundred miles to the international border with Mongolia, once known as Outer Mongolia because of its relationship to the Middle Kingdom. They planned to make the journey in a little over six hours, Yongli dropping them as close as possible to the border, allowing them to cross during the hours of darkness. But none of them had considered the possibility of a puncture three hours into their journey, or the fact that their pick-up would not be equipped with a jack.

Yongli kicked the tyre in frustration. He knew he should have checked there was a jack before they left. The brace would unscrew the wheelnuts, but they had nothing to lift the truck, allowing them to remove the wheel. Ironically, the spare was sound and well filled with air.

The pick-up sat at an angle on the camber of the road, tilting down towards the nearside rear wheel. Moonlight shimmered off into the distance among the endless swaying acres of grassland. The only sound was of the wind whistling through the grass. It was a wind soft on the skin and filled with the sweet scent of wild flowers. A vast black sky bejewelled with stars spread above them like a dome, the moon a brilliant silver orb passing through its firmament. The road vanished to distant points behind and ahead of them. They were stranded and exposed, with nowhere to go and nowhere to hide.

Yongli was almost beside himself with anger and self-recrimination. 'It's hopeless, it's completely hopeless,' he kept saying. 'It's all my fault.' Margaret was beginning to tire of him.

Li had instituted an exhaustive search of the vehicle – beneath the seats, under the bonnet in case the jack was strapped to the inside of the engine compartment, beneath the tailgate in case there was some hidden storage area. But they found nothing. And the back of the vehicle was empty. Nothing that might be of any use in improvising a jack. Li sat pensive and smoking at the roadside now, staring off into the distance. He had said almost nothing since the puncture.

Margaret had an idea. 'Where's the railway line?' she asked suddenly. 'We've been following it most of the way.'

'Over there.' Li pointed off to their right, but she couldn't see it.

'There might be old sleepers – you know, railroad ties – or bits of track lying around that we could use to lever up the truck.'

Li was on his feet in an instant. 'You're right,' he said. And he turned to Yongli. 'You head south, I'll go north. If you don't find anything within an hour, come back.' Yongli nodded and set off immediately at a jog for the railway line. Li said to Margaret, 'Will you be all right here on your own?'

She shook her head. 'No. I'm coming with you.'

At first they jogged up the line, but their pace very quickly reduced to a fast walk, Margaret struggling to keep up with Li over the uneven ground. They did not talk much, conserving their breath. Li reckoned they covered maybe seven miles in the hour, and they found nothing. The futility of that wasted time, and the further hour they would waste going back, was demoralising. It remained unspoken, but they both knew that if the truck was still there by morning, they were bound to be seen and reported. And it would only be a matter of time before they were picked up by the police.

Li turned, disheartened, in the direction they had come. Margaret caught his arm. He stopped, and for a moment they stood looking into each other's eyes, sharing their despair. Then he drew her to him and held her, feeling the contours of her body moulded into his. And they kissed. A long, hungry kiss filled with both passion and pain that left each of them aching with a desire they knew they could not fulfil. Not here. Not now.

By the time they got back to the pick-up, Yongli was there in a state of anger and frustration. 'Where the hell have you been?' he shouted at Li. 'I found a whole fucking pile of rail-road ties about a mile down the track. I came running back screaming my lungs out trying to stop you.'

Li shook his head. 'We didn't hear you.'

'That's nearly two fucking hours we've wasted!'

'Well, let's not waste any more,' Li said, annoyed. It was bad luck, but it was no one's fault, and he resented Yongli's attitude.

This time they ran all the way down the line to where the railroad ties were stacked, Li explaining to Margaret in between gasps for air what had happened. When they got there, Li surveyed the pile. 'We need two,' he said. 'One to run lengthwise between the wheels to provide a lever point for the other.'

Yongli said, 'They're too heavy for one person. I've already tried. We'll have to make two trips.'

It took another thirty minutes to get both railroad ties back to the pick-up. Margaret felt hopelessly redundant, a passenger, unable to do anything to help. She stayed behind to loosen the wheel nuts when Li and Yongli went for the second tie. It proved a lot harder than she had imagined. They had been over-tightened either by brute strength or by machine. She only began to make progress when she locked the brace on to the nut at a forty-five-degree angle and stood on the end of it, flexing her knees to bring repeated pressure to bear. The first grinding creak and half-turn felt like a major achievement. By the time the two men returned with the other tie, she had loosened all the nuts, taken all the skin off one of her shins, and was soaked in a fine film of sweat. But she wasn't about to complain. She saw the strain on their faces, and the rivulets of sweat that ran into their eyes and dripped from their chins.

Performing the remainder of the task turned out to be remarkably simple. The second tie was manoeuvred into position at right angles to the first, with the near end immediately below the vehicle's jacking point. Li and Margaret brought their combined weight down on the other end and lifted the rear of the pick-up by several inches while Yongli slipped the punctured wheel off and replaced it with the spare. When the nuts were in place, they lowered it again, and Yongli finished tightening them.

They had lost more than three hours, and the first light of dawn had appeared in the sky to the east. Yongli seemed close to panic. 'Come on,' he shouted, and he leapt up into the cab to start the engine. But Li stood where he was, panting, his face blackened and sweat-stained. 'It'll be broad daylight by the time we get to the border now,' he said. 'We're going to have to find somewhere to lie low until tonight.'

'Shit!' Yongli thumped the wheel in frustration.

CHAPTER FOURTEEN

I

Sunday

The world tilted to the east and the sun slid up over the far horizon. There was a strange, desolate beauty in this desert dawn, sunlight painting the edge of every swaying blade of grass yellow as the wind ebbed and flowed through the long stems like an invisible hand ruffling the still surface of a vast ocean. The grey pick-up rattled and bumped steadily northwards, a plume of fine dust rising from its tail then dipping to the west in the prevailing breeze. The road cut like an arrow through the high grasslands, straight and unbending, heading inexorably to the north and the mountains and deserts of Mongolia. They had not seen another vehicle all night.

They passed through two small villages, neat brick buildings and tidy flower-beds, streets lined with saplings. But there was no sign of life in either. It was still early, not yet six. Another hour, and the larger buildings of a town began to form themselves on the distant shimmering horizon. The sun was well up in the sky now, and the heat in the cab was building. Li was asleep, slumped against the door column. Margaret sat between the two men, staring off into the distance, lost in a fog of random thoughts and memories and regrets. Yongli lifted the map from the dash and glanced at it, keeping the pick-up one-handed on its undeviating course. This had to be Erhlien, which was no more than a kilometre or two from the border. Here, trains passing in either direction were shunted into huge sheds to have undercarriages replaced for the change of gauge between China and the old USSR. Yongli breathed an inner sigh of relief. They had made good time, were now perhaps only two hours behind their original schedule.

As they approached the town Margaret said, 'Could we stop here?'

Yongli looked at her, surprised. 'Why?'

'I need to go to the bathroom.'

For the first time in nearly three days she saw him smile with genuine amusement. 'This is not a good time to think of having a bath,' he said.

She laughed. 'I mean toilet.' She clutched her lower abdomen ruefully. 'I'm getting cramps. Probably all that fruit we ate yesterday. I'd say just stop at the roadside, but I don't see any bushes.' She grinned, embarrassed.

He smiled. 'Sure. We'll find you somewhere.'

Li still slept as they drove into Erhlien. It was a neat and tidy little town, with a post office, a large hotel, a shirt factory, a great railway shed, and rows of squat brick houses with tiled roofs. The population was already up and about – square, high-cheeked Mongolian faces, skin tanned and leathery. A group of workers painting a fence stopped to stare as the pick-up pulled up in front of the hotel.

'You should get a "bathroom" in there,' Yongli said, and he stepped down to let Margaret out at his side so as not to disturb Li.

A line of schoolchildren, with fresh faces and clean white blouses, gawped in amazement as the blonde-haired, blue-eyed *yangguizi* skipped across the road and into the hotel. A babble of excited chatter arose in the street. Yongli looked into the cab at the sleeping Li, hesitating for a moment before climbing carefully back in.

When, a few minutes later, Margaret emerged from the hotel, slinging her purse over her shoulder, a crowd of around forty or fifty townspeople had gathered in the street, word spreading quickly about her arrival. The twice-daily train from Mongolia was all that usually broke the monotony of their lives. This was unusual, something not to be missed. Others were hurrying along the street to join them and catch a glimpse. Margaret stopped on the steps, taken aback, uncertain how to react. She smiled nervously, but the faces that gazed back at her were blank. '*Ni hau*,' she said, and to her amazement received a spontaneous round of applause.

Li woke with a start, sitting up, blinking furiously, assimilating where they were. 'What the hell's happening?' he asked.

Yongli said, 'She needed the "bathroom".' Li frowned. Yongli explained, 'The toilet.'

Li looked at the crowds in the street. 'For God's sake,' he said. 'This is the last thing we need.' Margaret hurried across the street and Yongli jumped down to let her in. 'What the hell did you think you were doing?' Li snapped at her.

His words hit her like a slap in the face. 'I had to go to the toilet,' she said, defensive, hurt by his tone.

'And how long do you think it'll be before Public Security hear there was some blonde-haired, blue-eyed foreigner at the hotel? Now they're going to know where we are. We can't afford to wait till tonight. We're going to have to cross the border as soon as we can.'

Margaret sat in silence, pink-faced, stung by the rebuke, and realising the justification for it. But Yongli leapt to her defence. 'Lay off her, Li,' he said. 'She'd have created a much bigger stir squatting at the roadside.' He chucked the map at him. 'I've been looking at this. The main road crosses the border a couple of kilometres north of here. There'll be some kind of border post there. But if we take that smaller road west . . .' He leaned across to stab at it with his finger. '. . . we can probably get close enough to the border to see how the land lies without committing to a crossing.'

Li examined the route Yongli had pointed out. It made sense. He nodded. 'Okay.'

As they drove out of town, heading west on a road that was little more than a dirt track, he glanced at Margaret, wanting to apologise but not knowing how. She resolutely avoided meeting his eye. She felt guilty, and ashamed, and angry with herself for putting them so thoughtlessly at risk. She could easily have squatted down behind the pick-up out on the open road. After all, it wasn't as if there was any traffic, and she would have seen anything coming miles before it would have seen her. She felt his hand seek out hers and give it a tiny squeeze. She squeezed back, and wanted to kiss him and hold him and tell him she was sorry. But she didn't. She sat staring straight ahead through the windscreen at the immensity of nothing that stretched before them.

Erhlien had vanished into the shimmering heat haze behind them. The dust kicked up in their wake was blowing ahead of them now on the edge of the wind, reducing visibility to less than thirty or forty yards. Yongli fumbled to light a cigarette, and she noticed that his hands were shaking. 'Are you all right?' she asked.

'Sure,' he said, but he didn't look it. He was ghostly pale.

Suddenly a dark shape emerged from the dust up ahead of them on the road.

'What the hell's that!' Li sat bolt upright, and Yongli jammed on the brakes, bringing them to a skidding halt. The engine stalled, and the silence that followed was almost eerie, broken only by the whistling of wind through grass. They sat, without a word, watching as slowly the dust cleared to reveal a black Mercedes sitting facing them on the road, perhaps twenty-five yards away. There appeared to be a single figure sitting on the driver's side, a silhouette against the immensity of sky and grass beyond.

'Who is it?' Margaret whispered, as if the occupant of the other vehicle might hear her.

'I don't know,' Li said, but he had a sick, gnawing fear that perhaps he did.

Yongli stubbed his cigarette out with trembling fingers, and the occupants of both vehicles sat regarding one another without sound or movement for nearly a minute. Then the driver of the Mercedes opened the door and stepped out on to the track. Still they could not see his face. He wore a dark suit, the jacket flapping open, a white shirt and a tie, and he started walking, slowly, steadily, towards the pick-up. Li sat tensed, every muscle and sinew straining as he peered through the dusty windscreen, trying to bring form to the face of the approaching figure.

'Shit!' he hissed under his breath.

'What!' Margaret was very scared now.

'It's Johnny Ren.'

Ren stopped, almost as though he had heard, took out a red-and-white pack of Marlboro, and lit a cigarette. Then he resumed his progress towards them, his smoke whipped away in the wind.

Li reached under his jacket to remove his uncle's revolver from his shoulder holster. His fingers froze on the leather of its empty pocket. The gun was gone. He turned, slowly, to find Yongli pointing it at him. Margaret sat perfectly still between them, not daring to move. She had no idea what was happening here, or why.

'They said she would be shot,' Yongli said. A tear ran silently down his cheek. He was desperate for Li to understand, to know that there was justification in this. 'You said you would help, but I knew you wouldn't. And I was right. They came to me that day. Made it clear I had two choices. Lotus or you. She'd still have been there now, in some cell, if I hadn't agreed. Next week, next month, it would have been a bullet in the head.' Li *must* understand – there was nothing else he could have done. 'I had no choice,' he said. 'I love her.' His face was wet with tears now. 'I'm sorry, Li Yan.'

Johnny Ren arrived at the passenger side of the pick-up and pointed his gun in at Li. 'Get out,' he said. He had a large pink plaster across one side of his forehead. He was nervous, eyes dark-ringed and wary. Li remembered that face looming over him in the park, in the rain, the intent in those same eyes, the iron fist that had smashed repeatedly into his face. So they had won. He felt sick. All those wasted lives. For what? To buy a reprieve for those terrified executives at Grogan Industries, for Pang and his ambitions. To perhaps find a cure that would get them off the hook. He slipped out on to the dirt road, overcome now by a sad sense of despair in the knowledge that no one would ever know what he and Margaret knew. Guilty and greedy men would escape justice. Ren waggled his gun at Margaret and she climbed out after Li, who ached at the thought of a bullet piercing that pale, freckled flesh, spilling her blood in the dirt of this empty place. He hoped she would have no pain. There had been enough of that in her life. He glanced at her, but she had her eyes fixed on Ren, a strange, wild quality in them, the chipped ice-blue of her irises almost chilling in its intensity.

Yongli came round the front of the pick-up, the revolver

hanging loosely in his hand by his side. He was unable to meet Li's eye. Johnny Ren held out his hand towards him. 'Give me the gun,' he said, not taking his eyes from Li. Obediently, Yongli placed the revolver in his hand. Ren weighed it up and down for a moment, as if measuring its worth, then cocked the hammer, turned his head and shot Yongli twice in the chest. His eyes were on Li again before the young chef hit the ground. Ren had no need to check his handiwork. He knew that Yongli was dead.

Both Li and Margaret were struck by the shock of it as if by a physical blow. Moments earlier Yongli's face had been stained by warm, wet tears of pain and regret. Now they were turning cold in the wind that ruffled his hair as he lay dead in the dirt, blood spreading darkly around him. Life could be extinguished so easily, the human body such a frail vehicle for the weight of thought and pain and history that it bore.

Johnny Ren glanced at Margaret, meeting the eyes that never left him, and for a moment he was disconcerted by them. Then he smiled and tapped the plaster on his forehead. 'A lucky shot in the dark,' he said. 'Lucky for me. Unlucky for you.'

His eyes flickered back to meet Li's. Unfinished business to complete. Then, perhaps, a little entertainment. 'Goodbye,' he said.

Li felt the physical impact of the shot, watching in disbelief as blood trickled from the small round hole that had appeared in the middle of Ren's forehead. There was the merest hint of surprise in Johnny Ren's expression as his legs buckled under him and he tipped forward on to his face. Li saw that most of the back of his head was gone. He turned to see McCord's gun trembling in Margaret's hand. And still the wind blew, bending the tall grasses, whispering relentlessly through the empty spaces. The only sound, it seemed, in the whole world.

Margaret watched in silence for a long time from the cab of the pick-up as Li went through the Mercedes, very carefully, like a policeman searching for evidence. Which, she reflected, was what he was. She had no idea what he was looking for, or why. She suspected he was filling his mind with anything that would shut out his friend's betrayal, squeeze out the guilt and regret. They had not spoken since he had taken the gun gently from her hand and embraced her and told her to wait in the cab. She had done what she was told without question or feeling. She had never spilled living blood, and the shock of it was greater than she could have imagined. She felt numb now, but knew that the pain would come later.

Li emerged from the Mercedes, a dark object not much bigger than a cigarette pack in his hand. He seemed to be prodding it with his finger and then listening to it. It was a moment or two before she realised what it was, and she leaped from the cab and sprinted the twenty-odd yards to the car. She snatched it from him breathlessly and checked the display. 'We've got a signal,' she said.

He nodded. 'The battery's very low.'

She looked at him. 'Who do we call?' And even as she asked she saw the cable trailing in his other hand, and beyond him, on the back seat of the Mercedes, Johnny Ren's Apple Powerbook computer. She thrust the phone back into Li's hand and slipped into the seat, opening the laptop on her knees. It took several infuriating minutes for the operating system to load before the screen presented her with its options. She hardly dared look. But there it was. The Internet Explorer icon. 'Jesus . . .' She looked up at Li's perplexed face framed in the doorway. 'We don't need to call anyone. We can go on-line. We can put the entire goddamn story on the Internet and the whole world's going to know about Grogan Industries and Pang and RXV.'

Li understood at once the implications of what she was saying. 'Do you know how?' he asked anxiously.

'I think so.' She tapped a few keys and opened up a document template on which she could type up their story. 'It's crazy,' she gasped, her face shining with excitement. 'We're just about as far from anywhere as we can be . . .' She glanced out of the window at the endless expanse of grass and desert. '. . . and yet we can talk to anyone in the world – several millions of them simultaneously.'

The computer beeped and she froze.

Li leaned in, troubled by her consternation. 'What's wrong?'

'Battery's low on this, too.' A box on the screen told her she had less than fifteen minutes computing time left. 'God, how can I write it all in fifteen minutes?' She starting tapping furiously on the keyboard.

Li could do nothing but wait and watch, anxious and frustrated. He walked around the car, avoiding looking back in the direction of the pick-up. He still couldn't bring himself to think about Yongli, never mind look at his friend's body lying in the dirt. The incessant tap, tap of the computer keys punctuated the gentle whine of the wind. He saw, through the windscreen, the concentration on Margaret's face, the tension there. He heard the computer beep again and saw her despair.

'Less than five minutes. Jesus, I've got to get on-line! Give me the cellphone.' Her voice was shrill and insistent. He quickly rounded the car and handed her the phone. She plugged it into the modem socket on the back of the Powerbook and clicked the Internet icon. Almost instantly the melody of touch-tone numbers rang out, followed by the familiar white-noise sound of computers talking to each other across the ether – Ren's password and ID sent automatically by his software. Then she was connected.

Li watched in awe as her fingers rattled back and forth across the keyboard, her eyes flickering up and down between keyboard and screen, the occasional grimace contorting her lips. Then there was a gasp as the computer screen suddenly went black, and the single, high-pitched wail of a disconnected line emanated from the earpiece of the cellphone. She leaned back in the seat and closed her eyes.

'Well?' Li asked. He wasn't sure he wanted to hear her response.

She opened her eyes slowly and looked at him. 'I sent it to every website and bulletin board and e-mail address I could remember. It's out there now, Li Yan. It's not just our secret any more.'

*

The fence that marked the border ran off to east and west as far as the eye could see. Beyond lay Mongolia. A few miles to the north and east, the town of Dzamin Uüd, where it would be possible to catch a train for Ulaanbaatar. They stopped on a slight rise and gazed across the emptiness. They had left behind them, with the Mercedes and the pick-up and the bodies, the elation of sharing their secret with the world, and stood now facing a future of bleak uncertainty.

Li glanced back. China, in all its vast diversity, spread away to the south. His home. His country. In these last moments, as they had walked away, with every word of explanation, and with every step towards another country, his heart had grown heavy with the bitter burden of regret. Now he felt the eyes of his ancestors upon him, looking across five millennia. He had a responsibility to them, as well as to his country and to the oath he had taken as a police officer. He could not simply walk away. Margaret might have told their story to the world, but he had unfinished business in China.

He looked at her, her face stained by sweat and tears, her eyes strained by tiredness and death. And he put the flat of his hand on her cheek and felt it smooth and cool. He wished with all his heart it could be some other way.

He took a wad of dollars from his back pocket and pressed it into her hand. 'They'll take dollars,' he said. 'They always take dollars.' He gazed beyond her across the desolate wastes of Mongolia. 'It's only a few miles to Dzamin Uüd. Will you manage on your own?' She took the dollars without surprise and nodded. She had known he would not go to Ulaanbaatar with her. She had seen it in his eyes, had felt it in his touch. And she knew why. She understood. In his place she would have done the same.

'I'll always love you,' she said.

He could not meet her eye. How could he make her understand how hard this was for him? He took both her hands and forced himself to look at her. 'Even if they find a cure, what kind of existence would it be, living out my life in some foreign place, a fugitive from my own people?'

'I know,' she said.

He searched her eyes for understanding and saw only the reflection of his own pain.

'I've got to go back, to clear my name, to wipe away the lies. Would they ever believe me if I didn't?'

'I know.'

'I owe it to my uncle. I owe it to myself.' He knew it meant losing her. And that was the hardest thing he had ever had to do in his life. 'Margaret . . .'

'Just go,' she said, and she bit her lip to stop the tears.

They stood for a moment in silence, the wind tugging at their clothes, her hair flying out behind her, shining golden in the sun like a flag of freedom. He stooped to kiss her and they embraced, and clung to one another for a long time. Finally they broke apart, a little at a time, as if breaking the bond of a glue that held them. He turned without another word and started walking back towards the road through grass that ebbed and flowed like water on the shore. In the far distance he could see the black dots of the pick-up truck and the Mercedes where they had left them, the only break on a horizon that cut low across the immensity of blue overhead. His friend and his enemy lay dead there. His love lay behind him. Ahead of him, only uncertainty.

He waited for the call of her voice, turning in his mind's eye to see her running through the tall grass to tell him that she was coming with him. But there was no call, and he knew that if he turned he would not be able to walk away, to leave her to face a precarious journey across a hostile land on her own. And the urge to turn back was almost irresistible. He knew she would be standing there on the rise, watching him go. He glanced over his right shoulder, an entirely involuntary movement. Just one last look. But she was gone. Down the slope, out of sight and heading for the fence, resolute, determined not to weaken. He could almost see the set of her jaw. Then he heard a swish, swish, swish, and turned to his left to find Margaret keeping stride with him. She smiled and said, 'You didn't really think I was going to let you go, did you? I mean, I've always wanted to see the inside of a Chinese prison.' She held his arm and made him stop. Her smile faded. She said, 'Whatever future we have is for sharing.'

EPILOGUE

REUTERS:

DATELINE SUNDAY, 21 JUNE; WASHINGTON DC:

VIRUS CLAIMS BY US DOCTOR

The existence of a deadly new virus which may have infected up to half the world's population was revealed last night on the Internet by an American doctor working in the People's Republic of China.

Dr Margaret Campbell, a forensic pathologist from Chicago, claims that the virus, known as RXV, mutated during the development of a genetically engineered super-rice which was introduced across the People's Republic three years ago. The new rice, which increased yields by up to one hundred per cent and turned China into a major exporter, was developed during five years of research by the US-based company Grogan Industries.

A spokesman for Grogan refused to comment on the story which appeared on up to a dozen sites across the Internet late Saturday night, accusing the company of resorting to murder in an attempt to cover up the discovery of the virus.

Dr Campbell, who describes the virus as being similar to but more dangerous than AIDS, says that RXV is ingested with the rice and lies dormant in the body for up to five years before attacking and destroying the immune system. She claims the world could be less than two years away from a catastrophe unprecedented in human history.

To date there has been no official response from the Beijing government.

REUTERS:

DATELINE TUESDAY, 23 JUNE; BEIJING, PRC:

MEMBER OF POLITBURO ARRESTED

Rumours are circulating among US diplomatic staff here in Beijing today that Pang Xiaosheng, the man China watchers were tipping as the next leader of the People's Republic, has been arrested on murder and corruption charges.

It is believed that Pang, a leading member of the Politburo, was detained after a wide-ranging criminal investigation into a series of murders committed in the Chinese capital.

The authorities, however, have refused to comment, and there is now widespread speculation that Pang's alleged arrest is linked with the detention of five Beijing-based executives of the international biotech company Grogan Industries.

Pang was Minister for Agriculture and a leading proponent of the genetically engineered super-rice developed in China by Grogan during the nineties. Claims that the genetically modified rice is a carrier of a lethal virus which could have infected up to half the world's population have created panic in China and grave concern among the international community.

REUTERS:
DATELINE TUESDAY, 23 JUNE; BEIJING, PRC:
HIGH-RANKING LEGAL MANDARIN
ON CORRUPTION CHARGES

The second-highest ranking law officer in Beijing, Deputy Procurator General Zeng Hsun, was arrested here today on corruption charges.

Zeng, the equivalent of a US Deputy District Attorney, will face a closed-door trial to be held within the next three weeks, and could be executed if found guilty. The nature of the charges against him has not yet been made public.

REUTERS:
DATELINE WEDNESDAY, 24 JUNE; BEIJING, PRC:
CHINESE APPEAL TO WHO

The Chinese government today appealed to the World Health Organisation for help in tackling the fight against RXV, the virus carried in genetically modified rice which, it is claimed, could wipe out up to half the world's population within the next two to five years.

An international team of medical experts, set up by the WHO during the last forty-eight hours, is expected to leave for Beijing immediately. The Chinese authorities have promised unfettered access to the work that was carried out there during the development of the so-called super-rice.

With, potentially, more than a billion Chinese infected by the virus, the search for a cure will be a race against time, with the first symptoms expected to appear within two years.

REUTERS:
DATELINE THURSDAY, 25 JUNE;
LOS ANGELES, CALIFORNIA:
COMPANY OFFERS HOPE OF RXV CURE

The California-based biotech company Grogan Industries today announced a 100-million-dollar investment in the search for a cure for RXV.

The announcement comes just 24 hours after the company condemned and discredited its China-based executives currently held in Beijing, in the People's Republic, pending trial for murder.

A Grogan Industries spokesman said: 'While the company cannot accept any responsibility for the illegal actions of overseas executives acting on their own initiative, we feel morally obligated to take the lead in the search for a cure for RXV.'

He continued: 'To that end we are prepared to invest 100 million dollars of our own resources.'

With some of the world's leading geneticists and virologists at its disposal, Grogan Industries say they are confident they can make progress towards a cure in the two-year window of opportunity most experts believe exists before the virus becomes active.

Industry experts believe that a cure for RXV would generate multi-billion-dollar profits for the patenting company.

Ends . . .

ACKNOWLEDGEMENTS

This story is a work of fiction, but its background is authentic and its premise frighteningly plausible. It involved copious amounts of research in which I received invaluable help from the following people, all of whom gave their time and expertise with a willingness and generosity for which I will always be grateful: Dr Richard H. Ward, Professor of Criminology and Associate Chancellor of the University of Illinois, Chicago; Professor Joe Cummins, Emeritus of Genetics, University of Western Ontario; Zhenxiong 'Joe' Zhou, Office of International Criminal Justice, Chicago; Professor Dai Yisheng, former Director of the Fourth Chinese Institute for the Formulation of Police Policy, Beijing; Professor He Jiahong, Doctor of Juridical Science and Professor of Law, People's University of China School of Law; Professor Yijun Pi, Vice Director of the Institute of Legal Sociology and Juvenile Delinquency, China University of Political Science and Law; Professor Wang Dazhong, Director of the Criminal Investigation Department, Chinese People's Public Security University; Mr Chen Jun, Secretary-General of the Eastern Film and TV Production Centre, Beijing; Police Commissioner Wu He Ping, Ministry of Public Security,

Beijing; Steven C. Campman, MD, Forensic Pathology Fellow, Northern California Forensic Pathology; Robert D Cardiff, MD, PhD, Professor of Pathology, University of California, Davis, School of Medicine; Kevin Sinclair, writer and journalist, *South China Morning Post*; Liu Xu and his mother Shimei Jiang who were my tireless sherpas in Beijing.

I could not complete a list of credits without mentioning the biggest contributer of all – the Internet. Without it I would not have made contact with many of those who helped and advised. Nor would it have been possible to access so quickly and freely the information I required to build a detailed and authentic background to my story.